the
EUCALYPTUS
Blues

MARY BACHRAN

ASPEN GROVE
MEDIA

For Ray

Chapter 1

THE DAY BEFORE HER HUSBAND, Ernie, died, Jane booked a flight for Australia. While a nurse took Ernie's blood pressure and charted the course of his demise, Jane went to the bank, closed out all the accounts, and transferred the money onto a Visa debit card.

Ernie died at 7:46 the following morning. Jane met the undertakers with a money order and instructions about where to send the ashes. No memorial, no funeral, no graveside service, no mourners, no obituary, no tears, no flowers. Death certificates were to be mailed to her attorney, who would take care of the business of closing out the estate. She watched them load Ernie's black-plastic-shrouded corpse into the back of the hearse and felt numb. Her heart didn't twinge; no recriminations fell from her lips. She felt only a vague sensation in her stomach like a spring unwinding.

As the sound of the hearse receded into the distance, she grabbed her purse and toothbrush, slid into the driver's seat of her battered Subaru, and drove to Denver International Airport for a rendezvous with Qantas flight Q74. Two days later, forty-five-year-old Jane Mullet, clutching a canvas tote containing half a ham sandwich, a bag of peanuts, and her purse, disembarked in Melbourne somewhat disheveled, somewhat jet-lagged, and with a pressing need to find a toilet. Welcome to the other end of the earth, she thought. Welcome to Down Under.

Jane shivered in a steady drizzle outside a nondescript concrete building, a crumpled copy of a downloaded ad for Zeus Outback, "Australia's premier camper rental," clutched in her hand. Her short-sleeved T-shirt clung to her back, and her summer jeans felt sodden and leaden. In her tennis shoes, her sockless toes were icy while her arms sported a mountain range of goose bumps. In the light that sieved through the heavy clouds, the bedraggled bushes huddled in front of the building appeared cold and miserable. A faint pine-like scent exuded from them, reminding her of the mountains back home.

For some now-unfathomable reason, she had assumed Melbourne would be hot in October. After all, wasn't Australia known for its scorching weather? She'd read somewhere that it got up to 45 degrees. OK, 45 degrees Celsius. She wasn't quite sure how that translated into American degrees but was sure it was well over a hundred. This was not over a hundred. This resembled 45 degrees

Fahrenheit. She shivered again.

In front of her, a small sign in the window displayed a bearded god pointing a lightning bolt at a campervan under the words "Zeus Outback" in gold and navy blue. Instead of being inviting, the sign looked ominous, the god ready to zap the camper, occupants included, straight to Hades, particularly if they were middle-aged, female Americans who didn't think to research the weather or which side of the road Aussies drove on.

She about had a heart attack in the taxi on the way to Zeus when the first vehicle passed them on the right. She clutched the seat belt across her chest, eyes squinched shut, and braced for impact. It didn't come. Her eyes cracked open, and she realized they drove like the British—on the wrong side of the road. In that moment, it occurred to her that driving a camper around Australia might not have been her brightest idea, what with her conditioned driving habit of staying on the right side of the road while oncoming traffic remained on the left. Ernie had claimed she was a rotten driver and had seldom let her behind the wheel when he was in the car. If she was that bad in the States, down here she could be a four-wheeled campervan of destruction, leaving a wake of mangled men and beasts scattered across the country. And Ernie would love it if she crashed. He'd doubtless be doubled over in laughter on the other side, all his predictions about her confirmed: *worthless, hopeless, useless.*

Her nose tingled; raindrops spattered against her cheeks. Maybe she was brainless and incompetent. She sniffled, tears on the verge of erupting if she didn't do something. The last thing she needed was to stand in the rain in a strange country crying. Throwing back her shoulders, she marched to the door and jerked it open. This was the plan she'd hatched over months of .watching Ernie die by inches:

fly to Australia, rent a van, and drive around the country until her money ran out or they kicked her out. In hindsight, it may not have been the best plan, but the least she could do was try and carry it out. She wouldn't let his assessment of her be true. Not today.

The interior of the office was utilitarian, with faded posters tacked up here and there displaying what she imagined were various tourist attractions across the country. A bookshelf filled with colorful pamphlets stood against one wall, and a turquoise vinyl sofa snuggled against the opposite one. She wrinkled her nose. The place smelled old-mannish—musty and dusty and rarely cleaned. Stepping to a worn Formica counter with a couple of computer monitors peeking over the edge, she clutched her purse to her chest, protecting it from the grime all around. Through a row of windows to the left of the counter, she could see a garage full of vans, some with doors or hoods open. But not a soul in sight.

For a few moments she stood there, uncertain about the proper "Aussie" thing to do. Ring a bell? No bell in sight. Call out? That seemed crass and vulgar. Venture into the garage? Men rushing her and throwing her out spooled through her mind. Just about the time she'd decided to risk calling out, a man with skin the color of mahogany stepped out of a doorway to the right, a sheaf of papers in his hand. He was broad across the chest, narrow in the hips, with glistening black hair that fell in tight curls almost to his shoulders. His gray and red uniform shirt was pressed, knife creases arrowing down the short sleeves.

She sucked in a breath. Wow. No—double, triple, maybe quadruple, wow. On a scale of one to ten, he—well, there just wasn't a scale for him. She couldn't remember the last time the mere sight of a man had amazed her. Especially a black man. Maybe never at all. Ernie had never had that effect on her. She prayed she hadn't dropped into slack-jawed awe and pursed her lips and smiled.

He glanced up and smiled. "May I help you?" His voice was deep, with a hint of an accent. Not English but not what she considered Australian either.

She smiled back, acutely aware of her hair, finger-combed into a drooping ponytail, and soggy, rumpled clothes. "I'd like to rent a van."

"Do you have a reservation?" He stepped to a computer and poised his hands over the keyboard. What nice hands. So clean, with neat, trimmed fingernails. A stark contrast to the rest of the place. And he smelled of vanilla.

She shook her head. "Uh, no. Is that bad?"

He frowned. "That depends on what you want. Large, small, two-wheel drive or four-, basic or more upscale?"

"Oh, whatever's available. I'm not that picky." She shrugged and flashed him another smile, trying to look disarming and agreeable.

"Well, let me see. You're lucky this is the slow time of year, so we might have something that was reserved and not picked up. Let me just . . ." He pecked away at the keyboard with two fingers. Frowned, bit his lip, frowned, pecked, and frowned again. Clasping her hands together on the counter, she held her breath, the bedazzlement fading as anxiety crept in. This didn't look good.

At last he tapped a finger on the monitor. "Well, I don't have anything today. Not here anyhow. If you can wait for a day or two, I can have what you choose shipped down from Sydney." He glanced up. "You should've made a reservation."

"Oh." Her shoulders slumped, the anxiety ratcheting up a couple of notches. Why did she think she could just drop in and pick up a vehicle? What was she going to do?

"I can make a reservation for you now. It won't take long to get something here. Two or three days at the most." He slid a brochure across the counter. "Here. Why don't you look at the vans and decide what you would like."

She opened the brochure, trying to focus through a descending fog of jet lag and disappointment on the bright pictures and descriptions of different models posed in front of beaches and forests. Whatever adrenaline had gotten her through the airport to here sloughed away. Her brain felt muzzy, as if all the neurons had disconnected. Dozens of different types of vehicles filled the pages. A jumble of choices, and she was without a clue what she wanted or needed. Why hadn't she done more research? When she'd pulled the information about Zeus off the internet, she hadn't bothered to give its inventory more than a cursory glance. Why hadn't she looked a little closer? She could have at least decided on a size or if she wanted four-wheel drive. How could she have been so negligent? And now here she stood, too exhausted to think, in no condition to make any kind of decision.

Closing the brochure, she laid her hand on it. "Would it be OK if I took this with me and called you later to arrange something?"

His smile reemerged, and he seemed relieved. "That would be the best thing. If you don't mind my saying, you don't look so good. Are you OK?"

Oh God, she thought. Is it that bad? She straightened and ran a hand over her hair in an attempt to appear at least functional. "I just got off the plane from America, and I'm a little tired."

He shook his head, and she thought she caught a brief look of disdain cross his features. Her chest tightened, the same way it did when Ernie looked at her with disgust.

"Where are you staying?"

"I'm not staying anywhere. That's why I wanted to rent a camper." Her lips began to quiver and tears well. Stranger in a strange land. No place to go, nowhere to sleep. Nothing even to sleep in. Why am I here? Why did I think I could do this? Why did I choose to flee with only a purse and the clothes on my back? To be free of everything? I am such a fool.

His face softened. "What if I call you a taxi? You can go to a hotel, get a good night's rest, and figure out what you want to do."

Tears spilled down her cheeks in spite of her best efforts to hold them at bay. She wiped her face with the back of her hand and tried to look brave. "But I don't know where to go."

He laughed. "This is Melbourne. There are hundreds of hotels. Just pick one."

"Is there a Ramada?" It was the first name that popped into her head. Crap! I am such an idiot. Of course they don't have Ramadas here.

"Absolutely. Which one do you want?"

She blinked, dumbfounded. The fact that Melbourne had a Ramada Inn disturbed her in a way that was hard to explain. Ramada Inns in Australia? You'd think she was still in Colorado. Staying in an American chain motel was the last thing she wanted, but she also needed sleep—and did it matter in the end? She could find something more Australian tomorrow. With the palms of her hands, she dried her cheeks and straightened. "One close to a shopping center. Please."

A Ramada is a Ramada is a Ramada. Jane sighed, dumped her purse on the bed, and looked around. A queen bed with a gold, generic, patterned spread, end tables of dark, fake wood, a dresser/television stand of the same, stock paintings of stock flowers, industrial cleaner smell. Yup, she could have been in Anytown, America. The only difference she could see was a teapot where the coffeepot would be and beside it a large pitcher she couldn't identify, with a cord plugged into the wall. Now that she took a closer look, the electrical socket was different also: one straight hole with two above it canted inward. Good thing she didn't bring anything electric.

It felt strange to be divested of all property and possessions except for what her purse contained. Lighter but laced with fear. Nothing to fall back on, nothing to sink into, nothing to point to and say this was hers, nothing to anchor her. Her "real" life thousands of miles away. Wasn't that what she wanted? Wasn't that what she had been planning ever since Ernie, now ashes and a few bone fragments, was diagnosed with stage IV lung cancer? To leave the obligations of home, family, and friends in a jumbled pile in her past? To be free to do what she wished, go where she wanted, live her dreams? Well, here was the dream, and it was a Ramada Inn. Sigh.

Sinking onto the bed, she glanced at the clock. Three in the afternoon. She was dead tired and closed her eyes to think for a second. If she went to sleep now, she would probably wake up in the middle of the night. But maybe a short nap would be OK. Reclining into the pillows, she tried to relax. At once, Ernie's face invaded her thoughts, and memories of his last days, gasping, sweating, and accusing her of not saving him reeled through her mind unbidden. Her eyes shot open, and she bolted upright, dread constricting her chest, heart pounding. Better she should try and stay up.

Swinging her legs over the side of the bed, she rubbed her face. She felt grimy and sweaty and feared she stank. Though she wanted a shower, she had no desire to put on the same clothes she'd been wearing for the last two days. The taxi driver had pointed out a shopping center on the way to the motel that seemed a couple of blocks away. Maybe she should try and buy some clothes while it was still light out. When did the sun go down around here anyhow?

In the bathroom she splashed cold water on her face and washed her hands. She undid her ponytail and ran her fingers through her hair while she stared into the mirror. It hung to her shoulders, greasy and resembling limp, gray-brown spaghetti. The wrinkles around her eyes and mouth seemed accentuated with blue eyeliner while the fluorescent lights sucked all the color out of her face. Even the bags under her eyes carried bags. She needed washing; she needed sleep; she needed a cosmetics department. But she wasn't going to shower or sleep, and all her makeup was sitting in America. Tears began to well once more. With a snarl, she slammed her palm against the marbleized sink top. Was this any way to begin a new life? Was she going to melt into a puddle of self-loathing before she even had one adventure? Was she going to be everything Ernie said she was? Pulling her hair back again, she strode to the bed, threw her purse over her shoulder, and pulled open the door. Appearances be damned. If you don't have it, buy it.

She filled two shopping carts at a Kmart in the mall, which, while also disturbing (like Ramadas, she never expected to see a Kmart here), was at least convenient. By the time she made it back to the motel lobby, she was exhausted from the shopping and the walk back carrying all her purchases. She collapsed against the counter and blinked at the clerk. The elevator rendition of Black

Sabbath's "Iron Man" oozed from speakers behind his head.

"Do you have room service here?"

The clerk shook his head, eyeing all the baggage she hadn't checked in with. "Sorry, ma'am. But, no worries, there's a restaurant around the corner there." He indicated a potted fern standing at the corner of the wall.

Jane craned to the left and saw the beginning of a short corridor with a menu-clad sandwich board standing near an open door. She grimaced. She didn't want to dine with a bunch of strangers, but unless she wanted to starve or go out again seeking another restaurant, it seemed the only option. After thanking him, she trudged to her room, threw off her clothes, and climbed into the shower.

Ah, the wonder of hot, falling water. She stood with her hands against the wall, head hanging under the stream, luxuriating in the feel of it all. Water cascaded from her hair, threaded down her spine, unwound muscles taut from too many hours in planes, taxis, and malls. Liquid heaven. Her new shampoo smelled of roses, and the lather sluiced down her arms and tickled her armpits while she massaged her scalp. Some of her exhaustion seemed to wash down the drain with the bubbles. She hated to turn the knob and bring it to an end, but her stomach was beginning to complain. She found herself looking forward to eating in the dining room after all, remembering an exquisite sandwich she'd eaten at the airport. Roasted eggplant, pumpkin, and capsicum (aka red pepper) on focaccia bread, with olive oil and vinegar. Her mouth watered thinking about it. If airport food could be that good, maybe motel restaurant food could be even better.

It wasn't. The menu seemed transplanted from America, and the food tasted dry and bland, as if it had been flown in precooked from the States. It reminded her of the people in the Melbourne airport. They all looked so American. Not Aussie at all.

All her imaginings of Australia had been of a blood-red desert and midnight-dark Aborigines daubed in white paint, dressed in feathers, with flattened noses and yellow eyes. Of kangaroos and emus wandering freely, koalas munching eucalyptus leaves high in the trees. Of the Southern Cross and men dressed like Crocodile Dundee, including accent and attitude. She'd never considered it could be the metropolitan mélange of three-piece suits, high heels, polo shirts, Nikes, and Columbia jackets she had seen in the airport. She couldn't even tell who was Australian or just visiting. Now Ramadas and American food. It seemed Australia had turned into a mini-USA, and how rotten was that?

She finished her dinner, paid for the check with her Visa card, and waved goodbye to a couple of women with blond-streaked hair who'd been scrutinizing her during the whole meal. They resembled clones—with their long, painted nails, crew-necked sweaters, and cropped jackets. Odd Melbournian clones. At least they didn't look as if they'd materialized from a Denver Ramada. But if they were how the average Australian woman looked, she was going to stick out like a kangaroo in the Rockies.

Settled in her new flannel jammies, covers tucked around her shoulders, she flicked off the light, closed her eyes, and waited for sleep to engulf her. And waited. Turned on her side and waited. Turned on her other side and waited. Flipped onto her stomach and waited. Rolled onto her back and waited. Sighed and turned on the light. Not only was sleep hiding in the closet, afraid to come out, but Ernie had also joined her in bed and was now harassing her the way he'd done all their married life.

Earnest James Mullet. Dead, cremated, half a world away, and still around to haunt her.

Jane jumped out of bed and stomped around the room, hoping to drive his harsh, guttural smoker's voice out of her skull. What the hell do you think you're doing? he ranted. What a stupid plan—or should I say lack of plan. Jump on a plane without thinking anything out. Throwing away my hard-earned money on a bunch of stuff that's total crap. Why didn't you bring what you owned? You've got tons of clothes and other stuff. Closets full of stuff. Stuff you had to have. Stuff you never needed. And now here you are, sleepless. You were always so hopeless. A dead-assed bitch. Can't even run away from home right.

"Shut up," she hissed. "Shut up, shut up, shut up! You're dead. Get out of my head and go back to your urn."

She paused, closed her eyes, and pictured his face moments after he'd died. The flaccid features, skin pallid beneath the brownish tinge the tobacco had infused into it, thinning hair stretched across his bare scalp in a poorly attempted comb-over. She had poked his cheek after the last breath had oozed from between his parted lips. The skin felt warm, but the resistance was gone. It felt as if she could mold it into any shape she desired, now that no spark of life would ease it back over the bones. For a moment she was tempted to pull his mouth into a grin and bare his yellowed teeth. Instead, she stared, taking in the moment when her life changed. Taking her first breath of freedom. Then she jerked the sheet over his head and called the mortuary.

The memory seemed to quell the voice, and she crawled back into bed. Cradling a pillow to her chest, she curled into a ball. Tears welled and spilled onto the freshly laundered cotton fabric—tears for what, she wasn't sure. Not for Ernie. She had shed all the tears she ever intended to shed for or about him. Maybe for herself, for all the lost years and maybe for those still to be found. Maybe because she had left everything that was comfortable and secure thousands of miles away. And maybe, just maybe, just because.

Australian adventure, day two, was spent almost entirely in bed. Around midday she woke enough to wash her face, slip on clothes, and seek out food in the restaurant, after which, still exhausted, she lay on the bed and channel-surfed, too tired to even think about Zeus or her campervan. She briefly considered searching for a more Aussie motel but was too wrung out to even try. Then came a restless night laced with Ernie dreams.

It was raining outside her third day Down Under. She glared out the window at the drenched Melbourne skyline in the distance and wished for sunshine. Pulling a purple sweater closed across her chest, she climbed on the bed and unfolded the brochure for Zeus and her map of the country. Pictures of vans lined the pages. Big ones, little ones, tall ones, ones that resembled a regular SUV, ones that could have carried all Ernie's relatives and a few friends to boot. They came with and without toilets, showers, kitchens, air conditioners, refrigerators, and microwaves. At least they all had some kind of sleeping facility. After a few minutes, she set the brochure aside. How did she know what she wanted or needed? She didn't even know where she was going.

Turning to the map steepled on the bed beside her, she flattened it with a palm and then stared. The country seemed huge on paper. She remembered that she'd learned somewhere that Australia and the US were about the same size. That was a lot of country. With one finger she traced a road that headed up the center of the country from south to north—a very long road. Then she ran her finger along the eastern shore: Cairns and the Great Barrier Reef, Brisbane, Sydney. On the western shore, Perth. Darwin at the very top, Adelaide near the bottom. Lots of nothing in between.

Sighing, she leaned back. She wanted to see everything she could see before her tourist visa expired in three months. Ayers Rock, the Nullarbor Plain, the rainforest, the ocean, where koalas lived, Sydney Opera House. From the little research she'd done back when this trip was a vague dream, she'd learned that most of the country's population lived along the coast. That meant a lot of empty land in the middle and many, many miles (ahem, kilometers) to traverse. She wasn't sure that three months would be enough.

An antsy feeling enveloped her. She was wasting time waiting for the rain to stop. Swinging her legs over the side of the bed, she picked up the phone and dialed Zeus's number. After a few rings a deep voice answered. "Zeus Mobile. Geoff speaking."

"Hi, my name's Jane Mullet, and I was in your place a couple of days ago looking for a campervan, but you didn't have any available."

"Ah, yes." The voice resembled a smile. "I remember. Have you decided on the type of vehicle you want?"

Her heart skipped a beat. The black man. Now she knew his name. "No, Geoff, but I do have some questions."

"What do you want to know?"

"I want to drive into the outback, and I see on the map there aren't a lot of paved roads out there. Can I take the campervan on unpaved roads?"

14

"That depends on what kind of vehicle you're driving and where you want to go. There are places none of our vehicles are permitted to drive, but most of the roads are accessible. If you want to get off sealed roads, then you're going to need a four-wheel-drive camper equipped with an outback package." He sounded like a commercial.

"What's the outback package, and do I need it?"

"I think so, especially if you're traveling alone. Are you traveling alone?"

For no good reason, she felt defensive. "Yes, I am." A little too strong maybe. She took a breath.

"The Zeus Packer sleeps two, is four-wheel drive, and has a survival guide, air jack, recovery shovel, GPS, extra water and petrol storage, a satellite tracker with emergency connections, and all the usual items—cookware, linen, and dishes."

She gulped. Survival guide? Satellite tracker? How dangerous was it out there? She had pictured Mojave Desert dangerous, not ends-of-the-Earth, filled-with-poisonous-plants/animals/insects/floods/fire-and-wrath-of-God dangerous. Either Zeus stood to make a lot of money renting unnecessary items to gullible tourists, or this was going to be more of an adventure than she'd anticipated. "How much would all that be for three months?"

He quoted a figure with five digits before he got to the decimal. She'd never understood what it meant to have one's breath taken away until she heard the number. It was more, far more, than just a chunk of change. Though she could cover the amount with her debit card, she still had to worry about gas, food, and nonessential items that always cropped up. What would she do if she ran out of money? Then again, if she wanted to see more than the coast of the country, she'd have to rent a vehicle that was allowed on unpaved roads. Damn.

"So, what would it be without the outback package?" she asked, hoping for some huge reduction. The figure was less, enough less that she considered taking it, but still far more than she had expected to spend. "I don't know."

Geoff sighed. "Listen, miss, I've been in this business for many years, and I've seen people get into all sorts of trouble. If you can manage it, I'd suggest you take the whole package. You have no idea what can happen out there."

He sounded less like a commercial now and more like a salesman who didn't want customers to be angry when they got into trouble and didn't have the needed equipment. Or dead on the side of the road.

"I still don't know. Is there any piece of the outback package I can drop that would make a difference in price without hurting me?"

A long pause on the other end. "Well, I guess you could do without the satellite tracker. It is the most expensive piece of equipment and the least used. I suppose I could work up such a deal." After a couple of minutes of silence, he quoted another price—leaning toward the cheaper one but still high enough that she had to think for a couple of minutes. At last she shook her head. Was she going to do this or not? *Coward*, Ernie intoned in her head.

She straightened. "I'll take it. How long will it take to get the camper?"

"I can have one ready for you in a week."

"A week! I thought you said it would take a couple of days."

"That was before I knew you wanted this type of vehicle. I'll need to get one down from Alice Springs, and that's a long way." His voice hinted that the edges of his patience were raveling.

She tapped her foot. Did she want to hang around Melbourne for a week? She glanced at the open map on the bed. "What if I picked it up in Alice Springs? How soon could I get it then?"

"Let me see." She could hear computer keys tapping in the background. "I'm sorry, but it looks the same."

She opened her mouth to protest that his statement didn't make any sense, then decided it wasn't worth the effort. "Fine. I'll pick it up in a week. Here."

The next half an hour was spent providing all her information. When they were finished, Geoff rang off sounding downright chipper. No doubt because of the huge commission he was going to get off the booking, she snarked to herself. He might be happy, but she was frustrated—though, to be honest, also a bit excited. But stuck in Melbourne for a week. Drat. Throwing back her shoulders, she ran both hands through her hair. Well, if she was stuck in Melbourne, why shouldn't she see what there was to see? She grabbed her purse and jacket, stuffed the room key into her pocket, and headed out the door.

The lobby of the motel had a few brochures, and she leafed through them looking for something interesting. The National Gallery of Victoria, Cook's Cottage, Puffing Billy Railway, theaters, shopping centers, and on and on and on. Shopping she eliminated. She'd done enough of that her first day there to last her weeks. The Melbourne Museum and the botanical gardens caught her eye. It might feel good to be outside, even in the rain. After all, she wasn't going to melt.

With a little help from the woman behind the desk, she was able to figure out how to get to the gardens by tram. The woman also suggested a rental car, but Jane wasn't quite ready to take that leap. She would be driving soon enough and better she should be a dedicated and watchful passenger first. After thanking the clerk, she zipped up her jacket, stuffed the brochures into her purse, and stepped into the rain. Immediately she pulled the hood up over her head. It wasn't raining; it was pouring. At this rate she'd be soaked before she'd gone a quarter mile—no, quarter kilometer. Well, maybe shopping wasn't off the list. She hoped the mall carried umbrellas.

The Royal Botanic Gardens Victoria was gorgeous, even in the rain. The downpour turned into a steady drizzle, and she was able to put down her hood as she remained sheltered under the umbrella. She walked for hours trying to identify trees, bushes, and flowers from little placards scattered around the gardens. She wasn't sure she'd identified anything for certain and wondered if she'd be able to recognize any of the plants out in the wild—even something like the desert pea, so distinctive with its blood-red flowers and protruding coal-black centers circling a central stem. It looked more like a cell phone tower than anything.

While she strolled, she kept having the urge to comment on a flower or display to Ernie. It was weird. He would never have been interested in such a place, but she still would have told him all about it when she got home. He would have made a sarcastic comment, and she would have gotten angry and stomped out of the room. But he was gone, and the hole that had been chewed into her life gaped, black and empty. Who would she talk to now? Who would she tell about her day or the things she'd seen or what she'd felt? Even if

Ernie had rarely uttered a kind word, he'd listened and responded. Now her company was a void.

A wave of loneliness swept over her, catching her in its arms and carrying her to tears again. She collapsed onto a bench, head bent, grateful that the rain had corralled most visitors indoors. She had no desire for someone to stop and inquire how she was. She had no words to outline her heartbreak and the inherent contradiction in losing the man she had, for so long, wanted to die while still wanting the familiarity of his presence. It didn't make sense. She couldn't explain it to herself, much less anyone else, and she didn't want to try. Closing her umbrella, she turned her face to the rain and let it merge with her tears.

Time crawled by. Though she tried to fill the hours with sightseeing, eating at exotic restaurants, and watching movies and television, the moments alone piled one on the other, and it became harder to shush the voice and vision of Ernie during the last months of his life. He shuffled through her mind, skeletal, oxygen tube wrapped under his nose and trailing behind him like a tether tying him to the humming machine in the corner of their bedroom. He coughed and wheezed and edged away from life a breath at a time, all the while cataloging her faults and failures.

Not once in all that time did he admit he was dying. Not once did he allow a hospice worker or aide into the house to give her a hand—only the nurse who provided his painkillers. Even when she was so exhausted she could barely stand. And when he was in pain or couldn't eat or sleep, it became her fault. She was too loud; she didn't give him the right medications; her cooking was inedible. She prayed for him to die, begged God to take him, then ravaged herself with guilt for wishing such a thing. Now she was reliving it all again.

Slamming a fist into her pillow, she howled inside. This was not her new life. This was not what she wanted to be doing. She wanted to lock Ernie into the darkest corner of her mind and dissolve the key in acid. "Get out of my head," she snarled, fists pressing against her temples. When the memories still battered her, she grabbed her purse and fled to the street. She walked until the sun backlit the Melbourne skyline, until her legs ached, until her mind lapsed into silence. Then she crossed another day off the week of waiting and fell into bed.

It arrived. The day. Traffic be damned; today she was going driving.

Geoff wasn't anywhere in sight when she pushed through the glass door into the Zeus office. Instead, a skinny kid in a red-and-brown plaid cowboy shirt and horn-rimmed glasses stood behind the counter. He looked twenty years old, if that, acne still peppering his cheeks and forehead. She wondered if he had to shave more than once a week. And where was his uniform? Was this his first day on the job, and did he know what he was supposed to be doing? She wanted Geoff back. Heaving an inward sigh, she approached. "Hi," she said, plopping her purse on the counter. "I'm Jane Mullet, and I'm here to pick up my van."

The kid squinted at her, then at the computer screen in front of him. "What did you say your name was?"

"Mullet. Jane Mullet. I have a Zeus Packer reserved. It's supposed to be ready today."

He punched a few keys. "How do you spell that?"

She took a deep breath, closed her eyes, and spelled her last name. God, please, please, please let it be here.

He squinted some more, then looked up, smiled, and nodded. "Oh yeah. We're still doing some last-minute checks on it, but it should be ready for you very soon."

"Wonderful." She beamed back at him.

"Now, we just need to do a little paperwork."

The "paperwork" consisted of twenty pages of forms, each containing multiple blanks for her to fill out. As she worked, the kid tapped at the keyboard for a few moments, then headed into the garage. From the corner of her eye she saw him wander behind a huge camper and disappear. Pausing, she wondered if the behemoth on the other side of the glass was hers. She couldn't imagine herself negotiating Australian traffic in something as large as a tank. Gads! She hoped that one wasn't it.

By the time she finished initialing the last space, signing all the signature lines, and dating all the dates, the kid still hadn't returned. She fished her driver's license from her wallet, unfolded her proof of insurance on the Subaru back home, and slid them both inside her passport. Then waited. Five minutes. Ten. By the twenty-minute mark, she was drumming her passport on the papers, trying to decide if she should invade the garage in search of the kid. Just then, Geoff—thank the gods in all their incarnations—pushed into the office.

"G'day, Mrs. Mullet. How're you coming with that paperwork?" He smiled.

She pushed the packet with her passport on top across the counter. "All done. How's my camper?"

"Well, seems there's a little bit of a problem." He scanned the top form without looking up.

She felt her chest tighten. Not another week at the Ramada. "Problem?"

"Yes, the van they sent us has an oil leak, and I don't want you to be in the outback in any vehicle that isn't in top working condition. So I've upgraded you to a van we had a cancellation on." He glanced up. "Will that work for you?"

"That depends." From the corner of her eye she glanced out the garage window at the monster van. "What sort of vehicle is this and how much more is it going to cost?"

"Almost the same size but with a high top. No extra charge. Would you like to see it first?"

She nodded. "Absolutely."

He stepped out from behind the desk and opened the garage door for her. "Come then."

The garage reeked of diesel fuel overlayed with dust. The doors stood open, and the sound of semis rumbling past on the street outside combined with the whine of air tools in the garage made it impossible for her to hear what Geoff was saying. She caught a few words such as "enhanced" and "power" and "extra" but little of what lay between them. She figured it would do little good to protest until they were either inside the vehicle or back in the office. Then she could get him to repeat the whole thing.

They rounded the massive van, and he led her to something that looked akin to a Toyota Land Cruiser on steroids. Instead of a regular roof, it had a fiberglass top that looked to be at least four feet tall with windows. The tires were huge—at least thirty inches tall—and had treads that resembled teeth. The chassis of the vehicle was jacked up another four inches above that. It resembled something you'd see at a tractor pull rather than a campervan. She looked at the bottom of the door and wondered if she'd need a ladder to climb inside. A spare tire hung from the back door under the window. Geoff walked to the back and pulled open the two small doors.

"What do you think?"

She peered inside. A faux wood counter lined the right side of the vehicle, complete with sink and chest refrigerator. Round, silver buttons studded what appeared to be doors under the counter. On the other side, a bench seat with a bolster ran the length of the back, upholstered in blue serge with a table in front of it on a single pedestal. It smelled of Pine-Sol or some Aussie equivalent. The top made the inside appear tall enough to stand up in without stooping.

Geoff waved toward the interior. "Why don't you climb in?"

Jane approached the back, put one foot on the back bumper, and heaved herself inside. OK, it was doable without a ladder. Reaching inside, Geoff punched one of the buttons. It popped out and transformed into a knob, which he used to open the door.

"Here is your stove." He indicated a gas camp stove sequestered in the compartment. "You can take it out and cook with it on the counter or here." Reaching up, he pulled down a shelf that was folded against the inside of the right-hand door. He showed her where the gas canister lived and how to light the stove. Then he opened another compartment. Inside nestled pots and pans, lids, a tea kettle, and two skillets. Another contained plates, cups, glasses, and bowls, and another towels, washcloths, a bucket, and a clothesline with a dozen or so clothespins. In a drawer she found silverware and several tea towels. He walked her through how to set up the beds, top and bottom, and where to stow the linens and other bedding supplies. He pointed out the location of the water tank, batteries, hoses, extension cords, broom and dustpan, and finally, how to operate the lights.

She tried to remember everything he said, but it ran into a blur of opened doors and hidden compartments. Nonetheless, she was impressed. It seemed a tidy little home away from home, clean and well designed. If she'd had any doubts about being able to live on the road, they were extinguished. She ran a hand over the smooth surface of the seat and imagined herself leaning back against the window having tea. Yes, this would work.

Next, they moved to the front seats and vehicle operation. The steering wheel was on the right. She grimaced. Geoff opened the door for her. "Come on; up you go."

She climbed into the driver's seat feeling strange, and examined the gauges and signals. The turn signal was on the right side of the steering wheel, not the left side, and the lights and wipers were on the other side. This was going to take some getting used to. The vehicle had an automatic transmission and automatic four-wheel drive. She and Ernie had owned a 1983 Land Cruiser back when they thought driving old mountain passes was fun, but this thing made that one seem antique. The dials and gauges shone like something out of the space shuttle, and the conveniences (no more having to get out of the vehicle to lock the hubs, built-in GPS, CD player) were things no car of hers had ever contained.

It felt too good. A niggling sense that she didn't deserve all this ate at her. A part of her wanted to turn down all the luxury and get an old four-wheel-drive vehicle and a tent. Did she deserve to be touring Australia in a fabulous camper? She gripped the wheel and closed her eyes. For once in her life she was going to go first class. She was going to do something wonderful for herself, even if it killed her.

"Will this do?" Geoff stood by the open door looking concerned.

She flashed him a broad grin. "This will be perfect."

A relieved smile creased his face. "Good. Then why don't we go and finish the paperwork."

Back in the office, he found several more sheets of warnings and limitations for her to read, initial, and sign. One covered where she could and couldn't drive. She read it, her brow furrowing. "You mean I can't take this vehicle to all these places?" She pointed to a list of dirt roads that were restricted. "I wanted to see some of these places. That's why I got the four-wheel drive."

Geoff shook his head. "I'm sorry. You can purchase a waiver for these," he indicated the group at the top, "but the rest are strictly off-limits. If you are seen driving these roads, the fines are very steep."

She frowned. "And just how much is this waiver?" He quoted a price that was less than the hundreds of dollars she had imagined but enough to give her pause. She acceded to buying the waiver and handed over her debit card. The total price tag was substantial, and she crossed her fingers that it would go through. Within seconds the machine began to chatter while it printed out her receipt, and she sighed in relief once again.

It took another thirty minutes to get all the checks done, the paperwork copied and filed, and instruction manuals found and released before she was able to roll her suitcases out to the camper and stash them in the back. After she climbed behind the wheel, Geoff handed her several books filled with information about caravan parks all over Australia and a fistful of colorful brochures that hawked every attraction in the nation. Then he stepped back and gave her a thumbs up. She keyed the engine to life. "Remember how tall you are," he shouted from the rear of the camper. "And stay on the left side of the road!"

She smiled and waved, then put it into gear. Easing out of the garage, she whispered, "Left, left, left" as she approached the street. She flipped up what appeared to be the turn signal lever, and the wipers sprang to life. "Damn!" She switched levers, killing the wipers and initiating the turn signal. She stopped at the end of the driveway and planned her turn. Go right, cross the closest lane, and move into the far lane. Just like turning left in the States. She sucked in a breath, pressed down on the gas, and drove into the left lane. Grinning, she accelerated. One turn down. A thousand more to go.

Chapter 2

HAVING CONQUERED her first corner, she faced her second challenge: how to get out of Melbourne. She had mapped out her route before she left the hotel and had it sitting on the seat beside her, each road number and turn listed on a sheet of lined paper. The biggest problem was the roundabouts, traffic circles to her. She almost hit a tiny car the first time she encountered one, wanting to turn right while traffic was flowing left. Luckily, she hadn't made it all the way into the lane before the little gray car came zipping straight at her. She jerked the wheel and felt the Packer sway as she swung a hard left, avoiding the car and slewing into the correct lane. Her heart slammed into her breastbone, and her hands shook while she edged around the circle.

She was so upset that she drove around the circle five times before she could pull herself together enough to figure out which street she needed to take to get off it. When she pulled onto a straight street again, she found the nearest parking spot and stopped.

For a long while she sat with her head resting against the steering wheel, panting. Ernie laughed at her. "And you thought you could drive out here! You always were a stupid bitch." Tears streamed down her cheeks from beneath closed lids. He was right. Goddammit, he was right. What was she thinking—that she would be able to drive in Australia? She was a stupid woman. A very, very stupid woman.

She flipped the ignition off and lay her head back on the seat. Her hands still quaked in her lap, but her heart rate had dropped into a more reasonable range. The tears subsided, and she wiped her face with her palms, then ran her fingers through her hair. That was close. She'd never been that close to having an accident in her entire life. Here she was, forty-five, and had never even dented a fender. Her insurance company loved her. It made tons of money off her premiums and never had to pay a claim. Now she'd almost killed another person with her driving. And she'd had to travel to the other end of the world to do it. How sad was that?

She rose and climbed into the back of the van. From the small refrigerator she pulled out a complimentary bottle of water and took a sip. The cool liquid felt good sliding down her throat. Slumping onto the bench seat, she shoved her legs out to the line of cubbies on the opposite side and cradled the water on her lap. Now what to do? She could take the camper back, but Zeus wasn't going to refund any of her money. Page three, paragraph seven, sentence one: "All monies are to be paid in advance and are nonrefundable."

She remembered initialing that one. So, if she couldn't return the camper, she could stay here and live in it for the next three months. Parked on a side street in Melbourne. Bzzzz. Wrong. Or she could get back behind the wheel and try again. Her stomach lurched, but she knew she had to do it. She took another swig of water. OK, she could do it. She *would* do it.

She climbed to her feet and shuffled to the front. Once she was buckled in, she fired up the engine. Her hands were sweating a little. "Left," she murmured. Turn signal on, she checked her mirrors and pulled into traffic again. At the next roundabout, she waited at the intersection until she was certain she knew which way traffic flowed, then eased into it and emerged on the other side as if she'd been doing it her entire life. She smiled. She could so do this.

Once on the M1 heading for Geelong, she relaxed. Rolling green hills flowed by, and the highway was a multiple-lane affair, so there was no chance she was going to be in the wrong lane. She stayed to the far left since most of the slower vehicles seemed to drive there. Aside from the fact it felt strange to have cars passing her on the right, she felt almost normal again. She kept reminding herself she was still driving on the left and to stay there, but her confidence seemed to be returning.

Aside from a couple of sedans and a few large trucks that lumbered by, she cruised along by herself. Houses dropped away, and soon she was traveling through what appeared to be farmland and fields. She didn't see any cattle or farm equipment, but she'd lived in rural America long enough to spot fence lines and recognize crops in the field. Where trees clustered, they were tall and some-what gangly. Eucalyptus, she decided, or what the Aussies called gum trees. She remembered seeing them in the botanical gardens, lots of them. In lots of different varieties. What varieties were these, she wondered. Ghost gums, stringy gums, rainbow gums? Or plain old ordinary gums, if there was such a thing. At this distance, their leaves appeared bluish, so she decided she would call them blue gums no matter what a botanist would say.

Before she knew it, she was on the outskirts of Geelong. Her nerves ratcheted up when she realized she needed to change roads. She'd wanted to get to the beach and, according to the map, had to exit the highway near what appeared to be the center of town to catch the beach road. Palms sweating, she eased onto the exit ramp and into heavier Mercer Street traffic. It seemed she was driving a semi, though she knew it was only a little larger than an SUV. She felt blind and kept glancing in the mirrors on the side of the camper, checking and rechecking that she wasn't going to hit anyone before she switched lanes. The drive through the business section felt like trying to thread a needle wearing oven mitts. When she reached Western Beach, she breathed a huge sigh of relief as she pulled into the parking lot and shut off the engine.

She rolled down the windows and sat for a minute. Adrenaline hummed through her veins but faded, washed away by the smell of salt water and something faintly eucalyptusy. Ah, those gum trees. Pulling the keys from the ignition, she climbed out, flung her purse over her shoulder, and headed for the sea.

The sun warmed her head and shoulders while she ambled along the paved path by the ocean. A little greenery dotted the shore, but the place was generally flat and barren. She didn't care. She'd made it to her first destination intact—shaken but intact. She'd also come to the conclusion that her brush with autocide back in Melbourne was the best thing that could have happened to her. She didn't think she'd soon forget which way to turn when approaching a round-about. She'd be getting lots more practice at it; she was sure. The Aussies seemed to love dropping roundabouts into any convenient intersection, like M&M'S on a map. She much preferred the regular kind of intersection with stoplights and turn lanes, but she didn't get to choose here. In short order she was sure she'd be a pro at them.

By the time she reached the pier, she was famished. She had considered eating her first meal on the road in her camper, but instead she decided to walk out to the end of the pier and eat there. Her guidebooks said it was a great restaurant, and she was game.

Pumpkin was on the menu, and she ordered it, remembering the sandwich at the airport that had so thrilled her. She paused over the "bug and bacon" entrée, thinking it could be something exotic, but the "bug" part brought up visions of something black with multiple legs squashed on bread with a bacon slice on top. Ugh. She couldn't swallow her repulsion enough to ask the waiter what it was.

The guidebooks understated the quality of the food. Her pump-kin fritter melted in her mouth, and the iced coffee resembled a dessert more than a drink. It had ice cream in it, something she never would have imagined. She felt decadent while she sipped the rich, sweet concoction, surrounded by smells of grilling seafood and the gentle clink of silverware against ceramic in the background. Outside the floor-to-ceiling windows, gulls dipped and swayed over the aquamarine waters of Corio Bay.

Ernie would have hated all of it—the different food, ice cream in his coffee, driving on the "wrong" side of the road. Ernie hated so much. And because he hated anything new or different or outside his schedule, they had rarely traveled, always ate at two restaurants—one ten miles away—watched one television station, listened to one radio station, shopped at one grocery store. And on and on and on.

After their first few years of marriage, Jane had given up trying to convince him to broaden his horizons. When he was younger, he had been adaptable enough that when his favorite restaurant went out of business, he had allowed her to take him to a new one. At first, he had hated it, but he got used to the food and added it to his list of acceptable places. That had changed soon enough. The older he had gotten, the more rigid he had become. By the end, a steel girder would have displayed more flexibility.

She drained the last of the coffee from the glass. How had she remained married to him all those years? It was going to be twenty-five years this July. Twenty-five years. She shook her head. That was one anniversary she was not going to regret missing. Twenty-five years. Over half her life. When she looked back on it, it seemed more akin to a long prison sentence than a marriage. But no one had chained her to a wall. She could have walked out anytime she wanted to. And she had wanted to, hadn't she? Two months earlier, she would have answered with a most emphatic "yes." And now? Now it seemed more of a puzzle why, if she was so unhappy, she had stayed.

Oh, she had a list of reasons: money (she hadn't worked full-time since Ernie's promotion to the Cortez office), her family (her parents didn't believe in divorce), his family (they had said she would leave him, and she was damned if she would prove them right), friends (everyone said they had a model marriage), but most of all herself. She was too afraid to go. She didn't think she could make it on her own and was too afraid to try. Now here she was on her own. And thousands of miles away to boot. How foolish she had been. If only—if only—if only—if only—

With a sigh, she placed the glass back on the table and rose. Past. It was all in the past. Now she had a life and a mission to see the country. And traffic to deal with.

Fed and fortified, the return to the highway didn't seem so daunting. She stayed on her side of the road, turned into all the appropriate lanes, and felt reasonably competent by the time she was doing 80 kph on the road to Apollo Bay. Somewhere in the middle of the city of Torquay, the road lost a couple of lanes and morphed into the Great Ocean Road. Jane liked the sound of that. "The Great Ocean Road," she intoned, the name rolling off her tongue. It rang of ships, foreign ports, and adventure. She said it several more times, savoring the feel of it even if there was no ocean in sight. In fact, it looked downright landlocked, with clusters of gum trees and greening fields on either side of the road. She had so enjoyed sitting by the bay at lunch; as she drove on, she yearned again to see the sea, the ocean, the big water.

Colorado was not known for vast expanses of water and Cortez even less. A reservoir here and there was the norm. For a year when she was ten or so and living in Northglenn with her family, Jane had been entranced by stories of the sea. She'd read pirate adventures and stories of great voyages and dreamed of cruising the oceans in search of something lost or found. Her reading sailed the world, her imagination with it. Like the captains in the stories, she was mistress of her own fate, charting a course into her future, in charge of the world around her.

Then her reading choices began to land on strange continents filled with bizarre animals, plants, and painted natives, dark and strange with spears in hand and necklaces of teeth hanging down their chests. When she discovered Australia and the Aborigines, she felt she'd found her paradise. Surrounded by ocean, filled with desert, peopled by one of the oldest races on earth, she lived and breathed and dreamed of Australia for years. She fantasized about standing on a beach surrounded by men and women, mostly naked, dotted with white, chalky paint, and chanting while she let the waves lap at her feet. Ah, if only.

One chilly Saturday in November when she was twelve, she swore an oath to herself to go there. It was cleaning day, and all morning she had mopped and dusted, put clothes through the washer, and scrubbed bathrooms. Mikey, her eleven-year-old younger brother, sat in his room playing Nintendo. Blessed male, he didn't have to clean anything except his room once in a while. She hated him. Her older sister, Sally, was sixteen and had a job bagging groceries at the local Safeway. Saturdays were her long days, which meant she was gone from seven in the morning until four or five. That left Jane—too young to have a job and too female to be considered exempt.

That particular Saturday, her father had gone plinking with a couple of his friends. Plinking, according to her mother, was an excuse to drink beer and spend a small fortune on ammunition. Her father maintained that it was the only hobby he had, and after a grueling week at the packing plant, he deserved a little time out of the house. What it cost in ammo was little in comparison to what it would cost to deal with a nervous breakdown. What it was, Jane discovered one blistering July morning a couple of years earlier when her dad agreed to take her with him, was shooting at bottles out on the prairie. The beer-drinking part happened after most of the ammo was spent. The only therapeutic thing she could find in it was the joy at seeing a bottle splinter into a thousand pieces if you hit it just right. It was a glorious sight. Brown glass spraying outward in an explosion of shards. She'd managed to hit a few and had basked in the praise her father showered on her.

That morning after breakfast, her father collected his .22 rifle, the revolver he'd bought at a gun show in downtown Denver, a Luger that looked real but shot only pellets, his ammunition box, and a canvas vest with leather patches at each shoulder. He threw it all into the Chevy station wagon, and roared off without even saying goodbye. Her parents had been fighting again. Must have been one of the late-night ones, she thought, those held in snarled tones downstairs after the kids had gone to bed and left unresolved. Her mother's frustration had targeted Jane.

"Look at this house," she'd ranted before the sound of the Chevy's bad muffler had faded in the distance. "You kids have destroyed it. I work all week to keep things up, but in just one evening all my work is trashed. Well, I'm not putting up with it anymore. Janie, get off your butt and get to work. I want the kitchen floor stripped and rewaxed. Bathrooms too. I'm tired of living like this. Now, to it!"

She snatched Jane's half-eaten bowl of Cheerios from the table and dropped it in the sink. Mikey smirked as he scooped his bowl from the table and fled to his room before the sights of his mother's anger found him too. Jane opened her mouth to protest, but her mother spun and leveled a finger at her.

35

"Not one word from you, young lady. Not one word. I've carted you around all week without a word of thanks. Well, it's payback time. After the floors, I want everything vacuumed and dusted. And clean up that pile of dirty laundry in the middle of your floor. I am not your maid. It's about time you learned to chip in around here."

After four hours of "chipping in," Jane sat slumped by the toilet in the kids' bathroom, sobbing. The sound of her mother's sewing machine rumbled in the background. None of this was fair: her brother never having to do anything, her sister at work and not having to help out. She was the one who had to clean. She was a prisoner. Nothing more than a prisoner to her mother's anger.

She rested her head on the edge of the bathtub, feeling shackled to the toilet, to a life of misery. It was so unfair. Unfair as slavery. And that's what she was, nothing more than a slave to a family of ingrates. She couldn't take it anymore. She *wouldn't* take it anymore. She had to get out. She had to leave. And leave she would.

Dropping the toilet brush, she rose and slipped down the stairs. She grabbed her coat off the line of pegs by the front door and slid outside, the chugging of the sewing machine never missing a beat.

A chill wind ripped through the housing development. Jane clutched her coat, bent her head into the cold, and stomped down the street toward open ground. Their house sat at the edge of an older development skirting the prairie. Beyond the manicured lawns and tidily laid-out streets, dead grass the color of straw climbed hills and slid into ravines. The air smelled of dust and drying vegetation. Scattered in the deep places, cottonwood trees clustered near ephemeral stream beds, their roots buried deep in search of moisture. Crows, magpies, rabbits, and foxes inhabited the land, with an occasional eagle spinning lazy circles in the air, scouring the grass below for small rodents.

But not that day. That day the world lay hunkered in hollows and sheltered places, waiting for the wind to blow itself out. The prairie grass hugged the earth and the cottonwoods groaned. A hint of the coming winter scented the air.

Jane climbed to the top of a hill. Throwing back her head, she drew the hazy blue of the arching sky into her lungs. Coat unbuttoned and flapping around her chest, she stretched out her arms and reached for the sea, the place in her head where her dreams dwelled. She was a ship, forging through wind and wave for the distant shore. The Cape of Good Hope. The East China Sea. The Indies. A place so far that her world would disappear. A place so far that she could be free, slave to no one, her own person.

She returned home eventually, but that was the day she decided she was going to go to Australia, one way or another. It was the farthest point on the map and could be her land of freedom. Her home. Who could touch her there?

And now here she was, captain of her own campervan, off to chart lands she'd only read and dreamed about. A smile inched across her lips. Even though she could almost sense Ernie sitting in the seat next to her, sneering, she let the smile expand.

Forty minutes after she slid onto the Great Ocean Road, it veered seaward, and Jane caught her breath. To her left, the ocean, turquoise as the stones set in Navajo jewelry back home, lapped the horizon, glistening breakers expiring into foam on the beach. When she could find a place to pull off the road, she parked.

A wooden barrier, weathered gray, lined the parking area. She leaned against it, sucking in a salt breeze laced with the taste of strange green things, the sun warm on her bare arms and face. This was what she had always dreamed about. She felt transported into a novel, except it was far more beautiful than any seascape she'd imagined. From where she stood, a variety of bushes, some covered in white flowers, crept down to the sand. Their leaves shone in the afternoon light, tickled by the breeze, a perfect counterpoint to the rumble and gleam of the waves below.

She stood transfixed, the minutes sliding by unnoticed. She felt like she'd come home in some strange way—Cortez, Colorado, was the dream, and this, the reality. If she turned, she imagined she could see her house, nestled in the nearby village of Anglesea, her husband there, tall and tan, mowing the grass or sipping a lager out back on the deck. The red bricks of the house needed pointing in some places, and the windowsills were peeling, but the work could wait. Kids ran laughing down the street, baseball bats—no, cricket bats—in hand, headed for a park or playground. Her husband would smile when he heard them and make some comment about how it would have been nice to have a few of their own. She would nod, come and rub his back, and kiss the top of his head, inhaling his musk. No trace of cigarettes, just soap and the ineffable scent of male. Then, turning, she'd put some more shrimp on the barbie.

The sound of another car pulling next to the camper jerked her from her reverie. One more look, one more breath, and she would leave. She turned and realized she hadn't taken one picture of the sight that had entranced her so. Stepping to the vehicle, she dug her camera out of the back and returned to the railing. A young couple had climbed from a tiny gray car and stood near the edge, arms wrapped around each other, heads touching. Ah, lovers, she thought, and a twinge of jealousy pinched her. Were Ernie and I ever that in love? Would we have stood with our arms entwined in public staring at the sea or any beautiful scene? Did we?

For a moment she tried to remember when they first decided they loved each other, but it was like staring into a fog. She couldn't remember their first date or when they decided to get married. A few visions of the wedding and honeymoon remained, disjointed and washed out, like sepia-toned photographs in a dusty album. How strange to have it all disappear, she thought, troubled that she couldn't retrieve anything of substance. Did all the memories die with Ernie, or had she buried them so deeply in the drudgery of married life that she could no longer find them?

The couple kissed, and Jane turned away, feeling like a voyeur. She snapped a couple of pictures of the ocean and a spit of land in the distance, then hurried back to the camper and climbed inside. Flustered, she dropped the keys on the floorboard, and after retrieving them and starting the vehicle, she forgot to tell herself to stay on the left when she backed out of the parking spot. An oncoming truck reminded her.

As she drove along the coast, thoughts about Ernie faded into the background. The road had enough curves to keep her occupied, and the ocean, glimpsed lapping in blue-green splendor out her window, beckoned to her. An hour down the road, she found another pullout with no cars in it and parked the van. Camera looped over her wrist, she headed for the beach.

A narrow path snaked down an escarpment, steps hewn into the light, crumbly rock in places. Trees with long needles for leaves hung over the edge of the path and stood among an undergrowth of flowering bushes. She paused to finger the leaves of one of the bushes and wished she'd brought the reference book on Australia's flora and fauna that she'd purchased at the botanical gardens. The foliage didn't appear similar to anything she'd known in Colorado, and she couldn't remember seeing or smelling anything similar to it at the gardens. Kind of piney, yet not.

Sighing, she continued toward the beach. She had such a rotten memory. Airhead, Ernie always called her and insisted that she write all her appointments down and post them so that he could keep her on track and remind her where she was supposed to be. She complied because she did find it hard to remember everything, and he had saved her from more than one embarrassing moment. But on some deep level she was still a child, Ernie the surrogate parent chaining her to his demands and his life, not hers.

The beach sand seemed weird, like a flattened version of the cliff behind her. She wasn't sure what the material was, but it was white, grainy, a little chalky. Sand, or sand substitute, nestled up against the foot of the cliff in shallow depressions. The sound of the waves whispered to her as she walked toward the sea, snapping pictures, trying to capture the beauty that surrounded her. She was never much of a photographer, and the flat, off-kilter images that appeared on the tiny screen of the digital camera seemed to reinforce that fact. Shrugging, she let the camera dangle and examined the rocks at her feet. To her amazement, what she thought were black-flecked rocks, were, in fact, rocks covered with thousands of tiny crustaceans. Gasping, she turned and tiptoed her way back to the sand at the foot of the cliff, begging forgiveness for every creature she stepped on. Guilt for all the destruction she'd caused trailed her, mounting with each crushed sea creature.

Back on the sand, she sat in the shade, resting against a rock on the verge of tears. She tried to even her breathing and focus on the scene in front of her instead of on the thousands of little deaths she'd inflicted. One breath, two. While she composed herself, the beauty and serenity of the landscape seeped through her misery and filled her with a sense of wonder. She felt transported from the mundane into a world created of the finest dreams. A gentle breeze whispered through her hair, cooling the nape of her neck, while a billion sequins appeared to shimmer in the undulating waves. Scents of salt water and green, living things and something tangy yet dank she couldn't identify filled the air.

When she'd thought of Australia in her daydreams and musings, this kind of place had never even occurred to her. The coast she had imagined had been covered with red sand, kangaroos, and Aborigines. How naïve she had been. How could she have thought that a continent the size of the United States would be desert and a single species? Ernie was right. She didn't have a brain in her head sometimes.

A heaviness settled over her, the years with Ernie a chain around her neck. She could feel the weight of it dragging on her, holding her in place, shackling her thoughts and life to the misery she had endured for almost a quarter of a century. She brought her fists to her forehead and threw her head back.

"But he's dead!" she roared to the sand and waves. The sound faded like his final breath into nothingness. Dead in the flesh but alive and nasty in her mind. "No more," she muttered, straightening.

Grunting, she climbed to her feet and headed back up the path to the van.

As she climbed into the van, another kind of heaviness crept over her. She was tired. It had been a long day even though it was still midafternoon. She wanted a nap but felt too exposed to take one on the side of the road. Better she should find a place to camp for the night and rest. Pulling out from the glove box one of the complimentary books of caravan parks Geoff had given her, she flipped to Apollo Bay. Several were listed, and she decided it was time to try out the GPS.

She fiddled with the controls on the touch screen, trying to figure out how to enter the address she wanted and get the thing to guide her there. She couldn't get the address to enter; when she thought she had it set, the machine would blink to a different screen that seemed to have nothing to do with either the address or directions. After repeating the procedure with the same results several times, she pulled out the user manual and flipped through it.

She hated user manuals. They were never organized in a way her brain could understand and decipher. She searched for "address" in the index and found twenty-seven references, none of which seemed to tell her how to enter one. She looked under settings and got lost after the first sentence. Irritation bubbled to the surface. What she needed was something she could talk to, ask what to do, and have it answer her questions in understandable language, not this badly indexed tech manual that didn't seem to even be written in English. In frustration, she slammed the book onto the dashboard and banged her forehead on the steering wheel. How was she going to find places without the GPS? The maps in the caravan park book didn't look helpful at all. What was she going to do? She closed her eyes and tried not to break down into tears.

"Excuse me, but are you all right?" A voice drifted in through her open window.

She bolted upright and jerked around. A couple of girls stood next to the van, maybe in their late teens or early twenties, looking concerned. They wore bikini tops splashed with loud and clashing colors, tight, very short shorts, and sunglasses pushed on top of their blond heads. Lean and fit, they could have stepped out of an ad for suntan lotion. Behind them, a metallic, sky-blue convertible with the top down was parked a few paces back.

Jane felt old and frumpy. "Hi," was all she could think of to say.

"Are you well? You look a little ill." A crease furrowed the perfect brow of the girl on the right. She pulled the sunglasses off her head and tapped them against her thigh. "Are you alone?"

"Oh, I'm fine." Jane dredged up a smile and pasted it on her face. She didn't feel convinced by it on the inside but hoped it translated better on the outside. "I'm having a little trouble with my GPS."

"Is your husband around?" The girl looked even more concerned.

"My husband . . ." She trailed off, the word hanging like a rag caught on a bush. She tried to imagine what the end of that sentence could be that wouldn't end up sounding maudlin, self-serving, or needy. She didn't want to tell them Ernie was dead. That brought up visions of tears and sympathetic condolences and far more attention than she wanted or needed. But she couldn't think of a convincing lie either. That he was back in the States? That he was waiting for her in Apollo Bay? That he'd decided to stay in Melbourne and would meet her later? She opened her mouth then closed it. Better to avoid the subject.

"I can't get the GPS to work, and I need to get to a caravan park for the night. I'm tired." The smile was even more tenuous this time.

The second girl stepped closer and tried to peer into the van. She smelled of coconut, and Jane had sudden visions of Hawaii. "Oh, what model is it? Maybe I can help."

Jane sighed. "Oh, could you? I'd be so grateful. I can't seem to get the hang of it." She opened the door and climbed out. "I don't know what kind it is. It came with the camper."

The girl flashed a smile. "No worries. I deal with these things all the time." She hopped into the van and began flipping through icons.

"She's quite good at this." The other girl watched her friend. She smelled of vanilla.

Vanilla and coconut, Jane mused. The scents of dessert. She wondered if she smelled of anything besides sweat and frustration. Backing away a little, she moved to the side to let the other girl get a better view. "What does she do?"

"She works for Wallaby. Sells gear for campers. Are you from the States?" She turned and stared at Jane, her hazel eyes seeming to demand an answer.

"Yeah, I'm here on vacation." Jane dropped her gaze to her feet.

"I thought so." She nodded. "All by yourself or with someone?"

Jane pursed her lips. What was with this kid's need to know all about her life? "I'm traveling alone for now."

The girl smiled, showing a set of crooked teeth. "Good on you. I've been trying to talk my parents into letting me go to Cairns with Annie, but they are so retro. 'It's too dangerous,'" she mimicked. "But we could do just fine. That's what I tell them. They aren't bloody listening yet."

"It's a Growler 1500. An old model." A voice emerged from the interior. "Not the best on the market, and it's difficult to program if you don't know what you're doing."

Jane turned. "Can you show me what to do?"

"No worries. Here, I'll get in on the other side and show you how to use it." Annie scooted out, jogged around to the other door, and slid into the passenger seat. For her, arthritis and creaking joints didn't exist.

Annie swept her long hair back over an ear. "Here. All you have to do is hit this. Then enter the address. Where do you want to go?"

Jane showed her the ad for the caravan park and watched while the girl tapped the screen, then sat back.

"That's all there is to it. See?" She flashed a smile.

Jane didn't see. Annie had traced her fingers so fast across the screen that Jane couldn't follow. But she was too embarrassed to say anything. They would think she was stupid. "Uh, sure. You make it look so easy."

"Yeah, that's what Steph says too." Annie inclined her head toward the girl looking in the window.

"Yeah." Steph nodded. "But it's not. It's bloody hard. Show her again, why don't you, Annie?"

Jane sighed in relief. "Yes, please. And slowly if you don't mind."

"No worries. Here's what you do."

After Annie showed her step-by-step how to find an address, Jane felt she could do it herself. She grinned at the girls. "Thank you so much. You've been wonderful. I don't know what I would have done without your help. What can I do to thank you?"

Steph beamed and Annie shuffled at her side. "No worries," Annie said. "I'm glad we could help."

"Yeah, yeah." Steph nodded and pushed her sunglasses back on top of her head. "You set now?"

"Yes. I think I can find my way."

"OK then. I guess you'll be off." Steph grabbed Annie's arm. "Us too. Have a great trip." She tugged Annie toward the convertible. Annie waved at Jane and slid into the car. Steph revved the engine and peeled out onto the pavement without appearing to look in either direction. They disappeared around the corner with a roar.

Jane smiled and started the van. She could understand why their parents didn't like them traveling together. The two of them could get into a world of trouble just by being so pretty and engaging, not to mention the driving. Jane decided if they were her kids, she would keep them locked in the attic until they had developed a few wrinkles. After checking both ways and muttering her "keep left" mantra, Jane turned toward Apollo Bay.

Apollo Bay Camp Park nestled on a hill a couple of blocks from the beach. The Growler directed her straight there, requesting in a voice with an English accent that she turn at the appropriate streets and announcing in what Jane felt was a self-satisfied voice that she had arrived at her destination. The place looked great from the street, and it took only a little while to figure out where the office was and find a parking place.

Inside, the man behind the counter wore a bright green polo shirt emblazoned with a nautilus shell and the name of the park. He looked up from his computer when she walked in, accompanied by the raucous bleat of a door alarm. She startled at the noise and froze in the door while she figured out what it was, then marched to the counter hoping the door would shut and the racket cease. It seemed to take forever. All the while the man stared at her through horn-rimmed glasses. Brownish hair graying at the temples framed a long face with deep wrinkles scouring down from his eyes, nose, and mouth. The opposite of the girls, he looked like an ad for the necessity of using sunscreen.

When the alarm had fallen silent, she placed her purse on the counter and smiled. "I need to rent a camping space for the night."

"Powered?"

She blinked for a second, trying to figure out what the man was referring to. Then it struck her—did she want electricity at the site? "Yes, please. And water too."

He gave her a look that seemed to say, "What an idiot." She flinched but kept the smile pasted on her face. "Camper, trailer, tent?"

Again, it took her a minute to interpret. "Oh yes, I'm in a campervan."

He shoved a form at her. "Here. Fill this out." While she dug in her purse for a pen, he asked, "Grass or cement?"

She was flummoxed by that one. "I'm sorry. What?"

He sighed, pulled a pen from the side of his computer, and pushed it across the counter to her. "Do you want a grass site or a cement site?"

"Oh." She paused. "Is there a difference aside from the obvious?"

"No."

A man of very few words, she concluded. "I'll take a grass one." He dropped his gaze to the computer and began punching keys while she filled in her name, address, phone number, and the license plate number of the van. When she was finished, she handed back the form and the pen.

"That'll be forty dollars." He collected the form and, with his other hand, lifted a map to the counter. "Here's your site." With the pen, he outlined a rectangle on the piece of paper. He then tapped on another larger rectangle. "Here's the office. Cash or charge?"

She stared at the map, trying to figure out how to get from the office to the site. She was about to ask him when he asked cash or charge again. After locating her wallet, she pulled out the Visa and handed it to him. "Charge," she said while he swiped the card. She could be terse too.

After she completed the transaction, he gave her another sheet of paper covered in small print. "Read the rules." He handed her a receipt and turned away.

Well, she thought, somewhat taken aback by the abruptness of the whole transaction. I hope this isn't going to be the rule at these places. She walked back outside to the van, studying the map. If she turned it so it was oriented the same way she was, maybe she could figure it out.

It took a couple of trips around the park before she located a piece of empty grass with a small sign saying "18B." She pulled in under a large tree, grateful for the shade. The scent of ocean filled the air when she climbed from the van to scope out the place. Inhaling, she thought of whales and dolphins and sharks and the gentle lapping of the waves. If she had enough energy after dinner, she'd have another beach walk.

It was then that she realized that in her haste to leave Melbourne and get on the road, she'd forgotten to buy groceries. Her little cooler was bare, as were the cabinets and cubbies. At that moment her stomach chose to growl. Damn and damn again. The last thing she wanted to do was go shopping. She noticed a couple of shelves in the office stacked with boxed food items, but she didn't want to interact with Mister Only-Two-Consecutive-Words-At-A-Time again. That left eating out once more.

From the van, she pulled out another of Geoff's booklets and found several restaurants within walking distance. She wasn't sure which one she wanted, but she was certain she didn't want to drive to any of them. Enough left side of the road for one day. Purse on her shoulder, keys in her pocket, she headed for town.

Apollo Bay wasn't much of a town; at least there wasn't much to see from the main road. Seafood shops, restaurants, tourist kitsch shops, clothing shops, variety stores. Most of the places looked prosperous enough, even though there were few people on the sidewalk or on the beach on the other side of the road. Maybe it was too early for dinner or maybe too early for tourists. She had spent some time in the Ramada trying to equate Australian and American seasons and had figured out that instead of the heat of summer, she'd arrived in early spring, something akin to April back in Colorado. She wished she would have thought of that when she booked her ticket. No wonder it was so damned cold and rainy. And the timing explained why there were few to no tourists. School was in session all over the country, not to mention every other country that would be sending tourists to Australia. And older people wouldn't be out yet because of the weather. She was by far the exception.

She sauntered by the restaurants, reading the menus posted in the windows and trying to figure out if they were open or not. By and large they were empty. Maybe she needed to buy groceries after all.

At the end of the row of shops, a small café had a couple of patrons sitting at a cloth-covered table, sipping coffee. She didn't even check the menu before going inside. Open was all she cared about.

The couple nodded at her when she sat down, then went back to paying more attention to their drinks than each other. A large woman in a flowered skirt and loose cotton top placed a laminated menu on the table in front of Jane. "How are you today, luv? Can I get you something to drink?"

Jane scanned the menu and settled on a diet cola. She'd decided to try the barramundi, some kind of fish, according to the description, which came with rice pilaf and a salad. It wasn't the greatest meal she'd ever eaten, but it far outstripped everything she'd eaten at the Ramada. The pumpkin and eggplant sandwich was still her favorite. She had a dish of ice cream for dessert with a decaf "long black."

Coffee was a whole different world here. The first time she'd tried to order a cup of coffee with cream, she'd been completely confused. Long black, flat white, short black, none of it made any sense. The morning waitress at the Ramada had sat down across from her one day and explained it all. "Long black" equaled, more or less, what in America was called an Americano, espresso diluted with water. "Flat white" was something similar to a latte. Drip coffee was not to be had, and the only other thing available was the god-awful powdered coffee Jane had endured in the motel.

Once she understood, a whole new world of coffee enjoyment opened up. Previously she'd had one latte in her entire life, and she hadn't found it all that good. But in Australia, all the types of coffee were delightful, no matter the name. She ordered it often now, convinced she'd never go back to her Mr. Coffee.

Light still bathed the street and beach when she left the restaurant. Infused with energy from the food and coffee, she decided she would go shopping after all since she didn't want to face the morning with both an empty cooler and stomach at the same time. The IGA Express sat down the street from the restaurant. It was small by American standards, at least compared to the Safeway back home. She strode through the sliding-glass doors and pulled a shopping cart from the wire carts nested together near the front door. Before she was able to cradle her purse in the child's seat, the cart slid sideways and nearly crashed into a woman shepherding two toddlers into a cart on the left.

"Oh my goodness. I'm so sorry," she blurted, attempting to get the cart under control. But it swiveled in the other direction as if gliding on ice. Jane couldn't figure out for the life of her what was wrong with the thing and why it didn't behave. She felt her face reddening.

The woman glared at her. "You need to get your trolley out of my way." Both the kids were in the cart, standing with pudgy hands gripping the side and seeming to glare at Jane too.

"I'm sorry. I can't seem to make the cart go where I want it to." She pulled back and retreated a few steps to clear the aisle for the woman and her kids. The woman brushed by her, muttering something under her breath about "bloody tourists."

Feeling like a total fool, she steered the cart toward bins of vegetables. The thing still didn't want to track in a straight line. Before she ran into anyone else, she stopped and peered underneath to see if she could figure out what was wrong. All four wheels could swivel, unlike the ones back home where the back wheels were fixed and only the front ones swiveled. She straightened with a frown.

OK. The cart wasn't broken, and she had another kind of driving to learn—shopping cart/trolley driving.

The thought of calling them trolleys made her smile, and she imagined grocery carts traversing the hills and streets of San Francisco. She wouldn't forget the term now. Another new thing.

Though the store was laid out unlike anything she was used to, she managed to fill her cart with items that were mostly analogous to what she would have bought at home. The brands were different, of course, and some of the names she found confusing. The chips were called crisps, and fries were chips. Cookies were biscuits and biscuits, scones. Fish was flake; cantaloupes were rock melons; raisins, sultanas; ketchup, tomato sauce; and on and on. She resorted to buying packaging that looked familiar, no matter what it was called on the label. She was surprised, however, at the number of items that could have been pulled off the shelves of her local Safeway: Coke and Pepsi were the most plentiful, but there were items like Rice Krispies, with the same kind of packaging but called Rice Bubbles. Then there were the things she couldn't quite figure out. Thickened cream? Was that whipping cream or something else?

By the time she headed for the checkout, she felt confused and hoped she'd managed to buy enough to create a few edible meals. The bill felt astronomical compared to back home, and to top it off, she had to buy shopping bags to carry everything back to the van. Four shopping bags clustered at the end of the checkout by the time she was finished. She eyed them warily. How much did they weigh, and could she manage to carry them all the way back to the van without killing herself in the process? She wished she would have thought far enough ahead to have brought her backpack with her.

The clerk lifted them from the counter and placed them back

in the trolley. She wondered if she could wheel it all the way back to the van but decided that would be pushing things a little too far. Resigned to trudging, she parked the trolley by the front doors and lifted the bags.

Oh my God, she thought. She plopped them on the floor and flexed her fingers. They weighed a ton; then she wondered if American tons and Australian tons weighed the same. But no matter, she was going to have a long, long trek back to the van.

It seemed the longest trip of her life. Every hundred feet or so she'd drop the bags to the sidewalk, stretch her arms, and try to catch her breath. She kept hoping she'd see a bench or something she could rest on for a while, but to her right was sand and to her left were homes or businesses. In her head, Ernie commented on what an idiot she was and that her lack of planning was one of her greatest faults.

As she stood panting during the seventh stop, she had to agree. She was not the most organized person in the world. Ernie had planned all their vacations—all three of them—and while they weren't all that fun-filled and exciting, at least they got where they were going when they were supposed to; they ate in chain restaurants, slept in decent motels, saw everything that Ernie decided they needed to see, remained on schedule, and made it home with a day to spare before he had to go back to work so he could rest up and she could get the house back in working order. Utilitarian. Organized.

Standing under the waning Australian sun, the ocean breeze licking the sweat droplets on her forehead, she paused, as if someone had flipped a switch inside her brain, silencing it for a moment. In that silence a question arose: Was Ernie actually right?

It stunned her that she had never considered whether he was right about her—or anything else for that matter. Oh, she had ranted at what he said inside her head all the years of their marriage, but she had never questioned the veracity of the words that flensed her, that whittled her down, that dictated the breadth and height of her ego and self-esteem. Was he right? About her? About anything?

She wanted to sit down and think about it, to parse it out, to examine the evidence. However, in the middle of the sidewalk in Apollo Bay, Victoria, Australia, with the sun sinking and not sure how much farther she had to go, this wasn't the best time to settle in for a think. She bent and retrieved her bags, straightened, and began to walk again. But still—

The first time she could remember Ernie making one of his pronouncements about her deficits was when they'd first met. They were at a party thrown by a mutual friend one weekend during Christmas break. He plopped down beside her on a worn plaid couch covered by a musty, rumpled, crocheted afghan and threw one arm over the back of the sofa behind her head.

She turned and stared at him. His dark, wavy hair was tousled, brushing the tops of his ears and curling into tight loops above the collar of the blue oxford shirt he wore beneath a green V-neck sweater with Colorado State University embroidered in yellow on the left breast. The skin of his cheek was smooth, without a trace of five-o'clock shadow. Long eyelashes swept over gray eyes, and strong shoulders filled out the sweater, which covered a flat belly. He was the handsomest man she'd ever sat beside.

"God, this place is small," he said after taking a long pull on his Coors. "I could spit across it. And the music. Can you even hear me?" He turned his head toward her and smiled. White, even, perfect teeth shone between pink lips. She felt breathless.

"Barely." She smiled then held out her hand. "I'm Jane."

He caught his fingers beneath hers and brought her hand to his mouth, brushing the skin with a kiss, his breath warm on the flesh of her fingers. "I'm Ernest, but you can call me Ernie. It's a pleasure."

"I'm glad to meet you." She blushed and ducked her head, too shy to take her hand from his—then again, not wanting to. "You're going to CSU?"

"Oh yeah. Business major. Senior year and all that. Visiting friends for the holidays. How about you?"

"I live here. Grew up here. I just finished my associate's degree at Grand Community College, but I'd love to go on. Right now, I'm working to try and earn enough to do that." She was blathering but couldn't think of anything witty or charming to say.

"Too bad. I'm glad my parents can afford to send me straight through. They're in Europe for the season, visiting Mom's dying aunt. I'd have gone, but they won't return before I have to be back on campus." He stretched and took another swig of beer. "Besides, I figured it'd be a real downer, what with the old lady about to kick off and all that. How about you? Been to Paris yet?"

She shook her head. Paris. She'd love to go to Paris or London or Sydney or anywhere besides dumb old Northglenn. One of her secret dreams was to be a travel writer and visit the world, laptop under her arm, cataloging her adventures. But that didn't seem possible when her days were spent running a cash register at Roberts Drugs and Sundries and her nights were devoted to trying to keep up the house and take care of her parents, who had broken into pieces when Jane's brother died in a motorcycle accident two years earlier and had yet to put more than a couple of the pieces back together. She resented her older sister, whose husband had moved them to Scottsbluff in Nebraska, far enough away to never have to visit for long or to stay and help put the remains of the family back on its feet. Jane felt boxed and shelved like the packages of drugs she sometimes helped unload.

Ernie chuckled. "Eh, too bad. Stuck in the sticks. Must suck to have no future."

Jane could have melted into the weave of the afghan, she felt so ashamed. Here she was, next to a drop-dead-gorgeous guy, and she had nothing to offer or interest him. A small girl in a small town with no prospects. Total loser. "Yeah, it sucks," she somehow managed to say.

"Don't worry, kiddo. Stick with me and maybe you'll go somewhere. Want a beer?"

Bags cutting into the skin of her palms, shuffling toward the fading sun, Jane wanted to laugh. Go somewhere with him. What a joke. It was much later she found out that everything he'd told her that night was a lie. He'd never been to Europe or Paris or, in fact, anywhere outside of Colorado. His parents were back in Fort Collins that night, taking down the Christmas tree and slugging the last of the rum-laced eggnog. He was trying to impress her because he was so insecure that he couldn't admit his own life was pitiful too. She had to admit he had done quite a good job of impressing her—at first. By the time they'd been married a year, she knew when his version of the truth was larger than reality, though it took another five years for her to have the courage to amend his stories.

She thought she couldn't take another step when the entrance to the caravan park crawled into view. By the time she made it to the camper, her arms felt at least six inches longer, and she had a hard time moving her fingers to retrieve the keys from inside her purse. After dumping the groceries on the small table, she rolled her shoulders and swore to herself she would never walk to a grocery store again.

It took several minutes of searching, then observing another camper hooking up, before she had water and electricity installed for the night. Inside, she stowed perishables in the cooler while the rest of the food found homes in the various cubbies. Satisfied that her own little roving home was in order, she filled the electric kettle and pulled out a cup for tea.

Ensconced on the bench seat with the tea balanced on a plate next to her on the cushion, all the curtains drawn and the lights shining, her thoughts of Ernie resurfaced. Once again she wondered when he had been right about something. Dead right. Not just overly opinionated. And especially about her. Of all the things he had claimed about her over the years, were any of them real, or had she bought into his verbal diatribes the same way she had bought his line about having gone to Europe way back when?

The idea stunned her. She had defined herself according to Ernie's assessment for so long, it was hard to imagine who she could be if he wasn't there defining her. What if she came up with her own ideas of what she was good and bad at? That thought sent shivers down her back. But what if Ernie was right about her after all? She ran a hand through her hair. How could she know?

She pulled out her notebook and pen and drew a line down the middle of one of the sheets. On the top left side she wrote, "Ernie," and on the right she wrote, "True?" She thought for a minute and began to list all the things Ernie had routinely called her: lazy, disorganized, airhead, spendthrift, worthless, hopeless, useless, and, most of all, stupid. One by one she asked herself if she could demonstrate that most of the time she wasn't what he had claimed. Lazy, hardly. She worked the front desk and kept the books at the Hopi Motel three-quarters time, even after Ernie was earning enough so she didn't have to work; she also kept up the house and took care of all of his demands. The motel loved her, wanted her to become a full-time employee, and even encouraged her to go back to school in accounting.

So she wasn't lazy or stupid either. And the rest she discounted—all but one. Spendthrift. She did enjoy spending money; she had to admit. So maybe he had a point on that one.

She plopped her pen down by her tea. Angry and disgusted with herself for believing without question what he had told her, she wished she could flush his memory from her mind. But she had been trying that for the past weeks with little success. Maybe, she thought, if I get rid of anything I have that reminds me of him. She grabbed her purse and fished out her wallet. Inside she searched for any picture or other reminder of Ernie. Behind a picture of her sister and family, she found an old picture of Ernie with his parents and six siblings.

A pang of guilt stabbed her. She had called his parents after he died to let them know but hadn't contacted any of his brothers or sisters-in-law. She had assumed his parents would take care of that. They probably hated her for not having a funeral, even though they got his ashes. But then they all hated her anyway. It was obvious that by the time she and Ernie had been together for a couple of years, they were never going to welcome her into the family. She never quite understood what they had against her, aside from the fact that they blamed her for not being able to conceive a child even though they all knew, because she made sure she told them, that it was Ernie who was infertile and not her. Maybe that was it. That she spilled the beans about their favorite child. Even the nieces and nephews stopped talking to her after a while and referred to "strange Auntie Jane" in loud whispers when she was around. To hell with them, she thought. She pulled out the picture, tore it into small squares, and placed it on the plate.

The rest of her purse yielded nothing she could tie to Ernie. Now what should she do with the picture fragments, she wondered. Somehow just chucking them into the trash didn't seem final enough for the moment. Then she smiled, set up the propane stove, and fed the pieces one by one to the flame, vowing from then on to do the opposite of what Ernie would have done. Take that, Ernie, she thought. Burned you again.

Chapter 3

WITH ERNIE SYMBOLICALLY RECREMATED, Jane felt she could start her new life for real. Strangely energized by her little ritual, she wasn't ready to go to bed even though it was fast approaching her usual bedtime. She considered setting up the bed and remembered Geoff explaining the procedure, but she couldn't recall now how it was done. For a minute she thought about pulling out the manual, but instead she opened the novel she'd thrown in her cart on a whim at Kmart and lost herself in the travails of Sweetie Sommers.

It was close to midnight by the time she felt tired enough to sleep. Toothbrush in hand, she headed for the amenities block.

Block was the correct word for the place. Inside the cinderblock building, one wall had stalls enclosing the toilets, which, when she opened one, looked to be of 1950s vintage and well used. Another wall contained a long counter with half a dozen sinks in it. Around the wall in back of the toilets, a line of cubicles with curtains fronting them turned out to be the showers. They looked as old and worn as the toilets and smelled vaguely of mold. While Jane watched, a cockroach scurried from beneath one of the curtains, went around a corner, and disappeared into the darkness. A shiver skittered across her back and arms, and she fled back into the first room. She wasn't sure how dirty she was going to have to get before she'd shower in the place and hoped this was one of the worst caravan parks around. After emptying her bladder, washing her face, and brushing her teeth, she walked back to the van.

Despite her reservations, it took just a few minutes to assemble the bed once she took a close look at it. When she had the cushions in place, she realized she hadn't gotten the sheets out from their cubby, which was now covered by the bed. She took the bed apart, obtained the sheets, and started again. Putting the sheets on required crawling on the bed to tuck everything into place while fighting the cushions to stay put instead of folding into two sections. By the time she was done, she was more than ready to call it a day. Then she realized that her pajamas were under the bed, and worse, she had no place to change except for the amenities block or standing on the bed. She sat on the bed edge, her feet hanging out the open back doors of the van and sighed. She was sure the people in the next site had seen her making a complete fool of herself, and she couldn't bear to entertain them again while she disassembled the bed once more, retrieved everything she needed, changed, and remade the bed.

Forget it, she thought, and flopped back onto the bed. For the first time in her life, she'd sleep either in her underwear or clothes.

It was supposed to be an adventure, after all. She was too tired to even pay attention when Ernie began berating her for such uncouth behavior. Rising, she sat, rolled her legs onto the bed and pulled the back doors shut. Under the covers in just bra and panties, she flipped off the lights and rolled onto her side. Australian campervan adventure, day one, done.

"Congratulations, me," she whispered and shut her eyes.

The sound of a car revving its engine jerked Jane awake. Sunlight streamed through the cracks between the curtains, painting stripes of brilliance across her legs and upper body. She stretched, ran a hand through her hair, and considered going back to sleep for a little while. A glance at her watch shocked her out from under the covers. It was almost noon. She hadn't slept for twelve hours straight since she was—well, she could never remember sleeping that long at a stretch, even when she was sick. Throwing on her clothes from the previous day, she crawled to the back of the van and opened the door.

A glorious day fell inside. The sky was clear, and the temperature felt in the 60s, with a hint of sea breeze ruffling the eucalyptus trees lining the grass opposite her. She slid to the grass, bare feet sinking into the cool blades, and sighed. A dog was barking in the distance while her bladder informed her she had been sleeping far too long for it to endure any longer. Slipping on shoes and grabbing her keys and toothbrush, she headed once more for the amenities block.

It didn't look any better in the daylight than it had the previous night. In fact, it appeared even shabbier, with sunshine streaming through the high windows over the sinks, the paint chipped and stained near the floor, the worn linoleum tiles looking as if they hadn't been swept or mopped in a week, and flies clustering against the screens. She wanted a shower but felt dirtier even thinking about washing in the place. In her head she calculated whether she could make it through another day or two before she absolutely needed a shower. It would be at least three days since she was spending that day and the next in Apollo Bay before moving on down the coast, but there was no way to ensure that the next caravan park's amenities would be any cleaner or newer than this one's.

Grimacing, she walked back to the van, collected her towels, shampoo, and clean clothes, then returned to the block. They could all be this bad or worse. She'd better get used to it.

She found that if she closed her eyes while showering, she could imagine she was back in her own neatly tiled, spotless shower. Not that she wanted to be there, but it was enough to get her through bathing and dressing and back out into the park. Clean and well rested, she felt ready to take on the day—post-brekkie/lunch, of course.

Standing behind the camper, she was frying herself a hamburger when she first caught sight of a girl strolling between the campers. Her hair was a mass of red-tinged dreadlocks that jumbled over her shoulders down to the middle of her back, her skin darker than shadows at midnight, her face breathtakingly beautiful. She was so thin and frail that Jane could count her ribs below the lower edge of a T-shirt that was chopped off just under her small breasts. The shirt's sleeves and collar were removed to resemble a tank top. When the girl stooped to examine something on the ground, Jane noticed that her legs were as long as the rest of her body, and her shoulder blades jutted like bat wings from her back. Her shorts were ragged and looked like pants that had been ripped off above the knees. They hung on her hips, her belly concave above the waistband. A bag fashioned from old scraps of material bulged at her side, swinging forward when she bent and bumping her left hip when she walked. She looks half starved, Jane thought as the young woman ambled toward her and the van.

Jane's first impulse was to pull the pan off the stove, climb into the van, and shut the door. That's what they would have done if she had been with Ernie. Strangers were dangerous, especially black strangers, and they didn't get any blacker than this girl. Then she remembered her promise from the previous evening. If Ernie would turn away and hide, she would stand her ground and talk to the girl, even though she felt awkward and a little afraid.

The girl sauntered over, humming to herself in a manner that implied she had nothing else to do and nowhere else she'd rather be. When she approached Jane, she flashed a broad smile filled with crooked teeth. "G'day, ma'am." She nodded and paused. "Lovely day, no?"

Jane nodded back, clutching her spatula to her chest. "That it is. How are you?"

"Not so good," she replied, slumping against the side of the camper and shoving her hands into the pockets of her shorts. Her face looked drawn, and her eyes focused on the grass between the two of them. "Not so good at all. In fact, I'm downright buggered."

"Oh?" Here it comes, Jane thought, edging closer to the stove. She's going to hit me up for money or try and steal my purse or something.

"My mate up and left me stranded here. He sent me to buy him a pack of fags and split while I was in the store. Now I'm stuffed, with no money and no way to get home." Her accent was soft and lyrical, almost musical. Her eyes wandered from the ground to the hamburger cooking on the stove. "I was wondering if you could spare a couple of dollars so I could at least call my mum and let her know where I am."

Jane stared at the pathetic-looking creature, wondering if it was an act to get drug money or if any part of the story was real. With an edge that resembled Ernie's, the voice in her head demanded what the girl was doing out in the middle of Apollo Bay alone with some boy anyway? And what did she do to make him abandon her? Why wasn't she home and in school or working or something?

Tightening her lips, she squelched the voice and wondered instead when the girl had last eaten. Hadn't she heard somewhere that it was better to give a beggar a sandwich than a dollar? Since Ernie would never have done anything of the sort, dollar or sandwich, why couldn't she?

Jane tsk-tsked and lowered the spatula. "You look starved. How would you like a hamburger and some chips?" She shook her head, remembering her grocery-buying adventure the previous day. "Make that some crisps."

The girl's head dropped, and Jane thought she could see tears forming beneath her long lashes. "I couldn't . . . I couldn't bother you. I just need to call my mum."

Inside, Jane melted and felt her own eyes begin to water. "Oh, of course you can. I have more than enough. We'll see about getting in touch with your mum later. Come here."

Stepping forward, she wrapped one arm around the girl's shoulders and turned her toward the open door. "Here, up you go." She pointed her to the aisle between the cubbies and the bench seat. "You sit there, and I'll get you a plate and some food. Do you want crisps, or would you prefer some carrots or something? And what do you want to drink? I have some Diet Coke, milk, or water."

The girl cradled her face in her hands and wept. "I don't care," she stammered in a soggy voice.

Jane laid a hand on her back. "It's OK, honey. It's OK. I'll get you something, and you can leave anything you don't want to eat. How about that?"

The girl raised her head and wiped her eyes with the back of her hands. "Thank you," she said, sniffling.

With a heave, Jane climbed around the girl into the van. She grabbed a napkin and handed it to her. "Here. You can use this to blow your nose." Then she pulled out everything the girl might want or need from the cubbies and cooler. She plopped a bun on the plate and climbed back down to the stove. With a flourish, she placed the hamburger on the bun and handed the plate to the girl.

"Here. Take this inside and fix it the way you want. I'm going to put another burger on for me."

The girl took the plate in both hands, sniffled, then burst into tears once more. "I'm so sorry to be such a bother. I usually don't do this. I've never . . ." The tears drowned out the words.

"Oh dear. You poor thing." Jane took the plate and set it on the seat. Then she wrapped her arms around her and held her while the girl sobbed. "It's OK. It's OK. I'm doing lots of stuff I never thought I'd do either. Right now you need food more than anything. I'll bet you'll feel a whole lot better once you've eaten. Then you can tell me all about it."

She felt awkward and tense. She'd never hugged a black person before, though it felt the same as hugging anyone else. And she felt something else. Maybe "motherly" was the word for it. Was she doing it right? Would the girl think she was some kind of weirdo for grabbing her? Should she let go?

The girl's sobs ebbed, and she raised her head from Jane's shoulder and produced a wan smile. "I'm so sorry. I've gotten you all wet."

Jane laughed. "Not nearly as wet as you. Are you OK?"

The girl nodded and dabbed her eyes with the sodden napkin. "I think I can eat now, if that's fine with you."

"Oh, gosh. Of course." She grabbed the plate and handed it to the girl. "Now fix it before it gets cold."

The girl complied. Jane patted out another hamburger from the package of meat by the stove and threw it into the now-smoking frying pan. The meat sizzled and geysered grease spatters in all directions. Jane beat the air with the spatula, then watched the young woman while she sat on the edge of the bench seat and took a bite. Jane smiled.

The girl was finished eating by the time Jane's burger was cooked. She wiped her mouth with the same napkin she'd used to dry her tears. "Dear, dear. I think you need another napkin. More chips, I mean, crisps?" She handed the girl another napkin and the bag of chips—she took both.

Once seated, Jane took a bite while she watched the girl fish chips out of the bag and pop them in her mouth. Jane suspected the child could eat another burger at the very least. She wished she'd bought ice cream or some other dessert. Maybe she should cook another burger.

"That was wonderful," the girl said, handing the bag of chips back to Jane. "Thank you so much. How can I repay you?"

Jane pushed the chips back at the girl. "I don't want any. You eat them. And there's no reason to repay me. I'm glad I could help. You want a drink of something?" The girl shook her head and held the chip bag as if she wanted to keep eating but was afraid to. "Go on. Finish them off. They're not my favorites." Well, that was a lie, she thought, since she hadn't even tasted them, but if it made the girl eat more, she was glad she'd told it.

They ate in silence, the girl crunching chips while Jane finished her hamburger. Jane watched her out of the corner of her eye, trying to figure out how old she was. Under twenty-five. Probably around twenty. Still a kid by any estimation. Curiosity piqued, she had a thousand questions for her, beginning with her name, where her home was, who this mate of hers was, what she was doing in Apollo Bay. But the quiet sat thickly between them, and Jane wasn't sure how to broach any of the questions that pinged around in her head. She'd never fed a stranger in her home before and wasn't sure what would be the best question to ask first. She popped the last of her meal in her mouth, set her plate on the counter, and turned to the girl, who was folding the empty chip bag into a square.

"Now don't you feel better?" she said, smiling. "By the way, my name is Jane Mullet. What's yours?"

"Cleo. Cleo Steyn. You've been so kind. I should be going. Thank you." She started to stand, but Jane put a hand on her arm.

"Wait, can you? I want to find out more about you. That is, if it's OK with you."

Cleo shrugged, easing back into her seat. "You're a Yank."

"If by that you mean an American, you're right. I've been in Australia for about a week." Only a week. She shook her head. It seemed a month or more. The week trapped in the Ramada stretched endlessly in her memory, a thick black line that separated her old life—the one with Ernie—from her new life, free and on the road alone in a foreign land. "How about you? Where are you from?"

"Melbourne. That's where my mum lives with her husband. I shared a flat with a couple of friends in St. Kilda. That is, until Jonny." She glanced at her hands, embarrassed.

"Jonny?"

"Yeah, Jonny." Her right hand touched a ring on the middle finger of her left hand. The beaded circlet was about half an inch wide, edged in yellow with a wavy line wound around the middle in black against a background of red. Jane thought it looked interesting and assumed it wasn't a wedding ring.

Cleo shook her head. "What a mistake."

"Is he the one who left you?"

Cleo nodded again.

"That's rough. Had you known him long?"

"Not long enough." She made a sound halfway between a laugh and a sigh. "We'd been seeing each other for nearly a year. I thought he was a good bloke, and I needed to get to Adelaide and Alice. He said he'd drive me, and I thought, hey, why not? What a joke." She shook her head, looking on the edge of tears once more.

Jane reached for another napkin and handed it to Cleo. "What happened?"

She sniffed. "It's like I said. He sent me to buy him a pack of fags and drove off while I was in the shop. I didn't know he'd stolen my wallet, and when I couldn't find it to pay for the cigarettes, I went back out to see if I'd left it in the car. He was gone with all my money and clothes and everything. Even my jewelry." A tear wandered down her cheek.

"What an asshole." Jane patted Cleo's arm. "Did you call the police?"

She shook her head. "Police aren't going to do anything for a black girl like me. Take down my complaint and send me on my way, that's all."

Jane opened her mouth to reply that the police were there to help, then shut it. Did she know what the relationship was between police and black people in Australia? Maybe it was as contentious as it was in the States. She sighed. "How long ago did all this happen?"

"Two days."

Jane inhaled. "You've been wandering around without food or a place to stay for two days? That's just horrible." Cleo shrugged. "What are you going to do?"

"I don't know. We, that is, Jonny and I, were going to go to Adelaide, where I have some of my jewelry in a shop. They owe me some money, and I was going to pick it up and give them some more to sell. But Jonny's got all my bracelets and necklaces now, and I've got nothing to bring them."

"What about going back to Melbourne?"

"I can't." Cleo shook her head. "My friends rented my room to another woman, and I won't go live with my mum again. Her husband is nothing but a bludger and an alki. I hate him, and I won't stay in the same house with him."

Jane slumped back against the cushion and frowned. Cleo made it sound so hopeless. Part of her wanted to say, "Come with me. I'm going to Adelaide, and I'll take you there." But she was scared. Who was this person? And what did Jane know of Australian criminals? Maybe this is what they looked like, all sweet and innocent, with a sob story to break your heart until you let them into your life, after which they stole everything you had or murdered you in your sleep. Another part wanted to hand her a twenty-dollar bill and let her figure it out for herself, but that felt cold and heartless, like deserting a cripple on the side of the road.

She found herself rationalizing why it wasn't such a bad thing to do anyway. The girl had asked for money, and Jane would be doing what she was asked to do. But she could do more. She wanted to do more in a tentative, uncertain kind of way. What would Ernie do? She almost laughed out loud. Kick her out and drive away, then call the police to report a loiterer.

Abruptly, Cleo stood and placed the folded chip bag on the counter. "Thank you so much for everything, but I need to go now. I hope you have a good vacation." She turned to the open door.

"Wait!" Jane grabbed her arm. "Why don't you stay with me for a while? I plan on going to Adelaide, and I can take you there. On the way you can sleep here—there's another bed up top—and I'd be glad for the company." She instantly regretted her words but shoved the feeling aside. This would be her second non-Ernie act.

Cleo's brow furrowed. "I don't know. It's a huge imposition. I can't just have you taking care of me."

"I won't be. You'll be helping me." Frantically she searched for something the girl could do. "You can help with the driving," she blurted. "I'm not used to driving on the left side of the road, and frankly, it scares the hell out of me. You could do that, and I'd appreciate it a lot, especially once we get to a city. Honestly, the roundabouts terrify me." She hoped she didn't sound too needy.

"I don't know." Cleo touched the ring again. "It doesn't feel right to me." She glanced up. "Thank you, though, for the offer. I appreciate it and the food." Grabbing her bag, she slung it over one shoulder and stood. "Thanks, and good luck with your driving."

Cleo turned to climb down, and Jane touched her shoulder.

"Wait just a second. I can't let you go out there without some money." She retrieved her purse from the front seat of the van, took out a couple of twenties from the billfold, and placed them in Cleo's hand. "Here. Take this. I hope you can get in touch with your mom and find a place to stay."

Cleo turned and gave her a hug. Jane stood in shock for a moment before wrapping her arms around the girl and squeezing back. Oddly, it felt good to be hugged. She realized that no one had held her in months, not since her friend Rachael had heard about Ernie's diagnosis and that he was determined to die at home no matter the cost to Jane. Both of them had cried at the time. She felt her eyes begin to water, both at the memory and the yearning for touch that had been absent from her life for so long. Then she realized she hadn't talked to Rachael since before Ernie died. Rachael must be going crazy wondering what had happened to her. She needed to call her or something.

Cleo pulled back and jumped to the ground without a word. Jane watched while she walked across the grass, a lost waif, alone in the world, just like Jane. She wished Cleo hadn't left and felt surprised at the emotion. Maybe she was needy after all.

Feeling morose, Jane cleaned up her little kitchen and washed the dishes. She missed Rachael and wondered what the best way to contact her was. She didn't have a phone, and she worried that a card would take too long. Email was a possibility, but without a computer, how was she going to do that? Guilt trailing her, she grabbed her camera and purse, locked the van, and went to sightsee.

The guilt didn't abate as she walked up the hill to Mariner's Point, which overlooked the bay and surrounding hills. Guilt stood between her and two little girls wearing rubber boots and straw hats, playing on the side of the path in a little stream as she talked to them. Guilt wrapped its arms around her on the beach and when she scanned the shops fronting the road. Her behavior with Cleo added to the feeling, and she felt foolish for having invited the girl to join her. What was she thinking? Couldn't she see the girl was uncomfortable with her? She must have looked like some kind of predator or weird old lady. Her shame grew as she walked, and she barely noticed the statue of the seals that grew organically from the sand or the pines scattered across the grass next to the beach or the dunes or the turquoise ocean or the people in swimming suits draped with towels who walked at the water's edge. She wished she could go back to bed and start the day over.

As she passed a pharmacy on her way back to the van, she noticed several unoccupied computers sitting near the window. Could they be for public use? Inside, the woman behind the counter confirmed her guess and explained the charges and how to get online. Jane pulled out her Visa card, paid for thirty minutes, and after several failed attempts to navigate the Australian system, managed to find her email account and log on.

She sat for several minutes sorting through her inbox. It was mostly junk, but it was always mostly junk, with maybe a good message from someone she knew every once in a while. Her sister, Sally, was the most consistent, her emails arriving about once a month filled with chatty details about her four kids and husband, Terry. She rarely inquired about how Jane was doing, especially since the time Sally had begged her to leave Ernie, and Jane had refused, saying she couldn't desert him after all they'd been through. Sally had never forgiven her for choosing Ernie. Jane hadn't forgiven herself either, not that she ever felt she had a choice in the matter. She wondered how Rachael had gotten up the guts to leave her husband. What did Rachael have that she didn't? Courage, she supposed.

There were eight emails from Rachael, a new record. Besides junk and the usual inspirational PowerPoint presentations her six sisters-in-law had been sending her the past ten years in some hope of converting her to their idea of Christianity, there were several messages from Ernie's other family members. She scrolled past them, not wanting to read what was sure to be an indictment of her behavior since Ernie's death. Instead she opened Rachael's, beginning with the oldest.

"WHERE THE HELL ARE YOU? I'VE BEEN CALLING YOU ALL DAY. CALL ME!!!!"

Jane cringed. Rachael used all caps when she was upset. The email was dated the morning after Ernie died. She wondered if Rachael knew of Ernie's death when she had written the first email. But how could she know? Who would tell her? There was no notice in the paper at that point; that wouldn't happen until the Friday after his death, when the obituaries were listed. Or did she suspect something had changed or was wrong, the way she did sometimes? Frowning, Jane opened Rachael's emails one after the other, the tone more concerned and afraid with each succeeding one. The last one even threatened to call the police. That was yesterday. Jane wondered if she'd done it, and if they had gone to her home.

With a sigh, she pulled the keyboard closer to compose a reply. For a moment her hands hung over the keys motionless, uncertain how to begin. I ran away? I'm in Australia? Remember how I always said I wanted to travel? Well, guess what? I'm sorry I didn't tell you?

She sighed again. How do you tell your best friend that you've been keeping a huge secret from her? That you didn't trust yourself enough to share your plans even with her, with whom you have shared everything in your life? That you were a world away and weren't coming back for a long time?

She dropped her hands to her lap and stared at the screen. How could she not have called Rachael? Of all the people in the universe, how could she not have picked up the phone and said, "Ernie's dead. I'm going away"? Rachael would have understood, would have urged her on, would have helped her pack her bags or offered to water her plants or pick up her mail.

Oh dear. Her plants. Her mail. The bills. What had she done? Shit.

She sat dumbfounded, overwhelmed by the enormity of the step she'd taken without making even one sensible, rational, necessary arrangement. What had been going on in her head? OK. Ernie was dying, she was more than a little stressed out, and all she could think about was having enough money to buy an airline ticket and leaving. And it had felt so good to walk out the door, climb on a plane, and fly away. Still, couldn't she have done a little more? At least stopped the mail? Back home, life continued while she sat in Australia staring at Rachael's panic. The electric meter was running while her refrigerator cooled all the food she'd left in it. The gas was feeding the pilot light on her furnace and range. The mortgage would be due on the fifth no matter where she was. The water bill would arrive, the trash men would lift her cans twice each week, full or not, and insurance on the car would come due. How could she have been so blind to think she could just walk away, and everything would be fine and take care of itself until she returned? Just this once, maybe Ernie was right. She had been a total airhead.

Forcing her hands to the keyboard, she typed: "Dear Rachael, I'm so sorry I haven't gotten back to you. You see, I did this dumb thing after Ernie died last Wednesday."

The email seemed to go on forever. She told her all about leaving and everything she hadn't done before she left. She related the story of getting the camper, of driving on the wrong side of the road, the sameness and strangeness of Australia—all jumbled together like chocolate chips in meatloaf. She said how much she had missed her and how she wished Rachael was sitting beside her in the camper. And how glad she was that Ernie was dead.

She felt exhausted by the time she hit send. Back at the inbox screen, the emails from Ernie's family glared at her. Torn between feeling obligated to at least read them and dreading every single word they likely contained, she sat. The screen went blank. Her time was up.

Blessing the lady behind the counter who'd shut down her connection, Jane gathered her purse and the camera and stood. She smiled and nodded to the woman when she walked out of the store, feeling lighter than when she'd walked in. Confession was good for the soul, and she felt glad she'd confessed to Rachael everything she'd done and not done. It wasn't fixed by a long shot, but at least she'd told someone.

The sun reflected off the sea to her right, throwing a million shards of light into the sky. She paused and watched the sun dip toward the horizon, casting the pines in silhouette against a red- and orange-streaked sky. The oceanscape stunned her with its beauty, and she stood, savoring the world around her for what felt like the first time that day, recriminations and guilt banished. I want more of this, she thought. More peace, more beauty, just more.

She strolled back toward the caravan park, letting the sea breeze fill her lungs and the shadows crawl across her toes. In the back of her mind, she assembled a list of things she would need to think about, not having the faintest clue how she was going to take care of them thousands of miles away. For the moment she was content just to list them. They might wake her in the middle of the night tonight and hammer on her brain until she tossed and turned waiting for dawn. Right now, she didn't care. She took a breath and walked through the entrance to the caravan park and let them be. For this moment she was going to live in this moment.

Shadows engulfed the rental cabins near the entrance of the park and lay across the cement walks in zebra stripes. She smiled when she saw her little camper sitting in its spot; she felt glad to be "home." It looked quite cute, she thought, with its air scoop sticking up on the left side of the hood and its high-topped roof with the picture of Zeus on the front, holding his lightning bolt and smiling.

Her feet hurt from all the walking, and she was looking forward to putting them up and having a cup of tea before she fixed dinner. Thankfully, no new campers had arrived while she was gone, and her neighbors from the night before had departed sometime during the day, so she'd be alone that night to struggle with putting the bed together without observers.

As she walked up to the camper, she thought she saw legs sticking down at the back. Clutching her purse, she edged her way around the van to the rear, then stopped and grinned. Cleo, looking even more forlorn than that morning, stared back at her from the bumper.

"You still want a passenger?"

Chapter 4

"I DON'T TAKE CHARITY." Cleo dropped her purse on the seat and threw back her shoulders. "I want to pay my way."

Jane heaved herself up into the rear of the camper. "OK. I would appreciate help with the driving."

"That's not enough. What else can I do?" Her chin jutted out, and Jane was reminded of a toddler insisting she have her way.

Easing herself onto the bench, Jane leaned back. "Oh, I don't know. There isn't much to do that I can think of. What about cooking? Do you cook?"

"Sure. You like bubble and squeak?" Cleo's demeanor softened a little as she rested against the counter.

"I have no idea what that is."

"It's wonderful—potatoes and vegetables all mashed together and fried. I can make it for breakfast if you have any leftover veggies."

"That sounds great," Jane replied tentatively. It didn't sound all that good to her, but she was willing to give it a shot. "But yesterday evening was the first time I shopped, and I don't have any leftovers right now except the hamburger stuff we had for lunch."

"No worries. I'll fix extra for dinner, so we'll have what we need in the morning." She turned to the cooler and began pulling out bags of vegetables. Jane wanted to object. She'd never had someone invade her kitchen before or cook a meal in her own home, even if that home was a campervan. It was unsettling, and she felt both a poor hostess and lazy. But before she could object, Cleo turned around and waved a hand at the bags of veggies covering the counter.

"Is this all you've got?"

Jane frowned. She thought she'd bought too many vegetables, far more than she would have if she were home. "It's all I could carry back from the store."

Cleo made a face. "I'll see what I can do with this amount tonight, but no bubble and squeak in the morning. Not with this lot. We can pick up a few more things tomorrow."

With my money, Jane thought. So much for not taking charity. Immediately she chided herself. She didn't even know the girl. She sighed, swearing to stop thinking like Ernie. "Can I help?" She started to rise, but Cleo waved her hand at her.

"I need to pay my way. This is my dinner."

Jane wasn't sure she liked being ordered around by someone she considered to be a kid. Was Cleo bossy about other things too? She wanted a cup of tea but was uncertain about making it herself since

Cleo had taken over, and she felt awkward asking Cleo to make it for her, as if she were asking Cleo to be her maid. Her black maid. She cringed inside. Standing, she reached for the electric kettle.

"I'm going to make tea. Do you want some while you cook?"

Cleo took the kettle from her and waved her back to the seat. "I'll fix us both one. Where's your tea?" Jane pointed to one of the cubbies. Cleo made a grumbling noise when she pulled out the box of generic tea bags.

Jane's shoulders slumped. Now she doesn't like my tea. Do I do anything right? Had Ernie morphed into this girl with the intent of letting her know just how incompetent she was even from the grave? Edging toward the front of the vehicle, she asked, "Is it OK if I get my notebook and pen? Will I be in your way?"

"No worries." Cleo flattened herself against the counter to let Jane by while she continued to pump water into the teakettle from the spigot over the sink.

Jane slunk by and retrieved her notebook from a drawer near the front seats. After slipping off her shoes, she propped both feet up on the seat and wiggled her toes. It felt fabulous to be barefooted. She calculated she'd walked at least five or six miles that day, a huge distance considering that back home she hardly walked at all. She'd done quite a bit of trekking around Melbourne, but nothing compared to this. If she continued, she might lose a couple of pounds.

As she watched Cleo chop and wash the veggies, she felt grateful not to have to stand and cook. She would have just fried herself another hamburger for dinner, maybe thrown a couple of carrots sticks beside it, and called it good. Cleo was preparing a vegetarian feast. She had piles of onions, carrots, celery, peppers, and tomatoes lined up in a colorful array and was whisking together a combination of spices and soy sauce—for what, Jane couldn't fathom. She considered herself an adequate cook, but then Ernie's palate was limited to meat and potatoes, with either peas or green beans on the side. He'd tolerated a salad if it was smothered in ranch dressing.

During their first few months of marriage, she'd perused cookbooks and experimented with exotic and complicated recipes, but after watching him push his food around the plate, only to polish off a bag of chips in front of the television while she dumped his dinner into the trash, she gave in and cooked what he liked. His family's potlucks were for birthdays and holidays, and she always brought Jell-O with mandarin oranges and whipped cream, as it was the one thing they'd eat. She had long since gotten used to the basic diet, but coming here and eating that first sandwich in the airport had rekindled her desire to experiment, though she didn't have the skills to attempt anything more exciting than what she knew. Maybe, if dinner was good, Cleo could teach her a thing or two. Maybe she could pay her way by driving and teaching.

Feeling a little more at ease with the situation, Jane opened the notebook and began to list all the things she had left undone when she'd walked out the door a week before. Mortgage, utility bills, phone bills—the recurring monthly expenses went on one sheet. Other things—such as the renewal for the license plates on her car and magazine subscriptions—she wasn't sure needed attention, but she wrote them down with a note to check them out. Next there was the mail, which she knew filled the mailbox; the plants, which she was sure were wilted, were located in nearly every window of the house; the furnace, which needed to be turned on to keep the pipes from freezing (had it frosted back home yet?); putting outdoor things away for winter; and refrigerator items that needed to be cleaned out, including food that would be outdated or rotten by the time she got home. The list went on another sheet of paper with "Rachael?" written on top. She hoped she hadn't angered her friend to the point she would never speak to her again, much less not help her with some of the stuff on her list.

When she finished cataloging everything she could think of, she sat back and surveyed her work. A cup of tea appeared on the seat beside her. After thanking Cleo, who grunted in reply, she sipped the brew and frowned. The list looked daunting. She felt depressed and hopeless looking at it. Some things Rachael could do, if she was still talking to Jane, but for so many of the others, she didn't have a clue. What did other people do when they were planning on being gone for extended periods of time? She answered herself: take care of things before they left. Damn, damn, and damn. Her shoulders sagged, and a familiar ache of self-doubt settled in her gut.

Outside the camper, Cleo was humming to herself while she sautéed vegetables on the propane stove. It was a lilting tune Jane couldn't identify. It sounded happy and carefree, and Cleo looked so contented stirring and humming that Jane felt envious. The girl had nothing to her name except the clothes on her back and what little was in her purse, and yet she seemed happy. Jane had all this stuff that needed caring for and money to take care of it with, but she felt miserable. Why did she ever think that she would be blissfully happy once Ernie dropped dead and she left?

She sipped her tea, wishing it had sugar in it. She usually drank it black, but at the moment she needed a little sweetening in her life. She was on the verge of standing to look for the sugar when Cleo handed her a plate of steaming-hot vegetables, slices of Swiss cheese, and a few crackers tucked in around the edges. It smelled earthy and spicy and healthy all at the same time. Jane's stomach gurgled in approval.

"Thank you," she said, taking the plate and grabbing a fork from the counter. "It smells wonderful. You'll have to tell me what you did while we eat."

"No worries." Cleo filled her own plate and climbed in to sit beside her. "I fried up what you had in the esky along with some diced potatoes, garlic, soy sauce, pepper, and mustard."

Jane placed a forkful of the mixture in her mouth and sighed. It tasted wonderful. "Wow," she said when she had swallowed. "This is terrific. Where did you learn to cook?"

She shrugged. "Here and there. Mum was a good cook, so I learned some from her, but my roomie, Casey, worked in the kitchen of a restaurant and taught me most of what I know." She chewed and waved her fork at the counter. "You need more spices and oils. I can't do all that much with what you have now. After dinner we could pop down to the store, and I'll help you pick up what you need."

The sun had long since set, and Jane had turned the lights on halfway through making her lists. The prospect of shopping ranked right up there with having Ernie show up at her open door. "How about in the morning? I had a long walk today, and I'm tired. We could stock up before we leave town or even stop in the next town."

Cleo made a face. "But I know what you need right now. If I wait until morning, I'll forget some things."

Jane sighed. "I don't want to do it. Are you sure you can't remember until tomorrow? Besides, I can't drive at night. I have enough problems in daylight."

"I thought I was going to drive." Cleo looked defiant. "It'll be so much better to do it tonight."

Jane could feel her tiredness sink to her bones. She wasn't sure she could muster the energy to walk around the store, much less come back, put everything away, and still set up the camper for the night. But the girl was so insistent. She sighed again. "All right. After dishes, we'll go."

At the store, Jane pushed the skittish cart while Cleo filled it with, to Jane's tastes, exotic vegetables such as eggplant and pumpkin. Then came the spices, some of which (cardamom and turmeric) she'd never even heard of; a fat, round loaf of bread; three different kinds of oil; three vinegars; rice noodles; and tofu. Jane watched her choose and toss, not having a clue how to fix or use most of what was in the cart. When the tofu came off the shelf, however, Jane stopped.

"I hate tofu."

Cleo dropped it in the cart and moved away. "Not the way I fix it."

Jane stiffened, feeling like she'd been told to shut up and eat her green beans. "Not a chance," she muttered under her breath.

The cart was half full by the time they reached the registers. Cleo packed the bags Jane had bought the previous day while chatting with the clerk about some group called Volcano that Jane assumed was a rock band. They both agreed they were "fair dinkum" rockers and "beauts." Jane wasn't sure she cared to know what they were talking about; she was just too tired.

While Cleo drove to the caravan park, Jane stayed in back and tried to find places for all the stuff they'd bought. At least one bagful wasn't going to go into any of the available spaces. By the time they'd parked and reattached the electricity, all Jane wanted to do was crawl into bed. But the bed had yet to be made.

Cleo seemed to grasp instinctively how the beds went together, and she assembled both of them in less time than it had taken Jane to do one. The top one was without sheets or blankets, but Cleo insisted she didn't need either of those things—after all, she'd spent two nights sleeping outside without anything. She could deal with a mattress and pillow. Jane felt awful that she didn't have linens for the girl and vowed to get her some when she could.

Inside the amenities block, Jane washed her face while Cleo used a finger to brush her teeth. Jane made a mental note to get some necessities for Cleo along with the linens: a few clothes, underwear, shoes, everything the girl would let her buy. She suspected this was going to be a fight, but it was one she was determined to win. Back at the van, Cleo climbed into the top bunk while Jane slid into her own little bed underneath. She could hear Cleo breathing, and every time she changed position or rolled over, the whole camper would shift a little, like a mini earthquake. Jane wondered if she was going to be able to fall asleep between the noise and the movement, but before she knew it, the sun was shining through the curtains.

Cleo was still sleeping when Jane crept out of the van and headed to the toilets, towel and toothbrush in hand. The air felt cooler than it had the previous morning, and Jane wrapped her robe more tightly around her, sure that Cleo must have been very cold during the night. She had to get to some kind of department store before the girl froze to death.

By the time she returned, Cleo was still dead to the world. Jane wanted a cup of coffee, but there was no way to fix one with the beds still in place, and she didn't want to wake up Cleo. Though she also wanted to put on clean clothes, she decided to wear what she had on the previous day and walk to town to get her caffeine fix. Surely by the time she got back, Cleo would be up, and they could get a start on the day.

Taking her time, Jane found a bakery that sold coffee, and she sat and watched the crowds while she ate a croissant and sipped her latte. A local newspaper was on the table, and she scanned the articles, noting that aside from the strange names, the issues seemed similar to those any resort community would face. She lingered until she could stand it no longer, then strolled back to the park along the beach, wishing she had brought a light jacket to ward off the sea breeze.

Cleo was still asleep. This is ridiculous, Jane thought, sitting on the bumper. It was pushing noon. Was this the way it was going to be from now on? Then again, she rationalized, the girl hadn't had a decent night's sleep for days and probably was catching up on some needed rest. Jane decided to return to town and check her email to see if Rachael had answered her. Before she left, she scribbled a note about where she had gone and left it on the pillow of her bed. She figured Cleo couldn't miss it when she climbed down.

Rachael had emailed back. "OMG Jane. I can't believe you did it, just like you said you would. I never believed you, and there you are. I am so jealous I can hardly stand it. What's it like? What have you been doing? How are you doing with the asshole finally out of your life?"

Jane wished Rachael were with her. If she were, they would have been on the road for hours after a long breakfast and would be looking for a good place to have lunch. Just thinking of having Rachael with her brought a wave of homesickness and loneliness. She wished she could wrap her arms around her friend and hug and be hugged in return. She wanted to sit over coffee and tell her all about Ernie dying, how glad she was to watch him take his last breath, how disgusted she was at the sight of his body, and how she couldn't be rid of it fast enough. How the undertakers looked at her when they rolled him out on the gurney, his face exposed, the rest of him neatly zipped into the black body bag, and how she turned away and didn't even look at the corpse.

She would tell her about how she set her purse on the floor by the front door, plane ticket sticking out of the top of it, then had to move it so they could wheel him out and into the waiting hearse. How she watched them drive away feeling dead inside, her only desire being to run far away from the house and her former life. How she drove to Denver without seeing anything and climbed aboard the plane with nothing and, instead of feeling free, felt she still carried the world on her back, and how she now was sitting at this computer with tears running down her face in public, feeling homesick, of all things. Jane wiped her eyes with a tissue and blew her nose.

Crying again. Had she cried every day since she had arrived? She was tired of leaking water, tired of breaking down all the time. Where was the joy she should be feeling? Maybe she would never be happy. Maybe she was meant to be miserable. Maybe that's all she deserved. She sniffled again, stuffed her sodden tissue into her purse, and placed her fingers on the keyboard.

Half an hour later, she hit send and stood up, exhausted. Who knew writing an email could take so much out of a person? Purse on her shoulder, she thanked the clerk and walked outside into the sunshine. Aside from feeling wrung out, she felt a little better than when she'd sat down. Hungry, she wondered if Cleo had woken up yet so that she could go back to the camper and fix something or whether she should eat in town. If Cleo was still asleep, she didn't have the energy to walk back into town to find food. She stood on the street debating with herself. What would Rachael do? She'd told Rachael about the strange girl she'd picked up and wondered what her reaction would be to that piece of information. It was so out of character for her—would Rachael think she'd completely lost her mind somewhere over the Pacific? It was something she thought Rachael might do and hoped her friend would approve.

Finally, she decided to risk going back to the camper. If Cleo was still sleeping, maybe she could grab something to eat from the park office and take a nap.

When Jane opened the back door of the camper, she was shocked to see that both beds had been stowed and the sink filled with dishes. She stuck her head inside, but there was no sign of Cleo. Had she determined she couldn't tolerate being with Jane and taken off again? Jane shook her head and decided she wasn't going to jump to that conclusion quite yet. But still. There was no note, and her purse was gone. Maybe she was taking a shower or going to the bathroom. Jane wouldn't have left her purse in the camper without locking it, and she had the key, so maybe Cleo was in the amenities block.

The toilets and showers were empty. Stumped, Jane decided to fix herself some lunch. She'd figure out what to do if Cleo hadn't shown up by the time she'd eaten and cleaned up.

The cooler was so packed with food that Jane had a hard time sorting through it all and deciding what to eat. What if Cleo didn't come back? She'd spent over a hundred dollars on food the previous night, and most of what she'd bought, she'd probably throw away since she didn't know what to do with it. Tightening her lips and gritting her teeth, she pulled out the rest of the hamburger and the jar of pickles. Wouldn't that be her luck—to go out on a limb for someone and have that person turn around and stab her in the back? Sure, she had money, but not enough to throw away on food she wouldn't eat. And she had been planning to spend more on the girl to make sure she had clothes to wear and sheets and blankets to keep her warm. If Cleo had to desert Jane, then better she did so before Jane had dropped a wad on her.

She flipped her burger and sprinkled some salt and pepper on it. What was the girl thinking? Obviously, she wasn't very responsible; otherwise, she would have left a note or something. Maybe she did this all the time—take people for a ride by looking miserable, then running out on them. Maybe Jane got off lucky by taking her purse with her that morning; otherwise Cleo might have stolen her Visa and be charging hundreds of dollars on it, bankrupting Jane while she was out. Maybe their whole interaction was a setup from the start. Maybe the boyfriend hadn't left her and instead was waiting somewhere, and that's where Cleo was now, plotting with him to steal what she could from Jane. She'd walk back all sweet and innocent and make some excuse, then steal everything she could take in the middle of the night. Or the boyfriend would come and hurt her.

Jane plopped her burger on the bun, then squeezed the ketchup bottle with such ferocity that it splashed down the front of her shirt and across the counter. "Damn it," she swore, snatching a dish towel. This is what you get when you trust strangers. "Damn it to hell."

Her nose began to tingle and her eyes water. "Oh no." She stuffed the burger in her mouth and chewed through the tears, vowing that after she cleaned up, she'd take a shower, wash the shirt in a sink in the amenities block, then pack up and leave, no matter if Cleo was there or not.

But by the time she finished eating, she realized it was long past checkout time, and she owed for another night. Frustrated, she decided to stay. If Cleo came back, at least she'd get a little pleasure from kicking her out.

Cleo strolled up to the back of the van while Jane was propped on the seat reading her novel. Jane glanced up when Cleo jumped into the back and dropped her purse. She flashed Jane a smile.

"Hey, how are ya goin'?"

"Where have you been?" She dropped the book to her lap and glared at the girl. "I was hoping we could get out of here today. I wanted to see Cape Otway, then drive on to Warrnambool, do some shopping, and spend the night there. But now it's too late to do any of that. Why didn't you leave me a note?" She felt her voice rising, and the heat in her words made her feel uncomfortable. She was never good at expressing anger; it made her feel out of control, and the results weren't what she wanted. But she couldn't seem to keep her voice level and reasonable. She needed to shout. After all, hadn't Cleo wrecked her plans? Didn't she have a right to express her displeasure?

Cleo looked completely taken aback. She blinked a couple of times. "I didn't have a pen. I'm sorry."

Oh. Jane had not stopped to consider that maybe Cleo couldn't leave her a note. Her anger abated a little, and she realized that some of the conclusions she had drawn might not be correct. But still, she felt wronged and irked that her plans had been thwarted.

"OK. I understand about the note. But where were you all day?"

"Collecting." Cleo reached inside her purse and pulled out an odd assortment of objects: shells, pieces of string and wire, stones, and bits of plastic, paper, and glass. They heaped in a jumble of bright colors on the counter.

To Jane it looked like garbage. "Why?"

Cleo stirred the pile with her finger, then picked up an oval piece of glass and held it to the light. "To make jewelry. This is the kind of stuff I use. I thought I could get a couple of pieces made before we got to Adelaide, and that way I'd have something to sell so I could repay you."

Oh. Again Jane felt very foolish. Her anger-fueled imaginings of plots and larceny evaporated, and her cheeks reddened. She looked at her hands. "You don't have to do that. We have an agreement."

Cleo shrugged. "I know, but I feel bad that I can't do more. I've never had to be on the dole before, and I want to do everything I can to pay you back."

"Like I said, you don't have to do that. What you're doing is enough."

Cleo stared at her defiantly. "But you're angry. If it was all right, why would you be angry?"

Jane felt her cheeks flush more deeply, her anger slumping into shame. She bit her lip, then sighed. "I was wrong. I didn't know where you were and couldn't go without you."

Cleo laughed, and Jane jerked back, surprised. "Oh, this is a beaut. My boyfriend up and bails on me, and the stranger I meet won't leave without me. Am I a nong or what?"

Jane frowned. "Nong?"

"A fool, an idiot." Cleo shook her head. "OK, I get why you were upset. I won't run off without letting you know where I'm going. I'd prefer it, though, if you could let me know when you have something planned so I don't mess it up."

But you were asleep, and I didn't want to wake you, Jane wanted to say, then realized she could have included the information in her note. "I'll do that."

She set the book on the cushion and rose. "So what did you say you were going to do with all this stuff?" She poked at the pile. Some of the things did look interesting. One shell in particular had been eroded away to reveal the iridescent spiral inside of it. Jane held it to the sun.

"I'm going to make it into jewelry. Like these here." She cradled in her palm small, frosted ovals of green and white, maybe three-quarters of an inch long. "Sea glass. Beaches are the best because of all the sea glass and other things people leave behind. I'm going to make these into a bracelet using this to bind them together and these for dangles." She pulled a long greenish length of wire from the jumble and several small mottled cone shells. "And the one you're holding is going to be a pendant."

Jane wasn't sure she could conceptualize the bracelet Cleo described, but the shell in her hand would make a wonderful pendant. "I can't wait to see what you create." She placed the shell back on the counter. "Have you eaten today?"

"Yeah, I'm good." Cleo wound the wire around her hand.

"Were you warm enough last night? It got kind of cold, and I was concerned."

"No worries."

Jane frowned. "And what about clothes? You can't just wear those until we get to Adelaide. I'd be happy to get you some things."

Cleo glanced up, setting the wire coil on the counter. "You still angry?"

Jane shook her head. "No, not anymore. I'd like to get you a few things." She looked into Cleo's eyes. "No strings attached."

The girl stared back warily. "OK," she said. "There's an op shop by the grocery store. There might be a Salvos too. I can pay you back with what I sell."

Jane smiled. "We can figure that out later. I'll bet you'd love to take a shower and get into clean clothes."

Cleo nodded, her mouth set in a straight line. "But I will pay you back."

"Whatever. Come on; let's go before they close."

Jane let Cleo drive to the store, first stopping at the office to pay for another night's stay. The "op shop" turned out to be a secondhand store, and "Salvos," a Salvation Army store. Jane wasn't thrilled with the idea of buying used clothing. But there was no department store in Apollo Bay, and while she was willing to purchase some things for Cleo, she wasn't willing to pay a hundred dollars for a shirt at the tourist shops across from the beach, especially for someone who was more or less dressed in rags and seemed to prefer it that way. Still, she balked at the door.

"You sure this is where you want to shop?"

Cleo bounded through the door. "I love op shops. You can get the best stuff ever in them." Within seconds she was deep among the racks of clothing.

It didn't take Cleo long to find a couple of T-shirts, a pair of pants, and a light jacket. Jane wandered around shuffling through the shirts and slacks. Most of the clothes were in relatively good shape, and she was surprised to find several name brands. She thought about her stained shirt but still couldn't quite make herself pull something from the rack to try on. In the back room, however, she found linens she thought might fit the upper mattress, a blanket, a couple of towels, and a washcloth. For some reason she wasn't squeamish about buying used sheets. Maybe it was because they weren't for her—and would Cleo care? When they both arrived at the register, Jane looked over what Cleo had picked out and frowned.

"That's hardly enough to get through the next day or two. Why don't you get a couple more things, maybe some underwear too."

Cleo made a face. "I'd rather go commando than wear someone's used undies. But maybe some bathers." She turned and headed back to the racks. Another shirt, a bikini, and a pair of shorts later, Jane charged eighty-seven dollars to her Visa. She felt better with her angry outburst atoned for.

When they got back to the caravan park, Cleo made a beeline for the washing machines with all the purchases. While the machines were running, Jane loaned her shampoo, soap, towels, and a robe so she could shower. Cleo was still bathing when the washing machines finished their cycle, and Jane grabbed the wash and looked for a dryer. None. At least none that she could see. Perplexed, she rigged a clothesline by the camper, though she had to hang the sheets on the lines by the laundry room. She hoped everything would dry by dark, and no one would come and steal it all in the meantime.

Cleo was grinning when she returned to the van, Jane's robe enveloping her from ears to ankles and wrapping around her almost to the back. "I never thought taking a shower could be so good. Thank you for letting me use your stuff."

"No problem. Say, don't you use clothes dryers here? I couldn't find one by the washing machines."

Cleo shook her head. "Not so much. My mum has one, but I can remember using it only once."

"What do you do if it rains?"

"Wait to do the wash or hang it on racks indoors." Cleo bent over and squeezed water from her dreadlocks. "What do you do in America?"

"Put it in the dryer. I don't know anyone who hangs their wash outside. I can't remember even seeing a clothesline in someone's yard."

"Doesn't that use a lot of electricity?"

Jane shrugged. "I guess I never thought about it. We couldn't hang clothes outside in winter, what with the snow and freezing temperatures."

Cleo straightened and flipped her hair back. "Snow. What I wouldn't give to see real snow. Do you get a lot where you live?"

"Some. Maybe a foot once a year and three to six inches several times during the winter. What about here? Does it ever snow?"

"Nah, not much anyhow. There's a ski area in Falls Creek that my mum once went to and the Snowy Mountains, of course. I saw falling snow once in Melbourne when I was little, but it melted when it touched the ground. I ran outside in it in my jammies with my dad—my real dad, that is, not Reggie. My dad stood in the door laughing his butt off. He wanted me to catch snowflakes on my tongue, but I couldn't do it. We had such a great time, laughing and chasing around, and he wasn't even pissed. Wasn't often he was cold sober." She sighed and twirled one of her dreadlocks between her fingers. "It must be wonderful to have snow on the ground."

Jane laughed. "Yes, the first time it falls in winter. After about the fourth or fifth storm and having to shovel the sidewalks and contend with ice on the roads and sidewalks, it gets very tiresome. I hope I miss all the snow this year."

"I wouldn't mind it, no matter what."

Yes, you would, thought Jane. You'd grow tired of it, you'd be angry at it, you'd hate it, but you'd give in to the inevitability of it and get through. Hadn't she done all of that, over and over and over? And not just with snow and work and dealing with Ernie, but with Ernie's family too. Like their first Thanksgiving in their new house, which presaged all the others that followed.

Ernie had insisted they have his family over for dinner.

"All of them?" Jane stopped picking up the dinner dishes from the table. "Your parents and all your brothers and their families too? That would be what, twelve, fourteen, no, eighteen people. Here? There isn't enough room."

He threw his napkin on the table. "One of the reasons I bought this house was so we could have my family over, and now you're saying it's not possible. You don't want to have my family around."

"That's not true. I don't mind your family, but they don't care for me." Well, that wasn't strictly true. They hated her, and she felt the same toward them.

"Maybe if you treated them right, they'd like you more."

She felt herself wilt inside as she walked to the kitchen. Maybe she hadn't done enough for them or participated in what they liked. Maybe she should try a little harder.

The minute she agreed to the dinner, she felt exhausted, as if someone had placed a ten-pound sack of flour on her neck. It sat on her while she shopped, inquired about everyone's favorite dishes, got her mother-in-law's stuffing recipe, created centerpieces, and personalized place mats. Another sack landed on her Thanksgiving morning while she assembled the hors d'oeuvres, put the turkey in the oven, and ran a dust cloth over the furniture one more time. She found herself brimming with anxiety and dread, watching the minutes race away until they were to arrive.

An hour and forty-five minutes after they were supposed to be there and half an hour after dinner was scheduled to be served, George and Thelma, Ernie's parents, rang the front doorbell. George had a bottle of Chivas in his hand, and Thelma carried a pumpkin pie—even though Jane had told her that she had made two pumpkin pies and apple would be appreciated instead. The men clasped hands, and Thelma pecked Ernie on the cheek. They handed their coats to Jane without saying hello, then the men disappeared into the den, where the television was, and Thelma headed straight for the kitchen. She was prodding the turkey with a fork when Jane returned from hanging the coats.

"Looks a little overdone to me," she said, giving the bird another stab.

Jane narrowed her eyes and bit back the recriminations that sprang to her lips like fiery darts. "You may be right." She scooted the pie over to the other pumpkin pies and turned on the burner to reheat the potatoes. "I thought we were eating at four."

Thelma rolled her eyes and straightened. "Well, there's nothing to be done about it now. We're just going to have to eat a stringy, dry bird."

The doorbell rang before Jane could reply, and she found most of the rest of the family huddled on the front stoop looking surly. They tramped in, dropped coats on the floor when Jane didn't grab them fast enough, and milled into the den, Thelma in the rear.

"Wait, please." Jane touched Thelma's arm, which Thelma jerked away.

"What?"

"Do you think people would rather eat now or wait until halftime?"

"How am I supposed to know? You're the hostess." Huffing, she followed the others.

After dumping the coats, Jane sat and rubbed her forehead with both hands. Should she serve the hors d'oeuvres or dinner? What would cause the least amount of tension among the fewest people? She decided on the hors d'oeuvres.

While Ernie's family devoured the slaw, the crackers with salmon, and the guacamole and chips, she tried to salvage what she could of dinner. The turkey would be tough, the stuffing dry, and everything else overcooked, but at least she'd made a meal. And there would be more than enough pumpkin pie to go around.

At halftime the whole lumbering lot of them descended on the dining room. Jane had set up a buffet line so that the people sitting at the smaller tables in the living room wouldn't have to come to the main table for food. They filed past the food, taking portions that would leave a mouse starving and making snide comments about her decorations and what they figured the meal would taste like.

When they were seated, they joined hands, and George led grace.

"Thanks for the food and for Ernie letting us come over to his place for a change. If he'd listened to me and bought the Oak Street house instead, we wouldn't be so crowded, but at least we're here. I'm sure the food will be fine, and the Broncos will win."

"Hoo-yaw!" all the males intoned, raising their forks.

Charlene, the eldest sister-in-law, cleared her throat loudly. The men sighed and lowered their forks and heads. "And thank you to Jesus for blessing us with his grace. He is the source of all, and without his smile, we are less than the worms in the dirt. His joy is ours and his blessings bountiful beyond our understanding." She carried on in this vein for several minutes, the other sisters-in-law softly chanting "amen" at salient points in the prayer. When she finally wound down, everyone glanced up, as if waiting for another sister-in-law to start in as well, but after a moment of silence, they raised their forks once more and prodded dinner.

Jane was about to take a bite when Ernie snapped his fingers.

"You forgot the Chablis I bought for dinner, Jane. Go get it and the wineglasses too. We'll have a toast."

But there isn't nearly enough for everyone, she thought, trying to portion out a single bottle of wine among fourteen adults. And she had only six wineglasses and not enough other glasses besides what were on the table for water and soda. But she rose and fetched the wine and a corkscrew for Ernie and placed the wineglasses on a tray by his left elbow. Let him figure out how to divide it.

Ernie filled a glass for himself, his mother, and father and ignored the rest. Most of those left dry glared at her, silently accusing her of not buying enough for everyone. The toast was "Cheers!" Then, before Jane could sit, Ernie needed more salt. Then it was pepper. Then water. Then rolls. Then gravy. Then, the most humiliating, ketchup. Jane bounced up and down all through dinner, barely getting in a bite or two. She took some satisfaction in the fact that most everyone, with the notable exceptions of Thelma, George, and Ernie, got up for seconds and took decent portions too.

Dessert was eaten in front of the final half of the game while Jane struggled alone in the kitchen to put away the leftovers and begin the cleanup. After the Broncos lost, Ernie's siblings and their families filed out the door, showering Ernie with thanks and making tentative plans for Christmas. Thelma and George were the last to leave and stood in the open door while Jane shivered in the incoming breeze next to Ernie.

"Well, I can't say the dinner was good, but it was edible." Thelma pulled on her leather gloves one at a time. "I'd say we should do Christmas somewhere else, but then how would Jane get the practice she needs. Isn't that right, son?"

Ernie nodded. "I'm sorry it was such a mess. She'll do better next time. I'll see to it."

Kisses, hugs, and they were gone.

Jane wanted to smash a plate over Ernie's head when he turned from the closed door. "How could you? How could you say such a thing?"

He looked at her. "I don't know what you mean. You have to admit dinner wasn't all that great."

"Because they were late! Deliberately late to make me look bad. I told you they have it out for me, and this proves it. They staged all of this."

Ernie smirked. "Don't blame them because you messed up."

"I didn't mess up. Did you call them up and change the time

without telling me? Or was it your mother? That's something she would do."

"Paranoia doesn't suit you. Nobody changed the time; you got it wrong."

Jane wanted to wring his neck and those of his mother and father too. Too angry to form a coherent sentence, she stormed back to the kitchen and threw the pots and pans around until she was afraid she would break something. Then collapsing against the counter, she sobbed into a dish towel until she could produce no more tears.

Ernie was in bed and fast asleep by the time she finished cleaning up the kitchen, dining room, and den. She stood by her side of the bed near midnight watching the rise and fall of his shoulder and vowed she'd never cook another meal for his family. That vow lasted for a month and was broken annually for at least one holiday meal from then on.

Jane shook her head, remembering how she'd gotten used to the barbs and sideways comments about her ineptitude in the kitchen. If the turkey came out well, they all remembered the one that didn't. If it was a little on the chewy side, they nodded and reported that was just the way it was at Jane's. At some point she began to consider it part of the holiday ritual, and it didn't matter what they thought.

But watching Cleo sort through her treasures, she realized she had never gotten over any of it. When she thought about the way they had treated her, her chest and throat tightened, and her stomach roiled. She hated them. Maybe that was one of the reasons she'd left without calling. Maybe it was her way of getting revenge for all the things they'd done to her over the years. If it was, then it suited her fine.

"Are you getting hungry?"

Cleo swept her things from the counter. "Yes, I'm getting a little peckish. What do you want for dinner?"

"I don't care. You're the cook. I'll leave that up to you and go see if the sheets are dry." And I promise I'll appreciate whatever you make and tell you that too, she thought.

Chapter 5

JANE FELT EXHAUSTED and ready for bed by nine, but Cleo was stringing together shells and sea glass while she listened to rock music. At least that's what Jane thought she heard leaking around the earbuds Cleo had attached to her MP3 player. Jane couldn't understand how Cleo could stand the volume. If she could hear the music, how loud was it for Cleo? She wouldn't have been surprised to find the girl had lost half her hearing.

She watched Cleo humming and working and wondered when the child would want to go to bed. Probably not until some wee hour in the morning, considering she didn't get up until around noon. Jane wanted to say something but was afraid to. When she tried to figure out what she was afraid of, it seemed to evade definition, like a shadow flickering on the bottom of a stream. Yet the feeling persisted, and she couldn't make herself say anything. Instead she tried hinting by yawning and stretching, but Cleo was so involved in her work that she didn't seem to notice. With a sigh, Jane returned to her novel.

Jane had read her share of romance novels. She preferred story lines with implied sexual content instead of the bodice rippers Rachael adored. This one Rachael would have loved. The hero had a throbbing member that he thrust into the woman at every opportunity. Far more often than Jane ever considered having sex, even when she and Ernie were in lust and hot to do it everywhere.

Reading about the fictional couple's encounters left her feeling empty and lonely. Not the sex part, she decided, but the fact that in books the men worshipped the women and would do anything to win them. The women spurned the men until some final act of kindness or bravery drove them into the hero's arms. Jane had experienced neither scenario.

Ernie had been her only lover, and his ardor after the first few months of marriage was tepid at best. What would it be like, she wondered, to have someone ready to leap into the unknown for you? To throw himself in the path of danger, to be willing to give up his life to save you? She felt she'd done that for Ernie, at least on some level. Hadn't she given up any hopes of a career to follow him from oil field to oil field? Didn't she give up her own job to chain herself to his bedside from the moment he was diagnosed until he died? Wouldn't it be nice to have someone do that for her?

She rested the book on her lap and closed her eyes, trying to imagine how it would feel. Instead, she drifted into a montage of Ernie memories, ones she would have preferred to forget. Picking up the book to banish the barrage, she found she'd lost interest. She yawned again.

Cleo finished a bracelet and placed it on the counter. Jane picked it up and held it in her palm. It was lovely—not exactly beautiful, but unique and cleverly constructed. Jane could see herself buying something similar if she were twenty years younger. No wonder Cleo could make a living using junk.

"It's beautiful," Jane said, returning the piece to the counter. Cleo didn't look up. She didn't hear me, Jane thought. "It's beautiful," she repeated louder, but still Cleo didn't respond. Oh well.

Jane tried to read once more, but to no avail. She wanted to go to sleep. Needed to go to sleep. Why couldn't she say something to Cleo? It was her camper after all. Why not indeed?

Reaching forward, she touched Cleo's shoulder. "I'm tired. Can we please make up the camper and go to bed?"

Cleo glanced at her and pulled out one of the earbuds. "What?"

"I want to go to bed." She said it loudly, probably too loudly for the small space.

"Oh. It's so early."

Since Cleo didn't seem to own a watch, Jane wondered how she knew it was early. It didn't feel early to Jane. "I'm tired. Can we please make up the beds? If you want to keep working, you can do so on your bed."

Cleo glanced up. "It's too low up there to sit up, and I can't work lying down. Can you wait until I finish this?"

Jane glanced at her watch. Ten fifteen. "How much longer do you think?"

"Half an hour, forty-five minutes."

Almost another hour. Jane wasn't sure she could take it, but she didn't want to stop Cleo from working since she was doing it to pay Jane back. She wished she had the guts to say no, but instead she nodded, feeling like a failure and resentful to boot. She rested her head against the back of the front seat and closed her eyes. Was she this self-centered when she was a teen? She didn't think so. Maybe it was a racial thing or an Australian thing. Did all blacks stay up late and sleep in? Maybe that's why they couldn't hold down jobs. That's what Ernie had said—that they were all lazy and good for nothing. Maybe that's why Cleo didn't have a job. Then again—before she could find any answers, she drifted to sleep.

Jane woke to the sound of birds. Light leaked through the curtains, and outside she could hear the sounds of someone mowing grass. She tried to lean forward, but her back spasmed. She gasped, froze, then rolled forward to try and let the spasm undo itself. Doubled over, she wondered where Cleo was and why the girl hadn't woken her to make up the beds. Had Cleo climbed into her own bed and left Jane where she was?

"Cleo?" Jane croaked. She cleared her throat and tried again. "Cleo?" Silence responded. Where was that girl?

Carefully she straightened and twisted from side to side. The pain diminished. Glancing up, she noticed the upper bed had not been made. So either Cleo had put up her bed or spent the night somewhere else. Where could that be? Tentatively, she lowered her legs to the ground and stood, her anger rising. Thoughts about Cleo's lack of responsibility and wild behavior spiraled into a vortex of rage. There was no note telling her where Cleo might have gone—this after they had talked about keeping each other informed. The child was nothing but a spoiled brat who had no concept of personal responsibility or the feelings and needs of others. This was inexcusable behavior, and Jane wasn't going to put up with any more of it.

She grabbed her toothbrush and a towel and fumed to the amenities block. When she returned to the camper, the back door was open, and Cleo was chopping fruit inside.

"Where the hell have you been?" Jane didn't try to modulate her tone or volume. "I thought we were supposed to let each other know where we were. And why didn't you wake me up last night to make the beds? I woke up all tied in knots from sleeping on the bench. Where's your sense of responsibility? Your consideration of others? It's the least you can do after everything I've done for you."

Cleo looked stricken. Jane's stomach clenched, and rage melted into fear. What had she done? Now that the words had escaped her mouth, she could hear Ernie's voice and intonation in them. The condemnation. The belittling. The demands. The guilt.

Cleo dropped the knife on the counter and wiped her hands on a dish towel. "I'm going." Turning, she retrieved her purse from the seat, stuck her hand inside, and pulled out the pendant and bracelet she'd constructed the evening before. She dropped them on the seat. "It's not enough to repay you for everything, but it's all I've got." Slowly, she climbed to the ground.

Jane grabbed for Cleo's arm, but the girl evaded her and stormed away. "Wait. I'm sorry. I shouldn't have said those things." Cleo ignored her and marched on. Jane raced ahead of her, then spun and faced her. "Please, wait."

Cleo halted, arms wrapped across her chest. Jane swallowed

hard and bowed her head. "I was wrong to say those things about you. I'm sorry."

Cleo stared at her, one foot tapping the ground, counting out the seconds until she could run away.

Jane motioned toward the camper. "Please come back. I'll fix us something to eat, and we can work this out. Please."

Cleo's jaw clenched. Her foot stopped. "You're bloody mental. Are you finished spewin'?"

"I don't know. What does 'spewin'' mean?"

"Are you done getting me up?" When Jane shrugged and shook her head, Cleo planted her hands on her hips and glared at her. "You finished yelling at me?"

"Oh." Jane nodded. "I am. I know I shouldn't have done that. I'm so very, very sorry. Please come back and let me explain."

"Explain here."

Jane glanced around, feeling exposed. Thankfully, the park seemed deserted except for a couple of men standing on a stoop in front of one of the cabins. They both looked in Jane's direction. "Please, can we go back to the camper?"

Cleo began to tap her foot again.

"OK." Jane turned her back to the men and tried to look inconspicuous. "I woke up stiff and sore, and you weren't anywhere around. I thought you'd run off again without letting me know where you were, and that made me angrier. And I couldn't figure out where you slept last night or understand why you didn't wake me when you wanted to go to bed. I wanted to sleep in my bed and not on the bench.

"I know I wasn't being rational when I yelled at you. I let my emotions take control of me. I shouldn't have done that. I'm sorry."

Cleo pursed her lips and paused her foot. "You aren't my mum." Jane nodded. "I wouldn't let my mum yell at me like that, not in front of everyone in the park for no good reason. Try asking where I was instead of making assumptions and screaming."

Jane nodded again. "You're right. I should have asked instead of assuming. Will you come back to the camper now?"

"I don't know. Is this going to keep happening every day?"

"No." Jane sighed. "Oh, I don't know. I hope not. I don't want to keep doing this."

"Neither do I."

"I don't want you to go away. I don't. But if you feel that's what you have to do, I'll help you pack up your things and you can take them with you. But please, at least have something to eat before you leave."

Cleo relaxed a little and took a step toward the camper. Jane sighed in relief.

Inside, Jane finished fixing the fruit that Cleo had started. She pulled out some yogurt from the cooler, added some bread, butter, and peanut butter, handed Cleo a plate, and stepped back.

Cleo filled the plate and perched on the edge of the bench. Jane took a helping and sat beside her. "Thank you for coming back."

"I didn't say I was staying."

Jane held up a hand. "OK, OK. I'm glad you decided to eat something before you left. You're so thin, a breeze could blow you away."

"I've always been skinny," Cleo replied in a defensive tone.

"I didn't know that. I thought it was because you've been out on your own for a while."

Cleo took a bite. "There's a lot about me you don't know."

"That's true. And there's a lot about me you don't know, and some of that makes me act crazy at times, I think."

"Like what?"

Damn. Jane didn't want to bare her soul to this child. She felt ashamed she had been married to Ernie and had let him push her around for all those years—and even more ashamed her actions resembled his. It was bad enough that Rachael knew the truth. She'd listened to her friend tell her practically every week that she needed to get a divorce, and she didn't want another person, a virtual stranger, a girl who was dumped by a bad boyfriend, to tell her that she was a fool and wrong and wonder aloud how she could have put up with all of that for all those years. She just wanted Cleo to let it go. All of it. Jane's yelling and irrational behavior. Her history. Ernie.

Did she want this girl around enough to divulge her secrets, or at least some of her secrets? Wouldn't it be so much easier to let Cleo leave and call it good? Did she need to have someone drive her around Australia? She'd gotten out of Melbourne and to Apollo Bay all by herself, after all. She could do the rest of her trip by herself. Couldn't she?

But the truth of the matter was she didn't want Cleo to leave. She wasn't sure if it was the fact she'd invested money in the girl and wanted to make sure Cleo was going to take care of her investment or that she looked so vulnerable and brought out some latent mothering instinct in her that she'd buried or denied until now. Or that deep down inside, she was afraid of being alone and wanted someone along to keep her company and help her if she might need it, someone who knew the lay of the land. Or that she needed to demonstrate to someone that she was capable of making decisions

without a husband around to tell her what to do and what to think—
she needed validation she was doing OK on her own. Or maybe she
just needed to save someone so she didn't feel the need to be saved
herself. Or maybe it was a combination of all of the above.

She didn't know and couldn't begin to try and figure it out in
the moment. But she had the feeling she couldn't gloss over Cleo's
question if she wanted to keep the girl around. She'd have to tell her
something, no matter how embarrassing it was going to be.

"Well," she answered, "I was married to an awful man for a long
time, and sometimes I say the same kind of things he would say,
even though I don't mean to."

"Divorced?"

"Well, no." She pushed the fruit around her plate. "He died."

"How long ago?"

Jane closed her eyes and counted. Two weeks? Fifteen days?
Could it be that long ago? It seemed only yesterday she'd watched
him being rolled out the door in black plastic. Why was he still
hanging around her thoughts and tormenting her? When she'd
thought about living without him, she had always assumed she
could drop everything associated with him and his memory in a
day, two at the outside. But here she was haranguing another person
identically to the way Ernie always harangued her.

"A couple of weeks."

"That's all?" Cleo looked amazed. "How long have you been
here?"

"Almost a couple of weeks."

Cleo laid her fork on her plate and stared at Jane. "So you left the
States a couple of days after your husband died to come to Australia.
What about the funeral and all that?"

"Well . . ." Jane shuffled her fruit bits again, eyes averted. "I didn't have one. I let the undertakers have him, and they were going to do a cremation, then send the ashes to his family."

Cleo's eyes widened. "Bloody hell, that's cold. He must have been a right bastard."

"Right bastard," Jane snorted. "I think you nailed him. His family too."

"He beat you up? On the bottle?"

"Do you mean, did he drink?" Cleo nodded and Jane shook her head. "No. And he didn't ever hit me, though he threatened to once or twice. He just . . ." She couldn't seem to find the right word, if there was one. How could one word encompass all the things Ernie had done to her? Or at least the things Rachael had opened her eyes to.

She and Rachael had known each other just a couple of months the first time Rachael caught her crying in the bathroom of the library. They met when Rachael was a volunteer, shelving in the same aisle where Jane was looking for a book. They'd hit it off from the minute they started talking about books. Soon, they were having coffee together on Jane's days off from the motel or lunch when they could fit it into their schedules. They'd talked about many things, but never about Ernie.

That morning Ernie had cornered Jane again about her job. He hated the fact that she wanted to work, especially at the Hopi Motel, which in Ernie's book was the lowest of the low.

"Do you know what it looks like?" he demanded after devouring his morning eggs, bacon, and toast. "It makes me look like a loser. Like I can't support my own wife."

"But I like it." She folded her hands in her lap and stared at them.

"You like it," he mimicked, sarcasm whining through the words. "You like it. You like making me look like a fool? You like having the whole community talking behind my back? You like being some menial, good-for-nothing clerk in the slimiest motel in the Four Corners area? Even the goddamn, good-for-nothing Utes won't work there, but you *'like it.'* Why? That weenie manager, Dougie, giving it to you in one of the rooms? That why you 'like it' so much?"

Tears sprang to her eyes as she shook her head. "That's not true. Doug would never . . ."

"No wonder. Look at you. You're a fat, slovenly mess. No man wants to lay a finger on you. Not even me. You're disgusting." He pushed back from the table, plucking his pack of cigarettes from his shirt pocket. He lit one, grabbed his sports coat from the back of the chair, and threw it on. "I'll be home around six. Try to have something edible on the table when I get here."

She sat still as a stone until she heard the roar of his souped-up diesel truck fade into the distance. Then, untwining her hands, she stood. She took his words and sequestered them in a far corner of her mind while she tidied the kitchen. In the bathroom she avoided looking in the mirror for fear her reflection would bear witness to his declaration that she was disgusting.

She managed to bind herself together tightly enough that she could smile and laugh with the customers at the motel, and she didn't even cringe when Doug patted her on the back. It was only when she arrived at the library that all the bindings burst, and she dissolved into tears.

Rachael found her locked in one of the stalls, reeling out toilet paper and swabbing her eyes in a vain attempt to stanch the flow of tears. "Honey?" Rachael knocked on the door. "Are you OK?"

"Rachael, is that you?"

"Jane, what's going on? Are you OK?" Jane thought she sounded suspicious and worried at the same time.

"I'm . . . I'm . . . I don't know." She dissolved into sobs again.

"Look, why don't you come out here where I can see you? Can you do that?"

Jane nodded, grabbed a handful of toilet paper, and opened the door. Rachael took one look at her and enfolded her in her arms. "What's going on? What's wrong?"

Jane rested her forehead on Rachael's shoulder. "It's Ernie." She broke into sobs.

"What about Ernie?"

"He said I was disgusting. That no one wants me. That I'm the worst person he's ever known. That the reason I have a job is because I'm screwing the boss," she sputtered between sobs. "He thinks I'm terrible . . . and I'm not sure." She pulled back and looked Rachael in the eyes. "You've got to tell me truthfully. Don't lie to me. Am I an awful person?"

Rachael's mouth gaped for a second. Then she grabbed Jane's shoulders and stared at her. "You are the most wonderful woman I know. How can you think you are anything less?"

"But Ernie—"

Rachael shook her head. "But Ernie nothing. I haven't liked that man since the day I met him. He's a spoiled son of a bitch. How dare he say that to you? Don't you know that someone who acts like he does is emotionally abusive? You're better than he can see or imagine, and don't you ever forget it."

But Jane forgot it, over and over and over again. And though Rachael reminded her often, a piece of her always believed what Ernie said. Even the day he died. Even today.

"I guess he was just mean," she finished. Cleo looked at her skeptically. "What about you?" Jane asked, hoping to shift attention away from herself. "Tell me about, what's his name, Jason?"

"Jonny." Cleo's voice was cold. "Talk about your right bastard."

"What did you like about him? What drew you two together?"

"I thought he was cute." Cleo huffed. "Cute the way a platypus is cute until he gets you with his spur."

"Oh?" Jane blinked. She was under the impression that platypuses were always cute and didn't know they had a spur, whatever that was—it didn't sound good.

"And I thought he was nice. When he came by the flat, he was always bringing something with him: lollies, crisps, books, even flowers once. Now I wonder where he stole them. Anyhow, I guessed he was sweet on me, and I thought I'd play along just to see where it went. And he was good in the sack—that is, when he wasn't high or bombed out, which he was a lot. He was just like my dad that way. I guess I should have seen it coming, what he did to me."

"Did you love him?"

Cleo shrugged. "I guess, best I could, considering. How about you? You love your husband? That why you stayed with him?"

Jane set her half-eaten breakfast on the counter with a sigh. "I loved him at first. At least I think I did. He was never very nice to me, but I guess I thought he was the best I could find. He was successful and handsome, and we had a nice house. Everybody said I was lucky. Everybody, that is, except Rachael, my best friend."

"But if he was so mean, why didn't you leave him?"

Why, why indeed. Standing, Jane began to clean her plate into the garbage. "It's getting late. If we're going to see anything today besides the road, we need to get going." She turned to face Cleo. "Are you coming?"

"Are you going to chuck a wobbly on me again?"

"Am I what?"

"Going to go mental on me again?"

"Oh." Jane frowned. "I don't know. I can't promise I won't get angry again, but I'll try to be reasonable about it and ask before I jump to conclusions." I hope.

"Fair go. In that case I'll ride with you to Adelaide. I'm driving, yes?"

Jane smiled. "You're driving, yes. But if you're getting off at Adelaide, then I'm going to need some practice. You can help me be a better driver. Will that work for you?"

Cleo nodded and placed her plate in the sink. "Agreed."

Shortly after leaving Apollo Bay, the Great Ocean Road turned inland and wandered through a forest comprised of gum trees and ferns. Cleo claimed it was rainforest and a lot of the Otway Peninsula was covered with it. Jane held a map on her lap, by turns staring out the window, then tracing her finger along the map. It was amazing. She'd never seen undergrowth so dense, verdant, and varied. Everything was so green, rich with the scent of water and rot. There was a tinge of the aroma of the Vicks VapoRub her mother used to slather on her chest when she had a cold. Compared to Cortez or the mountains around Cortez, this was a jungle.

"You've got to watch for roos," Cleo said. "Especially at night. I remember one time driving with Mum and Dad when I was little, we hit a roo, and it wrecked the car. At least out here they're relatively small, not like the big reds in the outback. And there's wombats too. They're nocturnal, and you have to watch for them at dawn and dusk. Same goes for roos."

"Are they dangerous? Wombats, I mean."

Cleo laughed. "They do have sharp teeth and claws for digging, but unless you try to pick up an injured one, they won't hurt you."

Jane grimaced. "Why would you want to pick up an injured animal?"

"The native wildlife here are protected. If you hit one, especially a marsupial, you need to see if there are young in the pouch—if the mother is dead—and take them to a rescue facility."

"We have nothing similar in America. If you hit a deer or something, you just hope your car is in good enough shape to drive away."

Cleo glanced at her with wide eyes. "What about the animal? What if it's not dead?"

"Either it'll get up and get better, or it'll die." Jane shrugged. "I've never known anyone who hit a deer to bother to see if the animal was alive. Once I hit a mountain lion at night, and I sure didn't stop to check on its condition."

"Isn't that cruel?"

"I don't know. I never thought about it before now." Jane tapped a finger on the map. "You put your hand inside an animal's pouch and pull out the babies? That's disgusting."

Cleo huffed and tightened her hands on the wheel. "Not as disgusting as leaving an animal to die on the side of the road if there's something you can do to help it. If my dad heard that, he'd get the shits."

Jane's brow furrowed. "I don't understand. It's just an animal, after all. They don't have feelings."

"You gubbas." Cleo shook her head. "You think you're better than everything."

Jane reared back. "What's that supposed to mean?"

"My dad, he'd kick your butt if he heard you say that animals don't have feelings." She snorted. "Where'd you get that from? Your husband tell you that?"

"No." Her back stiffened and she frowned. "So your dad thinks animals are equal to humans?"

"No. In some ways they're way better than humans; they don't go around killing each other for no good reason. They don't try and run things or change things without seeing how they work first. They don't ruin the world."

Jane felt herself getting angry. "Oh, so the next thing you're going to tell me is that global warming is real and it's all our fault."

"Yeah. That's obvious."

Jane opened her mouth, then shut it without saying anything. It wasn't obvious, at least not to her. She knew global warming was a plot by environmentalists to destroy the economic prosperity of the world. Everybody knew that—except maybe Rachael. They'd had this discussion more than once and could never find common ground. Now this girl, this black girl, was telling her the same thing on the other side of the world. She didn't want to argue the point.

"Tell me about your dad. He sounds interesting."

Cleo's shoulders twitched. "What do you want to know?"

"Is he an Aborigine?"

"What makes you think that?" She glanced at Jane suspiciously.

"I don't know. I thought he might be because of the way you've talked about him and because of the way . . . you look." She cringed inside, as if she were sticking her toe in shark-infested water. She didn't want to come right out and say, 'You're black,' because she thought she might sound racist, but she didn't quite know how to refer to her skin color.

"Because I'm black, you think he's a black fella, and because he's a black fella, you think he's a native. That right?" There was an edge to Cleo's voice.

"Well, kinda," Jane said, hedging.

Cleo was quiet for a long time. Jane was about to broach another subject when she spoke.

"My gran is one of the Warlpiri people. When she was not much more than a girl, my dad says, she met up with this South African fella and fell in love. He took her to Sydney, where they lived until she got knocked up. He didn't want a kid and kicked her out without anything except what she wore. It took her a long time, but she made it back to Alice, where she had my dad and tried to raise him as best she could. So to answer your question, yes, my dad is an Abo."

Jane didn't know how to respond. Cleo sounded so uncertain about sharing the information that Jane wondered if there was anything she could say that wouldn't offend the girl. But she was curious about Cleo's father and what it was like to be an Aborigine.

"What did you mean that your gran was a Warlpiri person?" She hoped that would be an innocuous enough question.

"That's her skin and language group. They live around Alice Springs. That's where she grew up, and she still lives there. I was hoping to see her when I got to NT."

"NT?"

"Northern Territory. That's where Alice Springs is."

"Oh, I want to go there. Maybe we can go together."

Cleo pursed her lips and Jane thought, Oh no, what have I done now? She was about to take her offer back when Cleo shrugged.

"Maybe. Let's see what happens in Adelaide." She wondered what she meant but decided to let it drop.

Jane was watching the rainforest scroll by the camper window when Cleo braked. Jane grabbed for the dashboard. "What's the matter?"

"Hey, you want to see some koalas?"

"Uh, sure, I guess. Is there one here?" She glanced up at the gums across the road.

"No, not here." Cleo turned left onto a narrow road labeled Otway Lighthouse Road. "But down this way you can usually see them hanging out in the trees."

"At the lighthouse?"

"Nah, in the forest, especially on Blanket Bay Road."

"OK. I'd enjoy that."

As they wound their way through the trees, Jane craned forward, looking right and left for animals. Instead she saw cyclists and a few other cars but not much else amid the dense flora. At a signpost, Cleo took another left onto a gravel road that was narrower and closely flanked by trees. It also sported several sharp corners, and when they rounded one, there were several cars parked along the side and in the center of the road. Cleo jammed on the brakes, and Jane felt her seat belt dig into her shoulder. "What the hell?"

"Up there, look."

Jane tried to follow the direction of Cleo's pointing finger, but all she could see were people standing in the road and tree trunks. "I don't see anything."

"Wait." Cleo backed the camper up and pulled off the road behind the other cars. In one motion she pulled the keys from the ignition and bounded out the door. Jane unfastened her seat belt and followed, first looking up the road to make sure no one was coming. Ahead, Cleo was standing next to an older couple, both with binoculars pointing at the top of a tree. Jane joined them and looked up.

On a branch about halfway down the tree trunk sat a koala, a eucalyptus leaf hanging from its mouth. Jane caught her breath and stared. It seemed to stare back at her, wondering what the big deal was.

"It's so cute. Just like in the pictures," she whispered. Cleo chuckled. "Are there more?"

Cleo turned around, paused, and pointed in the opposite direction. Swiveling, Jane scanned the trees until she saw another one, this time with a lump on its back. She pointed. "That one? What's wrong with it?"

Cleo laughed. "There's nothing wrong with it. That's her joey."

"Joey?"

"Yeah, baby. That's her baby riding on her back."

Jane mouthed an "oh," then jerked upright. Her camera. She sprinted to the camper and fished her camera out of the glove compartment. It took a few minutes to find the best place to stand, but with Cleo's help, she managed to shoot several photos. By that time, most of the people had climbed into their cars and were heading back onto the road. Cleo grabbed Jane by the arm and dragged her into the brush.

"Let's get off the road and take a walk in the bush."

Jane glanced at the foliage warily. "You sure we won't get lost in all that?"

"No worries. I don't get lost."

"You sure?" Jane frowned. "I get lost crossing the street."

"I said no worries." Cleo pushed past Jane into the vegetation. "Come on. You said you wanted to see something besides the roadway. Here's your chance."

Tentatively, Jane followed Cleo as she forged a path through the ferns and bushes. For the first few minutes, Jane kept looking over her shoulder, trying to keep the camper in sight or at least see the general direction in which it was parked. But the foliage soon closed in around them, and with a sigh, she decided she'd have to trust Cleo to get them back to the camper safe and sound.

Once she relaxed, she began to notice birdcalls all around her. Little peeps and throaty warbles, songs that floated up the scale and others that hung and fluctuated around a couple of notes. Flowers— small, delicate, and hugging the ground or glowing in grand profusion, spilling over the surface of bushes—seemed everywhere. And the smell was something she'd never experienced before. She decided it must be the flowers, though she couldn't quite link a flower to a specific smell. As they walked, she identified some of the species she'd seen at the botanical gardens in Melbourne, particularly a grass tree, which she thought was wonderful. Most, however, just seemed odd.

Cleo didn't say anything while she led Jane through the rain forest. Jane watched her forge her way through the undergrowth, thinking she looked more at home than she had at any point in the previous few days. Must be the Aborigine in her, Jane mused, thinking about the Indians she knew in Cortez. She didn't know more than a couple, and those were on a smile-and-chat basis. They seemed like regular people with jobs and kids, though she did know they lived on the Ute Mountain Reservation about thirteen miles from town. Then there were the ones who hung out in the park and were eternally drunk. She had always assumed it was the proximity to booze that kept them in town, but now she wondered if it wasn't more complicated than that. Could it be that part of the reason they were drunk all the time was that it was the only way they could cope with living in the town? If that was so, it was really sad. Maybe that was the case with Cleo's father too. Cleo had hinted he was a drunk, and maybe he felt out of place in the city too.

Suddenly, Cleo threw out an arm, and Jane stopped. A large feline scooted across a clearing in front of them, jumped on a downed log, and disappeared into the bushes on the other side. Jane estimated it was about the size of a lynx.

"What was that?" Jane hissed.

"That was a feral cat."

"What's a feral cat? A type of lion or something?"

Cleo shook her head. "Nah. When the whites first came, they had cats on board their ships. Some of them escaped into the bush, and what we just saw is the result of about 250 years of unrestricted breeding in a country where they have no predators."

"But it was huge!"

"Yeah, that's what happens when food is plentiful and nothing eats you. Those things have killed off a lot of the small marsupials, to the edge of extinction in places."

"Wow."

"Yeah." Cleo sounded bitter and crossed the clearing without further comment. Jane scrambled over the log after her, wondering what she was thinking. Was she angry about cats let loose, about animals being killed, about white people in general? And if it was white people, what did she think about Jane aside from the fact she could "go mental" on her? Or maybe that was some racist perspective of Cleo's instead of Jane's problem?

She was lost in thought when Cleo burst through the brush onto a path that fronted the ocean near the edge of a cliff. Jane stopped on the path and drew in a quick breath. The ocean below her was magnificent, with its fringe of breakers peeking through the trees and ferns. "Oh my," she breathed out.

"Not bad, huh?"

"You can say that again. Where are we?"

Cleo looked from right to left along the path. "On the Great Ocean Road Walk, I think. It's a hiking path along the coast. If we go that way, we should come to the Otway Lighthouse." She pointed to her right.

"Oh. How far?"

"A couple of kilometers."

Jane wasn't sure she wanted to walk another couple of kilometers and then backtrack all the way to the camper. Though she had built up some stamina, whacking through the bush was tiring, and she wasn't looking forward to the trek back as it was. But Cleo was headed down the path at a steady clip. With a sigh, Jane followed.

After another half an hour, they began to descend the steep slope, Cleo jogging while Jane struggled to keep up. She watched the ground for fear she'd lose her balance or trip on something and go tumbling out of control down the hill. When Cleo suddenly stopped, Jane nearly bumped into her and then raised her head. In front of them, an expanse of sand was bisected by a river that merged into the ocean several hundred feet away—at least that's what Jane decided the flowing water was. She didn't know what constituted a river here, but in Colorado that would have been called a river.

"You up for a little wade?" Cleo bent, stripped off her tennis shoes, and rolled up the legs of her pants to around her knees.

"Wade? You mean cross that?" She stared skeptically at the river.

"Why not?"

"It looks deep and fast. Aren't you worried about getting carried away by the water?"

Cleo burst into laughter. "Not bloody likely. Looks like low tide, and the water's barely running here. Are you afraid of getting a little wet?"

Yes, Jane thought. And not just a little. But she didn't want Cleo to think she was a coward, so she bent and stripped off her own shoes and socks. Cleo tied her shoes together by the laces, draped them over her shoulder, and strode across the sand. After stuffing her socks in her shoes, Jane followed Cleo's example.

The sand was cold and soggy underfoot. Jane could feel herself sinking in, and fears of quicksand skirted around the edges of her mind. Cleo covered the distance to the river and plunged in. The water covered her ankles and, before she had gone ten steps, was brushing the bottoms of her pants. She turned back to face Jane, who was perched at the edge of the water trying to decide if getting to the other side was worth the risk of drowning.

"Come on. It's a bit chilly but not bad. Feels good."

Jane stuck a toe in the water. A bit chilly hardly described it. Goose bumps skittered up her arms, and she hadn't submerged one foot yet. "Come on," Cleo urged, taking another couple of steps.

"OK, OK," Jane muttered, taking a step forward. The water enclosed her ankle, and she shuddered but kept going. The force of the water flowing against her legs made moving forward difficult, and before she was halfway across, the river had risen above her knees, soaking her pants and sending more shivers up her arms. She looked up, and Cleo was on the other side, stamping her feet on the sand and wiping water from her calves. Her clothes were dry.

By the time Jane had crossed, her pants were wet to her crotch and she was shaking all over. Cleo grabbed Jane's hand and pulled her onto the sand, then rubbed her own hands briskly up and down Jane's arms.

"How'd you get so wet, woman?"

"I must have stepped in a low spot," Jane replied, her teeth chattering. "That or you're about a foot taller than I am."

"Not bloody likely. Here. Let's get you dried off." She wiped the water from Jane's legs and instructed her to remove her pants.

"Are you crazy?" Jane looked from side to side, scanning the hills for people. "What if someone comes by?"

"Then you'll show them how good you look naked. Strip them off and put this on." Cleo pulled off her long-sleeved shirt and handed it to Jane. At least she had on a tank top under the shirt, Jane noted, glad that Cleo wasn't going to be exposing herself. She complied and handed Cleo her pants after threading the shirt over her arms and buttoning it.

Cleo wrung out the pants and shook them. "Come over here out of the shade and sit down on the dry sand," she directed, shaking the pants again. Jane obeyed. The warm sand felt good against the skin of her legs, and she leaned back on her hands and let the sun warm her face and chest. Cleo set the pants on the sand beside her, rolled down the legs of her own pants, and put on her shoes.

"You stay here for a few. I'm going to reconnoiter."

"You're what? Why?" Jane felt panicked. She didn't want to be left alone out there in the middle of nowhere since she didn't have a clue how to find the camper again.

"Calm down. I won't be gone but a few. I'll be back. Promise."

Jane tried to control her breathing and calm down as Cleo turned and sprinted up the hill and onto the path just visible through the overhanging brush. In seconds she had disappeared.

Jane took a couple of deep breaths and closed her eyes, focusing on keeping some sort of equilibrium. She concentrated on the sound of the water wending its way to the sea, but it seemed to whisper that she was alone. She first tried watching the clouds, then gazing at the flowers and bushes, and then counting her breaths, but every second seemed to pile on the previous one in a teetering tower that threatened to collapse and leave her deserted. Was this what Cleo had planned for her all along? To lure her away from the camper and then take off and leave her to die?

How long before she began to panic? And what should she do then? Try and head back the way they had come? But how could she do that? Cleo had the keys to the camper in her pocket, so if she was able, by some act of God, to find the camper again, she'd never be able to get inside or drive it. And what would the Zeus people do if they found out she'd been letting a teenager drive their van, and what could she tell them aside from the fact that she had given Cleo the keys? Then they'd figure out what she'd done, and that would void something, or they'd charge her thousands of dollars for her negligence.

Or should she head in the direction of the lighthouse and hope that someone was there who could help her? If someone was even there—it could be some deserted monument to a previous time and have no one around—then she would be farther away from the camper and more lost than ever. And if someone was there, how could she explain where the camper was, and would that person believe her? And if so, how many roads were out here that the camper could be parked on? Somehow, saying, "It was by where we saw the koalas" didn't seem an adequate explanation at all.

She began to pant and felt her heart pound beneath her breastbone. She felt lost, abandoned, deserted, alone. Why had she ever trusted that girl? Ernie would have had a cow if he'd known what she'd done and would never have let her forget her stupidity. So much for doing the opposite of what Ernie would have done. If she'd ignored Cleo from the first moment she saw her, she'd be sitting somewhere safe, happy, and contented in her new life. Now she was stranded and at her wits' end. What was she going to do?

Jane was ready to put on her wet pants and charge off somewhere, anywhere, when Cleo reappeared high on the path, leaping and running down toward her, something white in her hand. Jane was so relieved, she wanted to cry. She never would have guessed that a skinny black girl could look so good. As Cleo approached, Jane saw the white something was a paper cup with a plastic cover. Cleo handed it to her.

"Tea. Careful. It's hot."

Jane blinked at her a couple of times, and wrapped her hands around the warm cup. "Where in heaven's name did you get this?"

"From the café at the lighthouse. I told you it wasn't far."

Jane closed her eyes to stop any incipient tears, took a sip, and sighed, gratitude and relief flooding through her. The warm liquid felt wonderful in her belly. She took another drink and looked up. "But what did you do for money? I thought you didn't have any."

"I had a few quid left over from what you gave me before. I'm glad I stuck them in my pocket this morning." Cleo looked at the ground and shuffled a foot. "I'm sorry I made you cross the stream. I never thought you'd get so wet or so cold."

In spite of her best efforts, Jane felt her eyes tear up. How could she have been so wrong about this young woman and her intentions? She had thought all those awful things, and yet all Cleo was doing was running flat out to get something to help her. She was stupid and a fool, but not in any way Ernie would have described. She was a fool for being so suspicious when there was nothing but the girl's skin color to base it on. She hung her head. "Thank you," she murmured. "You didn't have to do that."

"Yeah, but it was my fault you got all wet."

"No, it wasn't. I could have stopped. But thank you for trying to take such good care of me anyway. I owe you."

Cleo sank down onto the sand beside Jane. "Drink your tea before it gets cold. Then we should get moving before it gets much later."

Jane put the cup to her lips and sipped. The brew was bitter without any milk or sweetener, but it felt good nonetheless. By the time the cup was empty, Jane felt much warmer and was ready to walk again. Putting on the pants was a chilling experience, but she soon warmed with the climb up the hill and the damp pants felt quite good after the first few minutes of exercise.

They made it back to the camper, by way of the road, by late afternoon. Jane's stomach informed her she'd missed lunch and couldn't wait for dinner to eat. She cut up some cheese and peppers, pulled out a box of crackers, and served it all to a protesting Cleo. "I'm not hungry," she insisted, but then she devoured everything on her plate while Jane watched with a smile. After cups of hot tea to wash it down, they climbed back into the front seats, and Cleo drove back to the highway.

It was after sunset by the time they reached Portland and found a caravan park. Cleo seemed much more proficient than Jane at navigating the park grid to their assigned spot, and she had the camper parked and plugged into the utilities in a fraction of the time it had taken Jane in Apollo Bay. When Jane returned from freshening up in the amenities block, Cleo had dinner started, humming to herself while she stirred something in a frying pan on the stove. She handed the spatula to Jane with admonitions to keep stirring, and then she went to relieve herself in the toilet.

Jane stirred the chopped meat and veggies, her stomach growling in anticipation. She was tired but felt wonderful. It seemed like she had conquered Everest or boated down the Amazon or spent the winter in Antarctica—like she'd accomplished something important that day. She wasn't sure if it was the long hike, wading the river, or discovering how wrong she had been about Cleo again, but it felt momentous just the same. Like a huge step forward. Without knowing when it started, she found herself humming, quite contented.

After dinner, she and Cleo cleaned up together and assembled the beds. "Good night," Jane said when Cleo disappeared into the upper bunk. Cleo grunted in reply, and Jane felt the camper rock as the girl wormed her way under the covers and rolled around to get comfortable. Before the rocking ceased, Jane had fallen asleep.

Chapter 6

JANE FOUND PORTLAND depressing and decided she would rather push on than spend any time in the area exploring. She and Cleo unfolded the map and considered the options. Adelaide was about a six-hour drive, Cleo claimed, pointing to a route up the coast. Jane considered heading straight for the city, but she had to admit that she was reluctant to get there and face the possibility Cleo might decide she no longer wanted to travel with her. After Cleo's rescue of her the previous day, she wanted to keep her around at least a little longer. She hoped Cleo might want the same thing.

She scanned the map for something that would make a logical detour from a straight shot to Adelaide. "What's this?" She pointed to a patch of green on the map labeled Grampians National Park.

"Oh, the Grampians. You've got to see the Grampians. We could do some more bushwalking." Cleo gave her a sideways glance. "That is, if I didn't scare you off of that yesterday."

Jane smiled and patted the back of Cleo's hand. "No, I'd rather do some more bushwalking, which is hiking, right?" Cleo nodded. "Can we stay on the trail though?"

"Oh, you have to in the Grampians. We could see the Grand Canyon and climb up to the Pinnacle, maybe do the Jaws of Death, and they have a charming campground."

"The what? Jaws of Death? I don't think so."

"Not to worry. It's just a ledge that's challenging to get to. They call it the Jaws of Death because it looks like some monster's gaping mouth."

"Oh." Jane still wasn't convinced she wanted to get anywhere near something with so gruesome a name. "If they have a good caravan park, I think that sounds good. If you'll get the camper unhooked, I'll do the dishes, and we can make an early start of it."

The road to the park traversed hills filled with grass and herds of sheep. It looked idyllic, a pastoral scene from a picture book, and Jane was entranced. She had discarded her vision of a dry and desolate Australia and was beginning to appreciate the diversity of the country. Turquoise oceans, rainforests inhabited by koalas, rolling pasture lands—she loved it all. She also loved being a passenger, able to take in the landscape instead of gripping the steering wheel in fear she'd do something wrong.

After about an hour and a half of driving, Cleo turned onto a narrow strip of pavement, just wider than the camper, mottled green with two wide swaths of bare dirt on either side. Jane peered through the windshield, trying to figure out what the green on the road was. At that moment, another car sped toward them. At the last possible instant, at least in Jane's view, Cleo swerved to the left so that two of the wheels were on the dirt shoulder. The other car did the same thing. They passed each other, and Cleo moved back to the center of the road.

Jane was startled. "Is that supposed to happen?"

"Sure. I think they're built like this to save money on tarmac."

Jane raised an eyebrow. "OK. What's the green stuff on the road?"

"Lichen."

"Lichen?" Jane raised both eyebrows. "That would mean it's either very wet or there isn't a lot of traffic on this road."

Cleo tilted her head. "Probably both."

Jane leaned back against the seat and rested an elbow on the door. How strange. Was this another Aussie innovation, or did other countries do the same kind of thing? It made sense in a way, but she couldn't imagine for the life of her ever finding something similar in America. Everyone she knew would freak if they had to pull halfway off the road going the speed limit so they could pass oncoming cars.

Jane was musing about the vagaries of Australian roads when hills began to appear in the distance. They grew as the camper threaded its way through a long valley, but never to the point Jane would have called them mountains. At best they were gum-tree-covered tall hills, but even that was an overestimation, in her view. Then again, after living in the Rockies all her life, anything lower than peaks soaring five thousand feet above you covered with snow seemed understated. She had to admit, however, they were interesting and scenic in their own way. Kind of like the Appalachian Mountains, with eucalyptus trees instead of pines and maples. Not that she'd ever been there, but these reminded her of pictures she'd seen.

After passing a sign saying they were in Grampians National Park and skirting a lake—Lake Bellfield, according to the map—Cleo pulled the camper into a parking lot for Brambuk: The National Park and Cultural Centre and shut off the engine.

"What's this?" Jane asked. "The visitor center or something?"

Pocketing the keys, Cleo opened her door. "If you want to learn about Aborigines, you need to start here."

Puzzled, Jane climbed out of the vehicle and hiked her purse over her shoulder, following Cleo. They walked several hundred feet toward an odd-shaped building with an undulating roof covered in rust-colored, corrugated tin. Jane had never seen a building so wavy or made of such a mishmash of architecture. It looked cobbled together: Parts were constructed of stone, parts of wood, parts with rounded walls and no corners, and others seemed as if they were just walls of framed windows. Jane stood for a moment trying to make sense of the structure. She thought it resembled a bird on some level or, more precisely, a bird's wings extended and grazing the ground. Whatever it was supposed to be, it was strange.

Cleo insisted she see the video show, and Jane shuffled to the ticket booth and purchased a couple of tickets. She was curious but resented having a girl tell her what she should or shouldn't do. When she offered Cleo a ticket, Cleo waved it away. "No need."

"But I've already bought it."

Cleo looked around. "Why don't you give it to that man over there? I'd bet he'd enjoy a show." She pointed to a pasty-white, balding man whose T-shirt just covered his more than ample paunch. He had several cameras slung over his shoulder and was reading a pamphlet by one of the windows. Jane looked at him and shook her head.

"I think I'll try for a refund."

The woman behind the counter politely told Jane she couldn't take the ticket back, even when Jane said they should give it to the next person who came in. Sighing, Jane stuck it in her purse. She wasn't about to approach some strange man and would rather eat the cost. She reminded herself not to make assumptions about what Cleo would want to see in the future.

Jane looked around and saw that Cleo had wandered up a ramp that circled the room and spiraled up to a second story around a huge tree trunk that seemed to support the roof. On the wall, pictures hung every few feet with plaques beneath them. She wasn't stopping and reading anything, just looking and then walking on. Jane followed her but paused to read some of the placards.

She was surprised to learn that the building was supposed to be a cockatoo in flight—no wonder it resembled a bird. The walkway represented eels the locals ate, the wooden poles that held up the roof were the forest, the fireplaces were rock shelters, and a bench represented Bunjil, the creator spirit of the people in this part of the country. All the symbolism reminded her of Indian stories she'd heard, but she'd never seen artifacts presented in such a manner, and she was impressed.

At the top of the walkway, several panels resembling a room divider were covered with pictures. One of them caught her eye, and she paused to read the sheet posted beside it. She was shocked to find the panel was covered with stories of how white settlers had tried to kill off the natives with poison, through starvation, or by flat-out shooting them en masse. Story after story was depicted with photos in some places, line drawings in others, and the remembrances of the affected people throughout.

She found herself tearing up after the first panel. How could anyone have done such things? How cruel. Granted, she had heard some of the same kinds of things in regard to the tribes back home, but that history had never touched her the way these stories did. Maybe it was the photos. After the first panel, she couldn't read anymore and fled back down the ramp to the waiting area for the show.

She collapsed onto the bench that was supposed to be Bunjil, the creator, and wiped her cheeks. Why did it hurt so much that the settlers of this continent had done the same things her own people had done? If she was this upset about the treatment of the Aborigines, why wasn't she as upset about the Utes or Cheyennes or Navajos back home? What was wrong with her? Was Cleo right? Was she crazy or at least heading in that direction? What was next? Would she tear off her clothes and go screaming down the street until the men in the white jackets came and carted her away to a padded room? Did they do that in this country?

Wondering what the Australians did with insane people brought her back to a semblance of calm. She closed her eyes for a moment. When she opened them, the pattern of rafters supporting the planks of the ceiling seemed soothing and welcoming for some strange reason. Before she could try and formulate a reason, a voice over the speakers announced the beginning of the show. Jane looked around for Cleo, but she was nowhere in sight. Sighing, she rose and followed several people into the theater, choosing to settle near the back of the room on a wooden bench.

It was not what she was expecting. No big screen filled one end of the room. Instead, a huge emu head, a crow, and several other stuffed animals were situated around the walls along with paintings of Aborigines in dotted white paint holding spears. The show turned out to be an explanation of the creation myth of the Gariwerd Mountains, the Grampians, she assumed. The story included a gigantic, flesh-eating emu, a crow that tried to eat the emu's egg, a coward of a man who was turned into a possum, and a fight that resulted in the rivers and gaps that scarred the mountain range. Everybody in the story seemed to end up turning into stars, mostly the ones making up the Southern Cross.

Jane was glad it was a fairly innocuous fable, and nothing in it threatened to send her reeling into tears again, but it wasn't history, at least not the type of history she'd grown up learning—yet that's what the whole thing was billed as. She couldn't understand it.

She was still trying to figure out the story and being in a building that seemed more abstract art than architecture when Cleo reappeared from a side room.

"Well, what did you think?" she asked Jane.

"Have you seen the show?"

Cleo nodded. "A long time ago when I was a kid."

"Do you believe that's what happened? I mean, for real?"

"You mean instead of some bearded white guy making everything in six days?" Her left foot tapped.

"Well, yes. I mean, no. I mean instead of evolution and erosion and volcanic uplift and the rest?"

"That's just another story. In the end what difference does it make what we believe about how it all got put together, provided that we take care of the land and the animals and each other?"

But it does make a difference, Jane wanted to say, though she couldn't figure out why at that moment. It seemed wrong to her to rely on a history made up of man-eating emus and gods who turned themselves into eagles. She had never been a big fan of the Christian creation story either, but she could justify it in her mind by relating each of the creation days to hundreds of billions of years of evolution. That made more rational sense than what she'd just seen. Where was there room for science in the Aboriginal version?

She was about to try and put her thoughts into words when Cleo grabbed her arm and dragged her out the door. "I want you to see something else."

What now? Jane thought. A story about how river rocks were created by shitting kangaroos?

Cleo led her across a lawn and around a pond to another building. Under a covered patio, a series of upright stone tablets about four feet wide and seven feet tall stood, each side engraved with pictures of animals and plants.

"This is something else you need to understand about the people of this land. This tells about our seasons."

Jane felt less than enthused. She wasn't ready for another dose of myth, but she stepped up to one of the tablets and started to read. OK, summer. Well, not summer per se, but early summer, the season of the butterflies; unlike late summer, the season of eels. Then there was early spring (nesting birds) and late spring (wildflowers). The only seasons she could relate to were autumn (honeybees) and winter (cockatoos) because they seemed like what she was used to back home, but not the honeybees and cockatoos parts. She turned to face Cleo.

"Six seasons?"

"Sure. How many do you have in the States?"

"Four. Why do you need six?"

"It makes more sense."

Jane frowned. "Well, not to me."

"Maybe you need only four seasons in America." Cleo shrugged. "I thought you might want to see how our seasons are related to what the animals, bird, and insects are doing at those times and not just the weather. You can't separate the living things from the rain or the heat or the cold. It's all part of the same whole."

"Well, where I come from, all the animals are either hibernating or have migrated somewhere else when it gets cold. So you can ignore them." She felt irritated at being lectured to and was ready to either go inside the building or back to the camper.

"Oh. *All* the animals and birds and insects are gone?" Cleo's tone hinted of sarcasm and Jane bristled.

"OK, not every single living thing aside from people. Some birds hang around, and there are all the animals people own that don't go anywhere either. But they don't count. I mean they're not free to leave in most cases. And what they do doesn't change either. I mean cows still eat hay or grass, and the dogs and cats still live with people. So how's that supposed to be hooked up with a season?" Sarcasm tinged her voice.

"Don't get so upset. I was just trying to show you how my people see things." Cleo held up her hands and took a step back.

Jane tried to unclench her teeth and relax. Was she about to "chuck a wobbly" again, in Cleo's words? What the hell was wrong with her? She took a deep breath.

"OK, I'm sorry. I guess six seasons works better here than it would at home. Are we going to see what's inside or not?"

Cleo narrowed her eyes and considered Jane for a moment

before answering. "You can look if you want. It's just a café and gift shop. I'm not all that interested."

Not that interested? It seemed more interesting than the tablets about the seasons. "I'm going inside. Where shall we meet up? I don't think I'll be too long."

Cleo motioned her head back the way they'd come. "I'm going to walk back to the camper. I'll see you there."

"OK." Turning, Jane pushed through the double glass doors into the shop.

The inside was packed with the usual tourist paraphernalia: stuffed kangaroos, snakes, emus, and koalas; books, trinkets, caps, cups, toys, books, and on and on. Aside from the animals, it could have been a gift shop at any museum or big attraction in the States. Jane wandered for a while, not looking, grudgingly agreeing that Cleo was right and giving herself time to calm down.

She was distressed that she had gotten so angry about nothing after crying over some pictures. Her emotions resembled a Ping-Pong ball in a tornado, and she wasn't sure what was going to come exploding out of her from minute to minute. Cleo was wary of the way she behaved, and she seemed to be getting worse. Maybe she should try and see a doctor or something. Maybe she needed tranquilizers. Maybe she needed her head examined for real.

She wandered over to the café thinking about getting a latte or something, but the line stretched out the door, and she wasn't in the mood to wait. Instead, she pushed back outside, and sniffing at the stone tablets, wandered in the general direction of the camper. About a hundred feet after the pond, a path wound into the undergrowth on the left. On a whim, she decided to take it. Cleo could manage quite well without her for a while, and it felt good to be out walking alone.

The tweets and peeps of unseen birds followed her through the bushes. Overhead, the sun flashed amid fluffy clouds, bathing her in light and then shadow. The bushes opened up to a grassy expanse where several small kangaroo-like animals sat grazing. Jane stopped and stared. Her first kangaroos—if they actually were kangaroos and not wallabies. But since she didn't have a clue what the difference between the two species was, she decided she would consider them kangaroos. There were four of them, three in a group and one off to the side, all about the same size and brownish-gray in color, each bending over once in a while to take a bite of grass.

Jane couldn't decide if they were standing or sitting but wanted to see them hop around. Yet they seemed to prefer to put their little front paws on the ground and move forward on all fours. Not very kangaroo-like. She was tempted to clap her hands or something to startle them but figured that might make them hop away. Then they'd be gone, and she couldn't watch them anymore. If she waited long enough, they'd hop away anyhow.

She didn't have long to wait. A couple of young women in running shorts and halter tops jogged, laughing, out from the bushes on the other side of the clearing. Two of the animals raised their heads and then straightened and hopped away on their back legs; the other two went back to eating. Jane smiled. It wasn't what she'd seen on television or in her mind—quite a bit more casual and slow—but at least she'd seen them hop.

She stood and stared at the roos for a long time; then they all raised their heads in unison and hopped across the path and into the undergrowth. She held her breath until they disappeared and realized she hadn't taken any pictures. She reached inside her purse for her camera, just in case they decided to come hopping out again, and remembered she'd left it in the camper. She sighed and walked on, chastising herself for being so forgetful.

No more roos showed up on the way back to the camper; nor was there anything more exciting than a bunch of kids wearing backpacks. Cleo was sitting on the back bumper when Jane arrived, twisting something together.

"I saw kangaroos, I think," Jane announced. "At least they could have been kangaroos or maybe wallabies. I wish you could have been with me. I'll bet you know the difference."

Cleo looked up and smiled. "Are they the first you've seen?"

"Yeah. It was great. I didn't know they walked around on all fours. I thought they only jumped."

"I'm sure we'll see a lot more. They are everywhere."

"I'll take your word for it. I just don't want to hit any with the camper."

Cleo stood and folded her work into her hand. "Provided we don't go driving at night, we'll be fine. Are you up for a walk?"

"Sure, but only if it's not to the Jaws of Death. Where do you think we should go?"

"Let's try the Pinnacle. It's quite an uphill climb, but the view is worth it." Cleo opened the back of the camper and placed the object on the counter. "There's a car park that's closer. Why don't we move there?"

The parking lot was a couple of kilometers away and filled with vehicles. They had to circle several times before they found an empty space. Jane left her purse under the passenger seat but made sure to retrieve the camera from the glove box before she locked her door. "Will I need my backpack?" She remembered the long hike of the previous day and wished she'd taken it then along with water bottles and a snack, not to mention dry clothes.

Cleo paused for a second and nodded. "That might be a good idea. You might want to grab some water and food too; we could be gone quite a while."

Jane eyed her. "How long a hike is this?"

"I'm not sure, but the last time I did it with my dad, it took several hours. Like I said, it's quite an uphill climb."

"Several hours—as in three or thirty?"

Cleo laughed. "Not thirty. Maybe half a day. We should be back in time for tea."

"And when is that?"

"That's right; you Americans don't call it tea. How about dinner?"

"So, late afternoon."

Cleo nodded. "Yeah, that's about right."

Jane opened the back of the camper and climbed inside. "Food and water it is. You want a sandwich or something lighter?"

"A sanger's fine." Cleo ran her fingers through her dreads and leaned against the back bumper.

Jane set both hands on the counter and sighed. She was getting tired of not understanding the terms Cleo used and wished she would speak straight English and not slang. "A sanger?"

"What you said, a sandwich." She glanced up. "You want me to make them?"

"No," Jane replied, pulling bread and sandwich meat out of the cooler. "Anything special on your sanger?"

After fixing lunch and packing chips, a couple of granola bars, and bottles of water, Jane handed Cleo the backpack. The girl could carry it since she hadn't fixed the lunch. Besides, she had to be her junior by at least twenty years, and if they were going to be doing a lot of climbing, she preferred to let Cleo carry the load.

It took a few minutes to find the footpath, which climbed steadily after the first turn. Cleo strode ahead without effort, as if she did this kind of thing every day. Jane tried to keep up for the first quarter mile, then, panting, slowed down, pacing herself a little more. By the time Cleo turned around to see where she was, Jane was huffing along several hundred feet behind, using every opportunity to stop and catch her breath and take pictures of flowers and rocks she found unusual. Thank God, there were a lot of each.

She caught up with Cleo at a set of metal-grated steps set into the side of the mountain and winding upward, reminding her of a snake. Jane took a picture of them. "This is different," she said, following Cleo up, her steps ringing with each footfall. "We don't do this back home, at least not where I'm from. There you have to climb over the rocks or scramble up the side of the hill. This seems so civilized or something." Cleo harrumphed and kept climbing. Jane made a face and followed. Maybe Cleo thought she was criticizing the steps or saying she didn't approve. She thought the steps were a great idea and wished that some of the hiking paths she'd climbed with Ernie were so equipped.

That was one thing she had to give Ernie credit for—he had liked to be outdoors too. Even though he smoked at least a pack a day, he enjoyed hiking in the mountains, and they drove all over the southern part of the state, trying different trails. He was slow and needed to stop often to catch his breath, but he was game, and the pace suited Jane more than this rush up the side of the hill after Cleo. She was grateful for his openness to trying new places for a day's adventure compared with the rigidity that permeated the rest of their married life. It was one thing they shared. One thing that, until he got so sick that he could hardly walk a block without stopping, they could do together without fighting or him telling her what a loser she was. It was comforting now to remember they had had something in common.

As Jane rounded a large, grayish rock, Cleo was standing on the side of the path talking to a couple of young men. They looked to be around her age, early to mid-twenties, fit, with backpacks slung over their shoulders and the air of men who'd just accomplished something. It made Jane wonder how hard this hike was going to get. It also made her wonder again how old Cleo was. She'd been meaning to ask her but hadn't gotten around to it. The men, both white, seemed entranced by Cleo in spite of her very dark skin.

This seemed strange to Jane, who'd always assumed that whites were attracted to whites and blacks to blacks. She remembered stories about mixed marriages back home, and some of those had seemed happy. Then there was Geoff. Gorgeous Geoff. Sigh. Maybe it wasn't so strange after all. She was still trying to parse it out in her mind when Cleo waved her over and introduced her.

"G'day." Jane smiled, feeling proud she'd used the ubiquitous Australian hello. The guys didn't seem to notice.

"I'm Jack," the tallest of the two responded. "So you're from America."

"Is it that obvious?" Jane winced. She thought she was blending in quite well but apparently not.

"It's your accent."

"Oh." She winced again. So much for thinking she'd gotten the "g'day" down just right. "Where are you from?"

"I'm in school in Canberra but on break. Harry here, my brother . . ." The shorter man poked him in the ribs.

"I'll talk for myself, if you don't mind." He stuck out his hand for Jane to shake. "I'm Harry, and I'm on holiday. Unlike this layabout, I work for a living."

Jane took his hand. "Nice to meet you. What do you do?"

"I'm in IT for a trucking firm."

"I didn't know they would need one of those."

"Yeah, got to keep the trucks running on schedule and deliveries prompt. We're number two but working on being number one." He grinned and dropped Jane's hand, his eyes focusing on Cleo. Jack's were too.

"So are you guys going up or coming down?" Jane felt like she was talking to a wall.

"Down," Jack said. "It's quite a nice trek—just be sure and watch your step up at the top. It's a little slippery." He winked at Cleo.

"We'll be fine." Cleo smiled. "Unless you want to come with us and show us the way."

The men paused, and Jane took a step forward. "No, no. We'll be fine. There's no need for you to climb back up again. By the way, is it far?"

Harry looked relieved and disappointed at the same time and sidestepped out of Jane's way. "A couple hours up. Less down. You're going to the Pinnacle, I assume." Jane nodded. "Yeah, then a couple up."

"Thanks. Then I guess we should be on our way. Right, Cleo?"

Cleo shrugged and stepped onto the trail. "Bye now." She turned and started up the mountain again.

"It was very nice to meet you. I hope you do well in school and at IT. Be number one!" Jane let them walk around her before starting up the trail again. Both of them glanced back at Cleo's retreating form before turning back to the trail.

What was Cleo thinking? That she would invite those men to come with them? Jane wondered. While they might have been interested in spending more time with Cleo, Jane didn't want a couple of more strangers for company. It was one thing to be welcoming, but this seemed over the top. Maybe it had to do with the fact they were men. Was this something the girl did all the time? Did Cleo often invite strange men into her life, and was that what happened between her and her boyfriend? Did she get too friendly with another man, and that's why he dumped her? If so, what might she do while traveling with Jane? Would she wake up some morning to a new male face in the camper?

And the men. Jane shook her head. They couldn't keep their eyes off Cleo even when Jane was speaking with them. She could see that Cleo was striking, though skinny as a twig, but did the men have to be that obvious? She wondered if Cleo evoked this kind of response from men all the time. That could be part of Cleo's problem with men—they wanted her, and she wanted them, and it resulted in hasty, unstable relationships.

Jane fretted while she climbed, realizing how little she knew about Cleo and what was usual behavior for her. Though it was nice to have a traveling companion, having someone with serious problems could be far worse than dealing with things on her own.

Maybe Ernie had been right to be so wary of strangers. Playing it safe wasn't such a bad thing sometimes.

The trail followed the side of the mountain for what seemed forever before turning right and meandering through a forested section. Jane thought she'd entered a fantasy land. Ferns and mushrooms crowded around the foot of the trees, branches intertwined overhead, and wavy, papery growths sprang horizontally to the ground from the trunks. Flowers of yellow and red, purple and pink, white and blue skirted thick beds of moss and bobbed in a gentle breeze while rivulets seemingly sprang from rocks on the side of the path and disappeared again without a trace. The rocks looked ancient, gray, heavily eroded, and covered in lichen. Where the foliage thinned, she spotted sheets of reddish sandstone draped beneath the grayed tops of crags far above her head.

She took picture after picture until the camera blinked and the display window informed her she'd used up all the memory. She cursed under her breath. Now what was she supposed to do? It was fun to have a digital camera, but she realized she didn't have a clue how she was supposed to get the pictures off the camera or get them printed. And the rest of the hike would have to go unrecorded. The thought of dealing with the digital camera resurrected her problems back home. How could she have forgotten she still needed to deal with bills and banks? And what about Rachael? Surely, she'd emailed her in the three days since she'd been on a computer. Jane wondered if Rachael thought she had deserted her again.

Eyes on the ground, Jane trudged up a set of stone steps placed in the path. Cleo and the traveling and hiking had distracted her from what she needed to do. She wanted to turn around, get in the camper, and find the nearest town with a computer she could rent. Hiking and having fun were all well and good when business was taken care of, but business wasn't taken care of. Yet here she was on the side of a mountain instead of doing what she needed to do. This would have to be the last hike until she got some things settled.

Ahead of her, Cleo was nowhere in sight. The trail was well marked, but still she was nervous that her companion had disappeared. Maybe she was so far out ahead of Jane that she couldn't be seen. Cleo would wait for her, wouldn't she? Then again, maybe she had taken a side trail with some guys and assumed that Jane would know to follow.

At that thought, Jane stopped herself. This was the same train of thought that had driven her frantic. Chances were that Cleo was up ahead, around the next corner. She needed to chill.

But when she trudged on, she didn't see any sign of the girl or any indication that a side path branched off the main trail. She began to feel a little uneasy. Where was she? The path took a sharp turn to the right and disappeared into what appeared to be a field of boulders. Had she climbed on ahead?

Jane stopped and glanced up at the boulder pile with more than a little trepidation. Several hundred feet above her she could see people scrambling over the rocks and, above them, more boulders. No one looked anything like Cleo. And though she scanned around, there seemed to be no indication of where the path went and no one close enough to ask directions. In frustration, she plopped down on a rock, wishing she had carried the backpack. She was thirsty and hungry and more than a little aggravated with Cleo.

She sat for a few minutes trying to decide what she should do next when an older couple rounded the curve in the path and almost ran into her.

"So sorry," the gentleman said, leaning on a metal walking stick. "I didn't see you there."

The woman stepped to his side and planted both her walking poles in the ground between two rocks. She reached behind her and pulled a water bottle from a fanny pack, took a swig, and offered it to her husband. Jane surmised it was her husband. For some reason, they looked very married.

"Taking a break, dearie?" the woman asked Jane.

"Kind of. I've lost my friend and can't seem to find the trail. I'll bet she's up at the top waiting for me. And I'm stuck here." She sighed.

"That's too bad." The woman retrieved the water bottle from her husband and took another drink.

"American, are you?" The man peered at her like she was some sort of museum exhibit.

Jane nodded. What was it about her that screamed American? "Then first time in the Grampians, I assume." Jane nodded again. "Done much hiking while you've been here?"

"No, in truth, this is the second hike I've taken. I thought I was doing fine until I got here and lost the trail." She added, "And my friend."

"No worries." The woman stuck the bottle back in her fanny pack and retrieved her poles. "We'll show you the way, won't we, Mark?"

"Yes, it's not so hard. You just need to look for the blue arrows." He pointed to a triangle of blue plastic pointing uphill that was fastened to a rock several feet up the path. "They'll show you the way to go."

Jane stood and stared at the triangle. Why hadn't she seen that before? Probably because she didn't know they existed. "OK, thanks. But if you don't mind, I'll follow you, so I don't lose my way again."

"No worries. You'll see how easy it is once we get up a little ways. The arrows are everywhere, and once we're up, I'll show you the ones that point the way down." He planted his pole next to the boulder with the arrow and stepped up.

"It's ever so convenient." The woman smiled and followed her husband, teetering between her poles when she stepped on the boulder. "It's almost impossible to get lost. Especially with all the traffic. I prefer coming in the winter when the park is close to empty, but Mark loves the spring, so here we are. Coming, dearie?"

Holding her arms out for balance, Jane followed the couple as they weaved their way through the rock field and up the side of the hill. Mark was right about the obviousness of the markings, once you knew what to look for. When she got to one marker, she paused and looked around for the next, and there it would be, a few yards ahead, pointing the way. If only life had such neat little markers, Jane thought. Maybe she would have made fewer mistakes. When Cleo showed up, for example, a little marker could have told her whether she should have asked her to join her in the camper or let her go on her way. Maybe a little marker would have told her not to marry Ernie or to believe Rachael when she said Jane could make it on her own and to divorce Ernie or to have kids.

Jane had always been ambivalent about having children. After her only brother, Mikey, died in the motorcycle accident when he was seventeen, she watched her parents' response to the tragedy. They were devastated. Her mother wept constantly and blamed God for taking her son while her father, after a short period of rage, withdrew into himself and never emerged from his shell of grief until he died of heart failure four years earlier. If that's what it meant to have kids, Jane wasn't sure she wanted to take the risk.

Ernie, on the other hand, had wanted kids from day one of their relationship. "I want to be a father," he repeated at any provocation, "just like my dad." Jane thought this was sweet at first, until she learned more about his father. He was even more critical and derisive than Ernie. Jane wondered many times how Ernie or any of his six siblings grew up with any sense of self-esteem. What kind of father would Ernie make? She looked at his brothers, all harsh and unforgiving to their kids but better than their father, and wondered if Ernie would have done any better. He could be cold, cutting, and critical to her, but he did have his moments of kindness, though few and far between. The one place where he was the most gentle and kind was with respect to having children.

The first Valentine's Day they spent together, Ernie bought her flowers and cooked her dinner. Jane remembered sitting at the table while Ernie, balancing a plate filled with rubbery meatloaf and dry mashed potatoes, approached with a bottle of red wine under his arm. He slid the plate in front of her, filled her glass with wine, and kissed her on the top of her head. "For you, my love." It was the sweetest thing he'd ever done for her, and she had melted into tears. It became their annual ritual, and though the meal morphed into heated TV dinners and the wine disappeared, it still meant a lot to her that he tried.

That first Valentine's Day, he once again brought up the subject of children. They'd walked around the issue before, but that night he laid it out on the table with the meatloaf.

"When should we have kids?" He looked at her over the rim of his wineglass and smiled. "I think the sooner the better; after all, it's better to have them while we're still young enough to keep up with them. Don't you think?"

She toyed with a green bean. "I don't know. Isn't it a little soon? I mean, we're getting settled in together and are on pretty shaky financial ground. I can't see how I can quit my job and still have us make it."

"You worry too much." He waved a dismissive hand. "I'm on track for a raise, and there's no end in sight to the work."

Jane frowned. "But you're gone so much of the time. The roustabout job pays OK, but I worry about you out there on the oil rigs. It's such a dangerous job. What would I do if I got pregnant, and you were hurt or killed? Maybe we should wait until you can find something closer to home and safer."

"Worrywart," he chided. "I'm not going to get hurt."

She stared at her plate. She'd heard too many stories, and their best friends, Erick and Samantha James, were waiting to see what was going on with Erick's back after he'd fallen on the rig. He was still at home with no income while the doctors tried to make up their minds if it was work related or some physical defect that hadn't come to light before. She couldn't begin to imagine what it would be like to be pregnant or to have a baby if Ernie got hurt or, worse, killed. She remained silent, and Ernie let the subject drop.

That evening when they climbed into bed, he reached over and stroked her face. "Why don't you stop taking the pill? It'd make things more exciting—don't you think?"

She looked at him with a cocked eyebrow. "What do you mean?"

"I mean," he grinned, "we could make it a game to see if you got pregnant or not. I'd sure find it exhilarating to wonder if this was the time I'd filled you with a baby. Like maybe tonight."

But she'd already taken that day's pill. She couldn't imagine how being off birth control would make their lovemaking more exciting. She'd be so worried about getting pregnant that she'd never have another orgasm.

When her prescription ran out, she didn't think twice about refilling it.

Yet Ernie persisted, monthly when she got her period, weekly when he was in the mood, or whenever they'd been with friends who had kids. After they'd been married three years, Jane acquiesced and stopped taking the pill. Ernie was still gone for a week at a time out in the oil fields, but their financial situation had improved, and she was tired of feeling guilty every time he broached the subject. If it was going to happen, it was going to happen, and there was nothing she could do to stop it, she rationalized, though the fear remained.

After the first month when she got her period, Ernie was philosophical. "I've heard that sometimes it takes several months before the effects of the pill wear off. I'll bet you'll be faster. What do you want to bet?"

Absolutely nothing, she thought, and blessed her empty uterus.

The next month he was a little less sanguine. "Still getting back to normal, I guess." In the succeeding months, he became more and more frustrated and disappointed until the day he returned from a ten-day absence to find her bleeding.

"What is wrong with you?" he asked. "You're not taking the pill behind my back, are you?"

She shook her head, shocked. "Of course not. I wouldn't do that."

"Then something's got to be wrong with you. Why don't you go to the doctor and get tested or something?"

"But, honey, what if it's still the pills working out of my system? My sister took two years after she quit to get pregnant. Now look at her, with two kids and pregnant again. Why don't we give it more time?"

He was angry but relented. But not for long. The next month he insisted she see a doctor. Six months, a thousand dollars, and a battery of tests later, the doctor could find nothing wrong with her. She felt vindicated but a little angry Ernie had assumed it was her problem and not something wrong with him. When the last of the results came in, she handed him a copy of the lab tests.

"I'm fine. See, there's nothing wrong with me. What about you? Are you ready to get tested?"

Ernie stared at the papers and grimaced. "I don't know if I believe this. After all, no one in my family has had any problems conceiving or fathering a child. It can't be me."

"Then what is it? Tell me that." She snatched the papers from his hand.

"Maybe you're doing something wrong. Maybe it's working at the motel. Maybe it's got you so stressed out that you can't conceive."

Jane wanted to laugh out loud but restrained herself. That again. He'd never been happy with her working and used any excuse to try and get her to quit. This one was way over the top, even for Ernie.

"Maybe it's you. You made me do all the tests; now it's your turn. Prove to me that you're fertile, and maybe I'll consider quitting."

He grumbled and walked away. For months he let the subject drop, and she was relieved not to be badgered every month when her period arrived. Then, after a year of silence, one day out of the blue, he made an appointment with the fertility clinic in Durango and went.

The results were conclusive: low sperm count, low motility, low viability. There was no way he was going to be able to father a child.

Jane breathed a sigh of relief and thanked God that was the end of it. No children, no problem, but she had a few regrets, she admitted. Every once in a while, the sight of a baby nestled in a mother's arms would send a twinge of longing through her—until the child cried, at which point she would offer a silent prayer of thanks to the universe.

But it was not the end for Ernie. After months of depression, he came home one day from the rig with a handful of brochures about adoption. Jane was aghast. Bad enough to have a child of your own, but the thought of taking on the burden of raising someone else's child, from God only knew what kind of background, horrified her. She'd heard the stories of parents who adopted a child only to find out it was retarded or was a child from a drug-addicted mother who had all kinds of medical and emotional problems. Ernie had dropped the brochures on the table without a word, and the day he went back to the rig, she threw them all away.

She was surprised he never broached the subject again, not even to ask her about the missing brochures. She was never going to initiate talking about adopting a child, and the whole issue faded into obscurity over time.

Yes, she decided, a little marker at the beginning of their marriage that showed they would never have children would have saved them thousands of dollars and concern. Being around Cleo reinforced the idea that having children would have been a bad idea for her. While she was certain if she had a daughter, her daughter wouldn't behave like Cleo, the idea of having to deal with such behavior at all filled her with dread. Bad enough she had chosen to ride for a while with a girl like Cleo, but how awful to have to deal with it for years.

Following Mark and his wife up the rocky slope was not an easy task. The boulders were slippery, and Jane found herself having to resort to clambering on all fours at times to keep from falling. She watched the older couple with a twinge of envy. Their walking sticks seemed to help them balance and climb. She wasn't sure they would work so well for her though; she felt clumsy enough without having to manipulate something else besides her hands. She could see herself tripping over her own poles and rolling downhill. But they sure made it look easy.

It took the better part of an hour to make it to the top of the mountain. There, on a metal platform attached to the very top, leaning over a railing, stood Cleo with a young man behind her. The wind coursing up over the crag blew her dreadlocks back from her face, and the sound of her laughter floated by.

Jane narrowed her eyes and glared at the girl. So much for wondering what had happened to her. Some boy had caught her attention, and she had forgotten about Jane. If it wasn't for Mark and his wife, she might never have made it to the top of the mountain. What would Cleo have done then? Would she have come looking for her at some point or gone on her merry way?

After thanking the couple, Jane walked up the stairs to the platform. They were narrow and steep, and she grabbed the railing on both sides, hoping she wouldn't trip. The wind was fierce and whipped her hair and shirt, chilling her in the process. She wished she would have brought a jacket.

Cleo and her boy were still peering over the edge when Jane arrived.

"Oh, there you are," Cleo said breezily. "I was wondering when you'd make it."

Like hell you were, Jane thought, but she smiled and walked closer to the edge. There was hardly enough room for one person to look over the edge, and Cleo and the boy took up most of it. The view was grand, though far less so than Jane was expecting, considering the climb. The valley below wasn't very wide or deep. She could make out the top of Brambuk, the cultural center, and the shop next to it nestled in the trees. She wondered if she could see the platform she was standing on if she were at Brambuk. It didn't seem that far away from here. She'd have to remember to look up when they got back to the camper.

With a sniff, she turned to Cleo. "Could I get a drink from the pack? And I could do with some lunch."

"No worries. Here you go." Cleo stripped the pack from her back and handed it to Jane.

"What about you? You want to come down and have something to eat with me?"

Cleo shook her head. "I'm not hungry yet. I'm going to stay here for a while longer. You do what you want, and I'll find you."

Lips pressed together, Jane threaded the pack's straps over her shoulders and descended the stairs. She found a rock that was somewhat sheltered from the wind and sat down.

Damn that girl. She wanted to tell her what she thought about her running off without a word and leaving Jane to her own devices, but she didn't want to make a scene in front of all the people wandering around. She'd had enough of that in the caravan park in Apollo Bay and wasn't about to do a repeat performance. She chewed her sandwich, mulling over the things she would say to her when they were alone again. Maybe this time she'd ask her to leave. How many times should she put up with the same crappy behavior before she'd had enough? She should have learned with Ernie; she had put up with his shit for most of her adult life. Did she have to continue to put up with it from other people?

By the time she'd finished eating, Cleo and the boy had disappeared. Jane wondered if she'd headed back down the trail or taken off in another direction. There was a trail that led in the opposite direction from the one she'd come up, and she wondered if Cleo had gone that way. Still aggravated, she put on the pack and headed back down the hill on the path.

The trail didn't seem to be as well marked on the way down, and the rocks were even more slippery. Jane slid several times, landing on her rear end, much to her embarrassment. One man tried to give her instructions about what she was doing wrong, but she ignored him and trudged along, trying not to make more of a fool of herself.

By the time she got back to the camper, it was midafternoon. It was only when she stuck a hand in her pocket that she realized Cleo had the keys to the camper. Damn, damn, and damn again. What was she to do now? How could she have let the girl keep the keys? Why didn't she remember when she was at the top of the mountain to get them from Cleo when she got the backpack? When was she going to learn?

She plopped down on the grass in front of the camper and leaned against a tree. The list of all the things she needed to do back home crept back into her thoughts, and she cursed herself again for letting Cleo keep the keys. How long would it take the girl to get back, that is, assuming she came back at all? Would she take off with the boy and days later and miles away realize she had the keys to Jane's camper? And what should Jane do in the meantime? How long should she wait before she tried to find a policeman to maybe help her open the van so she could get her purse and try and contact Zeus about the problem? Would they have a way to help her? She couldn't remember anything in the sheaf of paperwork she signed about losing the keys. Could she be the first? She doubted that very much. They'd have some kind of procedure, wouldn't they? At least if she could get in the van, she'd be out of the weather and have a place to sleep even if she couldn't drive anywhere.

The sun descended in the western sky, and Jane found herself getting angrier with each passing hour. By the time Cleo sauntered up to the camper, Jane was in a rage. But somehow she took a deep breath and told herself to remain calm. She did, however, stand up.

"You took a long time coming back. I've been waiting here for hours."

Cleo looked nonplussed. "Oh, I went on a short hike down to the Grand Canyon. I didn't think you would want to come."

Jane gritted her teeth and fought to keep her voice even. "And what gave you that impression?"

"You looked pretty beat by the time you got to the top. When you sat down, I thought you were going to wait for a while, so Charlie and I took off. He said it wouldn't take very long, but by the time we got back, you had left."

"Why didn't you ask me if I wanted to come? Why didn't you tell me where you were going? Why didn't you at least give me back the keys to the camper so I wouldn't have to wait outside?" Her voice rose with each question until she was almost shouting again.

"Sorry." Cleo held up her hands and took a step backward. "Like I said, I didn't think it would be all that long."

"Well, it was. Please give me the keys." Jane's extended hand trembled.

Cleo fished in her pocket for the keys and dropped them into Jane's palm. Jane turned to the door of the camper as Cleo said, "No need to get all upset. It was a simple mistake."

Jane whirled. "No, it wasn't a simple mistake. It was rude and thoughtless. I thought we had an understanding about this."

"Yeah, I thought you weren't going to go mental on me all the time."

"I am not going mental!" Jane winced at the volume and anger in her voice. She took another breath and forced herself to slowly open the camper door before she turned back to face Cleo. "You need to let me know where you're going before you take off. Besides, you shouldn't be running off with strange men at the drop of a hat. What if he was a rapist or something? What would you have done then?"

Cleo burst into laughter. "Charlie? You Americans are so paranoid."

"I am not paranoid. I've just been around the block more times than you and have seen things."

"Oh." Cleo smirked. "Like what? Have you ever known anyone who was raped on a footpath in front of hundreds of people in the middle of the day?"

Jane pursed her lips and felt her hands tighten. "It happens. And there weren't hundreds of people out there."

Shrugging, Cleo tossed her dreads back over one shoulder. "There were enough. Nothing was going to happen. Nothing did happen."

"But it could have. You are just a kid, what eighteen or nineteen years old?

"Twenty-two, and I've been living on my own for five years." She crossed her arms and glared at Jane.

"Twenty-two isn't so old."

"Oh, and how long have you been on your own? A couple of weeks? You don't have a whole lot of room to be telling me how to live my life."

Jane felt a wave of shame rise to her face. She didn't have a lot of room to talk. She'd gone from living with her parents to living with Ernie without ever having experienced being on her own. She'd been more independent since she climbed on the plane than she'd been most of her adult life. In her gut, she felt she was right about Cleo taking off with any boy who crossed her path, but now she felt she lacked the authority to say anything about it. And had she pissed Cleo off to the point she would turn around and walk away from her, leaving her to fend for herself again? The prospect of being alone and driving on the wrong side of the road again loomed like a dark shadow.

"Look, I'm just tired and hungry. You're right. I shouldn't be telling you what to do." She glanced up, but Cleo's expression hadn't changed. "I'm sorry I yelled at you."

Cleo narrowed her eyes and stood in silence.

"Why don't we find a caravan park and get settled for the evening?" She pulled the door open and tossed the backpack inside. "I'll bet you're hungry after all that hiking."

Cleo didn't budge. Jane stared at her for a moment, trying to figure out what to do. She sighed. "Come on. I'll make you a deal;

if you'll stop running out on me, I'll stop telling you what you should or shouldn't do." Cleo still didn't move. "OK, what do you want? I'm sorry."

With a huff, Cleo dropped her arms and circled to the back of the camper. Jane watched her, feeling she had done something very wrong but not sure what. It was the same feeling she got whenever Ernie was on a rant, even when the rant had nothing to do with her. Maybe this had nothing to do with her either, aside from Cleo being angry because Jane had dared tell her she didn't appreciate what she had done. One thing was certain to Jane; she was tired of feeling like the bad guy.

They found a reasonable caravan park, and by the time Cleo had fixed some supper, she was back to talking to Jane. Jane was relieved. She hated conflict, and her relationship with Cleo seemed to be one conflict after another. She'd always thought that living with a woman would be easier than living with a man, but now she wasn't so sure. Having Cleo around was similar to being with Ernie, equal amounts of self-doubt and guilt included. What she wouldn't give for a whole twenty-four hours when she and Cleo got along.

Chapter 7

ALL HER UNFINISHED RESPONSIBILITIES poked Jane in the conscience when the sun crested the hills, jolting her into wakefulness. She lay for a few minutes cataloging everything left undone in the States and tried to figure out the best way to deal with each of them. She didn't have a clue about so much of it, bills and the like, but was certain of one thing; she needed to get to a computer, and the sooner the better.

Turning on her side, she glanced at her watch. Seven. With a sigh, she rolled onto her back and stared at the bottom of the platform where Cleo was sleeping. She was sure Cleo wouldn't be ready to get up, but she didn't want to wait for the girl to wake on her own. Based on their short history together, that would be midmorning at the earliest. Should she wake her or be patient? She fretted, waffling on the best course of action until her bladder and back began a duet of combined discomfort that spurred her into action. Trying to be quiet, she wormed her way out of the camper, clothes bunched under one arm, toiletries and towel under the other, and hurried to the amenities block.

At least this one looked clean enough to bathe in. She stood under a lukewarm shower for a long time, trying to work the kinks out of her back and legs from the previous day's hike while attempting to work up the courage to roust Cleo. Maybe it was time to try and get things going on her schedule instead of waiting for the girl. All she had done the last few days was wait for Cleo. Couldn't she make some demands of her own? After all, wasn't she the one footing all the expenses, providing the transportation, buying the food? For that, didn't she deserve to at least set some of the rules?

She turned off the water and reached for her towel, checking to see if this was how Ernie would react to the situation. He'd never have let Cleo anywhere near the camper to begin with, but if by some miracle she'd joined them anyway, he'd have made demands on her from the start. He'd never have let her take the keys with her, for one thing. He wouldn't have let her sleep in at all and would have insisted she go to bed when he did. He would have kicked her out rather than fall asleep on the bench seat waiting for her to finish a project. In other words, he would have done the opposite of what Jane had done, and while it would have been harsh, at least he wouldn't have had to suffer through all the rotten situations she had.

She sighed and wrapped the towel around her head before she dressed. Maybe doing the opposite of what Ernie would have done wasn't the greatest idea she'd ever had. Maybe it was time to try to be a little like him without going overboard. Perhaps by setting a few limits but not being overbearing. She sighed again. Did she know how to do that? So far, she'd been on the extreme edge of either being too strict or having no standards at all. She wished Rachael were there. She'd know what to do. She always seemed to know what to do.

Loneliness engulfed her, and she sank onto the worn wooden bench in the shower stall, burying her face in her hands. How she missed Rachael. Whatever made her think she could go charging off alone to the other side of the world and be OK? If Rachael were there, she wouldn't have had any of the problems Jane had with Cleo. Rachael would have known how to keep things going smoothly. Rachael would have set limits without going too far. Rachael would have protected her.

Tears moistened her fingers, slicked the palms of her hands, and trickled onto her wrists. Jane sat hunched and weeping, the ache inside growing until it filled her, overflowed, then drained away with the last of her sobs. Pulling the towel from her hair, she swabbed her face and hands dry. She leaned against the metal wall and stared at the ceiling. Rachael wasn't there and wasn't going to be there. She was on her own, and all she could do was muddle through. Maybe she should try being like Rachael instead of an anti-Ernie. Maybe that would work better.

Closing her eyes, she sat listening to the voices of the other campers as they wandered in to start their day. They sounded cheerful, chattering about plans for the morning, brekkie menus, what the kids wanted to do. Envy nipped at her. If she were closer to her sister, if she'd had kids, if she hadn't married Ernie and instead had met someone who loved and cared for her—then maybe she wouldn't be sitting here, all alone, not knowing what to do or where to go. Then maybe she'd be happy.

A hand jerked back the curtain covering the shower cubicle, and a little girl of two or three stared in at her. Jane startled, and a rumpled woman, obviously the child's mother, grabbed the little girl and dragged her back.

"Bad girl, Suzy." She slapped the child's behind and pushed her into the center of the room, glancing back at Jane. "I'm so sorry. She's such a brat sometimes." Suzy wailed, and her mother yanked her arm.

Bundling her towel into a ball, Jane grabbed for the rest of her things and stood. "That's OK. I was done."

Suzy's mother yanked at the child again and swung her around to face Jane. "Tell the nice lady you're sorry. Now!" Suzy wailed louder and tried to pull away.

Clutching her things to her chest, Jane sidled toward the door, her wet hair hanging in tangles around her face. "It's OK. She doesn't have to say anything. Honest." Her stomach clenched, and all she could think about was getting away. Before the mother could respond, Jane turned and fled the mother's yells and the child's cries.

Sunshine dappled the ground, and a cool breeze fingered Jane's damp scalp as she scurried back to the camper. She felt sad and angry and ashamed and dirty and useless all at the same time. She felt somehow responsible for the way the mother had treated Suzy yet outraged that a mother could be so awful to a young girl for such a little thing. She should have done something to stop the woman, but what? She'd been in similar situations in stores where she'd seen parents yelling at kids or hitting them without any visible reason. It always reminded her of how her mother berated her in public for the slightest mistake.

"Janey, you look like a bum—push your hair out of your eyes. Janey, only a slut would wear that kind of top. Put it back on the rack. Janey, that lipstick makes you look like a whore. Janey, you are the laziest girl on the planet. Stand up and help. Janey, if you had one working brain cell in your head, you'd be getting better grades than these. Janey, you're too fat. Janey, you're too thin. Janey . . . Janey . . . Janey . . ." She wondered what would have happened if anyone had tried to stop her mother, not that it was ever a possibility. She sighed and leaned against the camper. Nothing good. Her mother would have blamed her for the whole incident, and her life would have gotten harder.

Piling her towels and toiletries on the bumper, she ran a brush through her hair. The tangles reluctantly relented, and after several minutes she replaced the brush in the toiletries kit and reached for the back door. Time to grow a backbone.

"Time to rise and shine, Cleo. I have a lot to do today. Let's go."

A groaning issued from the top bunk, and the platform flexed as Cleo repositioned herself before lapsing into silence and immobility. Round one to Cleo.

Jane pursed her lips. "Cleo, it's time to get moving. Come on."

Another groan. "It can't be morning already. What time is it?"

"Almost eight."

"Bugger. It's too early."

"No, it's not. Come on, Cleo. I've showered and dressed and want some breakfast. Please get up."

Motion on the platform. "So go get some. I'll be up by the time you get back."

Jane gritted her teeth and took a deep breath. "I don't want to eat out. I want to fix breakfast here with my own food, and I can't do that while you're in bed. I need you to get up. Now." At the word "now" she cringed, remembering the mother in the amenities block saying the same thing to her daughter. Was she being too harsh? She sighed. She didn't think so, but maybe she should drop the "nows" from her requests for the time being. She took another breath. "I need you to get up so I can cook."

The platform creaked, and Jane could hear the rustle of blankets and a murmured "bugger." Round two, Jane. She pulled the sheets and blankets from her bed and folded them. In the upper bunk Cleo was moving around, muttering to herself. After several minutes, her feet appeared at the edge of the platform, slowly followed by the rest of her body. She scooted to the end of the camper, a pout planted on her face.

"Excuse me." She edged past Jane and headed for the toilets.

Jane followed her progress with a grin. Victory! She'd managed to get Cleo to do what she wanted, and she didn't have to yell or get angry or anything. Maybe there was hope after all.

By the time Cleo returned, Jane had folded the bedclothes from the upper berth and stored the platform. Cleo still looked miffed when she climbed in and settled on the bench. She leaned back against the window, arms crossed over her chest, legs extending to the cubbies on the other side, and closed her eyes.

"What do you want for breakfast?" Jane asked, stuffing the bedding in its cubby. "Oatmeal? Eggs? Fruit and yogurt?"

Cleo sniffed. "Nothing. I'm too tired to be hungry."

Well, if you went to sleep at a decent hour, you wouldn't be so tired in the morning. Jane bit her bottom lip to keep the words in her head instead of tumbling out of her mouth. "I think I'll have oatmeal with a banana and yogurt. And a cup of coffee too. Do you want some?" Cleo shook her head and slumped farther down on the bench. "OK then. Oatmeal for one."

Stepping over Cleo's legs, Jane pulled what she needed from the cupboards and set up her meal to cook. After a moment's consideration, she decided to have tea instead of coffee and filled the electric kettle. By the time her food was ready, Cleo had stretched herself out along the length of the bench seat and looked to be fast asleep again. Jane edged her legs off the bench, ignoring Cleo's whimper of complaint, and settled back to enjoy her breakfast.

Cleo managed to rouse herself before Jane had finished eating. In silence she made herself a cup of tea and folded herself back onto the bench.

"So, what's the big rush this morning that I couldn't have another hour in the sack?"

Jane took a sip of tea. "I have to take care of some unfinished business in a bigger town than this. I think Stawell isn't too far away."

Cleo frowned. "Stay-well? Where the bloody hell is Stay-well?"

"Here." Jane pulled a map off the counter and pointed to the city.

Cleo burst into laughter. "That's pronounced 'stahl,' not 'stay-well.' You Yanks don't have a clue how to speak English."

Jane gritted her teeth at the jibe but decided to let it pass. So what if they didn't know how to spell in Australia? "Whatever. I need to get to a computer. I left several things undone when I flew here and have to take care of them."

Cleo shrugged and sipped her tea.

Jane watched her for a minute, unable to tell if she was angry, sullen, or tired. She hoped that whatever Cleo's current mood was, it would be better after they were on the road.

Reaching forward, she retrieved the list she had made and stared at it. Email Rachael was at the top of the list, followed by gas and electric companies, the water, trash, cable, phone services, and the post office. She tapped a finger against her lips trying to think of anyone else she needed to contact. Maybe she could get Rachael to check on the house from time to time to make sure no one broke into it or vandalized it. The neighborhood was safe, but an empty house just begged for attention of the wrong kind.

For a moment she considered asking one of her neighbors to do it but realized she didn't have a clue how to get in touch with any of them. Both she and Ernie didn't do much socializing, and the most contact she had with any of the people living on her block was to wave if she saw them outside. Rachael would have to do.

When she had finished, she stood and washed her dishes while Cleo continued to sit and sip. "Look, I'm going to unhook the camper. If you want to cook something, I suggest you do it now."

Cleo grimaced but got up and heated more water while Jane put away her dishes. By the time she'd disconnected the water line and unplugged and stowed the electrical cord, Cleo had moved outside with a fresh cup of tea and a banana and was perched on the rear bumper. "Do you feel up to driving or shall I give it a try?" Jane asked.

Cleo took a bite of the fruit and chewed, as if considering a weighty question. Jane rolled her eyes. It wasn't that hard a decision.

"I'll drive," she said at last. "But do you think you could wait long enough for me to at least wash my face and brush my teeth before we leave?" There was a whining edge to her voice.

Jane folded the towels. "Sure. Just don't take too long, OK?"

Without responding, Cleo climbed into the camper and

returned with her purse. Jane watched her saunter to the amenities block, her long dreads swinging down her back in counterpoint to her hips. For a change, Jane seemed to be the grown-up in the relationship, not the irrational child. A smile lifted the corners of her lips. Now if both of them could act like adults at the same time.

By the time they were on the road, Cleo's mood seemed to have mellowed. She hummed to herself while Jane looked out the window for animals and interesting flora. The trees hugged both sides of the road, with fields occasionally visible in the distance. After about a half hour, they came to an intersection and what appeared to be a big blue building, which reminded Jane of one of the large building-supply stores back in the States. This had to mean it was a town of some size; at least that would have been the case at home. It also meant there was a good chance she'd be able to find a place to rent computer time.

Cleo slowed. "Left or right?"

Jane glanced at the map open on her lap. "Right, I think. I need to find someplace that has a computer I can use."

"Don't you have one of your own?"

"Yes, back home. I didn't think I'd need anything like that while I was here."

Cleo shrugged. "Why don't you buy one? You could get a laptop with wireless. Most of the caravan parks have wireless you can connect to, or you can sometimes piggyback off someone else's signal. That way you wouldn't have to go to a chemist's to rent time. And it would be far more secure."

Jane stared at Cleo. Why hadn't she thought of that? Probably because she was not a child of the digital age, and computers to her were a convenience, not a matter of necessity. "That's brilliant. Do you think there's a place I could get one in Stawell?"

"Sure. It might be more expensive here than in Melbourne, but I'm sure you can find one."

"That's great. So how do we go about finding where to go?"

Cleo gave her a what-kind-of-an-idiot-are-you look. "If you had a phone, we could Google it, but since you don't have that either, we can drive around looking for a pay phone or ask someone at a petrol station or something. By the way, we need petrol."

"I think I'd prefer the latter idea. Find us a petrol station, and I'll fill it if you'll ask."

A few minutes later they pulled into a BP station, and Jane jumped out. Cleo handed her the keys and walked into the convenience store while Jane puzzled through how to fill the camper and with what. The choices were myriad, not the unleaded, midgrade, and high-octane choices she was used to. There was petrol, diesel, biodiesel, autogas, and ethanol. She was still staring at the pump trying to decide which was which when Cleo returned.

"There's a couple of places, but the attendant says Big Frank's is the cheapest."

"That's great." She smiled and pointed at the pump. "I'm confused here. What do I put in the camper? We don't have any of these back home, except the diesel, and I know the camper doesn't take diesel."

Cleo rolled her eyes and pulled the pump handle out for petrol and stuck it in the tank.

"Oh, thanks." She felt silly but ran her card and pumped the gas. How was she to know? It could have been autogas or ethanol, couldn't it? At least she now knew what to look for and was happy she didn't have to go inside and appear like a naïve fool.

Cleo had gotten directions, and it took a few minutes to find the shop in what appeared to be the center of the town. The place was packed with computers, some new, some that looked used, lots in boxes stacked against one of the walls. The brands were the same ones she remembered seeing in Cortez. She had an old IBM at home, and the system she'd used in the drug store didn't have a name on it—at least she couldn't remember having seen a name on it—but it had seemed to work the same. She had some sense that Apple computers ran on a different system than she was used to, so she eliminated them from her choices.

She scanned the laptops on display, not understanding the differences between the machines except for the size of the screens. Cleo was chatting up the man behind the counter, and Jane looked at them, wishing the clerk would come talk to her instead. She was the one buying, after all. Then again, cute perkiness might outweigh a sale when you're a twenty-something male. After an eternity, Cleo wandered over when the phone behind the counter rang and the man turned to answer it.

"See anything you like?"

Jane sighed. "Do you know anything about these machines? I can't tell one from the other and haven't the faintest idea what I need or want, except not Apple. Help."

A smile spread across Cleo's face. "No worries. Tell me what you want to do on it."

"Well, I'm not too sure about that either. I want to be able to check my email and maybe do something with the pictures on my camera. It's full, and I still want to take more pictures, and I'm supposed to put them on a computer, I think. And then I've got all these bills I have to pay back home that I didn't think about when I left, and I don't know how to deal with that since I don't have any way of knowing how much I owe on them. But if I don't pay them, they'll shut off my electricity and water and cable and charge me an arm and a leg to get them all turned back on again, not to mention what it's going to do to my credit rating, which may affect my Visa card, I think. And I don't know what any of these machines do or how to do what I need to do, if I can do anything at all." Jane ran a hand across her forehead and sighed again. "Can you help? Please?"

Cleo placed a hand on her shoulder and smiled again. "Is that all? This is easy."

Jane looked at her warily and shrugged. Maybe for her. It seemed overwhelming to Jane, but if Cleo knew where to begin, she'd be grateful. "So what do you think I need?"

Pursing her lips, Cleo scanned the displayed computers. "Well, you don't need anything complicated or with a huge hard drive, RAM, or memory. I'm assuming you're not going to be gaming or video conferencing, right?"

Jane raised an eyebrow and shrugged again. "I don't think so. Is gaming playing solitaire or something else?"

Cleo laughed. "No, it's not playing solitaire on your laptop. It's playing interactive video games that require a high-end video card and the fastest processor you can get."

"Oh. In that case, no."

"OK then, so . . ." She walked down the display case, paused, then tapped on the glass and glanced at the clerk, who was standing a few feet away staring at her. "Tony, can we take a look at this one?"

"Sure." Pulling a key from behind the register, he unlocked the case and placed the laptop on the counter. "Pretty basic. You'll be lucky to load Monsters and Mayhem, much less run it. You sure this is what you want, luv?"

Cleo's expression turned icy. "Don't call me luv, luv. And yes, this is the one we want to look at."

"'Scuse me." Tony held up his hands and backed away.

Jane suppressed a smile. Well, the girl could set boundaries when she wanted to. Another assumption she'd made about Cleo that was wrong. Cleo punched the "on" button and frowned when the laptop didn't respond.

"Hey, can you plug this in for us? By the way, what's the OS?"

Reluctantly, Tony complied. "Windows 10. No word-processing software except Notepad."

"You may want to think about buying that," Cleo said, turning to Jane. "Notepad is a bitch if you're not used to it. Are you sure you don't want an Apple?"

Jane shook her head. "I wouldn't have a clue how to use it."

"It's not that different from Windows, and you don't have to worry so much about viruses."

"No." She shook her head again. "I can buy a virus protection program, can't I? That's what I did back home."

Cleo harrumphed. "No need. I'll download a free one for you."

After the computer booted up, Cleo checked the system specifications and the programs installed on the machine and nodded. "This should work, and the price is reasonable. The screen isn't very big though."

"That's OK. It's similar to the one I have at home, and that works fine."

"OK then." She glanced at Tony. "We'll take it."

After picking out a word-processing program, case, and backup battery, Jane handed over her Visa card. It was pricier than she expected, but if it would deal with all her problems the way Cleo thought it would, it was well worth the investment. Besides, she felt downright techy to now own a laptop. Ernie hated the whole idea of computers, and this would have sent him into an antitechnology rant. He had a personal secretary who did all his computer work. She left the shop feeling proud of herself for having taken another step beyond Ernie's limits.

Cleo jabbered all the way back to the camper about the benefits of having the laptop. She appeared happy for the first time since she had climbed aboard the camper, and Jane wondered if this was the first time Cleo felt she had contributed something to the relationship. Up to this point, aside from a little cooking, driving, and leading a trek through the bush, Cleo had been on the receiving end of everything and the subject of more than one tirade on her behavior. Maybe this would even out some of the rough spots of their association.

They drove around looking for a place to pick up a wireless signal that wasn't encrypted, but they ended up having to find a caravan park where they could buy time on the internet. Jane was content to remain in Stawell if it meant she could get her issues back home resolved. After hooking up, Cleo settled down in front of the laptop, installed the word-processing program, downloaded an antivirus program, and configured the system to Jane's specifications. Then she looked up.

"OK. What do you need done?"

Once again Jane outlined her problems dealing with the bills at home. One by one, Cleo walked her through setting up online accounts for each of the companies and automatic payments from her Visa account. While Cleo worked, Jane fixed lunch and then a midafternoon snack. She tried to follow what Cleo was doing but felt lost from the outset. In the end, all she cared about was being able to understand how to find out what she owed at any given time, how to make sure it was paid, and how to see how much she had left on her Visa card. That she could do any of this from Australia astounded her.

Shadows from the surrounding trees engulfed the camper by the time Cleo sat back and stretched. "I think it's all done," she announced, then yawned.

"Oh, Cleo, I don't know how to thank you." Jane sank onto the seat beside her. "What you have done for me is a miracle. To think of all the trouble I would have been in if it weren't for you. What can I do to repay you?"

Cleo shrugged and relaxed a little against the seat, but Jane thought she could see a faint smile cross her lips. Maybe she had underestimated her, and she had more character than she'd expected. Maybe all she'd seen was her youth and the impulsiveness that comes with youth, rather than some character flaw. She owed Cleo a great deal, not just for that day but also for taking on the driving and rescuing her after the river crossing.

"Say, enough hanging out in the camper. What do you say we try and find a movie or something? Have dinner in a nice restaurant. Drink a glass of wine. Kind of a celebration. My treat."

"I don't know that we'll find much here. This is rather a small town."

Jane waved a hand. "You're just used to Melbourne. This looks like the town I'm from back home, and there was a theater there.

Considering this is a tourist town, wouldn't they have a theater and some good restaurants? What do you say?"

Cleo looked up and straightened. "I guess we could look online."

"That's the spirit. You can show me how."

The restaurant they settled on looked classy by Jane's standards, and she was worried they would be very out of place in their casual clothes. Cleo brushed off her concerns, and when they arrived, Jane was relieved to see that no one inside was dressed any better than they were.

After ordering dinner, Jane lifted her glass of rosé to Cleo. "To a great traveling companion."

Cleo raised her glass and eyed Jane while she sipped. "So yesterday I was rude and inconsiderate, and today I'm a great traveling companion. Quite a leap."

Jane set her glass back on the table and ran a finger around the base. It seemed a huge leap to her too. Maybe she shouldn't have put it quite that way, but there was no way to take back the words, and anything she said now to modify the statement would sound as if she didn't mean it at all.

"It's just . . ." she began, then paused. "Well, I guess I've been taking a look at my behavior toward you and rethinking what I assumed you were thinking and doing too. You've accused me of being mental, and I guess I've looked that way more than once. I assumed you were being selfish and thoughtless when you'd take off, and now I wonder if that was the case. I realize that I don't know what you're thinking or feeling most of the time—"

"All of the time," Cleo interrupted.

"OK, all of the time. But the same goes for you. What I'm trying to say is this: Here we are, two women from two generations and different countries, who decided to travel together knowing nothing about each other and, surprise, surprise, we've had problems understanding each other. Today you've been so helpful and knowledgeable in ways I am not. It made me think I've been underestimating you because you are so much younger than I am, and I see how unfair that is. When I was your age, I could do lots of things my mother didn't think I could. Maybe I've been making the same mistake about you."

"Righto." Cleo lifted her glass, took a sip then, making a face, replaced it on the table and edged it toward Jane.

Jane's eyebrows lifted. "Are you angry with me?"

"Nah, just never quite got onto the taste of wine."

"No, I mean about underestimating you."

"Oh that. That's what I meant about you not being my mum. She was always telling me where to go, what to do, what to think, without ever giving a mind to the fact I might have a good idea about what was going on in my life. She'd bombed out in her life and was telling me what to do. What a laugh." Cleo toyed with her napkin.

"And I was doing the same thing."

"Like I said, righto."

"I already told you I married a jerk. Was your dad a—what did you call your stepfather?"

"A bludger."

"Yeah, a bludger, whatever that is. Was your dad a bludger too?"

Cleo shrugged, picked up a fork, and set it back down. "A bludger is a no-good layabout. Dad was a cot case, but when he wasn't drinking, he was OK. He wasn't around much. I guess he and Mum were doing fine until I was born. That's when he started drinking and things began to fall apart. I often wondered if Mum didn't give him a fair go, and he left because he couldn't stand her whinging."

"Whinging?" Jane cocked an eyebrow.

"Whining," Cleo clarified.

"But he was still part of your life, right?"

"If you could call showing up with stories and arms full of prezzies a couple of times a year, sticking around a few days, and then disappearing into the outback being part of my life, then yeah."

"Did your parents fight?"

"Like cats and dogs. Then Mum hooked up with Reggie, and I haven't seen my dad since."

Jane frowned. "How long has that been?"

"Five years. Next week." Cleo glanced at her hands, sadness seeming to close over her features like a dark cloud.

Jane's throat tightened. "That's a long time. You must miss him."

"Yeah." She said the word slowly, softly. "That's one of the reasons I wanted to go to Alice. His mum lives there, and I was hoping he'd be staying with her."

"You don't know?"

She shook her head. "He never said where he went when he was gone. I always assumed he went back to Alice. I may be way off, and he could be sitting pissed in some alley back in Melbourne for all I know."

"Not in Adelaide?"

"No. I need to go there because of my jewelry."

Jane sighed. "Well, after Adelaide, I planned on heading up

to Alice Springs. Maybe if we can be OK with each other, you can ride along."

"If I have some money coming in. I hate being baggage and not contributing."

"Well, you contributed today. Help isn't always about money."

Cleo tilted her head to one side. "Yeah, I know. I just wish I could do more."

"We'll see what we can do about that. OK?"

Leaning back against the passenger seat, Jane smiled to herself. The previous evening had been lovely, though they couldn't find a movie they both wanted to watch. Instead, Jane spent the rest of the evening composing a long email to Rachael while Cleo twined together junk into jewelry. Rachael hadn't written her back, and that bothered Jane. Was something wrong? Had she done something to anger Rachael too? She found that hard to believe. Rachael seemed unflappable.

Still, it had felt good to tell her about the troubles with Cleo, her insights on the matter, where she had gone and what she had seen, and the rest of her adventures. She also hoped Rachael would take her up on the request to keep an eye on the house. She wondered how it would have been to take this trip with Rachael, but she shelved that thought, feeling it might sour her budding relationship with Cleo with unfair comparisons. Instead, she focused on the landscape rolling by.

Jane marveled at the country closer to Adelaide. It was lush in a more conventional sense than the rain forest—fewer ferns and more hardwood trees. She was grateful again that Cleo could worry about traffic and exits, and she could sit and enjoy the scenery. She was doubly glad when they made it to the city, where the multilane highway they were on disappeared into a jumble of city streets. Jane didn't have a clue where they were going, but Cleo babbled about the shop and her success selling her jewelry there. Jane felt sure she would have had a heart attack trying to maneuver the camper through the heavy traffic on the narrow streets. Even being a passenger felt claustrophobic. She was grateful when Cleo parked the van on a shop-lined street with traffic zooming by on the right.

"We're probably not going to get any closer. The shop's down the road a little, but traffic can get bad, and there are no car parks anywhere." Cleo fetched her bag from the bench seat behind her and launched herself out of the van. "Come on."

The shops were small and abutted one another, as if one huge building had been segmented into small pieces. The whole place had an old feel to it, at least older than anything she'd seen in Melbourne. In fact, if Melbourne had sported similar streets, she never would have been on them.

She hurried after Cleo, who was almost bounding down the sidewalk. She hadn't seen the girl this excited, and it was fun to see her so full of energy and enthusiasm. Jane just wished she'd slow down a bit, as she was running to keep up and just managing to keep her in sight.

After a couple of blocks, Cleo stopped in front of a nondescript shop with a variety of kitsch in the window. "This is it." She scanned the display and then turned to Jane and smiled. "Nothing of mine in the window. Maybe it all sold. Mrs. Lancaster always puts my stuff in the window." Grinning, she pulled open the door and stepped inside.

Jane followed, breathing hard. Though the temperature was cool, she was sweating due to the exercise and mugginess of the air. She wished she had put on a cooler shirt—but then she hadn't expected to be chasing Cleo down the street.

The first thing that struck her was the smell, lavender overlaid with cinnamon and a scent she couldn't quite identify. Flowery and rich. She decided the owner must be a big fan of incense and was burning several types at the same time. The shop was an eclectic assortment of antiques, unusual clothing, bric-a-brac, kitchen supplies, hats, linens, candles, art, and greeting cards. The aisles displayed such a wide variety of items that Jane had trouble keeping track of what she saw. If it was strange or one of a kind, the shop seemed to have it tucked away somewhere.

Some of the items were fascinating, such as a set of salt and pepper shakers in the shapes of Elizabethan figurines—female for salt and male for pepper, she assumed. Next to them on a small, ornate table stood a stack of greeting cards that appeared handmade. She was fingering a brilliant silk scarf when Cleo called to her from the back of the room. Jane looked up and tried to see where the call came from and located the top of Cleo's head near a rack of slinky dresses.

As she approached, Cleo reached out and pulled her closer. "Mrs. Lancaster, I'd like you to meet Jane Mullet, the woman I've been riding with."

Jane held out a hand and took the small, soft fingers Mrs. Lancaster extended in her direction. She smelled of roses. "Nice to meet you."

"Likewise. I'm so glad you've been taking care of Cleo. I do worry about her out there on her own. She's quite the little artist, I tell you. I can't seem to keep anything she makes in stock. But she's such a wild child. I'm glad she's got an older woman to look after her."

Cleo shook her head and threw an arm around the woman. "You worry too much, Mrs. L."

Mrs. Lancaster smiled and laid her head against Cleo's. "Somebody's got to, dear."

They made an odd pair, Jane thought. Mrs. L. didn't stand much taller than Cleo but was at least three times broader, with a head of shaggy gray curls and a pair of reading glasses hanging from a beaded chain around her neck. If someone could epitomize Englishness, she felt, it could be this older lady in her chintz dress with the lace collar and gentle accent. It was obvious she cared a great deal about Cleo, and it made Jane glad to see the affection that flowed between the two. If Mrs. L. was happy Jane was in Cleo's life, Jane was equally pleased Cleo had Mrs. L.

"I love your shop," Jane said, glancing around. "It has so many strange and wonderful things in it. I could spend hours here looking through it all."

Mrs. L. beamed. "I'm so glad. It's been my little project since my Bernie died ten years ago. Keeps me out of trouble and off the streets. You're from America, aren't you, dear? What do you think of our country?"

There it was again. She wished she could fake an Australian accent and blend in better. "I like what I've seen so far. It's different from anything I'm used to and not what I expected."

"Have you seen a kangaroo yet? That's what most foreigners look for first, right off the plane."

Jane blushed. "Well, I have to admit that's one of the first things I looked for, but I was stuck in Melbourne for almost a week until my camper was ready, and there weren't a lot of them hopping around the streets. I did see what I thought might be some in the Grampians, and Cleo showed me some koalas out by Cape Otway, but that's the only wildlife I've seen so far."

Mrs. L. patted her on the arm. "Don't worry, dear. You'll see more if you go to Alice Springs. Cleo said you were thinking of doing that."

"Well, it's on my agenda, and I'm hoping Cleo will come with me." Cleo seemed to squirm, and Jane wondered if she'd changed her mind about Alice Springs.

"Did you sell all my jewelry?" Cleo leaned close to the woman.

Mrs. L. looked surprised. "Of course, my dear. I always do. Do you have more for me, I hope?"

"Just a couple of pieces, I'm afraid."

She patted Cleo's arm. "It will have to do then. Come on back, and let's settle up. You can show me the new things."

They turned and weaved through the jumble and soon disappeared. Jane didn't feel comfortable following, so she wandered the store instead, feeling abandoned for some strange reason. Was it that she felt usurped by Mrs. Lancaster or that she wasn't so special in Cleo's life or just that she wasn't Cleo's only friend out here? None of the reasons she could imagine rang true, yet the feeling remained.

She wished again that Rachael were traveling with her, standing by her in the shop, chatting over some interesting little thing she'd found on one of the shelves. But Rachael wasn't there and would never have come, even if Jane had given her the opportunity. Surrounded by kids and grandkids, with a job she loved, Rachael adored her life and home. When Jane had fantasized about running away after Ernie died, Rachael always said she wasn't the traveling type and that if she were in the same situation, she'd buy a comfortable chair and try to read every book in the library instead.

Jane lifted a pair of painted sticks and then set them back down. She wished she were happy with her life the way Rachael appeared to be. Even before she met Ernie, she didn't fit in her life. It wasn't big enough for her somehow. She needed more adventures, space, journeys, experiences—just something. When Ernie barged into her life, he seemed to fill the hole, at least for a while. But it didn't take long for the yearning to return, especially when Ernie was out in the field.

Her adult daydreams mirrored her childhood ones: travel, writing, climbing mountains, fording rivers, eating strange meals in stranger places. The fact that Ernie's idea of an adventure was a trip to Walmart or a short hike in the mountains fueled her imaginings. And now that she was on the big adventure with a strange and exotic young woman, she felt alone and lonely, and she wanted the comfort of a friend by her side. She shook her head. What a sad, pathetic creature she was.

By the window she stared at a stained-glass butterfly. Then again, maybe she was evolving, and this feeling of loneliness was realizing what she needed and wanted. She wasn't stuck in an empty marriage anymore. She wasn't confined to an unexciting job in a little town. She was living what she had always dreamed about. She was remaking her world. If it wasn't perfect, well, that was just life. Nothing ever was. But an emptiness still hung in her chest.

Cleo and Mrs. L. reappeared arm in arm and laughing. Jane felt the pangs of loneliness jab more acutely, but she managed a smile as they approached. "Got things settled?"

Cleo nodded. "I'm flush again." Then she turned to the older woman. "I promise I'll bring you lots more the next time I'm through."

"Well, I'll be glad to have it. You drive safely now."

Cleo settled in behind the steering wheel of the van. "We still have quite a few hours of daylight. Do you want to push on or see some of the city?"

She must be coming with me, Jane thought, and a sense of relief and contentment swept through her. She felt wanted, maybe even needed, and for some unfathomable reason, she began to tear up.

The expression on Cleo's face morphed into alarm. "What did I say? What's wrong? Are you OK?"

Oh shit. I'm going mental again. Jane wiped her eyes with her palms and shook her head. "I'm OK. I just . . ." She shrugged and smiled. "If you know someplace interesting, why don't we go there?"

Cleo's face registered disbelief as she sat watching Jane. At last she frowned and turned back to the windshield. "I don't like Adelaide. If you don't mind, I'd rather push on."

"That's fine with me." Jane tried to sound perky, though tears were still leaking from her eyes. "What's next?"

Cleo turned back to her, eyebrows knitted together. "You don't look so good. What's going on? Why are you crying?"

Wiping her cheeks, Jane tried to figure out how to put words around the emotions that seemed to flood through her. What would Cleo think if she told her how much she had feared Cleo would leave and how good it was that she'd decided to stay? The depth of her reaction didn't make any sense to her; why should it make more sense to Cleo? Would she assume she'd gone crazy again and desert her? And if not the truth, what could she say that would sound rational? To buy time, she took a couple of deep breaths and tried to compose herself.

"There was a piece in the shop that reminded me of my husband," she lied, figuring a dead husband was a good excuse. Ernie couldn't mind. "I guess it hit me harder than I thought."

Cleo's face softened. "Oh, I'm sorry. I didn't realize. I guess I assumed you didn't care about him after saying he was such a bastard and all."

"Well, he was a bastard. I'll grant you that. But we did spend a lot of years together, and I guess I'm still dealing with losing him, even if I'm glad he's gone."

"You sure you're going to be OK, or do we need to do something?"

Jane shook her head and sighed. The tears seemed to have stopped for the moment. "No, I'm fine. What do you want to do?"

Her answer seemed to mollify Cleo, and she turned back to start the engine. "I think we should get on the A1 and see how far we can go before dark."

"Sounds good to me."

Jane leaned back and watched the fields roll by while Cleo hummed to whatever was coursing through her earbuds. Jane's eyes still burned from the tears, and she felt tired. Still, she wasn't sobbing, and that was something. The lie about missing Ernie kept ping-ponging around in her head. Was it a lie, she wondered? She searched inside, looking for an empty spot where he once resided—or at least a residue of feeling attached to his memory that didn't include anger, betrayal, and guilt. Much to her surprise, what she found was a vision of herself stranded on a desert island, the boat she had clung to through skyscraper-high waves and drowning rains destroyed next to her. Had Ernie been that boat?

She had to admit that although he had treated her like she was his personal slave, he had provided for her through their years together. He had worked long hours out on the rigs so she could have anything she wanted. Then he took the promotion to the office because she wanted him to, even though he preferred being out in the field. Granted, he didn't want her to work, but she wondered now if that had more to do with his own sense of being able to give her a decent life than it did with wanting to keep her chained to the stove. Was it some kind of assault on his ego that she felt the need to have a job? Did her working make him feel less of a man?

A deep sadness arose in her at the thought. She never wanted him to feel like a failure, even when they found out it was his fault they couldn't have kids. His parents had done a good enough job of that. She wanted him to be happy, and not just because a happy Ernie was much easier to live with, but because it was her nature.

Deep down inside she'd always wanted everyone to be happy. She'd wanted her brother, Mikey, to be happy, even when the only way he seemed to get there was by being drunk. She'd wanted her mom and dad and sister to be happy after Mikey was killed in the motorcycle crash. After all, he was drunk at the time and did it to himself, and that's where the blame should have ended. But after the accident, there was so much yelling in the house and crying and blaming. Mom blamed Dad, Dad blamed Mom, and her older sister, Sally, blamed both of them and stopped speaking to them the day of the funeral. Then Dad climbed into his shell, and Mom fumed and lashed out at everyone.

Jane did her best to bring peace back to the family. She wouldn't argue with anyone; instead, she'd nod her head and agree with whomever she was talking to, no matter what that person said. She took on all the chores her mother usually performed—the cooking and everyone's laundry. If something needed to be done, she volunteered to do it. The hell of it was that nobody seemed to notice what she was trying to do—how hard she was working to make their lives easier so they could be a little happier. All her efforts didn't seem to make one bit of difference.

Looking at it now, Jane decided it was perfect training for living with Ernie. But she realized, too, that no matter what she did or didn't do, she could never have made him happy. If her default setting was toward happiness; his was toward misery. If she had quit her job, gotten pregnant, or let him work forever on the rigs, it wouldn't have made one whit of difference. And that was more tragic. That he spent all of his life down to his last breath locked in sadness, unable to move, unable to feel the joy she sought. She felt the tears begin again, and she leaned against the window with her face averted so Cleo wouldn't see. Then she let herself weep silently.

Chapter 8

THAT NIGHT THEY CAMPED at Port Pirie, an industrial town that sported a huge complex of grain silos and smelter chimneys. Jane was unimpressed and wished they could have driven farther up the coast to someplace a little more picturesque, but Cleo was bushed by the time they arrived at the caravan park. She declined Jane's offer of a walk after dinner and sequestered herself in the camper with her jewelry and MP3 player. Jane considered trying to take a turn around the town to see if she could find anything of interest but decided she would rather see if Rachael had answered her email.

No such luck. Her inbox was empty except for the usual junk and the emails from Ernie's family. She stared at them. One from each of the brothers' wives and one from her mother-in-law. None of them had attachments, so no PowerPoints this time. She debated opening them but just didn't want to face their condemnation, now or ever again. Though she had some guilt for not arranging a funeral for all his family to come to and weep copiously while deriding her for not taking better care of Ernie, it wasn't enough to prick her conscience often. She was sure they managed something on their own when they got the ashes in the mail. She was glad she hadn't had to witness it. Gritting her teeth, she highlighted the seven emails and then, with a decisive jab of her finger, deleted them. She grinned.

By the time the sun disappeared behind the veil of industrial smog, Jane was ready for a little reading and bed. Even Cleo looked like it would be an early night for her. By ten they were both in their bunks, Jane listening to the calls of the night birds as she drifted off to sleep.

The next morning they were up by six and munching bagels before the sun crowned the trees shading the east side of the caravan park. Jane was amazed that Cleo had bounced out of bed so early, but the girl seemed anxious to move on, and Jane decided that was the reason. Map spread between them, they scouted out a route that led to the Stuart Highway and right up the middle of the country. Cleo thought if they pushed it, they could reach Alice Springs that day. Jane looked at the map and frowned. She wasn't sure of the scale, and everything was in kilometers, but it seemed very far away to her. About halfway up the entire country.

"I don't know. Don't you think we should stop somewhere along the way for the night?"

Cleo sighed. "Well, I guess we could, but there isn't much out there to see along the way. Lots of desert and not much else."

"What about Ayers Rock? I want to see that."

Cleo gave her a withering look. "You must mean Uluru, right?"

"Uh, yeah, I guess." She shrugged. "Is that Ayers Rock?"

"It's the proper name, the real name, not the white fella's name." Cleo sat upright and stuck her chin out. "When we took the land back, we changed it. Same for the Olgas. They're called Kata Tjuta again, the way they're supposed to be."

"Oh." Jane looked down at the map, not knowing if she should apologize or something. She'd hit a nerve in Cleo but wasn't quite sure what it was all about. She wasn't certain she wanted to pursue the matter and hoped Cleo would let it drop. "Could we stop there on our way?"

Cleo pressed her lips together and crossed her arms. "That's a long way off the main highway. About a four-hour detour. Can't you go back after you drop me off at Alice?"

"I guess so," Jane said slowly. She kept her eyes on the map, the sense of abandonment she had felt in the shop catching her by the throat again. Until then she hadn't let herself realize that when they got to Alice Springs, it was likely the end of the line for Cleo. Somehow, she had assumed Cleo would be with her for the rest of her trip, no matter how unrealistic that idea was. She'd been in the country a little more than two weeks, and her visa didn't expire for another ten. She still had a lot of places she wanted to see, a lot of places Cleo didn't want to go to, like Ayers Rock. No, Uluru, she corrected herself. Places she would have to visit alone.

That thought sent another wave of sadness through her. And not just at the idea of having to drive on the wrong-sided roads or trying to find caravan parks, food stores, and attractions all on her own. She would miss Cleo. She would miss having another person in the van with her, having someone to talk to, to make decisions with.

Even though they hadn't been together all that long and had butted heads for most of the time, she liked having the girl around. And she still didn't know much about her, her life, or her people. She'd been traveling with a relative stranger, and in a day the opportunity to get to know her would be gone. She didn't want that.

Finally, she looked up at Cleo, who was staring at her expectantly. "I guess I kind of hoped you could help me understand places like Uluru. I assume they're important to your people, and I don't know anything about that. I was hoping you could help."

Cleo looked skeptical. "There's lots of information at the park. The people there can tell you a lot more than I ever could. Just because I'm a native doesn't mean I know everything about the sacred places of Australia. And I don't want to be a white American's teacher. You want to learn, then go out there and learn. I have a life to lead." She tossed her plate in the sink, stood, and then stretched. "You ready to go?"

Jane inhaled sharply and dropped her eyes. So she was some pushy white woman to Cleo and nothing more. A free ride to Alice. Although Cleo had given her a hundred dollars to help out, it wasn't close to half of what Jane had spent on gas and groceries and park fees since picking the girl up. Sure, Cleo had driven, and Jane reminded herself that was all she'd asked of her since the very beginning, but that didn't take the edge off the resentment and hurt that welled inside. She felt her nose prickle and tears begin to surface. With a vengeance, she chomped down on her bagel. She wasn't about to let Cleo know how she'd stung her. Let her abandon ship in Alice. Jane could find her own way.

"I'll be ready in a little while. I'm still eating." Jane took another bite and slowly chewed to emphasize the point.

Cleo rolled her eyes. "Whatever. I'll be unhooking the camper while you finish." She stomped out the door and banged it closed.

Dropping the last of the bagel onto her plate, Jane squeezed her eyes closed and let her head hang. Damn that girl.

Even though Jane dawdled, they were on the road soon after seven, Cleo again humming while she drove and Jane staring out the window, despondent. The landscape seemed to change to suit her mood, from farm ground to a more barren landscape, dotted sparsely with bushes and mountains looming in the distance. Cleo informed her they were the Flinders Ranges and a place for Jane to do some sightseeing on her way back to Melbourne. Jane gritted her teeth and tried not to break into tears again. She tried to focus on the scenery rolling by, but even the sight of several lakes that appeared to be bright pink did little more than register. They blew through Port Augusta and were driving on the Stuart Highway surrounded by a barren, red desert by nine.

The farther they got from the city, the more Cleo accelerated, until she was cruising at fifteen kilometers per hour above the speed limit. Jane protested that a ticket wouldn't be the best idea, but Cleo brushed her concerns aside.

"There are no police out here."

Jane stared at her while Cleo tapped her fingers against the steering wheel and pressed down on the gas pedal. "I don't believe you. I can't get a speeding ticket in this vehicle. I'll be in a whole lot of trouble, not to mention the trouble I'd be in if they found out you were driving and not me. Please slow down."

"No worries. No one's going to stop us."

"I don't care what you believe—slow down."

Cleo glared at her. "You're just trying to make sure we don't make it to Alice today, aren't you?"

203

"I am not," Jane protested, yet she wouldn't complain if driving the speed limit meant they had to stop for the night somewhere before Alice. "I just don't want to get in trouble. Or risk getting in trouble."

Cleo continued to glare but backed off the accelerator a little. Jane waited for a few minutes to see if she would slow to the speed limit, but when she continued to hover at five kilometers over, Jane decided it was time for more drastic measures.

"Cleo, either drive the speed limit, or I'm going to take over."

"Ha! You haven't been keen to drive. Now you're going to?"

Jane frowned. "If that's the only way I can keep from getting cited, yes, I'm going to drive. Besides, if you're leaving tomorrow, I need the practice."

Cleo eyed her. "And if I slow down?"

Jane sighed. "I still need to drive. Find a spot to pull over, and we'll switch." Even though it hadn't been her intention, she realized she'd have to take over the wheel at some point, and now was a good time.

Frowning, Cleo slowed and pulled over to the shoulder. Once they had stopped, Cleo turned to face her. "You sure you want to do this?"

Jane nodded, unfastening her seat belt. "I made it out of Melbourne by myself before I met you. How hard can driving on this straight, empty road be compared to that?"

"Fine, have a go."

They switched sides, Cleo mumbling to herself while she settled into the passenger seat.

Jane placed her hands on the steering wheel and tried to remember what she had learned the last time she'd driven: turn signal on the right, windshield wipers on the left, gas pedal on the right, and go. She shifted into drive and eased back onto the pavement, gravel crunching under the tires.

The camper felt huge and ungainly to Jane when she accelerated. As a passenger, she hadn't noticed the wind, but now every small breeze seemed to send the camper reeling, and she had to fight to keep it on the road. She edged the speed upward, but the limit of 110 kph seemed far too fast. She tried to console herself that it was kilometers per hour, not miles, but 110 kph felt like 110 mph, and she found herself gripping the steering wheel, her shoulders crawling up to her ears. The fact that Cleo had been driving at 125 amazed her. How did she do it?

From the passenger seat, Cleo stared at her, eyes narrowed, waiting for her to cave and surrender the wheel. "Is that all the faster you're going to go?"

Jane glanced at the speedometer. She'd managed to work up to 95 kph and was feeling pretty good about that. "I'm just getting the feel of the vehicle again. It's swaying in the wind, and I'm having some trouble controlling it. Did you notice the wind when you were driving?"

"Yeah, but it wasn't a problem. If you keep driving at this speed, a road train's going to pass you. You think you have wind now, wait for that."

"A road train? What's that?"

Cleo grinned. "It's a tractor with four or five trailers attached. You see them all the time on the Stuart Highway. I guarantee you don't want to be passed by one."

Jane scanned the road's two lanes, which didn't seem all that wide, and the shoulder, which barely existed. When Cleo had pulled off to let Jane drive, the passenger's side wheels were scarcely off the pavement and the driver's side was in the dirt. She didn't want to imagine what it would be like to have something as big as a train on the road with her. She gripped the steering wheel harder. "You've got to be kidding. That's huge. What happens if I need to pass one?"

"Mash the accelerator and go flat out like a lizard drinking."

The first thing that flashed into Jane's mind was a picture of her crashing into a car she hadn't seen while she was attempting to pass the monstrous road train. Wait, what if a gust of wind caught the camper and sent it reeling into the side of the thing? And then there was the possibility she'd get thrown off the road and—or—

She took a deep breath and tried to loosen her grip on the steering wheel, banishing to a quiet corner of her mind the myriad ways she could die on the Stuart Highway. "Tell me that there aren't all that many road trains on the highway. Please."

Cleo huffed. "Heaps. It's the way things get across the country. You sure you want to keep driving?"

"Yes. Since you're leaving, I have to do this."

Without saying anything, Cleo slouched and brought her heels up to rest on the edge of the seat. She wrapped her arms around her shins and stared straight ahead.

Jane watched her for a moment, wondering what was going through the girl's thoughts. Was she angry Jane wasn't going faster or resentful she had insisted on driving or anxious to get out of the van and be on her own again or bored or tired—or who knew? Jane wasn't in the mood to find out. She focused back on the road. If Cleo was right about a road train passing her, she'd better get brave fast and hit the speed limit. Ignoring the rocking of the camper, she pressed the gas down until the speedometer rose to 110 and prayed the only road train she would see would be in a parking lot. At least Cleo should be a little happier that she had speeded up.

They rode in silence, Jane scanning the rearview mirror for approaching road trains and taking in what scenery she could. It was strange, flat as western Kansas but without the vegetation. Scrubby bushes hunkered alone amid red sand and rocks. At one point they crossed what a sign declared was a creek, but it was several times larger than any river in Colorado. She began to feel more at home driving, and either the wind died down when the sun heated up the landscape, or she had gotten used to it.

She wondered what Rachael would make of it all: road trains, rust-red, flat land, the strange jargon. "Flat out as a lizard drinking." What an odd phrase. But Rachael would love it since language was her passion. Jane made a mental note to keep track of the strange words and phrases she heard and pass them on to Rachael. It's too bad she hadn't had a chance to share with Rachael her feelings about Cleo leaving. Maybe she would have had some good advice on how to keep the girl around—or how to cope without her. Rachael always seemed so good with kids, her own and other people's. There were times Jane wished that Rachael, or a Rachael-like being, had been her mother instead of the harridan she'd grown up with. Maybe then she never would have married Ernie.

Shortly after they passed the turnoff into a town called Woomera, Cleo straightened up and announced, "I need a dunny." When Jane didn't respond, Cleo added, "A lav, a toilet. I need to go."

"Oh. Can you wait for a rest area?"

"I don't think so."

"You want me to turn around and go back to Woomera?"

"Nah, pull over, and I'll piss by the van."

Jane stared at her. The last time she'd seen anybody urinate outside a bathroom was when she was out plinking with her father. He'd tell her to turn her back while he did his business. Even Ernie wouldn't pee in the woods when they were hiking. She'd never been able to go outside either, though a few times she had thought her bladder would explode before they made it home to a bathroom. "You're serious."

"Of course, I'm serious. Just pull over and let me get out."

Jane shook her head but complied. Once stopped, Cleo popped the door open and squatted down while Jane averted her eyes. She hoped no one would drive by, but while Cleo was fastening her pants, a big something appeared in the rearview mirror, moving very fast. It pulled alongside the camper while Cleo was settling into the seat and putting on her seat belt. A road train. Jane watched in amazement as the tractor trailer roared by, followed by four full-length trailers. It seemed to go on and on, the camper rocking in the wash from the vehicle. Though buffeted by the draft, Jane was thankful it had passed them while they were parked on the side of the road and not driving. She promised herself she'd risk getting a ticket for speeding rather than have one of those things pass her while she was moving.

The kilometers passed in silence. Cleo appeared to have adjusted to the fact of Jane's driving, and Jane tried to keep the camper traveling at the speed limit or a little more. She didn't see more road trains coming in either direction and was thankful for that. Trees appeared again alongside the road, and the bushes grew taller and more numerous. The ground looked redder than it had been, and the contrast between the red dirt, vivid greenery, and clear blue sky was picturesque and quite striking.

They stopped for gas at the hamlet of Glendambo, a little piece of nothing that seemed to consist of a couple of gas stations, a resort (though Jane in her wildest dreams would not have considered it a resort except for the sign), and a few houses spread among the scattered trees. Jane suggested they stop for lunch, but Cleo protested that she wasn't hungry and would rather stop at a rest area than the town.

While she was pumping gas, Jane noticed Cleo hunkering down in her seat, not making any move to leave the shelter of the camper. She wondered if it was because of the heat, at least 85 degrees by Jane's reckoning, or the fact that all the faces in the place were white.

As it turned out, there was a charming rest area not too far out of Glendambo. Though basic, the rest area had a tree that looked like it was out of a Dr. Seuss book in the center as well as flowering bushes growing in isolated clumps around the edge of the dirt parking area. She and Cleo ate in the camper with the back door open until the flies decided that inside was the perfect place to take up temporary residence. Within minutes, Jane and Cleo were swatting and shooing flies out the door, then closing it and opening up the screened windows to try and catch a breeze. After lunch, Jane insisted on taking a walk with her camera. It was too beautiful to pass by without taking at least a few pictures. But the flies outside were more irritating, and after trekking out a few meters, Jane fled back to the comfort of the camper.

Cleo laughed as Jane scrambled back inside. "I see you've decided you don't like Australia's national bird."

"Good grief, are they always this bad?"

"Nah, mostly in the spring."

"They sure are nasty. At least they weren't biting."

Cleo shook her head. "They don't do that though they will crawl in your ears or nose. That can be annoying."

"You can say that again. Doesn't make one want to camp outside."

"Agreed."

Back on the road, the greenery soon petered out, and the land became drier and more barren than it had been above Port Augusta. Low hills appeared on the side of the road. In the near distance sat mounds of dirt that didn't look natural, but there was no evidence of what could have made them. In the distance, Jane thought she could see machines, but they were so far away she couldn't make out what kind they could be. Cleo seemed not to notice the changes, and Jane wondered if she'd been through there so many times it wasn't novel or if this terrain just wasn't that unusual in the outback.

"What's all this about?' she finally asked.

"What?" Cleo looked at her.

"The dirt piles and machines in the distance. And look there." Jane pointed to a painted rectangle posted on what looked like a barbed wire fence. "That looks like a danger sign."

Cleo shrugged. "Oh, yeah. It's for the opal mines."

"Opal mines?" Jane glanced around looking for anything that resembled a mine. Nada.

"Yeah, they mine most of the opals found in Australia here. Actually, most of the opals in the world and some of the best too."

"Where?"

"Here. In pits." She pointed to berms of earth surrounded by large equipment. "There's one over there. They dig a hole, look through the rubble to see if they've found any opals or opal pieces, and if they have, they excavate the area and sift the dirt for the stones. Oh, and there's one of the machines they use in exploration." She pointed at what appeared to be a truck with a crane on the back of it, except the crane had a huge barrel-like attachment hanging off the end of it. "They drop that digger down, and it burrows into the earth. That's what makes all the holes around here with the piles of dirt beside them. They're rather deep, and sometimes people out looking for missed opals in the piles fall into the holes and get hurt or killed."

Jane's eyes widened. "Why don't they fill the holes back up?"

"I guess because fuel's too expensive to waste on that if there's no profit. Or they don't care 'cause it's so barren." Cleo shrugged. "Who knows why the white fellas do what they do."

Jane felt defensive. Cleo's reference to "white fellas" seemed to point directly at her though she wasn't a "fella" and had been in Australia only a couple of weeks. She seemed to blame everything negative on the whites, one of whom Jane decidedly was. It felt unfair, and Jane resented it and decided she needed to stand up for those of her color. "Well, it makes a lot of sense to me. This isn't what I'd call a picturesque landscape, and I'll bet it costs a lot to haul gas this far out. If people are falling in the holes, they shouldn't be messing around them. They should take responsibility."

Cleo gave her a hard look. "So it has to be pretty to you to make a difference?"

"What do you mean?"

"If the land doesn't fit your idea of beauty, then it's OK to trash it? It's not picturesque enough for you? What about all the things that live out there? What about the land itself? It's good if you can make money off of it; otherwise, it's nothing?" Her voice was shrill by the end of her questions.

Jane gripped the steering wheel harder and narrowed her eyes. "Well, aside from opals, what is the good of this place? What use is it? Would there be people out here if not for the gems?"

"Yes!" Cleo spat the word. "My people lived all over this continent before the white fellas came. Everywhere. Out here and everywhere the whites think is too hot or hard or dry to exist. But you came and killed us, drove us off the land, herded us like cattle, caged us in the prisons you call reserves, called us animals, nonhumans, and apes while you raped our women and castrated our men. You gubbas are blind and so self-involved you can see nothing except yourselves. You value nothing that can't be bought with a dollar. You live so far from the land and the wind and the sun that you can't feel the life that pulses through them all. You have dead hearts."

Jane shook her head. "You sound like the hippies and New Agers back home, putting trees and people on the same level. Well, they're not. God gave us this world to make something of it, and if we don't, then we're not fulfilling God's will."

"God!" Cleo crossed her arms and glared out the window. "Your god is an egomaniac and a pathetic excuse for raping and pillaging the land and people different from you with no remorse. Your people have committed thousands of atrocities in his name and have never taken responsibility for any of it."

"That's not true. That's not true," Jane sputtered. "God doesn't do that stuff, and he doesn't like people who rape and pillage, no matter if they are white or black or whatever. People everywhere have used God as an excuse for awful behavior, including blacks. You can't just claim it's the whites who are the problem. What about the black people who sit around doing nothing and then blame the whites for all their problems? What about that?" Her hands clenched the steering wheel and her teeth clamped together so hard her jaw ached.

Cleo opened her mouth to say something when a sign for Coober Pedy appeared on the right. Jane jerked the steering wheel in that direction. The camper rocked with the motion, and Cleo make a grab at the dashboard.

"What the hell are you doing?"

"I need to stop." Jane roared into a gas station, pulled alongside the building, and slammed the gearshift lever into park. Grabbing her purse, she bounded out of the vehicle, keys in hand, and stormed toward the front of the building without looking back.

The clerk behind the counter smiled at Jane as she charged toward the toilets. She sang out "g'day," but Jane made no response. Jerking open the door, she entered the small cubicle marked "Women," latched the door behind her, dropped her purse on the floor, and stomped back and forth in the cramped space. Her breath huffed. She wanted to grab something and tear it to shreds. On one level she didn't understand why she should feel so outraged. Hadn't Cleo voiced some of the same doubts she had herself about the unlimited benevolence of the Almighty when she was deleting her sisters-in-law's emails?

Or was it the indictment of her being one of the white people who had harmed Cleo's people? The Aborigines. The blacks. Even though she came from the other side of the world and wasn't alive when the awful things happened. How could she be to blame? What did she do? All she'd done since meeting Cleo was try and help her, and this was what she got in repayment? Abuse? Accusations? Rejection? What had made her think that she needed this mouthy black girl around her for anything? She was so much better off without her. She wished she were in Alice Springs so she could dump Cleo off on some street corner and be done with her.

After minutes of internal ranting and pacing, she rested her back against the door and took a breath. She needed to calm down if she was going to ride with Cleo to Alice Springs. But did she have to? She paused to consider the option. What did she owe the girl anyhow? She'd brought her all the way up the country from Apollo Bay, rescued her from starvation, bought her food and clothes, offered her a place to stay, taken her to Adelaide so she could collect her money, and put up with rude and childish behavior. In return she had gotten a few meals and dollars for her efforts.

Why not leave her here to hitch her way the last few hundred miles to her destination? Surely there'd be a black person or some other duped white woman or man who'd take her the rest of the way That idea gave her pause. She could see Cleo being taken advantage of, maybe raped, by some outback villain or outlaw. Or not even that. Just some horny truck driver who thought he'd get lucky out in the desert. She'd never hitchhiked herself for that very reason. She might be angry at Cleo, but she didn't want her to come to any harm.

She sighed. Placing her head against the cool metal of the door, she gazed at the bug-speckled ceiling. And she'd made a promise, damn it. Cleo might be a flake, but Jane was a woman of her word, and she would keep her word no matter how hard it was. She'd show her how white people dealt with adversity and conflict. Instead of getting drunk or abandoning Cleo as her father had, she'd deliver Cleo to Alice Springs as she had promised. That was how good people behaved. White or black.

Straightening, she looped her purse straps over her shoulder and opened the door.

Cleo was still sitting in the camper when Jane walked out the door, and she felt a pang of remorse. It had to be abominably hot in the van with the air conditioner off, sitting in the sun without a bit of shade anywhere and no way to roll down the windows without the key. She was surprised Cleo hadn't at least opened a door or walked outside, much less gone inside the cool store. Then again, maybe she was more immune to the heat than Jane was.

Jane strode to the camper and climbed inside. Sticking the keys in the ignition, she turned to Cleo. "You need anything before we get back on the road?" Cleo shook her head, her lips pressed into a dark, tight line. "Fine, then let's get going."

They sat in silence while the desert rolled past the windows and the mounds of mining dirt appeared in the rearview mirror, then not at all. The land remained flat, and Jane pushed the speed limit to the extent she felt comfortable. At least no road trains came by in either direction. With only the sound of the tires on the road and the swoosh of the air-conditioning to fill the space between them, Jane wanted to say something to break the monotony but couldn't seem to find a sentence inside her head that wasn't laced with sarcasm or anger. If she had to put up with Cleo, the least she could do was try and keep the peace between them until they got to Alice.

But she couldn't turn her mind off the argument they'd had, and the more she thought about it, the more she was convinced that Cleo was a reverse racist. Why else would she say the things she did? Why else would she make those accusations? Hadn't she appreciated everything Jane had done for her? The questions and anger circled her like vultures, pecking at her thoughts, making her bleed, inciting her sense of hurt and anger.

From time to time she questioned her own motives and responses to Cleo: going mental, making assumptions that were completely wrong. She remembered the loneliness she had experienced when she thought Cleo had deserted her, but they seemed so childish and self-indulgent now. Was she so weak and spineless that she needed this black girl around to feel OK? Ernie would have agreed with that assessment. Damn it.

The silence between them endured as the sun crept lower in the sky, washing over Cleo through the passenger window as it brushed the horizon. Not another town in sight. Jane was beginning to get worried and hungry. They hadn't passed the border into the Northern Territory yet, and Alice Springs looked to be three to four hours beyond the border. There was no way they were going to make it to the city that night, not if Jane had to drive, and she wasn't keen on relinquishing the wheel to Cleo. But if they were going to stop, they needed a caravan park.

"What towns are between here and Alice?" Jane finally asked.

"Why?" Cleo's voice was harsh and demanding.

"Because I'm tired and need to stop. I want to get something to eat and don't want to drive after dark. There are too many animals on the road, and I can't afford to have an accident in this vehicle. I want to find a nice caravan park and settle in for the night. We can make an early start of it tomorrow."

"Ha! There's nothing out here until we cross into NT. Erldunda is the closest thing after that, but I don't know how far away it is. If you had let me drive, we'd be fine. I've done this before and never had a problem."

"Well, I haven't, and I want to stop. Why don't you see if the GPS can give us any information? It's supposed to do that kind of thing. In the meantime, I'm going to look for a rest area or something."

Cleo narrowed her eyes but complied. She flipped through screens like a pro. She seemed to find something that she found interesting, and she scrolled up what looked from Jane's angle to be a map.

"Nothing, like I told you."

"Does it say how long until we get to Erldo . . . whatever that town was you mentioned?"

"Another two and a half hours."

Jane sighed and shook her head. "That'll be eight at least. We need to stop before that. I'm pulling off at the next rest area, and that's where we're going to spend the night. The guy at the camper place said I could run the electricity on batteries for a while without plugging in, and the stove doesn't need batteries at all."

"I think you should let me drive." Cleo crossed her arms over her chest and frowned out the window.

"And I don't. We're stopping. If you're so hot to get to Alice tonight, then hitchhike."

Turning to face her, Cleo lifted her chin. "I just might."

Jane frowned at her. "Do you want me to pull over now or wait until we find a rest area?"

Cleo tossed her head and looked out the passenger side window again.

They drove until the border marker to Northern Territory. The sun had slipped below the horizon, and Jane pulled into a parking area thankful for a stopping place, even if it wasn't a caravan park or anything resembling one. Cleo seemed to rouse herself from what Jane decided was a full-blown pout the girl had engaged in for the last hour and looked around.

"I don't think you can stay here. You can't camp just anywhere, you know."

Jane pulled the keys from the ignition and reached for her purse. "This isn't anywhere. There are picnic tables and restrooms. I don't see any cops and haven't seen anything about not being able to stay overnight. We're not going to be here for days, just until sunrise. Now I'm going to go to the bathroom and fix something to eat. You're welcome to join me or try and find a ride. Suit yourself."

She didn't see Cleo move as she walked to the back of the camper, but when she opened the back door, she heard the passenger side door slam, and Cleo appeared seconds later.

"I need to get my stuff."

"Fine." Jane stepped aside. Cleo climbed in the back and began rummaging around, stuffing things into her purse. Jane didn't know how she could identify anything in the gloom inside the camper but figured if she wanted a light, she'd have turned one on. If they worked. Jane hadn't tried using the lights without being plugged into an outlet. She reached up and switched on the one over the door, and much to her relief, it blinked on. Cleo didn't seem to notice.

Watching Cleo pull out the drawers and search through them, Jane considered that without Cleo around, she'd be spending the night all alone in the middle of nowhere. It didn't look like anyone else was setting up camp, and she had a vision of a carload of kids stopping and trying to rob her or something. The thought sent a chill down her back. Maybe she should try and get Cleo to stay.

Cleo straightened and shouldered her purse. It bulged with the clothes Jane had bought her, plus the bits of jewelry she'd been working on in the evenings. "That's it. If you find anything I left behind, you can keep it."

Jane stepped out of the doorway and back onto the pavement, Cleo following her. "You sure you won't have something to eat before you go? I can make you a sandwich or something."

"No, thank you. I appreciate all your help. Goodbye." Back straight, she marched into the waning light toward a couple of parked cars.

Well, so much for that, Jane thought, feeling somewhat miffed at the girl's rude departure. At least she had said thank you.

Jane watched her approach a couple of cars, look through the windows, then straighten and stride toward the stone marker emblazoned with "Welcome to the Northern Territory." Cleo approached a couple standing near the monument, and Jane could hear them talking, though she couldn't make out the words. The encounter lasted a minute before Cleo turned and headed for a group standing near one of the picnic tables. Shaking her head, Jane shut the back door and headed for the outside toilet, wondering how Cleo was going to find someone willing to take her with them. Those she had asked obviously said no and no one else was in the parking lot. How many people would be stopping in the dark? Not many, she surmised.

After using the toilet, she threw together a sandwich in the camper's dim light. Without an outside source of electricity, she didn't want to use more than one light since she wasn't sure how long the batteries would last. She ate her dinner, glancing from time to time to see if she could catch sight of Cleo. She hadn't heard any more cars come into the parking area and noticed the other two had left while she was eating. Had Cleo gotten a ride?

She cleaned up, pulled on her jacket, and stepped into the darkness. The sky overflowed with stars, far more than she remembered seeing in Colorado, even up in the mountains. In the distance she could hear the peeping of birds or some kind of night life, but aside from that, the silence seemed deeper than the universe arching over her head. Her eyes adjusted to the dark, and more stars appeared, along with the silhouettes of trees and bushes stretching away from the paved parking lot and canopied picnic tables.

Why hadn't she bothered to look up after dark before this? Was she so involved in whatever she was doing, be it walking to the amenities block or setting up the beds, that she didn't think about scanning overhead? How could she have missed all this? Leaning against the side of the camper, she absorbed the beauty of the night and searched for the Southern Cross, admitting to herself that she wouldn't have recognized it unless there was a huge arrow in the sky pointing it out. She decided she would do this more often from then on.

After a few minutes, she looked around to see if she could see any signs of Cleo. When she couldn't, in spite of her twinges of apprehension that something evil would grab her out there in the dark, she decided to risk it and walk around looking for the girl. Flashlight in hand, she locked the back of the camper and meandered to the monument.

Cleo was sitting on the "Welcome to South Australia" side of the sign, back resting against the stone, purse in the sand at her feet. Her eyes were closed, and she appeared to be sleeping. Jane stared at her for a moment, weighing the pros and cons of talking to her after her abrupt departure. She was still angry about the conversation in Coober Pedy and the way Cleo had left, but she also felt a little guilty she hadn't tried harder to get Cleo to eat something. She still wasn't looking forward to spending the night alone, yet she wasn't sure it would be worth an evening filled with tension to have her back. Finally, she decided the least she should do was try to get her to come and have some food. Whether she would stay the night was negotiable.

As Jane stepped closer, Cleo's eyes flew open and she straightened. "What do you want?"

Jane halted and stiffened. "Whoa. You don't have to bite my head off. I wanted to see if I could talk you into coming back and having something to eat."

"Oh." Cleo crumpled against the stone, shoulders sagging. She looked so pathetic that some of the anger and resentment leached away from Jane. It had been a long, hard day, and she bet Cleo was tired too. If she could let her hurt subside, maybe Cleo could do the same and get over her side of the argument and come back to the camper for some food.

"Come on. It's a bite of food. If a car comes by, you can dash out and try to get your ride. I promise I won't try and stop you. What do you say?"

Cleo sat motionless, then shrugged, and picked up her purse. "Just for a bite. I still want to make Alice tonight."

"Whatever you say. Let's go back."

They walked in silence, the oval glow of the flashlight high-lighting rocks and a few scuttling creatures that emerged with the disappearance of daylight. The cool air smelled of dust. Jane mulled over their argument in her head, trying to understand why she had become so upset when, on review, the actual words exchanged between them didn't seem all that awful. Sure, Cleo had demeaned her idea of God and implied that all whites were money-grubbing ignoramuses who didn't care about anything besides themselves. But hadn't she thought the same things occasionally, depending on the show she was watching on television or the latest book or email she was reading? Or did she become upset because she felt that since she was white, she had been implicated in all the wrongs ever perpetrated against any darker-skinned person, including all of Cleo's people and all of the Africans in the world too? She felt her neck tighten and her hand grip the flashlight a little harder.

It all seemed familiar. Her own assumptions about Cleo and her anger off and on during the entire time they'd been together. Going mental at little things. Deciding Cleo did what she did and said what she said because she was black or young or, even worse, a reverse racist. Wasn't that Ernie's way of categorizing people through and through? And hadn't she decided not to do what Ernie did ever again? And even though it felt unsettling, maybe Cleo had a point or two in her statements, and Jane was just too angry to admit it. What did she know about how a person of another race would think about the world? Rachael had called her on some of her attitudes in the past, and yet here she was spewing out the same rotten things she had heard her parents, Ernie, and his family say over and over. And when she was confronted about them by a real black person, all she could do was revert to the very words she purportedly hated. She felt ashamed.

Jane unlocked the camper, turned on the light, and climbed in, Cleo following. The girl dumped her purse on the seat and leaned on the counter. "You want me to cook?"

Turning, Jane managed a wan smile. "Thanks, but I've eaten. I can fix you something, or you can do it for yourself."

"I'll cook. I'll fix you a cup of tea in the meantime, OK?" Cleo opened a cupboard and pulled out the cutting board and teakettle.

Jane sank onto the seat, speechless for a moment. At last she said, "Thank you so much. That would be lovely."

The change in Cleo's attitude dumbfounded her. Five minutes earlier, the girl was ready to yell at her, and now here she was puttering in the kitchen and fixing her tea. Had she been reconsidering their argument too? Had she thought about her words and realized she was making unfounded allegations based solely on race—and she was wrong to do so? Was she sorry she'd stormed off or sorry about her words?

Jane watched while Cleo chopped ingredients for a salad as her tea steeped. With a smile, she handed Jane the steaming cup, filled her own plate, and plopped down on the seat beside her. For a few minutes she ate in silence, devouring the salad as if she were half-starved. Jane watched, sipping her tea and internally shaking her head in wonder. Cleo slowed down and paused, a forkful of lettuce resting on her plate.

"I appreciate that you came and got me. I was hungry."

Jane smiled. "I can see that."

"Yeah, I guess it's pretty obvious." She turned and flashed Jane a smile, but quickly sobered. Her eyes fell to her plate, her fingers playing with the end of her fork. "Look, I need to apologize for earlier. I shouldn't have burst out of here, and I shouldn't have gotten so angry before that. I just—"

Jane held up her hand. "You don't have to explain. I understand. I was way out of line and owe you an apology too."

"Yes, I do need to explain." She set her plate on the counter and swiveled to face Jane. "And you don't understand, if you don't mind my saying so. How can you? You aren't me. You haven't lived my life or experienced the kind of things I've experienced. Your world is so different from mine, and not only because it's on the other side of the earth. If you had been born and raised here, we still wouldn't inhabit the same world."

Jane felt herself becoming irritated and wanted to blurt out her own apology, but Cleo continued.

"I know you don't understand what I was trying to say, and I have to admit, I didn't say it well. I was angry and not just about you and what you said, but angry about a lot of things, most of which you know nothing about. It all got dumped on you, and I'm sorry about that."

"But . . ."

Cleo raised her hand and shook her head. "Hear me out, please."

Jane let out a sigh and nodded. "Fine. Go on."

"I know a lot of whites, and maybe one of them grasps some of the whole race issue, so I get it that you don't understand. There are so many things that come to you because you're white that I have to fight for all the time. Like hitching a ride. If you had asked the people who were parked here when we arrived, you'd be in Alice by now. But because I'm Abo, I'm assumed to be a drunk or lazy or violent, and nobody wants me in their car with them, not even for a couple of hours."

"But I took you in."

"Yes, you did, and I never expressed how grateful I was for that."

Jane nodded but let Cleo go on.

"It makes me angry when people see my kinky hair or black skin and not me. When I get treated like I'm nothing but a bunch of stereotypes. But more than that, it makes me angry when white fellas," she stared hard at Jane, "you included, dismiss anything that doesn't fit into the way you see the world as a myth or fable or something we simple black fellas made up because we don't know how things work. My people have never been taken seriously, though we've been on this continent for a hundred thousand years. And when you talk about God's plan and how we have to use up everything because it's the way God wants it, you aren't talking about my world and how it works but only your own. And see where that's gotten you. Global warming, environmental catastrophes all over the place, polluted air, land poisoned or ripped apart for gold or gems, dying oceans. That makes me angry, and it makes me angrier when people either deny what's happening or justify it with God.

"And I'm not just angry at you or the other whites. I'm angry at my own people for drinking or drugging, because all that does is make white assumptions about how primitive and unreliable we are seem right. And it hurts us all. It hurts me to see my dad pissed as a family fart and know my mum kicked him out because of it. And I'm angry that I let that asshole Jonny take advantage of me and steal from me when I should have known better. And I'm off to see my dad and don't know if he's going to be bombed out or sober, and that pisses me off too.

"So I'm sorry if I took out all my anger on you. I guess that's it." She picked up her fork and took a bite.

Jane sat still, the mug of tea warm in her hand. Finally, she sighed. "I was wrong. Until this moment I'd never considered that I got things that darker-skinned people didn't just by being white. I don't think you're right about me being able to get a ride to Alice, but I get your point. I'm less of a threat to the average tourist than you, a dreadlocked black girl, but unless the people had room and were going in the right direction and were used to picking up hitch-hikers, I'd still be sitting by the sign too." She sipped her tea, feeling the weight of all the mistakes she had made and the racist beliefs she had parroted enveloping her like a dark shroud. She sighed again.

"Thank you for telling me how you see things. My whole life I've heard awful things about black people, and I believed them without question most of the time. You are the first black person I have known, and now I see that I know only a little about you and your world. I have made some very wrong assumptions, and for that I am sorry. I still don't understand some of the things you were talking about, but I will think about them. I promise."

She lifted her cup to take a drink but lowered it again. Time to be brave. "And I want you to tell me when I'm being racist and unkind and judgmental and generally just a pain in the ass. I don't want to be that way anymore, especially not with you. I hope you can do that for the few hours we have left together." She raised her cup to her lips.

Silence grew between them, like tea steeping, unfinished, only waiting for the moment. Jane sipped and Cleo ate while the tension between them faded away. Finally, Cleo laid her fork on the empty plate.

"I'll clean up my mess and go."

"I would like you to stay. We'll leave at first light, and you'll be in Alice early. I haven't heard any cars come by, and chances are you won't be able to get a ride even if they do. Sleeping here would be far more comfortable than sitting out there." Jane looked at her over the rim of her cup, hoping she would take her up on the offer.

Cleo slid her plate onto the counter and sighed. She looked as if she were playing tug of war inside, part of her wanting to stand by her decision and part wanting to give in. She tapped a finger on the edge of her plate and looked up. "You're probably right. Besides, even if I caught a ride now, it'd be so late by the time I got into Alice that my gran would be asleep, and I wouldn't want to wake her." She turned to Jane. "One more night, OK?"

Jane grinned. "It would be wonderful."

Cleo seemed to relax and smiled in return. "I'll do my dishes, and we can make up the beds."

Jane nodded. "That would be perfect."

Chapter 9

THE ROAR OF A DIESEL MOTOR woke Jane. The sun beat against the curtains, indicating it was far past dawn. "Damn," she muttered, rolling over to find her watch and see how late she had slept. Above her, the boards shifted, and Cleo grunted. So she had also slept in. That was good, Jane thought, since it wasn't just her fault they weren't on the road. She didn't need to feel guilty at all.

"We overslept," Jane said, throwing off the blanket and edging toward the back of the camper. "It's almost eight. I guess we're not going to be in Alice early."

"Bugger." Cleo shifted, and her legs appeared over the edge of the upper berth. "You going to the toilet?"

"Yeah. Want to come or wait till I get back?"

"I'll wait."

Jane wriggled her way out of the camper, pulling up her pants as she did so. The day was clear and warming. Parked near the monument, a huge truck towing a camper disgorged an overweight couple and three kids, all bickering and yelling at one another. Shaking her head, Jane strode to the toilets, glad she wasn't part of the fracas and wishing they would have waited until she was on the road before they made their appearance. Not a nice way to start the day.

By the time she returned, Cleo had made both beds and was firing up the teakettle. Jane was still amazed at the change in attitude. Early to bed. Busy the minute she got up. Too bad Cleo couldn't have acted like that for most of the trip.

"Your turn." She climbed into the camper and slid across the seat to grab her brush. "You want something hot for brekky or just a bagel?"

"Make me whatever you're going to have. I won't be long." Cleo jumped out the back and disappeared around the side of the camper.

Jane pulled out a box of cereal and a carton of milk. Fast was better than hot and slow, she decided, while she filled the mugs with hot water and plopped a tea bag in each. The family members were still shouting at one another, and she didn't want to stick around to hear more of it than she had to. Maybe they'd leave quickly.

But they didn't, and by the time she and Cleo had finished eating, stowed everything, and backed out of the lot, the kids were digging in the sand in a shadow cast by the stone, and the parents had pulled out lawn chairs. Good riddance, Jane thought, and eased onto the highway, chanting "left side, left side" to herself.

The landscape became greener the longer they drove, with more bushes and trees, but beneath it all, red, red, red. Red sand, red rocks, red dust. It even smelled red. The dirt and sand had shifted to red after they left Port Augusta, but it seemed redder now against the contrasting foliage. In some places it looked almost purple. She mentioned it to Cleo, who replied, "Of course. They call it the Red Centre, after all."

Well, duh, Jane thought. I should have figured that one out.

It took an hour to reach Erldunda, and Jane glanced down the road that led to Uluru, wishing Cleo wanted to come with her to the sacred Aboriginal place. But it wasn't to be, and she made a note to herself that she would come back when she could, maybe right after dropping Cleo off if it wasn't too late. Then again, maybe she could get Cleo to show her around Alice Springs, and that would be worth spending a night or two in the town.

Cleo had pulled out her MP3 player and had her earbuds in, listening to something with a heavy backbeat and staring out the window. Jane glanced at her occasionally, wondering what made the girl tick. She had more than intimated that Jane didn't have a clue about her life or her world and, while Jane assumed that Cleo's world was more or less like the world Jane had inhabited when she was in her twenties, she now wondered.

Cleo's skin color probably did make a difference—and in ways Jane couldn't imagine. She had so little experience with black people. There were a couple of boys on the football team when she was in college, but she never met them, and one girl in her English 101 class her freshman year. She couldn't recall saying hello to her. Cortez had no black families. Indian families, yes, but no black ones. She didn't know any Indians and was most familiar with the Ute Mountain Ute Tribe through the stories about them being drunk in the park.

Ernie laughingly called them park rangers and wanted all of them thrown in jail. If he'd had his way, the whole population of Towaoc on the Ute Mountain Ute Reservation, twenty miles outside of Cortez, would have been thrown in jail and the town torn down and given to "hardworking" people, which meant anyone who wasn't a minority. Several of the men he worked with on the rigs were Mexican, and he never had a good word to say about them either. He even threatened to move when a Mexican family with six kids bought the house next to theirs. Even though they were exemplary neighbors and helped Jane out when Ernie was out of town, he never spoke to them or their kids and never spoke kindly of them either. She had thought he was foolish, but she never questioned the beliefs underlying his actions. In truth, she didn't have a clue what those beliefs were except that if you weren't white, you weren't worth anything. His family felt the same way.

Every so often, Rachael would make comments about some of the things Jane said about minorities. She remembered when she'd taken Ernie to Denver General Hospital for tests when he started to get sick. She'd come back and had coffee with Rachael the next day, just to blow off steam about the trip.

"It was a horror," she had said, sipping her latte, the hubbub of their favorite coffee shop so loud that Jane felt she had to yell to be heard. "He was such a jerk about everything. He fought with the guy who was doing the MRI and wouldn't let him touch him because he was black. He demanded that someone else do the test, and I thought they were going to sedate him he was so loud. I was so embarrassed."

Rachael shook her head and sighed.

"And the place was crawling with Mexicans. We had to go in through the ER, and the waiting room was filled with them, none of them speaking English. They wouldn't let me stay with Ernie at the MRI, and when I objected, they said it was a hospital rule."

Rachael frowned. "That doesn't sound right. When my Jack had his MRI, they let me go with him and only shooed me out of the room while they were running the machines."

"Well, that's not the way they did it there." Jane placed her cup on the table and looked up. "Maybe it was because of the Mexicans. Maybe they were worried about them carrying germs. Everyone knows they're dirty."

Rachael's eyes widened, and she placed her cup back on the table. "You can't be serious."

She shrugged. "What?"

"Did you hear what you just said?"

Jane shook her head, lost. "What are you talking about?"

Rachael took a deep breath and closed her eyes for a moment. When she reopened them, she gave Jane a hard stare. "Do you really believe that all Mexicans are dirty and carry germs, and that's why you weren't allowed in with Ernie?"

"Well . . ." Jane paused. Did she believe what she had just said? Maybe. Well, some Mexicans, maybe most, or maybe only the ones who came to the ER. She wasn't sure but felt there had to be some kernel of truth to her statement. Then again. "What do you think?" she hedged.

Rachael sighed once more. "Where did you ever come up with that notion?"

"I don't know. I guess I heard it somewhere or maybe read it."

"Didn't your mother ever tell you not to believe everything you read or hear?" Rachael gave her a wry smile.

Jane felt cornered. "So you're trying to tell me it isn't true."

"I'm not trying to tell you anything," she replied, shaking her head. "I want you to think about what you say about other people and maybe question some of your assumptions."

"So why do *you* think they wouldn't let me stay with Ernie?" Jane straightened and glared at her friend.

Rachael threw up her hands. "I don't know, but I don't think it was because there were a lot of Mexican Americans in the hospital. Maybe it was because Ernie was being a total bastard, and they felt they could control him better if you weren't there."

Jane opened her mouth to reply and then stopped. Ernie was being a total asshole that day, and sometimes he did behave better when she wasn't around. Could that have been the real reason? Or did Ernie say something about Mexicans on the drive home that she had sucked up as the truth instead of thinking about it at all?

She felt ashamed and wished she could sink into the floor. How many people had heard her remark and how many now thought she was some kind of racist? If she had those thoughts, didn't that make her a racist? And is that what she wanted to be?

Rachael must have seen the change in her because she reached out and placed a hand over hers. "Jane, it's OK."

Jane dropped her eyes and took another sip of her latte. She felt on the verge of tears and didn't want to lose it in public, and she was worried that if she said anything, the words would come out washed in tears.

"Jane, did I hurt you? I didn't mean to. It's just sometimes I don't understand where you're coming from."

"I'm such a fool." Her voice was a whisper, tightly wound around the words.

"Oh, honey, you're just learning." Rachael patted her hand. "Unless you grow up with parents who teach you to respect differences instead of demeaning them, how are you to know? Ernie hasn't been a shining example for you either. Now you're beginning to figure things out." She gave her hand a squeeze and smiled.

Jane wasn't sure how much she had learned since that conversation, and some of her interactions with Cleo seemed to indicate it wasn't very much—if anything. And now Cleo was leaving. How was she ever going to get better?

Erldunda was in the rearview mirror, and the highway ahead was a black slash through a red landscape. Jane tried to think of something to say to Cleo to strike up a conversation but was blank. She wanted to ask her more about her people and their traditions and ideas, but she couldn't think of a good way to broach the subject without alienating Cleo more than she had already. She hadn't been very open to talking about it in the past, and Jane didn't think anything had changed in that regard. She wanted their last few hours together to be pleasant, not frittered away in silence.

"Where does your grandmother live in Alice?" she finally asked, loud enough, she hoped, to be heard over the music.

Cleo popped one of the earbuds out. "What?"

"I asked where your grandmother lives in Alice."

"No worries. I'll show you when we get there." She started to put the earbud back in place.

"How much farther do you think it is?" Jane said quickly.

Cleo shot her a vexed look. "I don't know. A hundred kilometers or so. How far have we come since Erldunda?"

Jane peered at the odometer but couldn't remember what it read when they left the parking lot that morning, much less when they passed Erldunda. "Well, it's been about twenty minutes."

"In that case, it's going to take at least another two hours to get there." Cleo huffed and crossed her arms. "You feeling tired? You want me to drive?"

Jane was about to protest that she was doing fine, thank you, and then thought if Cleo was driving, maybe she'd have a better shot at getting her to talk. "Yeah. Why don't you take over? Then you won't have to give me directions to your grandmother's house."

Pulling the other earbud out and wrapping the wires around her MP3 player, Cleo sat up and looked interested. Jane slowed and pulled onto the shoulder, making sure she got all the wheels off the pavement. The last thing she needed was to be sideswiped by a road train while they were changing drivers.

Cleo settled in behind the wheel, looking happier than she had since Jane took over the driving. Jane smiled, glad such a small thing had made a difference to the girl.

"So tell me about your grandmother." She angled against the door so she could face Cleo.

"Whatcha want to know?"

"Anything, I guess. How old is she? Where did she grow up? Does she have any other kids besides your dad?" Jane half expected Cleo to shoot her one of her aggravated looks, but instead she appeared somewhat wistful.

"Nah, Dad was her only one. She had him when she was pretty

young, about sixteen or so, I think, and she told me she swore she'd have no more until she found a good man to help raise them. I guess she never found what she was looking for since it's just been her alone ever since I can remember."

"Has she always lived in Alice?"

Cleo cocked her head and seemed to think about it for a minute. "I think she was born somewhere west of Alice, maybe in WA. I think she said around Yuendumu, but I don't remember. All I know for certain is that I've never been there. She's been in Alice all my life."

"WA? Where's that?"

"Western Australia. It covers most of the west part of the continent. You should look at a map."

Jane frowned at the jibe but decided she wasn't going to let it get to her. "What's she like, your grandmother?"

"What's *your* gran like?"

Jane shook her head. "My maternal grandmother died when I was very young, so I never knew her. My father's mother lived on the East Coast, half a continent away from us. I think I saw her maybe four times in my life. She wasn't the grandmotherly type. She didn't want to cuddle me or any of us kids, and she didn't bake us chocolate chip cookies or anything. She'd married this rich Jew after she divorced my grandfather and moved to Florida, so she sat on the beach a lot and drank mai tais all day, I guess. How about yours?"

"I don't know what a mai tai is, but Gran never drank one. She never drank at all. I always kinda wondered why my dad took to the bottle the way he did when Gran was so sober. Maybe he was making up for her."

"You spend much time with her growing up?"

Cleo smirked. "You'd think not, what with Mum in Melbourne

and Gran in Alice Springs. But Dad took me to Gran's a lot, especially before he and Mum split up. We'd go out for a couple of weeks at a time, a couple or three times a year. I once spent a whole summer there. We got along splendidly, Gran and I."

"How did she support herself all those years? I'm guessing she's been on her own for a very long time."

Cleo shrugged. "She paints mostly. Sells some to the galleries but also hangs out on Todd Street, selling her work to the tourists. Gets a better price that way."

"Dot paintings?" Jane straightened. She'd read about the Aboriginal dot paintings and had seen a few in books and had always wanted to see more. Now here she sat with someone who was maybe related to someone who made them.

"Sure, among other styles. She has a few stories she can paint, but she does other things too."

"Stories she can paint?" Jane shook her head. "Can't she paint anything she wants to?"

Cleo glanced at her. "Well, sure. But some of the patterns of the dot paintings are sacred and can only be done by certain people. Gran can do a few, but that's not where she makes most of her money. She has lots of other designs she makes."

"I'd sure like to see some of her work."

"Maybe she'll show you some." Cleo shrugged. "That is, if she's home."

"She may not be home?"

"No worries. I have a key, and you can drop me off. I've been in and out of Gran's house on my own for years."

"Oh." Jane felt disappointed. Her chance to meet a real Aboriginal woman artist had come and perhaps gone in the space of a breath. She wished she would have asked Cleo these questions earlier instead of being aggravated with her. She should have taken more time to find out about her life. Ernie had always said she was too focused on herself, and here she had proved him right again. She sighed.

"So is she famous?"

Cleo burst into laughter. "You people. That's all you care about, being famous, making lots of money."

Jane felt indignant. "That's not true. I was only wondering if I'd maybe seen any of her work."

Cleo shot her a sideways glance. "How many native paintings have you seen, and did you ever try to find out anything about the artist?"

"Well . . ." She'd seen a few in books at the library when she was dreaming about Australia and what she'd do if she ever got there. But she'd never thought about finding out about the artist—not that she could remember if any of the paintings listed the artist. She wouldn't have searched out anything about a white artist either if she had seen a painting she liked. But she didn't approve of the tone of Cleo's voice, insinuating that she wouldn't do such a thing because her grandmother was an Aborigine.

"Ha, that's what I thought." Cleo tossed her head and smirked.

"It's not what you think," Jane protested.

"Yeah, what?"

She sighed, not wanting to get into another argument. "OK, I've seen only a few dot paintings in books, and I don't know who painted them."

"Like I thought. You white fellas think because you have a little knowledge, you know everything."

No, we don't, Jane wanted to counter but instead lapsed into silence. She couldn't think of anything to say that wouldn't further provoke Cleo and decided she'd prefer to ride the rest of the way without talking rather than fight. Slumping against the door, she watched the landscape roll by, wishing to see a kangaroo or some other exciting Australian animal to distract her, but nothing appeared except more bushes and trees and a few low hills.

Still, she roiled inside, part of her defending herself against imagined onslaughts and the other part deriding herself for being racist or at least too self-involved to have done more research before climbing on the plane. Ernie's voice seemed to intone the latter position, which left her feeling more unworthy. With each mile she seemed to feel worse—until she was afraid she would burst into tears again for no good reason. That's what she needed to finish off this relationship with Cleo, to break down like a crazy woman in the middle of the desert. If she were Cleo, she'd want to run away from her too. She prayed that Cleo's grandmother would be at home, so she could at least get to meet her and say hi. Providing, that is, she wouldn't say anything that would further embarrass herself.

Cleo seemed content to let Jane sit and stew while one hour bled into the next. The girl had replaced her earbuds after the first few minutes and tapped the steering wheel in time to her music. After what seemed an endless torture, a brown stone sign appeared, announcing they'd reached Alice Springs.

Cleo pulled off the Stuart Highway soon after entering the city and wound through neighborhoods of run-down clapboard houses with corrugated tin roofs; most of them needed a coat of paint and had lawns that consisted of dried grass or dirt behind chain-link fencing. It appeared depressing to Jane, and she hoped Cleo's grandmother lived in a better section of town. But Cleo pulled up in front of one of the dilapidated buildings and parked.

"Here we are," she announced. Opening the door, she bounced to the pavement, keys in one hand and purse in the other. Before Jane could get her seat belt off, Cleo had let herself through the gate and was on the doorstep. She didn't knock, but turned the knob and pushed on the door. When it didn't open, she reached behind a bush and extracted a key. Jane arrived in time to see her open the door and step inside, calling for her gran. Jane waited outside the fence, not wanting to intrude. A few moments later Cleo reappeared.

"Looks like she's not here. Must be down on Todd Street or just out. Too bad. I would have liked you to meet her. I'll get my stuff, and you can be on your way."

Crestfallen, Jane watched while Cleo opened the back of the camper and pulled out a few extra things she hadn't managed to stuff back in her purse from the night before. "I would have liked to meet her too," she said as Cleo glanced around the camper and shut the door. Cleo handed her the keys, and Jane brightened.

"Say, why don't I buy you lunch for a going-away present. Are there any places to eat on Todd Street? Maybe we can see your gran there, and I'll buy her lunch too."

Cleo shook her head. "Thanks, but no. I've had my fill of driving for a while and want to hang out until Gran gets back." Unexpectedly, she wrapped her arms around Jane and squeezed. "Thanks again for everything. I hope the rest of your trip is good. Maybe you'll come back sometime."

For the second time that morning, Jane didn't know what to say. She hugged Cleo back, a little awkwardly, then released her and stepped away. "I'm glad I got to know you. I just wish I'd done it sooner in our travels. Hope you have a wonderful life."

"Same to you," Cleo replied.

Jane watched Cleo as she trotted up the sidewalk and into the house before shuffling back around to the side and climbing in the van. She sat for a long while, staring out the windshield, keys dangling from her fingers, feeling lost and lonely. So much for that. Over a week of being together day and night, sharing adventures, and it all ends in a short hug and brief thanks. So abrupt.

Jane sighed. Now what? What should she do? Where should she go? A fog seemed to have invaded her brain and clogged up the neurons until she couldn't organize a thought or make a decision. The heat of the sun beating on metal roused her enough that she started the engine and cranked up the air-conditioning. The cool air revived her a little, enough to put the van in drive and edge away from the curb. She felt conspicuous parked in front of the house and worried that Cleo was staring at her from the window wondering if she'd lost it again. But she didn't know where to go or which way to turn to get back to the Stuart Highway. After wandering up and down a couple of blocks, she parked again and started searching for Todd Street on the GPS.

She barely remembered how to use the thing but managed to fumble through finding Alice Springs and punching in "Todd Street," though the latter didn't produce any usable results. Disgusted with herself, she almost turned it off when she remembered it had a map function. Once more she fiddled until she found a map of Alice and located Todd Street. It took a few more minutes to decipher where she was on the map and how to get to Todd, but once she had it, she headed out again.

Todd was closer than she thought, and after circling a few blocks, she was able to find a parking lot. She planned to walk down the street and see what there was to see, but as she was climbing out of the vehicle, she remembered Geoff's sheaf of pamphlets and adverts.

It took several minutes of sorting before she located anything to do with Alice Springs. The first one was a full-color trifold that contained a map with starred tourist attractions and short descriptions in tiny print on the bottom. Jane squinted at the text but gave up trying to read them and concentrated on the places where most of the stars were located. The Todd Street Mall. How convenient. Bundling up the other papers, she stuck the map into her purse and climbed out into the sunshine.

After the cool of the camper, the heat was searing. Though it was noon, it felt like a hundred degrees, and Jane didn't have an umbrella or anything to keep her the least shaded. By the time she found the trees on the mall, she felt cooked, though it was only a few blocks from the van. She wanted a cold drink and a place to cool off, maybe a bit of lunch, though she wasn't hungry. But it would give her something to do while she figured out what she would do now that she was alone again.

After passing several cafés, she decided on one with tables scattered under the trees with a good view of the people drifting up and down the brick walkway, poking in and out of the shops, and clustering in groups beneath awnings. She ordered a sandwich, latte, and water and then settled at a table facing the mall, the map open under her hand.

A sense of purposelessness washed over her, and there seemed no reason to move again—nothing to do, nowhere to go. She tried to find a word for the feeling—empty, lonely, lost, sad, depressed—but nothing seemed to fit. She felt she had been wrung out and left hanging over a tree branch, discarded, no longer needed or useful. At least when Cleo was with her, she had a destination and purpose, though that seemed to be shouting at the girl most of the time.

And when Ernie was alive, she'd had a purpose, even if it was just to wait on him like a slave and hate every minute of it. And when he died, she had a direction—south, south until there were kangaroos and koalas. Run away. Run away fast. Run away far. So here she was, far away at last, where she had dreamed of being, and completely alone.

Alone. Something she'd always thought she'd treasure. Something she had sought back home. Something she'd only shared with Rachael. But no Rachael now. No Ernie. No Cleo. No one but herself. And she didn't want to be alone with herself very much at all.

She wanted to collapse her head onto the table and sob, but propriety withered her tears and kept her back upright and straight. She stared, letting the grief and self-recriminations gnaw her insides bloody while the world swam by. It wasn't until a tanned youth with a 200-watt smile delivered her food and drink that she pried herself from her misery. She thanked him, amazed that he graced her with his smile, and she watched him walk back into the café, the rear end of his blue jeans winking from under the flaps of the calf-length apron wrapped around his waist.

As she sat, something shifted inside; an atom twitched and sidled away from the darkness, resettling itself in sunnier climes.

Just a single atom migrating. She drew in a breath, smelled the roasted pepper on her sandwich, the aroma of coffee drowned in milk, the hot green of the leaves overhead, the tang of red earth. She heard muted conversations, distant laughter, the bass rumble of a didgeridoo, the shuffle of feet on brick. She watched sunlight drench the russet boulders among the trees and the reflections from shop windows with yellow, black, and red flags festooned behind them. She took in dot-encrusted snakes in oil paints situated next to canvases festooned with whorls, footprints, or spiky flowers all exploding with color, and exhaled. She should call Rachael.

Chapter 10

TWO DAYS LATER, Rachael listened to Jane whine without comment about Cleo's leaving, how she was now all on her own, how lonely she felt, how she wasn't sure what to do. When Jane wound down, she said: "Well, kiddo, I guess it's time to grow up."

Jane almost dropped her new cell phone. This wasn't what she wanted; she wanted sympathy, understanding, help in figuring things out, not some off-handed remark. Didn't she understand how hard it was? Didn't she understand the gnawing aloneness? The lack of physical presence for days on end? She could feel the emptiness filling her chest, taking up residence in her gut, inhabiting her arms and legs. She'd never felt this before, and she didn't enjoy it at all. She sputtered for a second and said, "Thanks a lot."

A sigh issued from the cell. "Jane, haven't you got what you set out to get? You wanted to get far away from Ernie and your life here, and as I recall, you said in your first email to me that you needed to be on your own for a while to try and figure out who you were. Well, here you are. On your own. This is what you wanted. Now you want to bitch about it because it isn't what you expected? Give me a break."

Jane's shoulders slumped. Rachael was right. This is what she had set out to find; she just didn't expect it to be anything like this. She thought she'd be happy, feeling free, unfettered, and joyful bopping around Australia without a care in the world. Not sad, alone, and directionless. She felt tears well up. She wanted someone to hug. "I don't know what to do."

"Do what you want. Didn't you say you wanted to see Ayers Rock?"

"Uluru," Jane corrected, remembering Cleo's insistence that she use the Aboriginal name and feeling a little superior she remembered to use it to correct Rachael, who seemed to know everything.

"Fine. Uluru. Go see it. Go to the Great Barrier Reef. See the Sydney Opera House. Find a kangaroo. Whatever. The longer you sit and tell yourself how miserable you are, the longer you'll be miserable."

That wasn't what she wanted to hear either, though it rang true. She tried to muster a comeback but surrendered. "I guess you're right." She tried to put some enthusiasm into her voice, but it fell flat.

"Of course I'm right." Jane imagined Rachael throwing back her shoulders and shaking her head, her characteristic response when Jane conceded a point. "So, tell me, what are you going to do when I hang up the phone? Which is going to happen in about two minutes. I have to go to work, remember?"

"I guess I'll check out of the caravan park and head down to Uluru. But I need to go shopping first. I haven't stocked up since Cleo left, and that's been a couple of days."

"Good plan." Jane could hear Rachael fumbling with something in the background. "I'm so glad you called. I've missed talking to you more than I can say. Call me again after you've seen your rock and tell me what it's like. Or email me, but I'd rather hear your voice. Carry on, kiddo." And she was gone.

The phone made a funny sound, and Jane looked at the screen, wondering what was going on. But it seemed to be back at the home screen, like the salesgirl had shown her when she purchased the thing.

Even though she felt chastised, she felt so much better having heard Rachael's voice. It felt like she was just around the corner, except that the corner was about 10,000 miles and a day and a half away. This was so much better than email, and she chided herself for not having thought about it sooner. Even Cleo, the little tech girl that she was, hadn't mentioned that she could get a phone and call the States whenever she wanted. Jane felt a surge of pride she had thought of something Cleo hadn't. Maybe she wasn't such a loser after all.

Setting the phone on the seat beside her, she stood and glanced around her tiny home away from home. It was all hers again. It would be strange driving around without Cleo to tell her where to go or help out with the driving and cooking, but as Rachael had reminded her, it was what she had wanted in the first place. Still, the silence that leaked from the corners seemed filled with loneliness just waiting to grab her and sink her into darkness again.

She sighed and glanced at her watch. Almost three. Too late to check out of the caravan park without paying for a night she wouldn't use, and after shopping, it would be dark before she got to Erldunda, and who knows how late by the time she made it to Uluru. Maybe she could shop and then see what kind of nightlife Alice had to offer. She hadn't done much more than mope around the camper since she'd dropped Cleo off, and she wanted to do some exploring. She was sure Rachael would approve, though her own enthusiasm level was tepid at best. But better to move than let the sadness eat her whole.

In spite of the heat, Jane walked to the nearest Coles supermarket and filled her shopping bags. The trip back was exhausting but interesting. She'd passed quite a few dark-skinned people walking along the sidewalks who looked like Aborigines, at least what she'd come to think Aborigines looked like: darker than the darkest black person she'd ever seen, with wide noses, prominent lower faces, narrow foreheads, and hair that appeared coarse and unkempt in shades from black to reddish blond. All of them were barefoot. That in itself amazed her, considering the sidewalk and pavement had to be blistering, and some of them were wearing sweaters or coats in the heat. How they managed that, she couldn't fathom. It was hard for her to guess what the ages were, anywhere from early thirties to seventy, so she ended up wondering if each one she passed could be Cleo's gran. Did she walk around barefoot in a coat? Is that how she hawked her paintings?

When she'd gone to the Todd Street Mall, she'd looked for people selling their paintings on the street, but the one person who came close to filling the description was a man, and he had set up his work in the shade of a large gum tree on the grass in front of an official-looking building. If she were a braver person, she might have stopped and asked him if he knew Cleo's gran, but since she didn't know her name, she didn't think anyone would recognize the woman if she called her "Cleo's grandmother." And she wasn't brave enough to approach the man anyway. So she watched the natives walk by and wondered, feeling like a coward.

By the time she reached the camper, she was hot, sweaty, and thirsty beyond comprehension—not to mention tired. Again, she thought of the people she'd seen on the streets in bare feet and sweaters and shook her head. After showering and eating a quick dinner, however, she felt revived enough to screw up her courage and try the Todd Street Mall again. She figured if anything interesting was going on at night for the average tourist, that was the place it would be.

The evening crowd had settled into restaurants by the time Jane wandered down the brick walkway of the mall. She heard music wafting from the pubs and was tempted to go inside but decided she'd check the whole thing out before she settled on a particular place. It also gave her time to work up her courage. She couldn't remember ever having gone to a bar by herself, and she felt awkward and exposed when she thought about it. But she didn't want to go back to the camper without trying something new—and getting a drink on her own in a strange bar was new. Then again, maybe something more appealing would show up.

About halfway down the mall she saw a group of people milling about a storefront, as if they were waiting for something to happen. When she neared them, she heard the same didgeridoo music she'd heard the day she dropped Cleo off. At the time she thought she'd been imagining it, but there it was again, the low rhythmic buzz of it, mysterious and inviting. She smiled and quickened her pace. Maybe this was her adventure.

The store windows were filled with brightly painted, long wooden pipe-like things, CDs by an Aboriginal-looking man by the name of Jeshuar, decorated drums of various sizes, dot paintings in multiple sizes, boomerangs, and rocks. Jane looked at the rocks, trying to decide if they were there for effect or for sale. She wouldn't have spent good money on what appeared to be a plain, ordinary (OK, genuine Australian) rock, but there were probably a few gullible people in the millions of tourists who frequented Alice Springs every year.

As she worked her way closer to the door, she noticed a placard announcing a concert that evening, in about fifteen minutes. So that's what the crowd was all about. The Jeshuar guy was supposed to be playing "Authentic Aboriginal Tunes" with his band, which was also labeled as "authentic," all for a mere fifty dollars. She paused at the price, then thought, what the hell? It sure beat hanging out in a bar with strangers.

The girl taking the money was the least authentic person Jane could imagine, with her long blond braids, freckled nose, and ice-blue eyes. She collected Jane's cash and handed her a pasteboard square with a picture of Jeshuar on it above "Desert Sirens Theatre" in crooked lettering. She guessed that was supposed to represent "authentic" Aboriginal writing, but to her it just looked like a bad type font.

Following a couple conversing in what she took to be German, Jane entered a room about the size of a large living room; it was half-filled with metal folding chairs in front of a stage containing a couple of drum sets, several of the long wooden pipe things that

Jane decided must be didgeridoos, an electronic keyboard, and what appeared to be a badly stuffed emu. Somehow she doubted the keyboard and drum sets were all that "authentic." She found a seat near the back of the room in an unoccupied corner as people filed in until most of the chairs were filled. Her watch informed her the show was running ten minutes late.

The crowd was comprised of white people in various sizes and shapes, not a brown or black face among them. Was it only her, or was this a total rip-off designed for the ignorant tourist who was looking for some kind of native experience? She'd had her native experience with Cleo or a variation of an experience that included a native, well, part native at any rate. She felt at least one step ahead of the game.

Ten minutes later she was still sitting alone in her little corner of the room. Empty chairs were scattered here and there, and she wondered if they were waiting for a full house before they began. But a couple of minutes later, two men shuffled onstage and settled behind the drum sets; a third, looking very "authentic" in just a loincloth and white dots painted in crooked lines down his arms and torso, settled onto a stool in the middle of the stage. His skin was deep ebony, and his rather large potbelly hung over the top of his loincloth. One last man sidled around the back and took his place at the keyboards. Music flowed from the speakers, orchestral and dreamy—prerecorded, she decided, since no one had touched an instrument—while the house lights lowered and a spotlight illuminated the central figure.

"This is our story," he began in a voice whose timbre was far into the bass range. Instead of continuing to speak, he raised a didgeridoo to his lips and produced a sound so low and thrumming that Jane felt her sternum vibrate in harmony with it. Holy shit, she thought, and she closed her eyes to fully experience the sensations it evoked. Keyboards joined the burr, followed by drums, and before she could take a breath, the music gathered her up and dropped her in the land she'd read and dreamed about since she was a kid.

It wasn't so much the landscape she'd seen from the road, though that was enveloped in the music too, but this was a more elemental land—hot, red, and dry, with a pale, azure cup of a sky turned over it, the land that wavered like a mirage behind Cleo's words when she talked about her people. The land that the presentation in Brambuk cultural center back in the Grampians was trying to portray and that she didn't get—until now. One piece flowed into the next with little by way of introduction or explanation. She opened her eyes at intermission and was shocked to see a man seated on one side of her and a large woman in a flowered dress on the other side. She stood to go to the bathroom, feeling somewhat self-conscious that she hadn't noticed anyone come in after the show started. I guess that's what you call transported, she thought.

The second half of the show was also thrilling, though this time she kept her eyes open and saw that the music was accompanied by pictures and short videos projected onto a screen behind the musicians. Near the end, the performers passed out painted rocks and sticks to the audience members, who were invited to join in the last number by striking them together. Jane tried to stay with the beat but felt lost and embarrassed by her lack of rhythm. The man next to her seemed to be struggling too, and he shot her a nervous smile and a shrug at one point since they were banging along not in sync with anyone else. Finally, all the percussion instruments were collected, and Jeshuar invited them to tour the shop and purchase a CD—"only $22.95 each."

Amid the crowd, Jane shuffled out into the larger shop and wandered to a corner where a variety of didgeridoos were leaning haphazardly against the wall. Each was painted in bright colors with designs of animals and things she couldn't identify. Besides their being musical instruments, she thought they were works of art. She reached out to touch a carving when a voice from behind her startled her.

"You like the kangaroo dreaming?"

She whirled around to face the man who'd been seated beside her. "Oh dear. Sorry. The what?" For no understandable reason, she felt her cheeks flush and lowered her eyes.

"The kangaroo dreaming. That's the story that's emblazoned on that one." He smiled, his teeth even, straight, and exceptionally white under the dim lights of the shop. "Well, at least one of the dreamings." His accent was soft and lyrical, nothing at all like the Crocodile Dundee accent she associated with—albeit had yet to hear from—male Australians.

"What do you mean, dreamings?"

"Stories, tales, creation myths. How the kangaroo got her pouch. Why she has such long ears. And so on."

She brightened. "Oh, similar to the stories the Native Americans back home tell."

"Back home? Just where is back home?" He hooked his hands into the back pockets of his chinos and leaned forward.

Feeling crowded with nowhere to go except into the stack of didgeridoos, she pressed back until she felt them against her spine. At least he didn't call her an American. "Colorado, in the States. I live next to an Indian reservation."

"Colorado, eh?" He rocked back on his heels, and Jane took a deep breath, edging away from the instruments.

"Yes, a little town called Cortez."

"That wouldn't be near the Four Corners, would it?"

She paused, surprised. "Why yes, it is. Have you heard of it?"

"Heard of it? I've been there a couple of times. My ex adored Durango, and we took several vacations to the area."

"You sound Australian."

His grin widened. "From Queensland, actually. I have a ranch in the outback near the border with NT. Around Camooweal. Been there?

She shook her head. "I haven't made it that far. I've been driving the Stuart Highway up from Port Augusta."

"Too bad. It's lovely territory." He glanced around the room. "Are you planning on buying anything or looking around some more? If you're ready to leave, I'd love to take you to a great little pub I know. You can tell me about Cortez, and I'll tell you about outback ranching."

Jane's stomach flipped and filled with some version of Aussie butterflies. Or maybe just the good old American kind. Oh shit! She hadn't been out on a date or alone with a man besides Ernie since somewhere in the mid-1990s. What should she do? If she said yes, what would that mean, if anything? That she was some kind of loose woman because Ernie had been dead only a few weeks? Or just a grieving wife having a fling to forget? Or a woman released from a god-awful relationship taking advantage of her freedom? She wished she could whip out her cell phone and call Rachael for advice. She touched her hair, then her cheek, then thought, what the hell? No one here knew her history, so she could do what she wanted without judgment. She smiled.

"Well, I wanted to get one of the CDs, but I guess I could come back tomorrow. Where is this pub of yours?"

He extended his elbow toward her. "Just down the block. Follow me. By the way, I'm Neal. And you?"

"Jane."

"Nice to meet you, Jane."

They wound their way through the thinning crowd, smiling at Jeshuar behind the counter when they left. Outside, the temperature had dropped, and Jane shivered in the chill. Neal breezed along, not bothered by the cool evening air. He also was wearing pants and a long-sleeved shirt, while her top was sleeveless and flimsy, and her legs were bare below her shorts. Her goose bumps had fully blossomed by the time he led her into an impressive brick building and down a set of stairs. The lights dimly illuminated the steps, and she was grateful to hold Neal's arm while they descended. By the time they reached the bottom, her eyes had adjusted, and she could make out wooden booths lining the walls of the pub.

He settled her into one of the booths and headed off to obtain "two of Australia's finest lagers." Jane would have preferred a glass of wine or a Bloody Mary or margarita—not that she knew if they understood what a margarita was—but Neal hadn't asked what she wanted, and she didn't protest either. She figured she could make it through a beer. It felt a little like living with Ernie, except this man was more handsome, in much better shape, and seemed a whole lot nicer. And she was flattered that he had offered to buy her a drink. She felt old and frumpy and not the least bit attractive, especially to a good-looking man. That Neal would stop and talk to her did more for her ego than all of Rachael's pep talks.

Neal arrived with two mugs filled with foaming amber ale. He set them on the table and settled into the booth next to her. For an instant Jane's hackles rose, as if her territory had been invaded, but she let it go and slid a little closer to the far wall. Maybe this was normal Aussie male behavior. She had no idea but wasn't going to let a little thing ruin what could be a pleasant evening.

He raised his glass to her. "To a lovely lady."

She blushed and raised her glass also, trying to think of something clever to say. Nothing came, so she took a sip and gave him a smile.

"What brings you to Australia?" Neal took a hefty gulp of beer, settled back in his seat, and laid a hand across the booth behind her.

"It's someplace I've always wanted to see and after . . ." She paused and took a sip. At that point she didn't want to share the part about Ernie dying, especially if Neal asked how long ago that had happened. She didn't want his sympathy, nor, conversely, his derision. "Well, I found myself in a position to come, so I did," she finished, setting her mug back on the table.

"Good on ya." He took another large swig. "Last time I was in the States, I spent a week in Las Vegas then Reno. Great fun."

"Oh? You like casinos?"

"Yeah, Las Vegas has some great ones. I thought the ones in Reno were just smaller copies of the real ones and not nearly as good."

"I've never been. There's a casino close to where I live though. It's on the reservation. I've been there a couple of times, though just to eat. Not to gamble."

"What's the point then?" He emphasized his point, slamming his hand on the table, which shivered her mug sideways. "I mean, the shows are good, if you're into that sort of thing, but the whole point is to take a chance, spin the wheel, grab life by the balls, and go for it. That's my philosophy about gambling and everything else." He tipped back his glass and emptied it. "I'm ready for another. You haven't taken a sip. Come on, sheila, this is good stuff."

Jane stiffened. He didn't remember her name after she'd just told him. Maybe he was senile or something. She scrutinized him a little closer for signs of early onset dementia, though she had to admit she had no idea what that would look like. When her Aunt Mabel went to the nursing home because she couldn't take care of herself, her mother said Mabel had Alzheimer's and warned Jane to eat properly or she'd get it too. Neal didn't act at all like Mabel.

"Thanks, but I'm a slow drinker. You go ahead." She smiled at him and watched him cross the room to the bar. Maybe this wasn't such a good idea. He wasn't turning out to be Prince Charming, with his beer guzzling, hand slamming, and gambling-loving philosophy. Maybe she should finish her beer and go.

Neal returned, mug in hand, and slid in next to her, this time until his hip touched hers. His arm snaked over the booth behind her again too. She felt trapped but didn't know what to do about it.

"The States are OK," he said, after taking a swallow. "Nice mountains, but nothing like home. Queensland's about the perfect place, I think. My station's one of the three largest in the state. It's so big we use helicopters to gather the cattle, unlike the smaller ones that use quads and utes."

"Quads? Utes? What are they? Back home, the Utes are Indians." Jane took another sip of beer, thinking that when she finished, she'd make some excuse like going to the bathroom to get out and leave. Or at least sit back down on the other side of the table.

He guffawed, throwing his head back as if she'd said the funniest thing he'd ever heard. When he settled, he placed a hand on her arm. "A quad is a small four-wheel vehicle, an ATV. And a ute, my little sheila, is a truck. I take it you don't call them that?"

Jane eased her arm away. "No, we just call them trucks. And by the way, my name is Jane, not Sheila."

He laughed again, this time louder and longer, so much that his eyes teared up and he had to wipe them away with the back of his free hand. "Oh, that's a corker," he gasped. He patted her arm after swiping his eyes again. "Jane," he said when he regained his breath, "I know your name. A 'sheila' is an Aussie word for woman. That's all I was saying."

She felt her face redden and she averted her eyes. "Oh, I'm sorry. I didn't know."

"Hey, that's OK." He stroked her arm. "I made some whoppers, too, when I was in the States. Maybe I should coach you on Australian slang."

She shook her head and moved her arm away. "That's OK. I'm learning."

"No, no. You need help. Let me see . . ." He took a drink and ran his hand over his lips. "'Fair dinkum.' What's that?"

"I don't know." She sighed and pressed against the wall in a futile attempt to put some distance between them. Her skin was crawling where their hips touched, and the place on her arm that he'd stroked felt soiled. All she wanted was to get out of there—the sooner the better.

"It means real, true. Got that?"

She nodded and took a larger gulp of her drink. "Look, I think I need to go to the bathroom." She grabbed her purse.

He didn't budge. "Not bathroom. Toilet. Or loo. Or dunny. Or lav." He shook his head. "But not bathroom."

"Thanks, but I need to go to the whatever. Please let me out."

He relented and slid out of the booth. Then he extended a hand to help her stand. She tried to wave him off, but his hand wrapped around her upper arm and lifted her despite her protests. Tucking her purse under her arm, she wended her way toward the bar until she saw a sign for the toilets.

Inside, she braced her hands against the sink and took a deep breath, looking in the mirror. "You," she said to the image, "are one dumb sheila." How could she have been so stupid as to let this jerk take her anywhere? The thought of spending one more minute with him sent a wave of nausea through her. She thought Ernie was a bore and insensitive, but this man made him look like a saint.

She had to escape. But how? The toilets were in line with the table, and there was no way he was not going to see her walk back out unless he moved to the other side of the table or got so drunk in the next few minutes that he passed out. Though she'd give even money on his drunkenness, she knew she either had to try and sneak out while he wasn't looking or go back, make her excuses, and beat feet for the door before he could try and stop her. Thank goodness, she'd driven instead of walking. But she'd still have to make it to the parking lot without him following—if she could.

Dropping her head, she shook it from side to side. Why, why, why? Why did she let herself get into this situation? Was this Ernie's way of getting back at her from the afterlife for going out with a man so soon? Or was she such a fool that she let her loneliness drive her to allowing the first male who showed any interest in her sweep her away? Rachael would vote for the latter. Either way, she needed to make a move, and the quicker the better. If she stayed much longer, he'd likely come looking for her, and she didn't want any kind of scene.

Straightening, she pulled a brush from her purse and pulled it through her hair a couple of times. Then she used the john since she was there. After washing her hands, she looped her purse over her shoulder and faced the mirror again. Since there was no way to sneak out, she'd better face the situation, make some excuse, and leave. She sighed again. How she wished she could disappear. But no such luck. She took a deep breath, sucked in her stomach, and pushed her way out the door.

Neal was chatting up the waitress but waved at her before she'd taken two steps out the door. Her stomach clenched, and she could feel her hands quivering, but she forced herself to the table. The waitress turned when she neared, gave her a wink, and walked back toward the bar.

Her brow furrowed, and she paused for a second. What the hell was that for?

"Hey, it's about time you got back. Your beer's getting flat." Neal grinned and patted the seat beside him.

"Neal, I think I need to go. I'm not feeling well." She tried to look pathetic.

"No, no, no. That's no good. Come sit down, and I bet you'll feel much better in a minute."

She shook her head. "No, I have to go. Thanks for the beer and the slang lesson. I'll try and remember everything you taught me."

She turned, but he grabbed her arm and stood. "You can't go by yourself if you're feeling green around the gills. I'll walk you to your car."

"That's OK. I'll be fine. Why don't you stay and finish your beer?" She edged away from him, pulling at her arm, but he clung and followed.

"No, I insist." From his pocket he pulled a wad of bills, fished several out, and tossed them on the table. She took several steps toward the door when he dropped her arm to mess with his money, but he caught up with her and took her arm again before she could make it out.

She wanted to jerk away and make a break for it, but she felt the fool and didn't want to look like one, and that's what would happen if she jerked and ran. Even though she was cringing inside, she let him walk her up the stairs and onto the street.

Once outside, she pulled her arm away and stepped back. "I'll be fine from here. Thanks again."

"It's me, isn't it?" He stuffed his hands in his front pockets and dropped his head. He looked like a half-deflated balloon. "I was way out of line back there, laughing at you and being a nong generally. I'm sorry. Please don't go."

She stared at him, trying to figure out if he was playing another game with her or being sincere. Was he psychotic or what? Wouldn't it be her luck that the first man she had a drink with after being chained to Ernie all those years turned out to be crazy? At that point she didn't care. She was tired after the long day and wanted to go back to the caravan park, make up her little bed, and go to sleep. Alone. Enough with men for one night.

"Oh, it's not you," she lied, feeling bad about hurting his feelings. She could almost hear Rachael gagging in the background, but she continued. "I just don't feel well. I'm sorry to be such a spoilsport."

He glanced up. "Look. At the very least let me make it up to you. Let me take you to dinner tomorrow night. I promise you an excellent meal and will show you that I am a gentleman. Please give me a second chance."

"I don't know." She sighed, wishing she could walk away without regrets. Dinner didn't sound at all appealing after his show in the bar, but she couldn't seem to muster the courage to say no and walk away. "I'm too tired, and I can't think right now. Maybe we should say goodbye and call it good."

He reached out and touched her arm. "Please, no. I want to make things right. If you can't decide right now, why don't I give you my phone number, and you can call me in the morning instead. Would that be OK?" He looked so forlorn that Jane's heart melted—a little. Though she wanted to, she couldn't just walk away. What harm would it do to let him give her his number? Tomorrow she could let him know she couldn't have dinner with him because she was leaving or something. At least that way she wouldn't have to do it face-to-face.

"OK."

He smiled, pulled a small case from his back pocket, and extracted a business card from it. "Thanks. You won't regret this. I promise." He handed it to her, holding on for an instant after she reached for it. "Can I walk you to your car, just to make sure you're safe?"

She tucked the card into her purse without looking at it. "I'll be fine. It's not that far."

His shoulders seemed to sag even more. "OK. Till tomorrow then."

She nodded. "I'll call." She turned and strode toward the parking lot, not daring to turn around and see if he followed but feeling his eyes on her back until she turned the corner at the end of the mall. It felt creepy yet sensual in a weird kind of way. She was certain she didn't want to spend another minute with him, but the way he had looked at her when he handed her his card—so sheepish and regretful and hopeful—it plucked at the tender part of her psyche, the part that caused her to rescue abandoned kittens in the parking lot of Town Market and then hang around beseeching strangers to take them in until she found someone with a big enough heart to agree.

And there was a kind of sexual aura that surrounded him, with his broad shoulders and brash swagger, accentuated by his seeming vulnerability at that moment. She had the urge to stop and peek around the edge of the building to see if he was still standing there, looking lost and alone. Or had he resumed his asshole persona and was trying to pick up another woman wandering home in the dark? Resisting the impulse, she quickened her pace.

As she climbed into the vehicle, she breathed a sigh of relief. At least he wasn't enough of a creep to sneak after her, which was one point in his favor. Maybe he truly was regretful, and it was the beer talking in the bar. He had seemed to realize he'd been a complete jackass, which was another point in his favor, not that he'd come close to compensating for his boorish behavior. Despite that fact, he was at least one step above Ernie, who'd never apologized for anything he'd done in all their years together. She tossed her purse on the passenger seat and started up the motor, making up excuses why she couldn't make it for dinner in between toying with the idea of accepting.

The next morning Jane slept in. When she roused, she desperately wanted to call Rachael and fill her in about her adventure with

Neal, but after some calculation, she decided it was the middle of the night back home and it would be too cruel to call. Instead, she puttered around making breakfast and reviewing the evening's events. Neal still played the jerk in her memory—mostly. However, his face when he had handed her his card niggled at her, and all the questions from the night before still stood. The more she thought about it, the more intrigued she became. Who was this tall Aussie rancher, and did she want to find out or run away?

Her plan had been to pack up and head toward Uluru that morning, but noon came and went, and she was still puttering around the camper doing nothing of consequence except wishing she could call Rachael. She felt she should call Neal and let him know one way or the other about dinner, and she hated to string him along, but she didn't want to do it before talking to her friend. She also didn't want to call him so late that he'd already made other plans or wouldn't have time to make other plans if she decided to turn his offer down.

She glanced at her watch: two p.m. That made it seven a.m. back home if she had it figured right. Rachael wasn't what one could call an early riser; ten or later was her preferred wake-up time, but it was a workday and she'd have to be out the door in time to be at work by ten. The question was, would she be up at seven or eight or even nine thirty? And did Jane dare call her earlier than she normally rose? In all the years they'd hung together, the question of when Rachael got out of bed on a workday had never come up—nor had how grumpy she might be if she were awakened early. How Jane now wished that it had.

She tapped the face of her watch. If she waited until nine o'clock back home, that would be four in Australia. She shook her head.

Too late to decline or accept, at least in her estimation. She'd be livid if someone called that late about a dinner engagement. But she didn't think she could call Rachael any earlier. She tapped the watch again. Did she need Rachael's opinion? Wasn't she mature enough to make some decisions on her own? This wasn't going to alter the course of the planet, after all; it was just determining how she was going to spend her evening.

She fished Neal's card out of her purse and stared at it. Cream-colored with a gold embossed bull in the background, it stated the usual information in glossy black ink: Neal Stratmore, Urandangi Station, Camooweal, QLD. Phone number, mobile number, address, postal code. It looked impressive, as impressive as Neal had made it sound the previous night. Third-largest station in Queensland, he'd said, and, if she recalled correctly, Queensland covered almost a quarter of the country. Impressive indeed. If nothing else, he could afford a good dinner.

She flicked the edge of the card with her finger. Yes, he'd been a boor, but he'd apologized for his behavior and wanted to make up for it. He had invaded her personal space and made her feel uncomfortable and vulnerable, but that was in a booth where there was limited maneuverability and room to get away. He was loud and obnoxious and had used a demeaning term to refer to her—sheila. But maybe that was normal out here. Maybe it was acceptable, and she was being too sensitive. Hadn't Cleo called her on her cultural ignorance? Rachael, too, for that matter. Maybe she should give him another chance. If she made sure they were seated at a table where she could put some space between them, if she met him there so she could leave on her own, and if she called him on any rude behavior from the outset, maybe this could work.

She flicked the edge of the card again and reached for the cell phone. Part of her knew Rachael wouldn't approve, and a gnawing voice in the back of her head insisted that she was putting off calling Rachael for that very reason. She didn't want to get talked out of this. She wanted a date. She wanted dinner and wine and conversation—and to feel desirable to a man again, even if it was for a couple of hours in a faraway place with someone she'd most likely never see again. Maybe for that very reason. An anonymous fling. An irresponsible and self-indulgent fling with no one watching.

A thrill of anticipation skittered down her spine as she punched in the mobile number. While she waited for the phone to ring, she was already planning where she'd go to find a dress for the occasion and maybe a new pair of shoes. Did she have time to get her hair and nails done too? Probably not, but she'd look anyhow. She was going to make this exciting no matter which persona Neal showed up wearing.

Neal arrived at Seasoned Steak a few minutes after Jane. She watched him stride toward the double glass doors in his crisp white shirt, jeans, and leather vest, thinking he could have just stepped off any ranch outside of Cortez. Except, that is, for the leather hat she'd seen men all over the country wearing and the polished oxford shoes. My, oh my, was he handsome, she thought, feeling those Aussie butterflies invade her stomach again.

She smoothed the front of her new little black dress with its sequined belt, still amazed she had found something so sweet that fit so well in the Alice Springs Mall. She had lucked out at the hair salon too, a cancellation calling in just when she'd arrived. The spiky-haired blond woman with the tips of her hair dyed red looked too avant-garde for Jane's simple tastes, but she had adroitly swept her hair into a chignon with a few tendrils left curling at her temples and a rhinestone barrette sparkling in the back. Jane felt more chic and sexier than she had since her wedding day.

Neal pulled open the doors and then stopped and stared at her, grinning. "Wow. You look bonza!"

She blushed and touched her cheek. "I hope that's good."

"Good as gold. You're a ripper."

Her flush deepened when she reached out to take his extended arm. "You're looking quite handsome yourself."

"Why, thank you, ma'am. I hope you're hungry."

The maître d' seated them close to a wall of windows that overlooked the Todd River, which was empty and dry yet threaded through with gums and bushes. To Jane it looked barren and hardly what she would have termed picturesque compared with the wild Animus River back home, but she supposed it had its own sere beauty, especially compared with the Nullarbor Plain or the lands around Coober Pedy. It was just another facet of the desert she had never imagined.

She scanned the menu, looking for the signature dishes the internet had claimed the place served. And there they were—braised kangaroo, baked emu, curried snake, camel kabobs—next to the more standard chicken and beef dishes, all with price tags that nearly choked her. He must be well off to afford this, she thought, considering the shrinking assets on her own Visa card. At some point in the near future, she'd need to see what she had left on it. In the meantime, if he was willing to shell out the dollars, she was willing to let him.

Neal ordered steak and a beer, but she couldn't decide which of the exotic native meats she wanted to try. She finally settled on kangaroo medallions in a red wine sauce with new potatoes and slivered beets.

Neal shook his head when she'd finished ordering. "Kangaroo. Too gamey for my taste. If I have to eat native, I prefer camel. You want a drink?"

She asked about local wines and decided on a *rosé*, thankful that she didn't have to try and choke down another beer to be polite. So far, so good, she decided. He'd not pushed anything on her, had let her make her own choices, and was the perfect gentleman. She felt herself relax a little, only then aware of how tense she'd been since she'd accepted his invitation.

She leaned into the plush chair and picked up her wine. "So tell me about your ranch."

"Station," he corrected. "Out here, we call them stations." He proceeded to wax rhapsodic about the rolling grassland, the far mesas, the flat backs of his cattle, the sheen of their fur, their rotund bellies, the excitement of the muster, the rise and fall of cattle prices, the arguments for and against artificial insemination, the ebb and flow of water from the bore holes, the high price of hay, and the pitfalls of horse rearing. He continued through the soup, the salad, the main course, and several glasses of beer without needing a prompt, his verbiage peppered with slang terms and phrases, like "a possum up a gum tree," "long paddock," "poddy dodger," and "mulga."

She could figure most of them out in context, and she thought that those she couldn't figure out weren't worth the effort of interrupting to ask him what they meant. At least her dinner was one of the most flavorful experiences she could ever recall. While he carried on, she chewed and savored in silence. By the time he wound down as dessert and coffee (for her) and brandy (for him) were served, she felt exhausted.

Swirling brandy around a large crystal snifter, he laid his napkin on the table and smiled. "I've been doing all the talking. Now it's your turn. Tell me about yourself."

All during his monologue, she wondered if he'd ever ask about her, but now that he had, she wasn't sure what to say. She didn't have a rich or complex life like the one he described on the station, and she would have been embarrassed explaining she was a receptionist at a small local motel. Coming to Australia was the most exciting thing she'd ever done. That seemed even more mundane and bland considering she was in her mid-forties.

"There isn't much to tell," she said, sipping her coffee. "My life has been pretty simple up until I decided to take this trip."

"No, I don't believe that. Not a woman like you."

Her brow wrinkled. "What do you mean, a woman like me? I'm not very special."

He rocked forward and laid his hand on her side of the table. "That you're out here all on your own. And in a foreign country to boot. I don't know any women who'd be brave enough to try that."

She snorted. "Why? Is the Australian outback that dangerous?"

"Oh, that's good." He threw his head back and laughed loudly enough that she felt conspicuous. "No, no," he said, inhaling and shaking his head. "Not dangerous. Just most of the women I know wouldn't go off by themselves without a man around or at the very least another woman for company."

"Well, I guess I'm not like most Australian women." She finished her coffee and set the cup back on the table, wondering if the women's movement had ever made it to this continent. "I always wanted to travel; it's just life never gave me the opportunity until now. I'm having a great time on my own." Well, kind of on my own, she amended to herself, remembering that most of her time on the road so far had been in the company of Cleo.

"Well, I think it's grand. Good on ya." He nodded. "So, back home? Husband? Kids?"

Oh shit, here it comes. She delayed answering by flagging down the waiter for another cup of coffee, but that took only a couple of seconds. "Well," she began, fiddling with her napkin, trying to find words. "I was married, but he died."

Neal's face registered surprise that morphed into sympathy. "I'm so sorry to hear that. How long ago?"

She tugged at the napkin. Should she tell him the truth or make something up and hope the discussion never got back to it? And if she lied, what would be an appropriate time for Ernie to have been dead? Six months? A year? A couple of years? She didn't have a clue. "It's been a few months," she blurted, hoping the answer was ambiguous enough to satisfy him.

"That all?" He seemed shocked, and she wished she'd pushed it out a little further. "How are you doing with that?"

She shrugged. "It wasn't a happy marriage, and he was in a lot of pain at the end. I'm glad it didn't drag on any longer than it did." And that was true. For all his faults, it had been hard for her to watch Ernie suffer, especially when the pain and anxiety medications didn't take more than just the edge off. There were times she would have given him a lethal injection to stop the agony that was so evident in his sweating, moaning, writhing body. Late at night, during the bad ones, she lay in bed beseeching all the gods in the heavens to take him, to steal his breath, to still his heart, to let him go to heaven or hell or someplace in between—it didn't matter, provided the torment stopped. It felt like his pain wracked her body too, and the day he died was the greatest blessing ever bestowed upon her. Not only because it freed her from the loveless marriage she had come to hate, but also because the torture chamber their house had become had closed and she could flee.

"What'd he die of?"

"Lung cancer."

"Ooh, nasty death. Had an uncle who carked it from lung cancer. He was so drugged at the end that I don't think he realized he was dead until the drugs wore off." His lips twitched into a faint smile.

Jane matched his smile. "What do you say we change the subject? This one's too morbid for such a lovely evening."

"What do you say we change the venue? There's a dance band playing in the park. How's your two-step?"

Her smile broadened. A man who dances. Will wonders never cease? Ernie's version of dancing was to shuffle around the floor, groping her during the slow songs. He never got up for anything faster than a waltz and made fun of those men who did. Occasionally, after they were married, she'd dance with someone at a wedding or party, but that was the extent of it for most of her life. When she was in school, she was a popular partner because she could follow anyone; however, she hadn't been on a dance floor since the last century. Could she still do it? "My two-step's a little rusty, but I'm sure I'll remember once we get going. How's yours?"

"Never better." He pushed back his chair and extended a hand to her. "Shall we?"

The park turned out to be a botanic garden. Still wary, she insisted she follow him there in her camper, though he wasn't pleased with the arrangement. She parked behind him and let him escort her to a large tent that had been erected in the park, with a stage at one end and rows of folding chairs flanking a small dance floor. Jane felt conspicuous in her little black dress since most of the other people there were wearing shorts and T-shirts. She wished she could run back to the camper and change but decided she'd buck up and pretend all was normal. At least Neal also looked overdressed.

While they sat, the band settled on stage and the first chords of what was clearly country music wafted across the milling crowd. Jane had never imagined that she'd hear country music in Australia, though she'd never given a second thought to what constituted popular music there. Perhaps rehashed American or something akin to Men at Work. The lyrics had a distinctive Aussie bent, with mentions of roos and road trains, but the twang of the vocalists and whine of the steel guitar sounded the same. Country had never been her favorite genre, but she could dance to it, and that's all that counted tonight.

After listening awhile, Neal led her to the floor, joining several other couples, and he proceeded to shuffle her around the floor in a pattern that more or less resembled a two-step. Nothing fancy, no turns or promenades, only the basics, counterclockwise around the floor. Well, Jane thought, at least we're dancing.

They made it through a couple of songs, Neal perspiring more with each stanza. Even Jane was getting hot. She was thankful when he suggested they rest for a song or two, and he led her back to their seats. Once seated, he motioned to the back of the tent, where a makeshift bar had been erected.

"I think I'll get a beer. What about you?"

She shook her head. "I don't like beer, but if they have a cola of some kind, I'd love that." She smiled, hoping he didn't remember the way he'd ordered for her the previous evening and take offense.

"Sure thing." And he was gone.

Leaning back, she eased her feet out of her new shoes, half a size too small and far too narrow for her clodhopper feet. They looked great with the dress, but nowhere in the store did they have anything that would have both matched her dress and fit her feet. If she'd have thought she'd be dancing, she would have bought something less fashionable and more comfortable. She sighed, wiggling her toes in the grass.

If it wasn't for the fact this was at least the fourth beer Neal had downed, not counting the huge snifter of post-dinner brandy, it would have been the perfect evening. She wondered if slugging down a six-pack or more on a daily basis was normal for him or if he was using alcohol to ease any social distress he might be feeling. At least his behavior hadn't degenerated into what she had experienced before, and she was thankful for its absence.

Neal returned with a can of Coke and a larger can of a brand of beer she didn't recognize. He handed her the Coke and plopped down beside her, taking a huge gulp of his drink. "Bugger, it's hot out here. Not a lot of circulation in this tent."

She sipped the icy soda and nodded. "If you're from Queensland, what are you doing in Alice Springs?"

"Taking a break. I try to get off the station every couple of months. If I don't, I start going a little bushy." He took another gulp.

"Family? Wife? Kids?"

He shook his head and mopped his brow with the cuff of his shirt. "Nah. Divorced several years ago. Kids all grown, married, living in Brisbane or thereabouts."

"Oh? How many kids do you have?"

"Three, two girls and a boy. Boy just finished uni but hasn't found a job. He's living with his mother in Brisbane."

She thought she heard an undertone of derision in his voice. "And your daughters?"

"Both married. My oldest has two kids of her own, but the youngest says she doesn't want kids and wants to be a lawyer like her husband." He shook his head. "Can't understand that. Guess she's too much like her mother."

"Oh, in what way?"

"My ex decided to go back to school before she left me. She said she wanted a life of her own." He huffed and took another swallow. "Like she didn't have a life with me." He drained the can, crumpled it, and stuffed it under the chair. "Enough of this. How about another dance?"

They danced off and on until the band quit around midnight. Neal drank several more beers, and Jane watched him become increasingly less able to keep time to the music or walk a straight line. She was glad she had insisted on driving her camper to the park because she wouldn't have wanted to climb in a car with Neal in his current condition.

After their last dance, Neal staggered to his seat and collapsed. "I'm having too much fun to quit now. What do you say we find a pub? Or you could come to my hotel room for a nightcap?" He winked at her.

She thought she knew what the wink meant, and while she'd enjoyed being held in a man's arms, she wasn't quite ready to climb into bed with him. "Thank you, Neal, but I've had enough fun. Maybe another time. Thank you for dinner and dancing. It was all wonderful." She tucked her purse under her arm and stood.

He laid a hand on her arm. "What are you doing tomorrow? Maybe we could go golfing or something?"

She considered his proposal, but she'd never golfed and had no intention of starting at this late date—and in front of Neal to boot. The idea of spending more time with him was appealing, especially during the day when he might be sober. She liked feeling sexy, which is the way he made her feel, even if she wasn't ready to have sex with him or anyone. But she was tired of Alice Springs and did want to go see Uluru. "I was going to leave to go see Uluru in the morning. It's one of the things I definitely want to see while I'm here."

His face fell. "That's too bad. They have a great golf course here. Do you have to go tomorrow?"

She shifted from one foot to the other. What she wanted was to get brave and call Rachael and confess to her what she'd been doing. She suspected if she put the question to her, Rachael would tell her to get out of Alice and go see her rock. Being with Neal was fun, and though she hated to leave quite yet, she knew it would be better to go. "Yes, I need to go. I've had a wonderful time tonight though."

"OK." His hand dropped into his lap. "What do you plan on doing after that?" He looked up at her, hope glimmering in his eyes.

"I'm not sure. I want to go up north and see Darwin and the Great Barrier Reef, I guess. I hadn't planned much beyond Uluru."

"Look, you have my address. It's right off the Barkly Highway and right on your way to the Great Barrier Reef and Cairns. You could stop at the station, and I could show you around. Give you a real feel for what the outback is like. You could stay at the house." He held up a hand. "No worries. No pressure. There are lots of empty bedrooms. What do you say?"

She smiled. "That sounds good. I'd like that. When will you be back home?"

"I've got a couple more days off. Then it's back to work. Take your time at Ayers Rock, and call me when you're heading my direction." He grinned and stood. "I want to see you again."

She cringed at his use of Ayers Rock instead of Uluru but didn't want to correct him. "You too. Thanks again." As she moved to take a step back, he grabbed her in a bear hug. Worming her arms free, she embraced him too, feeling a rush of desire bloom. What would it be like to go to bed with another man? The thought was titillating and deserved more consideration. Consideration she could give on her way to Uluru.

"You what?" Rachael practically screamed into the phone. "At least you didn't go to bed with him. Please tell me you didn't go to bed with him."

"No, I didn't go to bed with him, but what would have been so bad about that?" Jane eased back in her lawn chair, her final purchase in Alice before hitting the road. At every caravan park, she had watched people lounging in the evenings in lawn chairs, chatting with one another or just having a cool drink. Jane had envied them and found a cheap folding chair on sale in one of the department stores downtown. At first it felt strange to be sitting outside in Yulara, in a caravan park near Uluru, with all the other people around her, but the evening breeze that tickled the back of her neck more than compensated for the awkward feeling.

She could hear Rachael sigh. "I guess if you need a postmortem swing, Australia is the place to do it. God knows you could use it after Ernie. But you aren't a teenager anymore, and the world has changed. You need to take precautions."

"Precautions?" Her brow furrowed, and she wondered if there was anywhere she could get birth control pills. She hadn't needed them with Ernie, but now, the last thing she needed was to get pregnant by a stranger who lived in another country.

"AIDS, sweetie. Make sure you have him use a condom. You don't know where his whanger has been."

She blushed clear to the roots of her hair. "Rachael, I swear. He's at least my age."

"Yeah, and who knows what he's been doing all these years. If he propositioned you on the first date, who's to say he hasn't been all over the country porking women in one-night stands. And does he use prostitutes? I'm sure Australia has a few of those."

"I don't think he uses prostitutes."

"Oh. And how well do you know this guy? Look, I'm not trying to cut him down; it's just you've barely met him. What does he know about you? Now figure that you know less about him. I want you to be careful; that's all."

She shook her head. "He talks an awful lot. I barely got a word in edgewise, and when he did ask about me, I told him about Ernie being dead. That was a real conversation killer. But I get your point. I'll be careful; that is, if I decide to see him again. I haven't made up my mind on that one yet."

"Good. Keep thinking about it. By the way, how's that big rock you went to see?"

She slouched deeper in her chair and gazed at the leaves shading her little camping spot. "It was wonderful. Oh, Rachael, you have no idea how amazing the thing is. It's got pockmarks all over it, and ridges, and clear pools at the foot, and trees and flowers growing all around. It's nothing like I expected. I want to walk around it tomorrow."

Rachael grunted. "Well, I hope you enjoy it. Maybe you'll find another nice man who maybe drinks a little less. Just don't get blisters."

She laughed. Rachael's idea of working up a sweat was walking two blocks to get a latte. Jane had never been able to talk her into doing anything outside, aside from having lunch together on the picnic table near the library. Her excuse had always been that she was wearing the wrong shoes and didn't want to get blisters. Not that Jane was a regular exerciser, but she liked to walk, and when she was much younger, she had gone on a couple of backpacking trips. She figured she had walked more since she'd been in Australia than she had in the last year.

"I'll be fine. I found out there's another whole set of rocks about thirty miles away, or is that kilometers? I still get confused. But I want to go see them too. I figure I'll be here at least another couple of days before I head out."

"To see Neal?"

"I don't know. There is the drinking thing. And I'm not certain about being way the hell out in the middle of nowhere at his place with nobody else around. It feels awkward."

"Good." She imagined Rachael nodding on the other end of the line. "At least you haven't completely lost your common sense.

I'm glad someone has taken an interest in you. You're a wonderful person, and it would be fantastic if you could find someone who told you that often and made you feel special. Someone besides me, that is. It'd do you good to have an affair."

"I don't know that I'm ready for that. I get the willies thinking about going to bed with Neal. I mean, it has its appeal, but it's intimidating. What if I take my clothes off and he's disgusted?"

A long sigh issued from the phone. "One of these days I'm going to find a way to suck Ernie out of your brain." Another sigh. "Look, no one is going to be disgusted by you. You don't have to believe it; take my word for it. I think your biggest problem is going to be falling in love with an Ernie clone just because it's what you're used to."

Jane shook her head. "Oh no. That's never going to happen."

"You'd be surprised. It happens to women getting out of terrible relationships all the time."

"Well, not to me. I won't let it."

"I hope that's true. Look, I've got to run. Call me before you leave. I'd love to hear what you decide about Neal."

"I will."

Jane flipped the phone closed, set it on her belly, and rested her head on the back of her chair. She felt miffed Rachael assumed she'd be attracted to another jerk instead of learning her lesson with Ernie. And she wasn't attracted to Neal. Well, not that much— was she? She liked the way he looked with his broad shoulders and strong jaw. The growing potbelly she could do without, but overall that was nothing. She liked the way he'd complimented her and seemed to appreciate her efforts to look good. She liked that he thought she was sexy. She let that thought run through her hormones for a minute.

On the other hand, she didn't appreciate his drinking, and she wished he would have asked a little more about her. It would have been nice to compare more where he'd been in the States with what she knew. Or to talk about what she liked and see if he liked the same things. While his monologue had been long, at the end of it, she felt she didn't know him any better. She'd learned more about raising cattle in the outback than she had about Neal the person. If she was going to see him again, that would have to change.

If she was going to see Neal again. That was the question, wasn't it? At that moment, watching the leaves above her shiver in the breeze, she didn't know. The pros and cons seemed to cancel each other out, leaving her in limbo. Maybe she'd have a better idea of what she wanted after she let it rest for a day or two.

She was up before dawn the next morning and driving out to see the sun rise over Uluru. The ranger at the cultural center seemed to think that was a smashing idea and assured her it was something not to miss. As she drove toward the area he'd indicated on the map, not even a cup of coffee in her system and her bed unmade, she wasn't so sure. It would have to be pretty spectacular to warrant all this effort.

It was a long drive to the viewing site, but she arrived in time to fix the bed and brew a cup of coffee before the sun made its appearance. The parking lot was half-filled with other cars, vans, and several large tour buses. People milled around, and some made their way to bleachers set in a hill. Jane chose to sit in the back doorway of the camper, her pot of coffee warm on the stove beside her, a blanket draped around her shoulders. She'd parked so the back end was facing east, or what she hoped was east. Beside her, a group of four dreadlocked twenty-somethings had pulled out a portable grill and were frying up eggs while they waited for the sun. They laughed and cuddled, and Jane felt a pang of jealousy. It would have been so nice to have someone to cuddle with. Maybe even Neal. She wondered how he would have responded if she'd invited him to come with her.

Suddenly her eyes filled with tears. An overwhelming sense of loneliness engulfed her, a feeling of being unrooted and unwanted, wandering like a lost dog looking for a master who'd moved across the country. Her vision blurred, and she retreated into the camper and huddled in a corner of the small space, weeping, while outside the sun edged over the top of Uluru without her. She tried to figure out if she was missing Ernie or missing the sense of being in a couple. Having someone there, even if he wasn't always helpful or caring—just being there. Another presence. Another warm body in the room. This felt like losing an arm or a leg. Having a piece of her cleaved away.

Maybe it wasn't Ernie she was missing. Maybe it was all the hopes and dreams of her childhood. Ernie was supposed to be part of that, and he was to the extent that he had shared her bed, played the role of husband her family and society demanded, provided for her, and from time to time, especially at first, been a gentle and tender lover.

Now she was a widow. That idea brought her up short. It was the first time she'd applied that word to herself, and it felt strange. Widow. It brought up images of women in long black dresses, their faces covered with heavy veils. Women living in darkened houses filled with ghosts and memories, dust and ashes. Old women.

Wizened women. Women coursing through life like the living dead.

She shuddered, and the tears began anew. She was too young to be a widow. Widows were in their seventies, with gray hair and lined faces. Widows sat around drinking tea and reminiscing about the past. Widows forgot who they were and what they once wanted. Widows were the refuse of a society that valued men and marriages more than old, single women, alone and no longer able to bear children. Widows were useless surplus.

She wasn't any of those things. She was young enough to still have a kid—well, barely. Her periods were still regular though not heavy, and she suspected perimenopause was around the corner. She wasn't home tatting or fondling old photographs; she was in the Australian outback by herself, much to the surprise of at least one native, Neal.

Jane wiped her eyes and blew her nose on a dish towel since she'd forgotten to buy tissues in Alice. She didn't have to let a word define her. It was her decision. So if she didn't want to be a widow, how would she define herself? She thought back to her conversation with Rachael—how she had said Jane was worthwhile and needed someone to tell her that often. Maybe that someone could be herself. And Rachael when needed. But she needed a watchword, something that would encapsulate all that she was and hoped to be, something that could send her forward into her future with confidence and courage, something wonderful.

Blotting her eyes with the towel and drying her cheeks, she sat upright. Her mind was blank. Not one single appropriate word bubbled to the surface, and nothing popped up when she delved a little further. OK, maybe she needed a bit more time to find it. After all, she was still new at this business of being alone and forging a future. Because that's what she intended to do, forge a future for herself on her own terms for a change. But she didn't need to figure all that out immediately.

Today, right now, she had a rock to walk around. Tomorrow she'd come back to see the sunrise for real and then investigate the other formation, Kata Tjuta, maybe kick around the national park and see what else there was to see, and spend some time thinking about what she wanted to do with her remaining time in Australia. Neal was on that list, but he was not the only item. And that was another thing she didn't have to deal with today.

For the next three days, Jane hiked up and down the rock formations in the park, read all the signs, attended presentations and activities, fought the busloads of tourists who teemed in waves along the walks like packs of lemmings following the tour guides. Most of them seemed to be from Japan or some other Asian country, though there were the clots of Germans and well-dressed couples with English accents too. She watched the buses arrive, disgorge the fifty or so passengers who would then march, en masse, down the trail to whatever the attraction was, snap a few photos, turn around, hike back, and climb on the bus, which then raced away to the next site.

She'd seen the tours advertised in Alice that promised visits to Uluru, Kata Tjuta, and Kings Canyon in a weekend. For her, just Uluru and Kata Tjuta would take a whole weekend alone, and that wasn't including driving from Alice. She had no idea what Kings Canyon was, or where, but she imagined one would have to do everything at a dead run to see it all in the time allotted. She was grateful she chose to investigate things by herself at her own pace.

From time to time while walking the trails, she wondered what Cleo would have said about what she'd seen. Did she believe what the rangers said about the pockmarks and rockslides of the Uluru being due to fights between huge ancient animals, among other mythic events? One of the signs she'd read invoked tourists to take home the stories of Uluru, not pictures, because they were the true representations of the rock. Would Cleo have agreed, or would she have found some middle ground between science and myth?

And how would she have felt about all the tourists? According to the presentations at the cultural center, both sites were sacred to the natives, and it was only through their generosity (and an agreement with the Australian government when the sites were given back to the natives) that the general public was allowed to see them. This was especially true of Kata Tjuta, which was a holy place for men only. That the natives allowed women anywhere near the sacred rocks smacked of a beneficence Jane couldn't imagine entering the mind of the average American. Like letting women visit the bedrooms of cloistered monks.

And then there was the whole issue of climbing on Uluru. A metal cable still snaked to the top of the rock to accommodate past climbers, but the practice had recently been banned. A ranger said that climbers had soiled the top of the rock so much with their rubbish and toileting habits that native children swimming in the pools at the bottom had contracted E. coli from the seepage down the rock. Even then, the natives didn't close access but arranged to let people climb until 2019. If someone had gotten sick back home from the negligence of visitors, the attraction would have been closed, no questions asked, and lawsuits filed. It made her marvel at the natives. What kind of people would react with such restraint and accommodation in the face of the risks to the health of their kids?

She'd always believed what she'd heard from both her family and Ernie's—that dark-skinned people were disrespectful and self-serving, sucking off the whites and giving nothing back. But here was the opposite; the whites were the ones defiling a sacred object at the expense of others for a little climb. She thought about the conquest of the American West and the multiple massacres of natives to cleanse the land so the white settlers could carve it up for their own use. Wasn't this a smaller example of the same thing? And the natives here didn't react with retribution, but rather with reason and understanding, trying to forge good relationships with the whites. Maybe everything she'd heard all her life about other races, and what she had believed without question, was wrong. Maybe it was the whites who were the ones who took what they wanted at the expense of others. Who didn't respect anything but their own desires. And maybe she'd been acting the same way. Maybe some of her own thoughts and attitudes toward Cleo were more of the self-serving attitude of whites she had absorbed with her ABCs in school and her Post Toasties, fed to her as reality when it was not.

How much of what she'd assumed about Cleo's behaviors were her own irritation at having her plans and desires foiled? How much was a focus on her own selfish needs without consideration for what was going on with Cleo? The thought that she had been acting no better than those who peed on top of Uluru shamed her. She wished she could tell Cleo how sorry she was. She thought about stopping back in Alice on her way north and tracking the girl down but realized she didn't have a hope in hell of ever finding Cleo's gran's house again. Given that fact, she vowed to try and be more accepting and understanding of other races from then on.

During her last evening in Yulara, she spread her maps of Australia on the table. Neal was correct in that it would be right on her way if she decided to drop by his place on her route to the coast. She could make a right turn at Tennant Creek, head for Brisbane, and drive right by his station, or if she wanted to bypass him, she could keep going straight up the Stuart Highway to Darwin and then follow the coast back down.

Rocking back, she sipped her tea and stared out the window. To Neal or not to Neal, that was her question. Was it better to carry on alone or, as Rachael put it, have a little postmortem fling? She didn't know, and Rachael hadn't been a whole lot of help either in their last conversation. She'd put it back in Jane's lap. "Do what you want to do. No one's out there looking over your shoulder."

But she felt like the whole world *was* looking over her shoulder. It was as if the eyes of her mother and sister and all of Ernie's family were lasered in on her, even if she was on the other side of the world and they didn't have a clue where she was or what she was doing.

She stopped and considered that for a moment. Was she that neurotic? Did she have to imagine lectures and guilt trips from everyone she was related to? Was that a necessity? What if she did what she wanted—and screw all of them? If she never told, how would they ever know, and what business was it of theirs anyhow?

She straightened. What business of anyone's was it, but hers? So what if she decided to sleep with Neal (using condoms, of course, after Rachael's chiding)? So what if she decided to live with him in sin or have a one-night stand and move on or get married? It was her decision, and she'd be the one who'd live with the consequences or lack thereof. So fuck them.

She still wasn't sure what she was going to do, but at least she was sure she wasn't going to let the ghosts of people not there decide for her. She had at least a day before she had to make any decision. It'd be a long day just to Tennant Creek if she could make it that far. She'd have lots of time on the drive to figure out what she wanted.

Chapter 11

DESPITE HER INTENTIONS, she ended up back in Alice for another couple of days to fill the fridge where it was a little less costly. She even got the same site in the caravan park she'd used the first time, and in a strange way, it felt like coming home. She'd planned on spending only the one night, but an elderly gentleman walking a basset hound stopped and talked to her while she was relaxing in her lawn chair and convinced her to see the Museum of Central Australia in the Araluen Cultural Precinct.

At first glance, the place seemed bleak and barren except for several largish buildings with a huge metal sculpture amid them that resembled a strange bug. The "bug" turned out to be a caterpillar, for the caterpillar people of the region, with lots of dot paintings and recorded singing being played inside it. Jane was entranced and took time to read all the plaques, learning of song lines and tribal space and the mythic creatures that once roamed the land and formed the mountains and valleys. The more she learned about the culture, the more she wanted to learn. She'd never been much interested in the tribes back home, and her interest surprised her.

The museum was also fascinating, though it didn't have a lot to do with the native population; it was more about the geology and vegetation of the central part of the continent. But she watched an interesting film about the natives' use of fire-stick farming, peri-odically burning the vegetation, and how that changed both the flora and fauna of the country. She found herself still wandering the exhibits at closing time and vowed to come back the next day to see the rest.

That evening she went back to Seasoned Steak in her little black dress, but she found the place a little tacky this time, the waitstaff slow and gruff, and the food mediocre. Her memory of the place was of elegance and exquisite dining. Or was it being in the company of Neal that had imbued the place with such cachet? Whatever the case, she didn't enjoy herself and rushed through dinner without even having dessert before she paid the check and fled into the night.

The restaurant sat on the edge of the Todd River, and with a full moon lighting the way, she wandered under the stars, remembering the feel of Neal's arms around her while they danced, the way he hadn't tried to kiss her even though she would have liked him to, how he was so gracious when he hadn't pressed her about Ernie or his death, how he had seemed so sweet when he invited her to come see him. She had enjoyed his company, and it felt good to have him take such an interest in her. She couldn't remember the last time a man had taken a second look at her, and she blushed when she remembered Neal's comment of how she looked "bonza." She still didn't have a clue what it meant, but it felt good nonetheless.

She walked for nearly an hour, listening to the crickets and the calls of some night bird. When she wandered back to the camper, her thoughts filled with Neal, and taking a right turn at Tennant Creek seemed inevitable.

Though she returned to the museum the next day, her heart wasn't in it. After spending the morning looking at the most magnificent dot paintings she'd ever seen and wondering if one of them was done by Cleo's gran, she left the museum, checked out of the caravan park, and headed north again on the Stuart Highway. For one fleeting instant, she thought she recognized the street Cleo had turned on to get to her gran's, but then the next one looked the same, and Jane gave up any shred of hope that she could find Cleo to apologize. Too bad, but she guessed it was meant to be.

The road was straight and the landscape barren, and Jane found herself wishing that Cleo was along to talk to or at least to do some of the driving so she could take a nap. She stopped for gas at a roadhouse that could have been the Bates Motel of Australia— ramshackle and seedy, with a bar that had graffiti all over the walls and no chairs. It gave her the creeps, and the guy who insisted he pump her gas creeped her out too. She used the restroom and escaped back to the safety of the road and the van.

She took a short break at Devils Marbles Conservation Reserve, or Karlwe Karlwe, the native name. She felt Cleo would have approved that she preferred the native name. Huge round rocks were scattered over the landscape, and she could understand why someone would consider the place sacred because it was so strange.

The information board explained the geology of the formation, but she wanted more magic involved than fracturing and erosion. After what she'd learned at Uluru and the museum in Alice, she wanted someone to tell her the story of the rocks, sing her their song. But all she saw were sunburned tourists snapping photos and climbing on the tumbled boulders. Disappointed, she climbed back in the van.

She arrived at Tennant Creek late in the afternoon. Just in time, she thought. She had passed a couple of large, dead kangaroos on the road and decided she needed to find a place to stay before she ended up being a kangaroo killer too. The town was small and dirty, poverty seeming to ooze from its dusty streets and alleys. Tin-roofed, cinderblock buildings lined the streets, looking shabby and worn. She found a caravan park, though it resembled a field of dust and sand rather than what she had come to expect. Not wanting to search for other accommodations, she secured a spot under one of the few trees and attached the electrical and water lines to her vehicle. A hot wind rustled the leaves of the tree, and Jane wished she had skipped the museum that morning so she could have made it farther. Still, it was better than killing Australia's national animal. She pulled out her lawn chair but repacked it when a gust of wind blasted her face with dirt. It was a good evening to be inside.

She went to bed early but was kept awake by the couple in the camper in the next spot arguing loudly and incoherently enough that all she got was the noise and not the substance. She tossed and turned, feeling thankful that at least she and Ernie hadn't been big fighters. Screaming and yelling wasn't their style. Icy silences, cutting remarks, and snide references were their weapons of choice and in play most of the time.

And it wasn't just Ernie; she'd done her share of sniping and backbiting in lieu of coming out and discussing the issue at hand. It made her feel ashamed, and she wondered if she could ever be in a healthy relationship—would she always revert to form? How long would it take her to start nipping at Neal? She already had a partial list of his faults, drinking foremost among them, and she could see herself making disparaging comments when he reached for another beer or opened a second bottle of wine. Maybe it would be better if she didn't call him and continued on to the coast. Save them both a lot of heartache.

The fighting ceased around midnight, and Jane fell into an uneasy slumber, her cheeks and pillow damp from remorse and fear of making the same mistakes again.

She woke up hot, grumpy, and still tired, with the sun beating through the shades, making the inside of the camper feel like a dry sauna. The amenities block was shabbier than anything she'd been in before, and she felt dirty despite a long shower, during which she spent most of the time standing under the steaming water, letting it course over her head and down her back.

A cup of coffee woke her a little, but when she looked for her morning cereal, she found she'd used up the last of it at Yulara and had forgotten to buy more before she left town. Nothing else in her little cupboard appealed to her. What she wanted was a huge cinnamon roll, swathed in icing, still steaming from the oven. Fat freaking chance of finding that here, she thought, pulling on her shorts. Still, breakfast out, even at some greasy-spoon roadhouse, sounded better than anything she could concoct on her own.

Much to her surprise, she found most of the town closed. Only then did she realize it was Sunday, and her only hope of food was at a gas station at the edge of town. Depressed and hungry, she drove through town, noticing that it greened up a little and didn't look quite so poverty-stricken the farther in she got. She even passed a caravan park near the far end that looked green, neat, and inviting, unlike hers had been. Finally, a BP station appeared, and she pulled off.

Breakfast consisted not of a steaming, freshly baked cinnamon roll but a microwave-heated meat pie and a watery cup of coffee. At least it was real Aussie food, she consoled herself while trying to punch through the rubbery crust of the meat pie. She wished she had made herself a salad or almost anything else. The pie was edible in the broadest sense of the term and filled her stomach, which was more than she'd expected when she first saw it, and she could tell Rachael that she'd eaten one at last, though she wasn't planning on repeating the experience anytime soon. Still feeling disgruntled, she filled the van and turned right, heading east toward Queensland and Neal—possibly.

If anything, the land became drier and more barren, with huge termite mounds scattered like misplaced bowling pins across the fiery sands. She wondered how anyone could make a living running cattle in such a landscape. But if Neal was to be believed, you could—and make a decent profit at it. She would have to wait and see. That is, if she chose to go see it.

She still wasn't certain. Too many questions and muddled feelings crowded out the path to a clear decision. For instance, why did he really get divorced? Did his wife go back to school, as he claimed, and choose to dump him? Or did he decide he didn't want to be with a woman who had plans outside the home? And did they still get along, or was it one of those awful things? Were his kids still talking to him? Was she the first person he'd dated since the divorce? If not, how many others, and did any of them still keep in touch? Did he sleep with any of them? Did he sleep around on his wife? And then all the drinking. She'd heard that Aussies were a hard-drinking lot, so was Neal's consumption considered normal? Or was it more than usual due to nerves or being away from home? And what was usual for him anyway?

She shook her head, trying to shake the swirling questions away, but they edged back in. Flipping on the radio, she searched for a station to drown them out, but the only thing filling the airways was static. She wished she had Cleo's MP3 player. Then she could plug her ears with noise and maybe drown out what was going on inside her head

Sighing, she slumped forward and attempted to focus on the road. That didn't stop questions about the decision she had made without seeming to realize it. After all, wasn't she on the road to Neal's? She could have kept going north on the Stuart Highway, but she'd turned without a second thought. Shouldn't that count for something? The logic seemed impeccable, but it didn't translate into fewer questions. Now she ended up questioning her motivations too. Was she trying to get laid? Was she trying to fill the Ernie-shaped hole in her life with another man? Shouldn't she be grieving or something instead? Was she doing this to prove to herself that she wasn't over the hill and a wasted old widow? That she was someone who still had a lot of years and life ahead of her? She didn't know. She didn't know about any of it, and it was driving her crazy.

She scanned the surrounding landscape and blinked. When did all the trees and bushes disappear? All around her lay a flat and treeless land, similar to the Nullarbor, but this time covered in a grayish-green grass. Hints of possible trees poked above the grass in the far distance, but she couldn't be sure without binoculars, which she didn't have. She remembered passing something called 41 Mile Bore that reminded her of a windmill without the blade structure; it had been next to three very long poles that were leaning against one another. She realized she didn't have the foggiest idea what a "bore" was, even less why one would be called "41 Mile Bore." What else had she missed while she was debating to death the whole Neal issue?

Just then a huge sign announcing she was entering Queensland appeared in the distance. That's it, she thought. I'm taking a break. I need to make a clear decision here, and I don't seem to be doing so well while I'm driving.

The tires spit gravel when she pulled off at the foot of the sign. Keys in hand, she jumped to the ground, locked the van, and strode back down the highway. She marched until the van was no longer visible in the distance and then turned around. By the time she arrived back at the van, she was hot, dusty, and tired—and no nearer to making a decision than she had been before she climbed out of the van. With a sigh, she opened the back and climbed inside. She hadn't eaten anything since the meat pie, and her stomach was registering complaints.

She fixed herself a salad and sat on the back bumper, watching the grasses bend and sway in the breeze and waving to the occasional vehicle that passed her. Maybe she should call Rachael. She glanced at her watch and added hours. Back home it should be about eight in the morning, Saturday morning that is. She wondered if Rachael slept in on Saturdays. Had they never gotten together over a weekend? Probably not. By the time they became friends, Ernie had weekends off, and if she wasn't tending to his needs, she was at work at the motel. Her friendship with Rachael was a Monday-through-Friday affair, during daytime, with perhaps a call in the evening, but nothing more than that. Should she risk waking Rachael, wait for another hour to be sure, or make up her mind on her own and go?

She popped the last piece of lettuce into her mouth with a sigh. She knew what Rachael would say: "Make up your own mind, damn it." She sighed again. OK, it was time to choose. She considered pulling a quarter out of her purse and tossing it, but she knew no matter what side came up, she'd do what she wanted. And deep down, below all the recriminations and doubts, below the guilt and self-flagellation, she wanted to see Neal again, no matter what happened—or didn't—between them.

She pulled out her cell phone and dialed his home number. Instead of ringing on the other end, her phone buzzed. She glanced at the screen. No bars. Well, that solved that problem, at least until she got to Camooweal. But once she found a cell tower or pay phone, she was going to call.

"Urandangi Station." The voice on the other end of the phone sounded female, older, and grumpy. Housekeeper or wife, Jane wondered, feeling a twinge of regret and/or fear in her stomach.

"I'd like to speak to Neal Stratmore," she managed to blurt out over a tongue as dry as the land around her.

"He's not here. Try his cell." The phone clicked off, and Jane blinked a couple of times in surprise. Huffing, she punched in the cell number on Neal's business card and waited.

He picked up on the third ring. "Yeah?"

Neal? It didn't sound like him—too gruff, with a surly edge. "Neal? It's Jane Mullet. I'm here in Camooweal and I ..."

"Bloody hell, it's good to hear your voice. I was so hoping you'd call." His enthusiasm gushed through the phone in such contrast to the way he had answered that she wondered if it was the same person. "Where are you?"

"In Camooweal. At the BP station."

"In Camooweal? That's wonderful! How long are you going to be there?"

She paused and bit her lip. Had he forgotten his invitation to come to the cattle station or had he changed his mind? Was she supposed to find a place to stay, go, or hang out for another dinner? She didn't know how to answer, and before she could figure it out, he was back on the line.

"Damn. You must think me such a nong. You must come out here and see the place, stay for a few days, or longer if you can. That van of yours have four-wheel drive?"

"Yes, but I've never used it."

"Well, now's the time. How are you with directions?"

"That all depends on the directions. Is this going to be complicated, because if it is, I'll get a piece of paper." She reached for her purse.

"Well, on second thought, you got GPS?"

Jane thought of the last time she had used it and felt her frustration rise. "Kind of. It's a long story."

"Never mind then. You need to get back on the Barkly heading west, then go for 8.2 kilometers to a road marker that's been broken.

There's a two-lane dirt road heading north around there, and you take that— You know what? You wait there, and I'll come get you. How's that sound?"

She sighed in relief. By the time he'd hit the road marker, she was lost. "That would be wonderful. About how long will it be?"

"Hour, hour and a half. I'll hurry."

"I'll be here." She disconnected, relieved yet a little nervous. She patted her hair and glanced down at her shirt. It was rumpled but clean. Mentally she scanned her wardrobe, wishing she'd taken time in Alice to do some laundry. This was the best clean thing she had, so it would have to do. Hopefully, Neal would let her throw in a load of clothes at his house.

She looked at her watch. Almost five. With an hour-plus to kill, she decided she'd take a turn around the town. Walking would feel good, and she'd be less likely to wind herself into a ball of nerves if she kept moving. She slung her purse over her shoulder and picked a direction. North, she assumed, considering the sun was walking toward the horizon on her left. Not that it mattered. Since the town of Camooweal appeared just a block long and wide, she decided she couldn't get lost in it no matter how hard she tried.

She'd underestimated the size of the town. It was about five blocks long and three, sometimes two, blocks wide. At the end of forty-five minutes, she figured she'd walked every street and seen every house, business, and eucalyptus tree. The only thing left was to walk out to the airport, and that held no appeal. She settled herself on the back bumper and hoped Neal would be there in the hour estimate, not the hour and a half.

But an hour and a half went by with no Neal. Then another hour. The sun was brushing the horizon, and she was getting panicky.

What if he didn't show up? She thought she remembered a sign for a caravan park back near the beginning of town at the Puma petrol station, but she couldn't remember for sure. Should she try and find it and get a spot before it got dark or wait another hour or so and then go? She ran a hand through her hair. She was getting hungry. The salad hadn't lasted very long, and she wished she'd eaten something more substantial. With a sigh, she rose and opened the back of the camper. At least she could get a snack while she waited.

From the cooler and cupboard, she pulled out crackers and cheese and sat inside eating and watching for headlights. Had he gotten in an accident? Was he messing with her and didn't plan to come get her at all? Was she being ten times the fool for calling him in the first place? She had no answers, just questions, and no way to answer them in the moment.

It was nearing eight in the evening when she put away the food and decided she could wait no longer. She climbed into the driver's seat and revved the engine. She was putting the van into gear when a white Land Rover covered in pink dust roared to a stop inches from her bumper. A man dressed in a plaid shirt and jeans and wearing a straw cowboy hat jumped out and strode to her door. He looked about thirty, and his clothes and face were as dusty as his car. This was not Neal. He knocked on her window, and she rolled it down.

"Are you Jane?" His was the broadest, most-Crocodile-Dundee accent she'd heard yet. She nodded. "Good. Neal said you'd still be here."

She raised an eyebrow. "Oh, did he?"

"Yeah. He told me to apologize and show you the way to the station."

"What happened?"

The man shook his head. "It's way too complicated. I'll let Neal fill you in. If you want to follow me, I'll get you there before you know it." He turned and walked back to his vehicle before Jane could protest about driving at night among kangaroos and other wild beasts. Before he climbed inside, he turned and shouted: "You better kick that thing into four-wheel drive."

Jane glanced down at the dashboard and controls, trying to remember what Geoff had said about that. There was a knob on the dash with 2H, 4H, and 4L written around it with the knob pointing at 2H. Two-wheel something beginning with "h" she surmised. Maybe she should try the 4H. She looked up and saw the Land Rover's taillights disappearing down the road. Shit. Well, 4H it was. She didn't notice any difference as she cruised down the highway after the Land Rover and prayed whatever she'd done would get her to Neal's with no problems.

As she drove, she smiled to herself that he'd sent someone to get her. It was kind of sweet. He could have called and told her to find a place to stay for the night and he'd come for her in the morning. The fact that he took the time to have someone fetch her demonstrated at least a modicum of courtesy and caring. She would have preferred that he had called to say he was going to be late and was sending a man, but this was better than the alternative.

It felt a whole lot longer than the eight kilometers Neal had mentioned on the phone before they took a hard right onto a narrow dirt track that didn't look wide enough for two cars to pass each other. The camper slewed in the loose dirt, and she slowed down in fear the thing would turn over or something. The Land Rover didn't ease off at all, and the taillights were fast becoming pinpricks in the night. Just when she thought she'd lose them, the Rover stopped and she was able to catch up. The man was standing on the side of the road when she arrived.

"You doin' OK there?"

Jane nodded. "It's acting a little squirrelly in the dirt. I'm not used to driving off-pavement. I'm sure I'll get used to it, but could you slow down a little for a while?"

He shrugged. "You got it in four?"

"I think so." She pointed to the knob.

He craned his head in the window and nodded. "Yeah, OK. I'll take it easy, but it's going to take a month of Sundays that way."

"Thank you. I'm sure I'll be able to go faster in a few miles." She gave him one of her best smiles, but he shrugged again and returned to the Rover.

He tore off at what seemed to be the same speed, and she pressed down on the accelerator trying to keep up. The camper skidded and she felt it rock back and forth, jouncing over invisible ruts that felt at least a foot deep and jolting her into the seat belt across her chest. Her palms were sweaty against the wheel, and she felt like she was fighting to stay in the dusty tracks that tied her to the Rover. At least she didn't see any kangaroos, but if they were out there, she was so focused on the road that one could have jumped over the van and she wouldn't have seen it.

She trailed the Rover through a landscape so dark she couldn't make out anything, not even the horizon, the odometer clicking away with no buildings in sight. She wondered if they were still rolling across those fields of grass she'd seen on the side of the road stretching into forever—or if they'd passed some of the trees she'd seen in the distance. Finally, the Rover slewed around a fence post and pulled to a stop beneath some good-sized trees outlined in light spilling from the windows of a large, low building. She parked beside him and climbed out.

"You got a suitcase or something?" She startled to find the man standing inches from her.

"Uh, not put together. I can grab a few things though."

"You might want to do that before we go inside." He nodded toward the back of the camper.

Jane took his advice and stuffed her pajamas, a bag of toiletries, and a change of clothing into her suitcase before reemerging. The man took the case from her hand and led her over a stone path to the front door.

They were climbing onto the covered porch when the door flew open and Neal burst out, arms extended, a smile creasing his face.

"Jane, Jane, Jane. I thought you'd never get here. Welcome to Urandangi." He wrapped her in his arms and squeezed so she could hardly breathe. When he released her, she stepped back and took a deep breath.

"Neal. I'm glad you're OK. I was worried when you didn't show up."

"Aw, it wasn't anything more than life as usual on the station. I'll bet you haven't eaten. Come on in, and I'll get Gretchen to find you a plate. You want a beer?" He laid a hand on her back and urged her forward. The other man disappeared inside with her suitcase.

She shook her head. "No thanks." She wanted a drink after the harrowing drive and searched her memory for something she'd had before that wasn't too complicated but tasted good. "But a gin and tonic would sure work."

"Gin and tonic it is." Neal's voice boomed as he ushered her into a spacious room. "Have a seat and I'll fix one for you." He crossed to a bar on the far wall.

Jane scanned the room for a seat where she wouldn't have to worry about fending off Neal, at least until she'd finished her drink. Large, overstuffed leather chairs and sofas were scattered around the perimeter, all of them big enough to seat at least two people. She settled into one of a pair that flanked a small mahogany table with a lamp and jade ashtray on it. It was still huge, and she felt swallowed alive, but she compensated by tucking her legs under her.

Neal presented her with a tall glass garnished with a lime wedge and cocktail straw jutting out at a jaunty angle. She took a sip.

"Oh, that's good. Thank you."

He eyed her in her chair, sat in the one next to it, and placed his beer glass on an agate coaster he pulled from a drawer. He set another one near her. "I'm sorry you had to wait. I hope it wasn't too bad."

She shook her head and took another sip. "I was more worried about you than anything. I thought you might have gotten in an accident or something."

"Nah, no such luck." He chuckled. "Would have rather though. One of my prize stallions has been off his feed, and I found him staggering around his stall about the time I was going to leave to get you. I had to call the vet and get some mash made before he went down. Turned out the vet was fifty kilometers away and had just finished with a job, so he was able to come right over. I didn't feel good about leaving until the horse had been seen. I knew I couldn't make it to you at any reasonable hour by the time the vet got here and finished the exam, so I sent Sam."

306

"I appreciate that. How's the horse?"

He shook his head and took a swallow of beer. "Not so good. Can't tell yet if he's got a torsion or is plugged up or what. Vet gave him a shot and will check in the morning. Meantime, I've got some of the boys walking him all night. I'll also take a turn, so it might be an early evening for us. I'll talk to Gretchen about dinner for you and make sure you have a good room. Then, I'm sorry, but I'll have to go back out. But first tell me how you did coming out here."

"Not so bad. I was worried about hitting a kangaroo but didn't even see one. Sam sure drives fast though."

Neal laughed. "Righto. I should have thought of that. He's like a rat up a drainpipe in that Rover. Sorry."

She waved a hand. "Not to worry. We made it, and that's all that counts."

He finished his beer in one long swallow. "I hate to leave you, but I do need to check on that stallion. Come, and I'll introduce you to Gretchen. But first, let's see where Sam put you."

He held out his hand, and she took it, stood, and followed him down a long hall lined with heavy wooden doors. Third one from the end. He opened it, peeked inside, shook his head, and tried the next. "Ah, here we go." He flung the door open to reveal a brass double bed covered with a hand-quilted bedspread in a floral design and an old-fashioned dresser with a pitcher and bowl on top of it and a framed mirror over it. By the bed nestled a matching night-stand with a lamp resting on a lace doily. Her suitcase sat on the bed. "I'm sure you'll be comfortable here."

"It's wonderful." She smiled at the homey comfort. It was cleaner and far more charming than anything she could have offered him in her own home. "Thank you."

"No worries. Now let's find Gretchen."

Gretchen turned out to be a fifty-something woman with gray-ing brown hair pulled back into a loose ponytail at the nape of her neck. She looked like she could have come from Poland or environs and was hefty, at least twenty pounds heavier than Jane. She was dressed in jeans and a purple T-shirt with a rampant horse embla-zoned over the words Urandangi Station, Camooweal, QLD. Her deep brown eyes squinted when Neal introduced Jane. She was sizing her up—and not approvingly. Jane stroked her hair and real-ized she hadn't actually run a brush through it since that morning. Neal instructed Gretchen to fix supper for Jane and make sure she had "all the best." Jane felt very self-conscious.

He stepped to Jane's side and placed his hand on her back. "I don't know how long this'll take, but if you get tired, snuggle in and I'll see you in the morning." Bending, he pecked her on the cheek and bustled out the kitchen door.

Jane blushed as she touched her cheek. Gretchen squinted at her once more and turned to a long tile countertop lined with kitchen appliances. "I can reheat what the men had or fix you something else. What do you want?"

"I'll take what everyone else had, if you don't mind. I appreciate your going out of your way to do this for me."

"It's my job." She pulled open the door of a gigantic refrigerator and began jerking containers from it.

Jane tightened her lips and crossed her arms. The woman oozed discontent, but Jane wasn't sure if it was disapproval of her or if it was her usual demeanor. "Can I give you a hand?"

Gretchen shook her head. "You'd be in the way. Go find a seat at the dining table, and I'll bring things out to you when they're done." She waved toward a door opposite from where Jane and Neal had come in.

"If you say so." With a grimace, she edged out of the kitchen and into a room that was filled with a huge dining table, eight chairs, a sideboard, and dish cupboard. Fresh flowers graced the center of the table; they were situated on a doily, reminding her of the one on her bedside table. She wondered if Gretchen crocheted them, or maybe it was Neal's ex. She walked around the table once, trying to decide where to sit. She felt like Goldilocks in the three bears story except that everything was too big. She chose a chair near the kitchen end of the table and sat with her gin and tonic cradled between her hands on her lap. The table looked so polished that she was afraid to set the glass down for fear of making a ring. She hoped Gretchen would bring a place mat with the food.

If nothing else, Gretchen was prompt in delivering a steaming plate of ham slices, au gratin potatoes, green beans, and a roll that looked homemade. The meat was stacked high, and the green beans were few and tucked mostly under the mound of potatoes. Gretchen pulled a plastic, woven place mat from the sideboard and set Jane's dinner on it. Butter, a pot of jam, and a dish of applesauce completed the meal.

Jane looked at the plate in awe and wondered if this was the usual portion at the station. She might be hungry, but she would never, ever be hungry enough to eat this much food. With a smile, she thanked Gretchen, who scowled in return and stalked out of the room.

She sawed her way through one of the ham steaks and half of the potatoes before she felt she couldn't cram in another bite. She pushed herself back and carried the plate and her silver to the kitchen. Gretchen was nowhere to be seen. With a shrug, Jane unburdened herself onto the counter and went back and collected the rest. She was turning to leave when Gretchen burst in through a door to the outside and eyed her.

"Food no good?"

"Oh no," Jane replied shaking her head. "It was wonderful. I just couldn't eat any more."

"Too bad. There's peach cobbler with ice cream for dessert."

Jane's stomach grumbled. There was no way cobbler was going down, no matter how wonderful it sounded. "Sorry. Not tonight. Do you think I could fix myself a cup of tea though?"

Without speaking, Gretchen filled the electric teakettle and set it to boil. From an overhead cupboard, she pulled out a couple of cans of tea and set them by the kettle. "What do you want?"

"Something decaffeinated or herbal."

Gretchen frowned. "I don't have anything like that."

"Whatever you have then." What the hell, Jane thought. With her stomach so full and tired from the long day, she'd fall asleep even if she drank a double espresso.

From one of the tins, Gretchen filled a tea ball, dropped it in a mug, and filled it with steaming water. The aroma was that of Earl Grey, Jane thought, but she couldn't read the front of the tin and didn't want to aggravate Gretchen with questions.

"Milk? Sugar?" Gretchen held the cup out to her.

"A little milk, please."

From a box in the cooler, she filled Jane's mug almost to the brim with milk. Jane stared at her cup, wondering if all Aussies brewed their tea with the milk in it. She thanked her and asked if she could take it to her room.

"Suit yourself," was the reply muttered from a turned back.

It took her a few minutes to find her room again. Her tea sloshed over the cup rim and singed her fingers. She was careful not to let any drop onto the polished wood floor or the rugs, but she was grateful to place it on her nightstand on top of one of her hankies.

Slipping off her shoes, she settled onto the bed, sinking into the comforter and mattress. The place smelled of old lavender, the kind that has almost completely dried out and melds a dusty aroma to the original scent. It made her want to sneeze. Head resting against the headboard, she sipped her tea and tried to relax.

She felt so out of place—as if she'd been dropped into a castle wearing rags and was expected to dance with the prince. If she'd imagined that Neal lived in such a huge house with servants—well, at least one—she wouldn't have called him. She was not a servant kind of person, and that's likely what Gretchen felt and was reacting to. Then again, maybe she was being overprotective of Neal, or maybe she had a crush on him and didn't brook any competition. Whatever the case, Jane didn't feel welcome in her kitchen—or the house, for that matter. Maybe she was being overly sensitive, and everything would be fine in the morning.

Before her tea was gone, Jane felt ready for bed. She slipped out to find a bathroom and ended up wandering up and down the hall clueless before opening a door and finding the toilet in a small enclosure but no sink for brushing her teeth. She decided she'd take her chances and spit into the toilet instead of heading out on another search; she'd also worry the next day about washing her face.

Back in her room, she slipped between the sheets and reached for the light switch just as someone knocked on the door.

"You still awake?" Neal murmured.

Jane pulled the covers over her chest before answering yes.

He cracked open the door, smiled, and stepped inside. "Glad I get a chance to say good night." He plopped down on the edge of the bed, and Jane jerked back, pulling the covers higher. Another Aussie quirk or an amazing lack of manners—or was this the prelude to something more? She had the urge to crawl up the headboard and perch on it.

"I'm so glad you're here. You've been on my mind since the dance, and I can't seem to get you out. I don't get a lot of company out here, not since Tish left, at any rate. She always was having parties and friends over for drinks or cards, but my mates all have wives and don't get out much. Not that I've got the time myself. Raising cattle and running a station are a full-time job and then some. The trip to Alice was the first time I've been off the place in months." He shrugged. "Can't say I miss all the entertaining; that was Tish's thing. But I do miss the woman's touch around here. Someone to have a squeeze with in the evening, you know?"

Jane didn't know. She and Ernie hadn't had sex for at least a year, since the day he was diagnosed. Right at the moment, she had no desire to be Neal's evening squeeze, at least not like this. She wondered if that was going to be part of the picture. She hadn't ruled it out, though she was so out of practice she was sure she'd be a lousy lover, not to mention the fact she was nervous about the whole thing. And taking her clothes off in front of a man other than Ernie felt like a betrayal—though she felt no loyalties to Ernie or his memory. Or did she?

Neal patted her knee, and she realized she'd missed the last few sentences of his part of their dialogue. Had he said anything important?

"I'll be going now. You look tired, and I'm totally knackered. Things get started early around here. I'll be up before sunrise, but you take your time. Brekkie's served around seven or so. You can meet most of the mob then." He bent over and gave her a peck on the cheek. "See you in the morning, luv."

Jane forced a smile. "Good night, Neal."

As he closed the door, she sank deep into the bed and sighed. Did she have to be up and looking decent enough to meet his "mates" or crew or cowboys or whatever they were called here at seven? At least she didn't have to roll out at sunrise. That would have been too much. She sighed and turned off the light.

She didn't have to worry about not waking up in time. Neal clomped past her room when first light squeezed through the curtains and what sounded like an enormous pack of dogs started to bark, accompanied by the mooing of hundreds of cows, not to mention the rooster. Jane couldn't have gone back to sleep if she'd taken a Valium or twelve. After tossing for fifteen minutes, she rolled to a sitting position and rubbed her eyes. This was not her idea of how to start the day.

She decided to take a shower and gathered her things and searched for the bathroom. Next to the room with the toilet, she found a shower and a tub inhabiting a room of their own. The shower was fronted in glass and tiled with pristine, glassy white tiles. A line of thin black tiles ran around the enclosure at eye level, and the whole thing smelled of lilacs, with not a water spot in sight. She felt bad about messing it up, but the thought of bathing in a shower not shared with a whole caravan park with room to open her arms wide and not have to worry about using excessive water was too good to miss.

She luxuriated in the hot water, letting it run over her head and soaping herself not once, but twice. When she shut off the water, she felt cleaner than she had since she left the Ramada in Melbourne, and she was energized, ready to take on the day.

Gretchen wasn't in the kitchen, though bacon sizzled on the stove, and the aroma of freshly baked bread wafted on a cool breeze from the open window over the sink. Though she still felt stuffed from the night before, all her senses pricked up at the aroma of brewed coffee, and her taste buds tingled. A nice hot cup would be the perfect start to the day. She wondered if she would be tempting the wrath of Gretchen if she found a cup and filled it on her own. Just then, Gretchen lumbered in through the kitchen door, her apron gathered up and holding a couple of dozen brown and pale-blue eggs.

"Here, let me help you." Jane reached out and tried to clear a space on the counter for the eggs, but Gretchen elbowed her aside.

"I've got it. Go sit in the dining room. Brekkie will be done shortly."

Jane backed away, feeling scolded. "May I have a cup of coffee?"

Gretchen glared at her but pulled a cup from one of the cupboards and filled it. "You need cream and sugar too?"

Jane wanted both but was too intimidated to do more than shake her head and retreat.

The dining room looked bigger than it had the evening before. The last thing she wanted to do was sit alone at the huge table waiting for someone else to show up. If breakfast was served when Neal had indicated, she had at least a half an hour to wait. With a toss of her head, she took her coffee and made her way to the front door and outside.

Though it was still early, the air felt warm, laced with a dusty smell she couldn't quite identify. The cows had quieted, also the rooster, and the only sounds were the soft voices of men in the distance and the rustling of eucalyptus leaves. In the daylight, the place looked grand. The house was clapboard with a broad porch that stretched around three sides and a tin roof that curled down at the lower edge into a quarter arc. The lawn was greening but only in spots, unlike the raised beds that flanked the brick walkway leading to the house, which were overflowing with foliage; she assumed at some point they would be covered with flowers. Both lawn and planters were in stark contrast to the surrounding land. Aside from the few trees shading the house, the land rolled forth in a mixture of bare dirt and more of the grayish-green grass she had seen beside the road. Corrals and outbuildings were scattered to the east and south, mostly unpainted and looking worn and used.

She sat on the edge of the porch and sipped her coffee, listening to a weird birdsong, a kind of warbling screech she couldn't remember hearing before. She hoped a kangaroo would hop by, or a wallaby or a wombat, but the only animal that came near was a shaggy, black-and-white dog that approached her cautiously from the outbuildings. After sitting at the end of the walkway for several minutes, the dog—she and it eyeing each other warily—bounded over and tried to lick her face. Obviously it decided she was okay. She fended it off without spilling her coffee, a major accomplishment. Dogs were fine with her, but the smaller the better, and this one was way over her limit.

"I see you met Charlene."

Jane looked up to see Neal striding up the walkway, one of the brown bush hats she'd seen for sale everywhere shading his eyes. She pushed the dog back and smiled. "Is that her name? She's quite friendly, boisterously friendly even."

He laughed. "That she is, once she decides you're OK. You've made the cut. Glad to see you're up and about."

She wanted to say, "How the hell could I sleep with all the racket?" But instead she smiled. "Are you coming in for breakfast or off to do something else?"

"Brekkie it is." He helped her to her feet and held the door for her.

Gretchen was setting out plates and silver, six places, around the table. Neal excused himself to go wash up, and Jane wandered around looking at the blue delft dishes in the china cabinet, thinking they seemed very out of place in this dry and dusty land. Gretchen returned with a covered dish that she set in the middle of the table. On repeated trips she placed stacks of toast beside it, along with pots of jam, another covered dish smelling of bacon, and a plate heaped with tomatoes.

Before she had finished, men shouldered past one another, hanging hats in the entryway and settling around the table. Most nodded at her, and she smiled in return. One of the last was the man she'd followed out there the previous evening. Sam, if she remembered correctly.

Neal arrived, sat near the head, and patted an empty seat next to him for her. She sat, and he put his arm around her.

"Everyone, I'd like you to meet Jane." Around the table heads nodded. "Jane, this is Jim, Harry, Ewan, Niles, Sam, and George." He pointed to each and, one by one, they either smiled or barely nodded—all except for Sam, who didn't respond at all.

They were a dusty, unshaven lot, dressed in plaid or chambray shirts with the distinctive curved plackets and pocket flaps she'd come to associate with cowboy clothing. All were tan and lean, with the exception of Harry, who looked a couple of decades older than the rest and sported a sizable beer belly.

"Glad to meet you."

She felt she should have said something else, but she couldn't for the life of her figure out what. However, it didn't seem to matter because after the introductions, the men began reaching for the food while Gretchen filled coffee cups. She lingered for a few minutes at Neal's side and paused to offer him things not on the table. When he said thank you, she glowed.

Aside from some discussion of the tasks for the day, they ate silently, the mounds of scrambled eggs, tomatoes, bacon, and toast disappearing rapidly. When the plates were once again empty except for a few stray crumbs, they rose and filed back out the door.

Beside her, Neal finished the last of his coffee and rose. "How would you like a tour of the station?"

"That would be great. Should I bring a hat or something?"

"Sure, if you have one. If not, no worries. I can find you something."

"No thanks. I've got one in the camper. It'll take a second for me to find it." She stood as Neal pulled out her chair for her. She smiled, thinking what a gentleman he was, while deep inside a twinge of unexpected gratitude surfaced. She felt cared for, a feeling she hadn't experienced in a long time, a warm feeling but edged with a touch of tension that hinted there would be payment required at some point. She brushed it aside.

Outside, he opened the door on an aging pickup truck, once red but now fading to pinkish orange, covered in dings and scratches with a few rust patches around the wheel wells. The station's name was painted on the side in white, though barely visible and mostly chipped away. In some places, brighter red paint still indicated what letters had once stood there. She slid in, the striped fabric of the seats intact though covered with papers, bits of twine, and the odd tool. There was neither seat belt nor headrest, and the dash was metal without the pretext of covering. All was layered in reddish dust.

They roared off in a cloud of dust, pausing for a minute for Neal to shout directions at a man standing in a corral surrounded by red cows with white faces and flat backs. The man waved back, and Neal shook his head and drove on. "That man is never going to be a stockman."

"Oh?"

"He spends more time guffing off than anything else."

She wanted to ask him what "guffing off" meant but was afraid he'd launch into his Australian slang dictionary the way he had that first night in the pub, and she didn't want to hear it. She assumed it was bad and let it go.

For hours they cruised pitted, red dirt roads, occasionally passing a small herd (he called them a mob) of cows or some free-ranging horses but little else aside from the vegetation, which in itself seemed pretty sparse. The only place where trees and other plants flourished was around the occasional water holes. Neal kept up a constant commentary, pointing out what made good feed for the animals and what didn't, how many acres and months he needed to bring a cow to market, predation on the calves by dingoes, issues with horse breeding and sales, the vagaries of stock prices, why he no longer raised sheep (the things seemed prone to keeling over for no good reason and tended to make tasty morsels for the various roaming carnivores in the region), and why being a stockman in the Australian outback was the greatest profession in the world.

He also rattled off a list of inventions that supposedly had come from Australia, including corrugated-tin roofing and collapsible clotheslines, and he stated that if anyone was paying attention, they could see that his country had been underrated across the board. She thought he sounded like a Russian at the height of the Cold War, when everything worthwhile had been invented in the USSR. But all she could do was "hmm" appropriately from time to time and stare out the window.

They stopped for lunch at the Camooweal Roadhouse, a combination gas station and convenience store with a small café that held three battered tables and five chairs. She looked at the menu hanging on the wall, remembering the meat pie she'd had and vowing to become a breatharian before she had another. Meat, meat, and more meat, with beef varieties primary among the choices. There didn't seem to be a green thing served, unless you counted the possibility of a wilted leaf of lettuce on a steak sandwich. A bored-looking twenty-something girl with scraggly blond hair tied into a rough knot on top of her head sported a denim miniskirt, tank top that reached the bottom of her ribs, and cowboy boots. She stood behind the counter picking her teeth with the point of a pencil covered in tooth marks.

Neal winked at her when he stepped up to the counter and ordered a hamburger, one with a fried egg and bacon on top, and a beer. She grinned back and jotted his order down on the bottom of half a piece of notebook paper.

What Jane wanted was a salad. When she asked the girl if she could get one, Neal threw one arm around her and laughed. "Salads and vegetables are what food eats. Tell her, Terry."

The girl nodded and grinned as if Jane's request was the most outlandish thing she'd ever heard. Feeling foolish, Jane ordered a hamburger, without Neal's greasy toppings, and a soda.

They sat, and the girl returned with Neal's beer in what appeared to be a forty-ounce can. Well, he's a drinker on or off the ranch, Jane concluded, hoping his consumption would stay at one. She had no desire to drive back with an inebriated man on the treacherous roads crisscrossing his place.

The burger turned out to be quite tasty but didn't contain even the single wilted lettuce leaf Jane had predicted. Neal wolfed his food down as if coyotes were going to rush in and steal it off his plate, while she ate slowly, hoping that the effects of food and alcohol would equalize in Neal's blood with a little time. When he raised his hand with the empty beer can in it for a refill, she bolted the rest of her food and stood.

"Why don't we go see the rest of your place?"

He looked disappointed but stood too.

Most of the rest of the afternoon mimicked the morning, with the exception that they ran into a few more mobs of cows and Sam on horseback, herding (mobbing?) a group of calves and their mothers somewhere, she assumed. Not that she could see anything resembling a corral or water hole they might be headed for. The ways of the Australian stockman appeared mysterious at best. Sam tipped his straw cowboy hat at her when the truck bounded by, and she smiled in return.

By the time the house came into view, she was hot and dusty and ready to be out of the truck. It felt like she'd seen more of Australia that day than she had in the past three weeks of driving. Well, maybe a small portion of Australia intensively. She had no idea how many miles or acres they had seen, but Neal intimated that most of the station didn't have roads, so access was either by four-wheeler, horse, or helicopter. Where, she wondered, did he have a helicopter stashed, and was it for checking out the north four thousand?

Neal muttered that he needed to take care of some chores and check on the stallion. He jumped out of the truck and strode toward some distant outbuildings, leaving Jane to her own devices. She felt deserted, like she'd been dumped at the end of a disastrous blind date. She thought he'd had a good time driving her around and telling her all about station operations, even if she was bored after they passed the second mob of cows. She hoped she hadn't shown it, but maybe that's why he took off so quickly. Maybe he felt slighted that she wasn't thrilled by his life. She shrugged and shook her head. Well, at least she knew where her room was, and maybe she could straighten things out after dinner.

The cool of the interior enveloped her when she shoved open the front door, a breath of air-conditioning exhaling to greet her. A nap would be wonderful, but a shower was more of a necessity, as she felt coated in dust from her crown to her pinky toes. She could hear clunking in the kitchen as she walked toward her room and assumed that Gretchen was hard at work turning meat into the evening meal. Maybe there would be more than a couple of green beans included tonight.

Once she found her room, she realized she didn't have any clean clothes to change into after her shower. Her choices were to put on what she wore the day before, not to shower, or to ask Gretchen for the use of the washer and dryer. The latter seemed the most sensible but also the most intimidating. She had no desire to ask Gretchen for a favor since the woman behaved as if she loathed the very space Jane occupied. But considering she would have to either wear the same clothes the entire time she was there or beg for laundry privileges, the choice was obvious.

With a sigh, she trudged out to the camper and collected the rest of her dirty clothes and, arms brimming, walked into the kitchen. Gretchen was stirring a bowl of something yellowish, her broad back to Jane.

"Excuse me," Jane said. "Could I borrow your washer and dryer to do a load of laundry? I would appreciate it since I'm out of clean clothes."

Gretchen turned around, her frown deeper than normal. "We don't have a dryer."

Drat. She should have remembered that one. "OK, then just the washer and some clothesline?" She tried a faint smile.

With a harrumph, Gretchen led her onto the porch to a battered washer that looked like it was new in World War II, with hoses running from the back of the machine into the sink. "You need detergent?"

Jane shook her head. "That, I've got. Thanks. I think I can figure it out. You can go back to what you were doing."

Gretchen growled the harrumphing noise again and departed.

Jane loaded the washer and ratcheted a few dials until the sound of water began. Back in the kitchen, Gretchen was scraping the last of what must have been cake batter into an oblong aluminum pan. Jane smiled at her.

"Looks like you're making a cake for dessert."

Gretchen grunted.

"What are you making for dinner tonight? I enjoyed last night's ham." Jane ventured another smile and hoped she could thaw Gretchen out with a little small talk.

"Pot roast, mashed potatoes, pumpkin, green beans, rolls, lemon cake." She muttered the list so fast it sounded like one long word.

"Wow. Sounds wonderful. You're a good cook. I wish I were so good."

Another grunt.

"I never realized pumpkin could be a side dish before coming to Australia. I thought it only went in pie for Thanksgiving and Christmas. Now I enjoy it. How are you fixing it?"

Gretchen spun to face her. "Look, I have work to do. I don't have time to yabber. The men will be coming in and supper has to be done. So if you don't mind, let me do my job." Snatching the cake pan from the counter, she slammed it into the oven.

Jane hung her head and whispered, "Sorry." Then she slunk out of the kitchen and back to her room. She sat on the edge of the bed feeling chastised, like she was twelve again and the butt of her mother's anger. Her bottom lip quivered, and tears sprang to her eyes. Again.

With a growl, she wiped them with her palms and stood. She wasn't going to let some overbearing Slavic cook make her feel like a naughty child. She was a guest in this house, at Neal's invitation, and she deserved at least a little civility, if not respect. It wasn't her fault Neal wasn't interested in Gretchen, even if it was obvious that she had a crush on him—which he either didn't notice or didn't care about. If Gretchen wanted to play the adoring servant to the ignorant master, that was her problem, and there was no reason to take it out on Jane.

Marching into the bathroom, she splashed cold water on her face.

Chapter 12

THAT EVENING, while Neal and Jane sat out on the patio (him sipping beer, her having a glass of red wine), watching the stars blink on and batting at the occasional fly, he reached out and took her hand.

"It's wonderful having you come out here. I can't begin to tell you how pleased I am. It's been ages since there's been a woman around, and the place can use one."

Jane wrinkled her brow. "What about Gretchen?"

"What about her?"

"Isn't she a woman?"

He brushed aside a fly and shrugged. "You know what I mean. A female who doesn't work here. A female who . . ." He trailed off and gave another shrug. "You know."

"Like a lover?" She said it very quietly, tentatively, testing the word against the possibilities of the relationship.

He turned to stare at her. "Yeah, like that."

She felt herself blush from her hairline to her shoulders. "What are you trying to say?"

"I thought that maybe . . ." He took a long pull from his beer. "I mean, you came all the way out here, so there must be some attraction. You have needs and I have needs. Maybe we could do something about that."

She blinked at him. That was the most unromantic proposition she'd ever had. Even Ernie had done better on his first try, and he hadn't done much besides take her to dinner, buy her candy, and tell her how beautiful she was while he was feeling her up in the front seat of his father's Caddy. Was this the way middle-aged people got to it? With a statement about meeting needs? No mention of appeal, of wanting to be with someone, of even liking someone?

She sipped her wine and gazed at the Southern Cross, which Neal had pointed out, broaching the horizon like a shy child. What was it she wanted from him if it wasn't to go to bed? Not a statement of undying love; that was too ridiculous at this point, especially considering she didn't feel that way toward him. So, what? Validation that she was desirable, framed in better words than their mutual "needs"? To be pampered, wined, dined, and shown off to the hired help, even if at least one of them seemed to hate her? To prove to herself she could attract a man? To see if there were better men than Ernie out there?

She took another sip and glanced at Neal. He'd laid his head back against the cushion of his patio chair and stretched his legs out in front of him. At least he wasn't pressing her for an answer because she wasn't sure what she would say if he did. Right now, it was good enough that the question had been broached and hung between them, answered or not.

They sat in silence as, one by one, the lights in the outbuildings blinked off, and only the light spilling from the kitchen remained. She finished her drink and set the glass on the paving stones, feeling contented with an edge of anticipation. She was tired after all the driving around and needed to stand up and say good night, carry her wineglass into the kitchen, and wend her way to bed. A snort startled her, and she realized Neal had drifted off to sleep and was snoring. A smile spread across her face. He looked quite cute lying there in the starlight, the beer still resting upright on his belly. She could almost kiss him.

Rising, she picked up her glass, reached out, and gently tugged on Neal's beer bottle. He startled and jerked upright.

"Wha—"

She patted his hand. "It's OK. You were asleep. I'm going to bed and was going to take your beer in with me."

"Oh." He glanced down at his empty hand and then up at her. "Oh. Well, I'm flaking out too. I'll walk you in." He rose with a groan and held the door for her.

She set the things on the counter and headed down the hall to her room with Neal trailing behind. At the door she paused and turned. "Thanks for a wonderful day. I'll see you in the morning."

He blinked a couple of times and pecked her on the cheek. "Till then."

Undressing, she felt disappointed. Did she expect him to try and sweep her off her feet or something? The peck on the cheek was anticlimactic at best. She slipped on her pajamas with a sigh, climbed between the sheets, and turned off the light, not knowing if she would have invited him in if he had asked but wishing he would have anyway.

She was lounging in a pool of warm water, her arms outstretched along the cool tiles, her head resting on the edge, the water caressing her back, her sides, her belly. It felt so wonderful, so arousing. When she opened her eyes, through the steam she saw a tall, lean man swim to her, place his hands on her breasts, and kiss her neck. She arched to him, yearning to feel him enter her, wanting it, desiring it, needing it.

Panting, Jane woke up throbbing with excitement and unfulfilled desire. For a moment she lay perfectly still, letting the dream unwind around her. She didn't want it to end. She wanted the man, wanted him to have her, wanted to go back to sleep and finish it. But the dream drifted away, leaving her feeling frustrated and needy.

She rolled onto her back, stared at the ceiling, and thought about Neal. He was down the hall. She could climb out of bed, walk to his room, and deal with both of their needs. At the thought, a wave of panic coursed through her. What was she thinking? How could she do such a thing? What would he think? How could she face him in the morning? And she couldn't go through with it even if she made it out of her bed and into his. She was terrified that she wouldn't—couldn't—respond to anything he did. Then what would he think of her?

She gritted her teeth and banged her head against the headboard a couple of times. Why couldn't she be one of those liberated women who went after what they wanted, consequences be damned? What would Rachael think if she could see her right now? She'd be shaking her head and tutting at what an emotionally immature person she was. You can have sex, she'd say, and not feel guilty about it. You can even ask the guy. It's a new century, girl!

Edging up to sitting, she turned on the light, hoping it could dispel some of her aggravation and disappointment in herself. It might be a new century, but she was the same old girl caught in the same old rules her mother had sewn so neatly into her soul. Women were pursued; they didn't do the pursuing. That was the man's job. A woman who chased a man was a slut, plain and simple, and men didn't respect sluts. She banged her head against the headboard again. What did you do if you wanted to pursue, to ask, to get, and to still be considered a good person? What could you do?

A light tapping at her door startled her out of her thoughts. "Yes?"

"Are you OK in there? I thought I heard banging.

She sat up straighter. "Neal, is that you?"

"Yeah. You all right?" He cracked open the door and poked his head inside.

"Sure. Yeah. Nothing's wrong. Come on in." She waved him into the room. He came and sat next to her, his chest bare and legs encased in wrinkled, green-striped pajama bottoms.

"I was up reading and thought I heard something."

She pursed her lips, composing a suitable lie. "Well, you did. I banged my head on the headboard, then hit it a couple more times trying to turn on the light and sit up. I'm sorry I bothered you."

"Oh, no bother. I'm glad you're OK." He put a hand over hers. "You sure you are?"

"Absolutely." She covered his hand with hers. "It was sweet of you to come check. I appreciate it a lot." She gave his hand a pat and then, without thinking, leaned forward and kissed him on the cheek.

In an instant, he wrapped his free hand around her head and pulled her to him. His lips were soft against hers, but the kiss was deep and urgent. She returned it with fervor, snaked her arms around his back, and pressed his chest to hers. They fell back against the pillows, and she wished she were wearing something sexier. At the moment it didn't matter, since Neal's fingers were under her pajama top, and anything she'd had on would have been a brief impediment. One that she would have helped eliminate.

Consciousness edged closer, swaddled in warmth and contentment. Her eyes opened to bright sunshine flooding through the sheers covering her window. She didn't want to move. Every cell in her body seemed content to luxuriate in the softness of the sheets, the gentle pressure of the mattress against her side, the pillow cradling her head, the smell of bacon and coffee wafting from under the door, and the feel of Neal's arm draped over her hip, his breath soft against the nape of her neck.

Oh, fuck. What the hell did I do?

She knew exactly what she had done, and while the regrets and second thoughts were beginning to form a small mountain in her head, the sheer depth of ease and comfort she felt at that moment superseded all of them. With one exception. She had to go to the bathroom—and urgently.

She tried to slip out from under Neal's arm without disturbing him, but his eyes opened the second she moved; he dreamily regarded her.

"Trying to escape?" He grinned then kissed her shoulder.

"Toilet," she muttered and shifted toward the edge of the bed.

"In a second." He tightened his arm around her waist and pulled her toward him. This kiss was planted on her lips, his tongue moving inside her mouth, as the hand restraining her edged over her right breast and kneaded it.

She pushed him away. "Neal, if I don't go right now, I'm going to have an accident." He loosened his grip and looked disappointed. "I'll be right back. Promise."

"OK, but hurry."

She gathered her robe from the end of the bed and swathed herself in it before peeking out into the hall. She could see no one, but the voices around the table were distinct in their wondering where the hell Neal was. Someone made a lewd suggestion and the rest of the group guffawed, but Jane figured it was a pretty accurate description of the previous evening's events. She ducked into the toilet.

Neal was still under the covers, dozing, when she returned. For a man who seemed to be up before the sun, this was an unprecedented sleep-in and, considering the response of the men to his absence at the morning table, one that rarely, if ever, happened. No wonder they nailed the reason.

Even though she didn't want to go back to bed now that she was up, she draped the robe over the footboard and slipped in beside him. He wound his arms around her and brought her in for what she assumed was round two. This had been a favorite tactic of Ernie's, to grab her and put his morning erection to some good use. But Neal held her to his chest, letting her head rest in the small bowl beneath his collar bone and caressing her hip with his free hand.

"Last night was wonderful," he murmured. "Thank you."

She wrinkled her brow. Thank you? She'd never been thanked for sex before, and it felt somewhat distasteful, as if she were a hooker and that when she arose, she'd find a couple of hundreds on the dresser. She wasn't quite sure what to say in response but settled on, "It was great for me too."

He gave her a squeeze. "I'm glad. I'm kind of out of practice, if you know what I mean."

She laughed. "Me too. I think the last time I made love to anyone was sometime in the last decade. Ernie wasn't interested after he was diagnosed." He stiffened, and she pressed her lips together. She shouldn't have brought up Ernie or anything to do with him at that moment. "Sorry. I shouldn't have said that."

He patted her head. "That's OK. Let's leave him out of our pillow talk from now on, and I won't bring up my ex either."

Relief unclenched her stomach, and she relaxed into his arms. "You sure this is OK?"

"OK?" He pushed her slightly away and gazed at her face.

"Well, I mean still being in bed and all when everyone else is eating breakfast and getting to work. Won't they be mad at you?"

He laughed. "If they are, they'll be looking for work. I'm the boss. I get to take a morning off if I want."

"But what about Gretchen?"

"Gretchen? What the hell has this to do with Gretchen?"

She sighed. He was clueless. She wished she hadn't broached the subject since the last thing she wanted to do was tell him about Gretchen's crush. It was better that he didn't know, considering they seemed to be getting along fine the way things were. What would happen if she enlightened him about Gretchen's feelings? Would it change things? Was it any of her business?

She shook her head. "Oh nothing."

"Come on—give."

She sighed again, trying to think of something that wasn't about the crush. "Well, won't she be angry that you missed breakfast?"

"That's her problem if she is. Again, I'm the boss."

The tone of his voice indicated the subject was closed. She wished she could think of something to say. She didn't want to go back to sleep but wasn't certain she was ready to make love again. However, she was beginning to get restless lying there. Cuddling was fine, but it was time to move.

"What should we do today?" She twirled one of his chest hairs around her finger. "Is there more station to see?"

He squeezed her shoulder. "I prefer this."

She suppressed a groan. "I want to get up and do something. It looks like a great day out there. What does one do in this part of Queensland on a beautiful day?"

"Are you trying to tell me you're bored? I can think of something to do right here." He grinned and reached around to fondle her breast again.

She wanted to push his hand away but instead smiled faintly. "No, I'm getting achy and want to get up. I'm also getting hungry. That bacon smells good."

He sighed. "I guess we should get up." But he didn't move. He caressed her breast with his right hand then bent down and kissed her while rolling her onto her back. Before she could protest, he ran his lips over her mouth, down between her breasts, and across her abdomen. Hand between her legs, he scooted down and licked her above her pubis.

Jane arched her back reflexively, not interested in the slightest now in getting out of bed. What Neal was doing with his lips and tongue between her legs was a new adventure. She had read and talked to other women about cunnilingus, but Ernie would sooner have given up sex entirely than give it a try. Of course, he expected her to suck him off, but return the favor? Never. This was extraordinary, and she was so aroused by the time he moved to enter her, she came immediately on his initial thrust. The rest was anticlimactic, at least for her. Neal seemed to be enjoying himself immensely, but she was glad when he finished and rolled off of her, both of them covered in sweat and panting.

He fell asleep immediately while she stared at the ceiling, remembering the wonders his tongue had done to her desire. If he'd do that to her every time, she'd stay in bed with him until they were both on the edge of starvation. She speculated about what else she had been missing since her first sexual encounter with Ernie a quarter of a century ago. To his credit, Ernie was a responsive lover, if somewhat rigid and formulaic. Sex was reserved for Friday evenings and Sunday mornings, unless he had Monday off, in which case the act was postponed until Monday morning.

She could pretty much predict how the encounter would unfold, from the first kiss to climax, though he did surprise her from time to time with changes in position that added a little spark to the proceedings. Most of the time he brought her to orgasm, and when it didn't seem to be happening, he would delay his own finish to help her come. But after this one, well, two sessions with Neal, the doors felt flung open, and suddenly she had a desire to crack open the Kama Sutra and see what lay amid those fabled pages. Maybe she should try some test runs on a few of the positions. And maybe a few more lovers too—to compare styles and techniques.

She was still considering the possibilities when Neal's eyes popped open. "I'm starving," he announced. Then he swung his legs over the side of the bed and grabbed his pajama bottoms. "I'm going to take a quick shower. Then let's go see what Gretchen can whip up for us. I'll meet you in the kitchen in fifteen."

She barely had time to blink before he'd donned his pajamas and disappeared out the door. Stunned, she stared at the closed door, attempting to shift gears from lying in postcoital bliss to a dead run into the day. Shaking her head, she grabbed her robe and headed for the other shower.

Neal was in the kitchen pouring himself a cup of coffee, with Gretchen at the stove, spatula in hand, doling strips of bacon into a cast-iron frying pan, her lips pressed into a bloodless slash across her face.

"Good morning, sleepyhead. It's about time you were up and about." He grinned at her, pouring cream into his cup.

She stared at him as if he'd gone insane. Did he think Gretchen would buy the fact that both of them had coincidentally slept in? Had he said that because he had picked up on his cook's displeasure, which was more than she'd given him credit for.

"Good morning to you too. That coffee smells great. May I have a cup?" She made her tone light and airy, as if this was the most normal morning in the world.

"Righto." He pulled a mug from the cupboard and filled it from the still-brewing pot.

Sipping, she glanced over Gretchen's shoulder at the spitting bacon and other skillet of scrambled eggs. "Looks wonderful. Thank you for taking time to make this for us so late."

Gretchen's back stiffened and her knuckles whitened on the handle of the spatula. Jane took a quick step back, fearing that the woman would spin around and slap her on the side of the face with the hot spatula. She sidled over to Neal. "What's the plan for the day?"

"After the stallion, I should check fences on the north boundary. We've lost a few cows up there recently, and I need to make sure it's because of broken fences rather than predators."

"Sounds interesting." Well, kind of, she thought. Better than hanging out in the house with the raging cook from hell. "May I tag along?"

"Sure. I'd love the company."

That response didn't seem to make Gretchen any happier, and Jane was relieved when they'd finished eating and headed outside, leaving Gretchen still slamming dishes around in the kitchen. She found her way to the truck while Neal checked on the stallion, and leaned against the passenger door, letting the sun warm her face.

Neal returned in a couple of minutes, smiling. "He's back up and running. Shifted the whole wad in the night."

"Oh good," Jane replied, assuming the horse had just taken a big dump and that was the problem. They climbed into the truck, Neal whistling under his breath.

"Gretchen was in a bad mood, wasn't she?" Jane shifted in the seat trying to get comfortable.

He grunted. "She's probably up on blocks."

"What?"

"She's probably having her period. That's why she was spewin.'"

Jane stared at him, making sure her mouth wasn't hanging open in disbelief. Even Ernie wouldn't have been so blind and sexist, and that was saying a great deal. Did Neal really believe that? If Rachael were sitting here, she'd slap the man silly. In fact, Jane had the urge to climb out of the truck, pack her things, and go roaring off in her camper. But he'd put the truck in gear and was bouncing, at what she considered a reckless speed, down a lane that more resembled a cow path than a road. She grabbed the dashboard and hung on.

They rode in silence for almost an hour, the rattling of the truck and complaints of the springs making conversation impossible. When Neal pulled up next to a long line of barbed wire fence stretching into the distance in both directions, she sat back and flexed her hands to work out the cramps. He turned and paralleled the wire, driving slowly.

"How long is this thing?" she asked after half an hour's travel hadn't shown any signs of a corner post or end to the fence.

"Thirty kilometers, more or less."

"Wow, that's amazing. I've never seen anything like it back home."

"This isn't the States, babe."

I know that, she wanted to retort but bit her lip and watched the fence roll by.

What a change. Yesterday the man wouldn't quit talking, and today she couldn't seem to get anything but sexist platitudes and grunts out of him. Was he withdrawing because of Gretchen's display that morning, or was this his normal mode of interacting, and yesterday was another form of foreplay? Showing off to make her think he was a good catch? She wasn't thrilled with either mode but didn't want to put out the effort to engage him in conversation when he so obviously wasn't interested. She wished she had stayed back at the house, tucked in her room away from Gretchen.

After thirty more minutes of the same view of fencing, in the distance she thought she could see a post leaning sideways. At least something was canted off-line or leaning against the wire. He pressed the accelerator, and the truck bounded over bunches of spinifex grass and small bushes until the break was visible.

"Aw, bugger," he muttered. He threw one arm over the seat back and pulled out a small toolbox and a hoop of wire. "Best see what we can do about this."

Jane followed him to the downed wire. The ends coiling together in the dirt appeared to be of different lengths. "Guess it wasn't cut," she ventured. "What do you think happened?"

"Looks like something big went right through. Might have been Max."

"Max?"

"Yeah, my Gelbvieh bull. Has a tendency to wander and take a few girls with him."

By girls she assumed he meant cows and nodded. "Do we need to go find him and the girls?"

"Not in this ute. I'll get Sam or one of the other station hands to track him down on horseback." He dropped the toolbox on the ground and extracted a pair of heavy pliers and leather gloves. With the hoop of wire slung over his shoulder, he began to pull the broken ends of the barbed wire together.

She watched for a minute as he struggled to grab two ends and join them. "Can I help?" She figured she could at least hold one of the ends for him.

"Nah. Got this." He jerked the wire but lost hold of it when he tried to bend one of the ends. "Bugger."

Without saying a word, she stepped forward and plucked the end from the ground. "Here, let me hold it for you."

A look of frustration flickered across his face, replaced with a smile that looked forced. "Sure. Just keep it while I get this end ready." He bent the end, turning it back to form a loop, which he secured by winding the broken end around the main body of the wire several times. "OK, now hold this one." He handed her his work and repeated the procedure on the next piece. Finally, he lopped off a section of new wire and joined the two looped ends.

"There, one done." They each reached for the next strand, and he repaired that one and the following two efficiently. As he was joining the last pieces, he waved toward the truck, aka ute, she corrected mentally. "There's a shovel in the back. Can you get it for me?"

"Sure." She was glad he asked her to do something and hoped she had proved herself at least marginally useful.

The bed of the truck was littered with boards, pieces of cardboard, and various tools. She pushed aside a section of plywood and located a shovel nestled against the wheel well. It took a bit of tugging, but she freed it and carried it to Neal.

"Here you go."

He grasped it and handed her the pliers and coil of wire in return. "Put these back in the ute and see if you can find a sledge in the bed."

The toolbox weighed a ton despite its small size. She staggered back to the truck and hoisted it with both hands, putting it behind the seat and sweating with the exertion. She stirred the contents in the bed but couldn't see any kind of hammer, much less a sledge. "I can't see one," she shouted.

"It's there. Look harder."

Mouth set in a tight line, she rummaged through the mess again with no luck. Just to be sure, she climbed in the back and lifted or moved everything. "Nope. No sledge."

"Bugger. OK, I'll have to make do." He dug around the first slanted post, straightened it, tamped the dirt back around the base with the end of the shovel, and moved to the next one. She watched him work, thinking it would have been a better idea to set the posts before splicing the wire. But then, she was no stockman, so what did she know? After the posts were in place, he glanced up and held out the shovel toward her.

"Here. I need the toolbox again."

Grabbing the shovel, she rolled her eyes internally. Why couldn't he have figured that out before he had her put it away? Shovel in the back, she muscled the toolbox back out. "You want the wire too?"

"Nah. Just need a hammer and some staples."

She hefted the box back to him and dropped it at his feet. "Here you go."

He removed what he needed, proceeded to use U-shaped nails to attach the wire to the posts, which he had her lean against while he banged the staples into the wood. Then he dropped it all back into the box. "Done," he announced, shedding his gloves. "Let's see if there's more."

They drove for another hour along the fence, but no other breaks appeared. Apparently satisfied, he turned the truck around and followed the wire back to the dirt track and home, not uttering a word.

The sun was near the horizon when they pulled up to the house. Jane was covered in dust, hot, sweaty, and more than a little irritated at the silent ride home. She'd tried to engage him in conversation a couple of times, but he didn't respond to her questions—either because he couldn't hear them over the rattling or didn't want to talk. To her it didn't matter. His behavior was ill-mannered at best and more likely outright rude. Before the truck came to a full stop, she'd flung open the door and made a beeline for the shower, mouth set in a grim line.

While mist from the steaming water fogged the mirrors and filled her lungs with blessed moisture, she tried to relax. The day had started out magnificently, but her thoughts kept circling back to his silence and misogynous opinions about Gretchen's behavior. Part of her wanted to dry off, pack her things, and leave, no matter if she faced rampaging kangaroos after dark or not. The other part was fabricating excuses for his behavior and looking forward to having his head between her legs again. The parts were more or less evenly divided, and she vowed she would stay in the shower until she could make up her mind.

Unfortunately, Gretchen's knock on the door and her insisting the hot water was running out forced her to grab towels instead of a decision. She dried off, brushed out her hair, dressed, and decided to give Neal another chance. The man might be clueless about what made women tick, so maybe he needed someone to point out a few things to him. Perhaps his bedroom behavior was more indicative of how he felt about women than his words. After all, her mother always said actions speak louder than words.

Dinner that evening was livelier than the previous day, with the men all exchanging anecdotes about their day and plans for what needed to be done the next. Even Gretchen seemed in a good mood and joked with several of the hands while she served another huge meal. Neal winked at her at one point, which sent some undecipherable emotion racing across her face before she retreated back to the kitchen.

The man on Jane's left asked her about Cortez, America, Indians, and the American brand of ranching. She felt flattered by his attention and, after a glass of wine wheedled from Gretchen, happily related story after story. A couple of the other men chimed in, and before the end of the meal, she found herself addressing the entire table about what it was like to live in a small, Western town. She was flushed and beaming by dessert, and when Neal led her outside to sip coffee under the stars, she was glad she'd decided to stay.

She went to bed alone and pajamaless but kept her light on and tried reading, hoping Neal would knock at her door before she fell asleep. The house settled into silence, and the minutes ticked into quarter hours then halves, then wholes, and still no Neal. She wondered if he was waiting for her to come to him. That seemed too far a step for her. She'd accept him back into her bed but couldn't picture herself sneaking into his. At least not yet.

When she was about to give up, close her book, and flick off the light, a soft knock sounded at the door. She climbed out of bed and pulled the door open. He swept her into his arms, his mouth planted on hers before he'd made it inside the room. Shuffling toward the bed, he kicked the door shut with one foot.

Jane rolled over and flung an arm, unseeing, in the general direction she thought Neal was lying. It hit the sheets and nothing else. She cracked open her eyes and stared at the head-shaped hollow in the pillow and sighed. Wasn't this the classic movie postcoital abandonment cliché? She hated playing out bad movie scenes.

Rolling onto her back, she stared at the ceiling and the dusty fan that hung there, a couple of cobwebs dangling between the blades. Maybe she should tell Gretchen. Then again, this was the first thing out of order in the entire house, and it felt good to see that the woman wasn't the perfect housekeeper. It would be her little secret.

As she watched the cobwebs swing in the imperceptible air currents, she wondered what had happened to Neal. After yesterday's thrilling start to the morning, she was expecting another early morning orgasm to begin her day. Now, alone between the sheets, the sun brightening the sky beyond the curtains, she felt sad and lonely. Just like in the movies. Why had he left so early? When had he left? The last thing she remembered was sweat beading on his back while he snored post-climax beside her. She had drifted off to sleep herself, savoring the feeling of his hands on her flesh, him moving inside her. She had assumed he would be there when she woke up, but nada. She sighed again.

Outside she could hear the sounds of men's voices, and she wondered what the fuss was about. Maybe that's why Neal was gone. Maybe something big had come up, and he had to go take care of things. She should go see. With a sigh, she swung her legs over the side of the bed.

Gretchen was at her usual post in the kitchen, breakfast sizzling, spattering, boiling, and baking all around her. Though Jane wanted a cup of tea or coffee, she felt like the proverbial elephant in this delicately timed operation and decided she could wait rather than invoke the wrath of the cook. Slipping out the kitchen door, she tried to locate Neal's voice among the others. Most of the commotion seemed to be coming from a set of outbuildings to the north of the house, so that's the way she pointed her feet.

The noise emanated from behind the buildings around a corral attached to the largest one. Ringing the corral, tethered horses twitched while a couple of the station hands brushed and groomed them, tack lying over the top rail in front of each of the steeds. Four other men fussed with four-wheelers, and behind it all, Neal was pumping fuel into a helicopter.

She blinked at the sight. Since he had first mentioned it, she had never believed that he owned a helicopter. It seemed too indulgently ludicrous. But there it was, a bright red machine with its top rotors balanced on a small tower attached to the bubble-shaped passenger compartment. And there was Neal, one hand placed lovingly on the side, gas nozzle in the other, a contented smile on his face.

Suppressing a grin, she circled the commotion to Neal. "Good morning. Feeding your baby?"

He looked up, startled, and grinned. "G'day. Nice to see you up and around so early."

A prick of annoyance jabbed her. "So early?" As if she was a lazy layabout who had forced herself out of bed. As if he wasn't the reason she'd stayed in bed so long yesterday. She gritted her teeth and forced a smile. Let it go, she told herself. He didn't mean it that way.

"Nice bird you've got there. Going flying today?"

He nodded. "Just as soon as brekkie's over. Need to muster the cows that'll be calving soon and get them in the paddock before they start dropping their calves all over the bush. You want to come?"

344

His grin widened, and he raised his eyebrows a couple of times.

She paused, her smile frozen on her lips. Flying. In that thing. It didn't look all that stable and didn't have any doors. She could imagine herself falling out at ten thousand feet to an untimely death among the kangaroos. But he looked so excited, like a kid with a new toy wanting to show it off. Cautiously, she nodded, praying this wouldn't be one of the times her motion sickness kicked into high gear. Did she have any meclizine in the camper? "Sure. Why not?"

That seemed to please him, and he took her arm after putting away the nozzle and led her to breakfast.

Gretchen had either come to terms with Jane's presence or decided she'd be gone soon enough, so she didn't have to worry about her cutting into her territory. In either case, she smiled when she handed Jane a plate of ham slices. Jane felt a chill run down her back, as if the meat had been presented by an ax murderer making nice-nice before committing the dreaded act. She preferred the grimaces and smoldering glances Gretchen was so good at. She thanked the cook and passed the meat on.

The men were excited and talkative as they divided up the range lands and formulated a plan of action for bringing in the cows. Ewan and Niles were going to ride horses with some men hired for the day to help out. The other four hands were on the ATVs, and Neal would supervise and guide in strays at the outskirts of the operation. They teased her and called her Neal's copilot, then guardian angel, then personal aide station. That sent a roar of laughter around the room, and she blushed while Neal looked proud. Gretchen poked her head into the room and retreated with a scowl. So much for smiles.

The food was consumed in short order, and before she could brush her teeth or collect a hat, Neal guided her out the door and to the helicopter. He helped her into the narrow seat on the left and pointed out the seat belt. By the time Neal had rounded the other side, checked the back rotor, and climbed in himself, she was belted in but still felt exposed, wishing the copter had a restraint system like a racing car.

"You ready?" He snapped his seat belt into place and reached for the controls. Before she could answer, he started the engine and let it rev higher and higher. He handed her a pair of headphones with a mic circling around from the left and donned his own. Once she had hers in place, he gave a thumbs up. "Testing, testing. Can you hear me, luv?"

His voice was filled with static and barely understandable, though it seemed to sit in her ear canals. Still, she doubted she could have made out a single word amid the roar of the engine without them. "I can hear you."

"Good. Then we're off."

She gulped and glanced at the other men outside, either mounting or mounted on their various conveyances, and wished Neal was piloting an ATV instead. But she turned back to him and produced a confident nod in spite of the churning in her stomach. The rotor's whine inched up the scale, and then they were rising above the rest, a cloud of dust and dirt the only reminder that they'd been on the ground a moment before.

She clutched the side of her seat with one hand and the edge of the plexiglass window with the other when he banked left and took a quick turn around the house, outbuildings, and corrals. A steady vibration coursed through her, reminding her of one of those cheap motel beds that pulsated, supposedly erotically, when fed the appropriate number of quarters. She wasn't turned on. But she found herself entranced by the view as they climbed higher and the sweep of the land grew around her in shades of ocher and muted green, with swaths of rusty red.

Beneath them, swales of low hills undulated across the land, and the courses of small streams were marked by lines of more verdant vegetation. Nestled among the rounded curves of the hills stood rocky outcroppings shaded from black to red to cream, and across it all fences marched in rigid lines. They circled upward, and she could see the dust plumes from the ATVs bouncing across the fields and the dots of the men on horseback following behind.

"We're going to head up toward Jackert's place first. Niles said he spotted a good-size mob out that way yesterday."

She nodded, not understanding what direction that was but figuring that acknowledging his words would be helpful. They flew in silence for a few minutes; then he tapped her on the arm and pointed.

"Look. Roos. Let's have some fun." He banked sharply to the right and angled steeply toward the earth. She gasped at the sudden move and tightened her grip on the window as he plummeted toward the ground until he was fifty feet above the tops of the bushes. The kangaroos scattered, breaking into groups of two or three, and hopped in a mad dash for the cover of the sparsely distributed trees. He laughed and pulled up.

"Those do-gooder animal rights people hate that. Call it wildlife harassment. But I say they're on my land, so they're my roos, and I can do anything I damn well like to them."

She smiled weakly, remembering Cleo's beliefs about the worth of everything and, inside, siding with the do-gooders. It seemed like a waste of gas and time to go buzzing wild animals for the hell of it. It reminded her of the tales some of her classmates told of cow tipping or of the out-of-state hunters back home who killed to collect the head and antlers of deer or elk. It left her queasy.

They continued in silence for about fifteen minutes until he pointed out three red-and-white cows grazing near one another in the distance. They all looked fat and contented to Jane, though she amended that, thinking maybe the appearance of fat was really a calf. Her earphones crackled.

"Got some at . . ." He bent over a GPS unit on the dash and ran a finger along the display. "91degrees, 34 minutes, 37.18 seconds by 138 degrees, 8 minutes, 23.6 seconds. Got that?" After a moment he nodded. "I'll send them your direction."

She assumed that someone had answered him, but she wasn't plugged into the frequency the men on the ground used or some such thing. She felt left out and wished she could have heard the other half of the conversation, even if it was a one-word response. Before she could think more on the subject, he whipped the copter around and dove for the cows. Her stomach grumbled.

With more care and finesse than he'd shown chasing the kangaroos, Neal got the cattle moving back the way they'd come. Before he got very far, however, he swung the machine back the other direction.

"What's happening?" she managed to croak out over the protests of her stomach.

"Another mob over there." He jerked his head toward a more heavily wooded gully, what she would have called an arroyo back home, where she could make out the backs of several more cows. Quickly, he rounded up the cattle and sent them trotting off in the same direction as the first group. After a few minutes of shepherding, the two groups had joined and were met by the men on ATVs, who surrounded them and urged them forward.

"Watch those buggers on the left," Neal shouted into the mic. One of the ATVs split off and headed toward a couple of cows that looked to her as if they were doing fine. But then this was her first muster, and Neal probably saw something she did not.

The helicopter rose and veered around back toward the trees and gully, rousting out more cattle and flushing them into the open. Each time, the cows were met by the ATVs, and each time, Neal found something to complain about in the performance of the men on the ground. He began to swear at them although she could see nothing wrong. After about an hour, the herd had grown to sizable proportions, and the men on horseback began driving them home while frenetic dots—the cattle dogs—roamed the edges, maintaining the group's cohesion.

But Neal seemed far from pleased. He berated the men constantly, calling them bloody fools, drongos, or stuff-ups. She couldn't hear what the men replied to his abuse, but at one point she thought she saw an upraised hand with the middle finger extended at the copter. She agreed with the gesture. The longer she sat in the copter, the more it seemed she was riding with an Ernie clone and the more she wanted out.

The day wore on without any breaks. Jane was sure they must be out of fuel by now and prayed they would be forced to return to the house, and she could abandon ship. But the fuel seemed endless, as did the cows that were scattered like strewn confetti across the land. She was thirsty and hungry and her stomach unhappy with the dips and swaying. Her butt tingled from the constant vibration. Neal, however, seemed in his element. She could have sworn he got a thrill out of yelling at his men. He seemed to get a charge out of brushing the tops of the trees and bushes as well. She didn't think a helicopter could fly so low, raising clouds of dust and sending small animals skittering for cover. When she wasn't nauseated or bored, she was scared out of her wits by some of his stunts. She swore that if she survived the trip, she would never, ever, ever ride in such a machine again.

It was midafternoon by the time the herd had grown to several hundred and was meandering home. She could have kissed Neal when he tapped the fuel gauge and announced they needed to get back. Slumping back in the seat, she sighed, watching the herd disappear into the distance. She didn't envy the rest of the station hands, who still had to get the cattle back to the paddocks and settled with food and water. She just hoped she could land and stay landed.

But they didn't stay landed. Neal insisted she remain in the chopper, relenting only when she pleaded for a bathroom break. She bolted for the house. Sitting on the toilet, she tried to think of reasons why she couldn't go back up. Vertigo? Nausea? Plain fear?

Just then, the banging of pots and pans in the kitchen viscerally reminded her that with Neal gone, Gretchen ruled the house. The thought of spending hours alone with Gretchen made her break out in a cold sweat. She realized she would rather careen around in the sky than be at that woman's mercy.

Without even grabbing a drink, she raced back outside in what she considered record time. Neal, on the other hand, seemed to think she had dawdled.

"I finished refueling five minutes ago. What the bloody hell took you so long?"

She ducked her head and climbed aboard. "Sorry. I went as fast as I could. I didn't even stop for a drink of water."

He huffed and churned the blades back into motion. She had barely gotten her seat belt fastened when he pulled back on the lever and they soared into the afternoon sky. Jane clung to the seat feeling chastised. His anger at her seemed irrational, but then neither of them had had anything to eat or drink since breakfast, and she could feel her own mood darken in response to thirst and plummeting blood sugar. He must be feeling much the same. Better they should get this task done quickly.

It took another three hours to drive the herd into the paddocks, three hours filled with Neal berating his men and growling at her when he wasn't yelling at them. She wished she had a parachute and that they were high enough that she could bail, but she was stuck for the duration. So she plastered a weak smile on her face and kept quiet.

It was dark by the time the stock tanks were filled, the hay scattered, and the paddocks shut. Neal landed back at the fuel tank, so close she was sure the rotors would hit it and ignite them into a ball of fire large enough to go down in history. She opened her mouth to protest his approach, but she reconsidered and let him land, her fingers and knuckles white in a terror grip. The blades swooshed into silence, and she sat and forced her fingers free of their clutch and climbed out on shaky legs. He also descended, looking haggard and several years older than he had when they'd taken off that morning.

Dinner was a silent affair, the men shoveling down Gretchen's steaks accompanied by bottle after bottle of beer. By the end of the meal, Jane was tempted to sneak out back and see how many bottles filled the trash. Whether the drinking was a normal response to a hard day's work or a way to deal with Neal's abuse, she couldn't tell, but she was glad when they filed out the door into the night.

As Gretchen cleared the table, Neal wrapped one hand around his beer bottle and reached for Jane with the other. "Why don't we sit on the veranda for a few?"

She evaded his grasp but nodded. "Sure. Just for a little while. I'm exhausted."

He opened the door and followed her to the wicker chairs set against the side of the house. Collapsing into the nearest one, she stretched out her feet and sighed. He took the other and scooted down until the back of his head rested on the chair.

"What a long day. Is it always like this when you gather the cows?"

He took a long swig from his bottle. "Today was a corker. Things went without a hitch. Usually it takes days to get done what we did, and we seem to always lose one or two on the trip back. You saw one of the good days."

She pressed her lips together and stared into the night. If today was one of the good days, how was he when things went badly? She couldn't imagine the kind of language and imprecations he would heap upon his help if he was really displeased. His remarks got him flipped off at least once that day. Would his men stick around if it was worse, or would they ride off leaving him to do things alone? Somehow she couldn't imagine this, but then she couldn't imagine them staying for it either. Maybe jobs were scarce enough a man would put up with almost anything to stay employed. God knows, she had stayed through some horrible abuse because of family pressures, her doubts that she could make it on her own, and the guilt associated with the thought of leaving after Ernie got sick. Maybe these men had some of the same pressures on them, and that's why they stayed. But for all she knew, this was the way things were done on cattle stations in the outback. She didn't have a clue what normal was out here.

She sighed again, the meal filling her belly and the rest of her with drowsiness. She closed her eyes and then opened them when she heard the clunk of glass against the boards of the veranda and a gentle snore emanate from Neal's chair. He'd fallen asleep.

Smiling, she rose and crept into the house to her room. She doubted she'd have a midnight visitor that night; at least she hoped that would be the case. She didn't have enough strength to muster one hormone, much less the army of them she'd need for a late-night tryst. Besides, she was still unsettled by Neal's behavior and wasn't sure she wanted him around for a while. She flicked off the light, briefly considering leaving in the morning but concluding she was too tired to make a decision. Tomorrow would sort itself out.

Chapter 13

NEAL TAPPED ON HER DOOR while she was finishing getting dressed. She opened it, still fastening the last button on her shirt.

"Hey. Good morning. Heading for breakfast?"

He shook his head after planting a kiss on her cheek. "No brekkie for me this morning, I'm afraid. I was going to grab a cup of tea and then go see why there's no water in the tank out by the northeast bore. All the cattle we drove to that paddock yesterday are going to be very thirsty if I don't figure things out. You're welcome to come." He flashed a smile.

Yesterday. She remembered his interactions with the hands and cringed. At least they would be going out alone, or so she assumed.

She didn't want to hear him raving again. And what about leaving? That was high on her agenda the day before. Now his smile and the gentle touch of his hand on her arm initiated a whole line of argument why she should stay another day. He looked cute this morning.

"Sure, sounds interesting. Do you think I could get a bite of toast while you have your tea?"

"No worries. I'll get Gretchen to fix you a slice with Vegemite. Come on." He laid her hand in the crook of his arm. "You've had Vegemite, right?" She shook her head. "Ah, then you're in for a real Aussie treat."

Gretchen beamed at Neal like he was the sun after a week of rain—but her beam went into eclipse the instant she caught sight of Jane. Mouth a tight slash, she filled a battered travel mug for Neal and scraped a dark substance onto toast for Jane and handed it to her with narrowed eyes.

Jane sniffed the bread and took a bite. It tasted of salt and something vaguely like beef bouillon in paste form. She chewed, wishing she could spit it out, but Neal stared at her while Gretchen glared, daring her to hate it. Swallowing she put on a smile. "I've never tasted anything like that. What is it?"

"It's a yeast extract. Our version of Marmite, the British one."

"Oh. You mean other people eat this stuff too, not just Australians?" She wanted to add "why" but forced herself to take another bite instead.

Neal shrugged and grabbed his cup. "Sure. You ready?"

"Could I get a drink of water first?" She looked around for a glass and then thanked Gretchen when she pushed one at her. The water washed some of the taste out of her mouth, but unless she carried a full canteen with her, there was no way she was going to make it through the rest of the toast. She set the toast on the counter while she drank and then placed the glass next to the bread and turned to leave, hoping Neal wouldn't catch on that she wasn't going to eat it all.

He didn't seem to notice and pushed out the screen door with her in tow. Gretchen, on the other hand, made a low grumbling noise as Jane followed him into the sunshine.

"We'll take the ute. Climb on in while I grab a toolbox." He gestured toward a different dusty pickup truck. She walked to the right side then sighed and circled around to the other when she saw the steering wheel. Was she ever going to get used to having the driver on the right?

The truck jounced, and a noisy clunking startled her. Then she realized it was Neal adding his tools to the bed in back. He grinned at her and climbed behind the wheel. "Off we go."

Dust from the road created a rising reddish cloud behind them while they bounced along again at what she thought was an unreasonable speed, especially considering her head hit the roof a couple of times as they jounced over deep ruts. Still, it could have been worse; they could have been in the copter. She tried to ask him about the tank and what a bore was, but the rattling of the truck, the roar of the engine, and the crashing of the toolbox against the side of the bed made it impossible to carry on a conversation. Again. Instead, she looked out the window, hoping for a glimpse of wildlife or a cow or two. The land rolled by flat and red, highlighted occasionally by bushes or patches of the funny-colored grass.

About an hour later, they halted in front of a huge windmill that reminded her of something out of a picture of 1930s Kansas. The dust following them caught up, and she emerged from the truck coughing and trying to swoosh it away with her hand.

From the back, Neal pulled out the metal toolbox and set it on the ground by a large, round stock tank, which was dented and empty.

"So this is a bore," she said, eyes climbing up the side of the tower on which the windmill sat, its blades motionless in the morning breeze.

"No, that's a windmill. The bore's the well into the aquifer." He bent over the tools and extracted an oversize plumber's wrench from the box.

"Oh. I wondered what a bore was. What do you think's wrong with it?"

"One of the arms has likely broken off the drive gear or seized up. I'll have to go up and check it out." He gazed up at the wheel high overhead and then down at her. "You can give me a hand. I'll take a rope up and you can tie the tools I need on the end of it. That would save me a lot of climbing up and down."

She shrugged. "Sure. I hope I can figure out what tools you need."

"No worries. It'll be easy." With a grin, he handed her the wrench and grabbed a coil of rope from the truck.

The wrench weighed a ton. She almost dropped it and then struggled to keep it at waist level rather than look like a wimp and let it fall to the dirt. Neal looped the rope over one shoulder and climbed up the tower, his feet making scraping noises on the wooden slats of the ladder. She watched him ascend, feeling a little vertigo herself. She never could have made it to the top of the platform, much less have done anything, since she would have been hanging on for dear life.

When he got to the top, he yelled down at her. "I'm dropping the rope. Watch out." She took a step back as the braided yellow rope uncoiled and then plopped at her feet in a puff of dust. "OK, now attach the spanner to it."

"The what?" She glanced around for something she thought could fit the description of a spanner—to no avail.

"The thing in your hand." His tone sounded aggravated.

"Oh." She placed the wrench in the dirt and wound the rope around it a couple of times to where she didn't think it could slip off. "OK, it's ready."

He pulled the wrench up, hand over hand, one leg wrapped around the supporting strut of the windmill tower and the other on the top step. She shaded her eyes, watching him bang at something on the back of the blade assembly, the metallic clunks sounding very far away.

"OK, now I need a screwdriver."

"What kind?"

"What do you mean what kind? A screwdriver." Again, he glared down at her.

"Flat-head or Phillips and what size?"

"Phillips, the bigger the better."

As she bent and rummaged through the toolbox, she caught a glimpse of the rope falling to her left. It landed with a thunk. She pulled the biggest screwdriver she could find from the box and tied the rope around it. "OK, it's ready," she shouted up at him.

He jerked on the rope, but before the tool was halfway up, the screwdriver swung, handle down, and slipped out of her knot. She jerked back from the falling metal and thought she heard a muttered curse.

"Sorry." She grabbed the screwdriver and wound the rope around it several times and knotted it. Before she let go, she shook it a couple of times to make sure it wasn't going to fall out again. "OK," she said at last and waited for him to haul it up. This time it made it to the platform without incident.

More clunking and sounds of metal hitting metal, punctuated by swear words. She stared upward, concerned that he was having problems. "Is everything OK?"

"Bugger."

That didn't sound good. "What's the matter?"

"Driver's too big. This one's coming down—find one that's smaller."

She jumped backward when the screwdriver slammed, point first, into the ground where she had been standing a moment before. The rope followed. She cursed under her breath. If she hadn't been looking up, the thing would have impaled her. Didn't he look before he tossed it? Teeth clenched, she located a smaller screwdriver and wound the rope around it. It disappeared up the tower.

For a long time she stood, eyes shaded, staring up at Neal while he worked, still muttering. Occasionally she could make out a "bloody hell" or "damn," but most of the time it seemed he was either talking to himself or the windmill. She was getting hot and hungry. Her stomach grumbled, and she wished she had finished off the Vegemite on toast no matter how bad it tasted. Glancing at her watch, she realized it was noon and the repair job looked nowhere close to being finished. Even if they left now, by the time they got back to the house, it would be close to midafternoon, so lunch was history, just like breakfast.

"Fuck!" The word drifted down to her, and her jaw clenched. "God damn it to hell!"

"What's wrong?" she shouted.

He swung the wrench against the top of the platform with a resounding clang. "God damn it, the arm broke. Fuck." He wiped his forehead with the back of his hand, his face looking beet red even at that distance. Suddenly, he slammed a fist against the platform and then straightened. After a few minutes, during which she hoped he was trying to calm down, he looked down at her. "OK, I need you to fetch me another arm from the back of the ute." His voice sounded strained.

Her eyes widened, and a panicky feeling gripped her stomach. She didn't have a clue what to do, and this was going to be far trickier than the spanner. "What does it look like?" she managed to shout back, hoping it would have a distinctive shape or color or something.

"Long and thin, about 300 centimeters long with holes at both ends."

Shit. How long was 300 centimeters? Long and thin with holes, that could be damned near anything. She walked to the back of the truck, hands perspiring, and glanced inside. It was awash in various tools and pieces of metal, from gears to horse tack. Reaching in, she pushed things around, trying to see anything that even vaguely matched his description. When nothing did, she opened the toolbox and looked in. It was crammed full of wrenches, screwdrivers, rolls of wire, and tools she couldn't identify. She looked up again. "Where do you think it is?"

She could hear muttering from the top of the tower but couldn't make out the words. The tone reminded her of Ernie's when he became irritated with her—just before he exploded. She didn't want to say anything else and began to search through the truck bed again.

"It's in the bed at the front." His tone was angry.

She moved toward the cab and stood on tiptoe, reaching her arm over the side and into a clutter of metal pieces, none of which resembled what he described. The pieces were heavy, and she could barely flip them over to look beneath.

"Farther up." He waved toward the cab, and she shook her head and moved forward more. "No, by the cab!"

She thought she was by the cab, at least her arm was. She realized she was never going to find it like this. Maybe if she got inside, she could get a better look. She moved to the back of the truck and was trying to figure out how to open the tailgate when he shouted again.

"What the bloody hell are you trying to do?"

She froze, feeling like a deer in the headlights. "I can't see from the side. I thought I'd get in and see if I could find it."

A long pause. "Well, get to it then."

Not bothering to try and lower the tailgate, she used the rear bumper to hoist herself over the side and into the bed. It looked more of a mess from this angle. She threaded her way to the cab and began to shuffle things around, eyes straining for anything that matched his description.

"Well?"

"I'm looking." She pushed a bucket of nails to one side.

"It's right there. You can't miss it unless you're blind. Come on."

Her movements became more frantic, but nothing looked right. She had searched the whole front of the bed by the cab and was moving backward when she heard grunting and looked up to see Neal descending the tower.

Oh shit.

He stormed over to the truck, his face red and sweaty. He didn't look at her, just pushed a rimless tire back from where it sat midway

362

down the bed of the truck. From behind it he extracted a piece of metal about a foot long and two inches wide. He held it up and shook it in her face. "This is what I was talking about."

Jane jerked back, fear arrowing through her. The part was inches from her, and she could see the anger boiling off him. For an instant she was sure he was going to strike her, but he spun and climbed back up the tower.

Jane cringed in the back of the truck, feeling incompetent and worthless. She felt she was back with Ernie but worse. No matter how angry Ernie became or how many times he threatened her, she never worried he would hit her. With Neal, that threat felt very real.

Shaking, she climbed onto the ground and wiped her sweaty palms on the legs of her pants, leaving dark smudges on her thighs. On one level the situation felt so familiar, an angry man showing her what a useless human being she was and her responding with self-loathing and acceptance that what he said was the truth. It was accompanied by fear that she could never measure up, never be anything more than a bumbling idiot of a human being, not worth the food it took to feed her, not worth the air she breathed. She leaned against the side of the truck, tears coursing down her cheeks, and ran her hands through her hair and took a deep breath.

Damn it, she didn't want to be that woman anymore. She wasn't that woman anymore. She'd done so many things on her own since she'd gotten there, things she never would have tried when Ernie was alive—and she'd done them well. She'd figured stuff out and had begun to acknowledge she had some abilities aside from cleaning house, doing laundry, and greeting people at the motel. She didn't want to feel worthless and less than dirt. Hadn't she made a vow somewhere during this trip that she wasn't going to go there again? Or at least not let someone else make her feel valueless. And yet, here she was.

Throwing her head back, she set her jaw and glared at the tower, Neal atop it, and swore that when she got back to the ranch house, she'd pack her suitcase and leave.

The ride back to the house was a long silent one. It had taken another couple of hours of Neal wrestling with the windmill, then waiting while the stock tank filled to make sure everything was working, before they could leave. But once he was off the tower, his mood improved and his language too. She wasn't thrilled standing around in the heat listening to water splash into the tank, but at least she didn't have to put up with a continual string of curses, and he was busy enough puttering around that she didn't have to put up with him either. She tensed up when they climbed into the truck, not wanting to be in an enclosed space with him, but the tension eased with the quiet miles.

At one point, Neal tried to make conversation, but Jane forced herself not to engage him and looked out the side window, counting the minutes until they were back. He gave up rather quickly and settled into an uneasy silence. *Maybe he understands what he did wrong,* she wondered. *Maybe that's why he's not saying anything—because he feels ashamed.* She hoped so, though a twinge of guilt that she was making him feel bad sprang up.

The sun was behind the horizon, and the sky was darkening by the time they pulled up next to the house. She was famished. Two missed meals and barely a sip or two of water had left her feeling depleted and tired. She wanted to grab her suitcase and go, but she knew she was courting trouble if she did that. Unsure of the way back to town, especially in the dark with all the wildlife roaming about, she would end up hitting something or getting lost. Though it set her teeth on edge, she decided she'd brave another supper under the glowering eye of Gretchen and leave at first light.

Inside, the aroma of roasting potatoes and lamb set Jane's stomach to cramping. All she wanted to do was sit down, grab a plateful of food, and eat like there was no hope of ever eating again, but she opted for a quick shower instead. By the time she was toweled dry and dressed in clean clothes, most of the men were around the table, and Gretchen was delivering platters of food. Neal's chair was empty. She wondered about it, and when she approached the table, she heard someone mutter: "Took the chopper to Tennant Creek." She ignored the comment and decided Neal must have taken a shower too. She smiled at the hands as she took her place beside Neal's chair and asked what they had been up to that day as they all waited for him to arrive.

Five minutes passed, then five more. "Don't you think we should eat before it gets cold?" she asked no one in particular, not sure if she could tolerate sitting in front of everything without taking a bite.

"We wait," Gretchen announced from the kitchen door.

Jane turned toward her. "Do you know where Neal is?"

"He will be back in a minute." She folded her arms and leaned against the jamb.

Jane grimaced. "Would it be OK if I had a glass of water then?"

Gretchen seemed to consider this for a moment and nodded. Jane grabbed the nearest water pitcher and filled her glass, drained it in a single swig, and reached to fill it again. She was lifting it to her lips when Neal sauntered in from the kitchen.

"Sorry to have kept you waiting, but I had a little errand to run. Let's eat." He sat, placing something on the floor beside his chair. Jane couldn't see what it was but was too hungry to dwell on the mystery.

The food traveled from platter to plate to stomach without a lot of conversation getting in the way. She filled her plate twice before easing back in her chair with a contented sigh. Gretchen was a piece of work but an excellent cook and seemed to have outdone herself that night. One by one the men also sat back, nursing bottles of beer and chatting. Only Neal remained silent after he pushed his plate away. He had one hand wrapped around his ubiquitous beer and seemed to be deep in thought. She watched him for a moment, wondering what was going on with him. Finally he rose and clapped his hands.

"Quiet, blokes. I have an announcement."

The room stilled. The only noise she could make out was the buzzing of a fly doing loop-the-loops around the light fixture. What the hell was up?

"I can be a bit of an arse, as some of you are aware." The room broke into uneasy chuckles, and Neal raised a hand. "And some days are worse than others. Well, today was one of those days, and my friend Jane here took the brunt of it." He glanced at her and winked. "I wanted to apologize to her in front of everyone." He turned to her and held out a hand.

She sat, uncertain of what to do. Did he want her to take it? To stand up beside him?

Bending, he clasped her hand and drew her to her feet. Her face flushed, and her first impulse was to jerk her hand away and flee outside, but instead she lowered her head and pursed her lips.

"I'm sorry for the way I behaved today, Jane. I hope you'll forgive me." His hand felt hot and sweaty in hers. He pulled her toward him and moved to kiss her.

Without thinking, she ducked. For some reason she hugged him instead, kicking herself all the while for allowing him to touch her in the first place. She was furious that he was putting her on the spot, embarrassed that he was doing it in front of everyone, ashamed she had hugged him instead of walking away, and, on top of it all, guilty. Guilty that he was trying to make amends and she was too angry to let him. Guilty that she might have done something to make him think he could just say sorry and everything would be OK again. But most of all, guilty that she had let herself get into this situation by sleeping with him.

She wanted to cry. She wanted to scream. She wanted to run away. But she stood with her face pressed against his chest, the fine meal she had eaten churning in her belly.

After a few moments, he pushed her back and reached down beside his chair. "I hope you'll accept this token of my apology." He handed her a bouquet of roses, red and white, with sprays of baby's breath setting them off in glory.

Jane gasped. "Oh my. They're beautiful." She laid them in her arms and sniffed. "Thank you." She was so touched, tears clouded her eyes, and this time when he bent to kiss her, she let him.

He beamed at her and those around the table. The men sat expressionless, some fiddling with their silverware, most with eyes downcast. Smiling, Neal turned to Gretchen, glowering in the door. "What have you made for dessert tonight? Hope it's something special."

Jane sat, placing the flowers on the table beside her. "Where did you ever find roses out here? Certainly not Camooweal."

He winked at her. "Never mind. You deserve them."

She blushed, feeling undeserving. She had done nothing to warrant this kind of attention. The gesture confused her to the point she wasn't sure what she thought or felt. It was hard to reconcile his behavior out at the windmill with his apology and roses here. The two actions seemed contradictory, and she was left feeling she didn't know what was going on.

Gretchen arrived with a layer cake frosted with chocolate icing. She set it on the table and proceeded to carve out huge hunks of it for each of the men. Jane's slice was smaller, but she didn't complain since she wasn't sure she could eat what she was given, much less what the men were served.

While she ate, she tried to sort out her feelings and make sense of it all. She found herself still angry at Neal for the way he had acted, but the anger was muted now and not the burning rage she'd felt most of the afternoon. She appreciated the flowers and realized that he must have fired up the chopper and taken it to Tennant Creek after they got back to the house. That's the only place she could think of big enough to have a florist shop, aside from Alice Springs, and there was no way he had time to get there and back by supper. The fact that he would do that for her pleased her in a way that felt strangely uncomfortable. She wanted to stay angry. She wanted to have a reason to leave. Even though his gesture was kind and generous, it felt odd, odd in a way she couldn't quite put her finger on.

She finished her cake and sat back.

Neal sighed and patted his belly. "Why don't we sit on the veranda? Gretchen, would you please bring us a couple of cups of tea outside?" Then reaching out, he took her hand and lifted her to her feet.

Jane was following him when he stopped and turned back to the table. "Don't forget your roses." He pointed to where they still sat by her empty plate.

"Oh yes." A twinge of resentment nicked at her as she retrieved them. The glow of their beauty had worn off, and she would rather have left them for Gretchen. It felt awkward to haul them outside, as if she needed a reminder sitting beside her that Neal had gone to great lengths to get them for her. Maybe he was the one who needed the reminding.

The thought stopped her dead in her tracks. The roses weren't for her. They were for him. For him to feel exonerated for being a total asshole, for his yelling and cursing, for almost hitting her, for showing his men what a great guy he was. Nothing in his flying off to Tennant Creek was about her. The same went for his apology. That was all a show too. Neal Stratmore, humble man, willing to take responsibility for his actions. She wondered if the station hands had bought any part of his act. Was he sorry? Maybe, but she would never know for sure, and somewhere inside she doubted it. He didn't care for her any more than she cared for him. Maybe less, which was saying a lot.

That he wanted her to stay was obvious from his actions that evening. For what? Sex? Probably. Gretchen seemed to fill all the other roles he might need a woman for. Why Gretchen would still want him after his crappy behavior toward her was unfathomable.

And what about his flaunting of Jane like some show cow? Oh, that too. Maybe that's what he needed Jane for. To be his arm candy when he went to town, to make him feel desirable and virile to the men who worked on the station and to anyone who knew him. If this is the way he had treated his wife, no wonder she was gone and the kids with her. No wonder they didn't want to have much to do with him. It all made sense to her now.

Outside on the veranda, Neal was leaning back in one of the chairs and rubbing his belly. Jane felt a sudden wave of revulsion. She could see Ernie superimposed over him; they were the same man in so many of the ways that counted. Why she couldn't see it before amazed her. But see it she did, and she knew what she needed to do. She could never find the strength to leave Ernie, but today was different.

She placed the roses on the table beside Neal. "Thanks for putting me up these last few days. I've learned so much, but I need to get going. I don't have all that much time left on my visa, and there's a great deal more of the country I want to see before I go home. It's been a pleasure." Before he could respond, she turned back to the house and strode into her bedroom, threw her things into her suitcase, grabbed her purse, and headed for the door.

Neal was waiting for her by the front door, the roses hanging upside down in his left hand, his expression a cross between fury and hurt. She paused for a second, afraid of what he might do or say. She wished the rest of the men were around for a kind of protection, but everyone was out of sight—including Gretchen. Jane would have been grateful even for her presence. Gathering up her courage, she stepped forward, hand sweaty on the handle of her suitcase.

Neal blocked her passage with his free hand. "Where do you think you're going?"

The comment struck her as ludicrous, and she burst out laughing. "Wherever I want to. I'm not your wife, not even your girlfriend. We had a couple of laughs between the sheets, but I'm ready to move on. Now please get out of my way."

He didn't move. "You can't just up and leave like this."

"Why the hell not?"

That seemed to stump him for a moment. "Because you owe me," he blurted.

She felt her face redden and flush with anger. "For what? A few meals, a helicopter ride, a roll in the hay? If I knew you were charging, I never would have called."

"I put myself out for you. I might have made some mistakes, but I apologized in front of everyone and bought you roses." He raised the flowers and shook them.

She narrowed her eyes and gritted her teeth. "Why don't you give them to someone who cares? Gretchen, for example. She's in love with you, and you can't see it. On top of that, you treat her like a slave. She'd be thrilled."

He opened his mouth, and his eyes widened. Then his expression snapped shut and he lowered the bouquet. "Go on, if that's what you want to do. You Americans are so selfish and whinging."

"Thank you. I will. It's been a learning experience. Thank you for that, and g'day." She forged past him, her shoulder brushing his chest as she stormed to the camper.

"That's not how you say g'day!" he shouted when she unlocked the door and threw her suitcase in.

"I don't give a rip," she muttered, shoving the key in the ignition and flicking on the lights. In a cloud of dust, she roared down the road in what she hoped was the right direction, kangaroos be damned.

The highway seemed as distant as America. She followed the dirt track, eyes straining for movement at the edges of the headlights in case any variety of wildlife was lurking there, ready to jump in front of her. Her nerves felt frayed, and her mind either ranted at Neal for being such a jerk or at herself for getting into the situation in the first place. By the time she hit pavement and turned left toward Camooweal, she was exhausted.

She considered pulling into the caravan park there, but it felt too close to Neal. The last thing she wanted was for him to get an insane urge and try to track her down. Camooweal would be the first place he'd look, especially since she'd told him she preferred to stay in caravan parks and that was all she'd done since she'd gotten her van. Better instead that she should push on and find a rest area and camp there.

About an hour after zipping through Camooweal, she saw a wide spot in the road at the intersection with Thorntonia Yelvertoft Road. Gratefully, she pulled onto the dirt and parked close to the trees. Shutting off the engine, she leaned back and sighed. The energy that had impelled her to this point dissolved like mist in the morning sun, and she wasn't sure she could make up the bed, much less move from her seat. But her mind was still whirling, and she mustered the strength to climb out of the cab and into the back, aided by the moonlight. She tried to turn on the lights, but they didn't respond. Stunned, she stood in the back and stared at the places where they should be shining. Ah, the batteries. She realized that while she was playing with Neal, the cooler running in the back of the hot camper must have drained the auxiliary battery packs. Shit. And she'd so wanted a cup of tea.

She collapsed onto the bench seat. She didn't have the heart to open the cooler and see if anything inside was still edible, and without a flashlight it wouldn't have done much good anyway. Better to leave it closed until morning to keep any smells at bay.

As she lay on the bench, her head resting on one hand, she stared at the ceiling, replaying her time with Neal like a bad movie. In retrospect, she could see the warning signs from the first time they'd met. His bluster, his needing to control things, his drinking, his anger. Part of it she'd seen at the time but either wasn't able to put it together or was unable to find the courage to let it go and leave.

It reminded her so much of living with Ernie. She'd been clueless about how awful her situation was until Rachael had befriended her and shown her there were other ways of viewing and thinking about her life. Until that time, her marriage, in her mind, was the way people lived with one another. It was the way Ernie's family behaved and to a certain extent her own. She couldn't ever remember her parents being kind or loving to each other. An unspoken but hostile truce was the norm. Without Rachael, it's likely she'd have gone to her grave never knowing there could be another way. Even now, knowing what she did, she'd still walked straight into the trap an abusive man had set for her, smiling the whole way. Was she so broken that this was all she could ever hope for?

That thought sent a lonely wind blowing through her. She wrapped her arms over her chest, rolled to one side, and pulled herself into a fetal ball. Her insides felt cramped, as if a hand had clenched them and squeezed hard. She could barely breathe. She felt her eyes water and wished she could talk to Rachael.

Forcing herself upward, she wiped her eyes and cheeks with one hand while she located her purse on the passenger seat with the other. She dug around in it by feel until she found her cell phone and then flipped it open, hoping that it still had a charge. The screen lit up. The clock indicated it was one in the morning, which meant it was still early enough back home for Rachael to be awake. But no bars. No signal. No hope in hell of having someone to talk to.

Her hands dropped between her legs, the light from the screen puddling around her feet. She took a breath and raised her head.

It was not all her fault. She remembered the roses and how she realized that Neal's actions had nothing to do with her. Ernie had been the same. He hadn't done anything different than what he knew growing up. He had treated her the same way his father had treated his mother and just like his mother had treated him. Probably he hadn't known what he could have done differently. He'd never had a Rachael to show him that life didn't have to repeat in endlessly hurting cycles. So he went on behaving as he was programmed to, reacting not to her but to the voices instilled in him by his parents, who'd been programmed by their parents, and on and on. And she'd responded to him through her own programming.

But now she knew. Now she saw. And if she made the same mistakes once again or twice again or many times again until something new became her instinctual way of being, it never needed to be the way it was with Ernie or Neal or the next guy. And there would be a next guy, maybe in Cairns, maybe in Cortez, but there would be one; of that she was certain. She might not catch the clues at first that he wasn't a good guy, but she would sooner the next time. Or maybe she'd learned enough this time around to not be attracted to another jerk, or at least to evaluate any future attractions a little more skeptically. She was breaking the pattern and, though it hurt, it was better.

She was breaking other patterns too. Cleo had shown her that her ideas about people with skin darker than her own were stereotypes she'd been fed all her life—that one didn't need a job to be hardworking, that people weren't the only valuable things on the planet, and that she had a great deal to learn about most things—including herself and who she was. Including being a widow. Widow. Again, that word.

Suddenly she smiled and chuckled in the darkness. She didn't need a new word to define herself; no single word was large or complex enough. She could be many words, ideas, or beliefs, anything she could collect and accept. She could be large or small, and she could change anytime she didn't like the woman who stared back at her in the mirror. Truly the mistress of herself and her fate.

She glanced down at the phone when the screen went dark. She pressed one of the buttons and the light blinked on again. She grinned. She might not be able to call anyone, but she could use the light from the phone to fire up the stove and make tea.

Acknowledgments

AS WITH A CHILD, it takes a village to write a book. The following is not an all-inclusive list of everyone who helped this book come to fruition. Since this novel took over ten years to progress from idea to print, that would be a book in itself. The following people are only some of the contributors to that journey.

Eternal thanks to the people who took time to read the entire rough manuscript and provide me with invaluable suggestions: Daoine Bachran (yes, my daughter, the brave soul), Warren Duncan (the Aussie connection), Cathy Davis, Sunshine Knight, and Carmella Courtney. For the editors who polished my punctuation and caught errors in plot and continuity: Angela Renkoski and Tom Locke. Thanks to Victoria Wolf for the magnificent cover and interior layout, to Amanda Miller for shepherding me through this process and Polly Leftoski and Bobby Haas for their encouragement. To my sister, Virginia Egger, for her financial support, and to all the members of the Paonia Writers Group over the years. These hardy souls trudged through many of my words without praise or pay and offered me feedback I very much needed. They are a resilient group.

Finally, I cannot stop without thanking my children, Corwin, Daoine and Tristan, for hanging in there with me through all the years. They are my heart and soul.

About the Author

MARY BACHRAN was born and raised on a small family farm in western Colorado. After bouncing around the United States for twenty years, getting married and having three kids, she went back to school and earned a doctorate in clinical psychology with an emphasis on the psychology of indigenous and minority populations. She and her late husband finally settled in Paonia, CO, a little mountain town, where they lived off the grid for five years. She has traveled to Australia and India and currently occupies her time hiking with her dog, Shanti, writing novels and short stories, and serving as the town's mayor.

Invite Mary to Your Book Club!

As a special offer to The Eucalyptus Blues readers, Mary has offered to visit your book club either virtually or in person.

Please contact Mary directly to schedule an appearance at your book club.

MaryBachran1@gmail.com

Made in the USA
Columbia, SC
05 August 2021

42718643R00231